Praise for *Hidden Pe...*

"Hannon combines intrigue and restrained romance to create a story layered with multiple intertwining mysteries."

Publishers Weekly

"Top-notch and probably one of Hannon's best to date. If you like mysteries or thrillers, what are you waiting for? This one is a real winner and one I am happy to recommend to all ages."

Bookworm Banquet

"Skillfully written, and the characters are nicely defined. Readers will find plenty to enjoy here."

Booklist

Praise for *Dangerous Illusions*

"The suspenseful conclusion and believable romantic element will leave readers eager for the next installment."

Publishers Weekly

"Races full speed ahead, spinning out a twisty plot. The author's many fans will devour this work."

Library Journal

"Hannon is at the top of her game. *Dangerous Illusions*, the first in the Code of Honor series, will satisfy any suspense reader."

Christian Market

"Intricately plotted with a large number of unexpected events that will keep readers guessing."

RT Book Reviews

DARK
AMBITIONS

Books by Irene Hannon

HEROES OF QUANTICO

Against All Odds
An Eye for an Eye
In Harm's Way

GUARDIANS OF JUSTICE

Fatal Judgment
Deadly Pursuit
Lethal Legacy

PRIVATE JUSTICE

Vanished
Trapped
Deceived

MEN OF VALOR

Buried Secrets
Thin Ice
Tangled Webs

CODE OF HONOR

Dangerous Illusions
Hidden Peril
Dark Ambitions

That Certain Summer
One Perfect Spring
Hope Harbor
Sea Rose Lane
Sandpiper Cove
Pelican Point
Driftwood Bay

DARK AMBITIONS

IRENE HANNON

Revell

a division of Baker Publishing Group
Grand Rapids, Michigan

© 2019 by Irene Hannon

Published by Revell
a division of Baker Publishing Group
PO Box 6287, Grand Rapids, MI 49516-6287
www.revellbooks.com

Printed in the United States of America

Library of Congress Cataloging-in-Publication Data
Names: Hannon, Irene, author.
Title: Dark ambitions / Irene Hannon.
Description: Grand Rapids, MI : Revell, [2019] | Series: Code of honor ; 3
Identifiers: LCCN 2019006996 | ISBN 9780800727703 (pbk.)
Subjects: | GSAFD: Mystery fiction.
Classification: LCC PS3558.A4793 D37 2019 | DDC 813/.54—dc23
LC record available at https://lccn.loc.gov/2019006996

ISBN 978-0-8007-2778-9 (cloth)

19 20 21 22 23 24 25   7 6 5 4 3 2 1

To my husband, Tom—
as we celebrate our 30th anniversary.

Thank you for sticking with me
through happy times and sad,
for putting up with my episodes of writer's angst,
for your unwavering fidelity, love, and devotion . . .

And most of all, for being my hero—and friend.

I love you more than words can say.

PROLOGUE

"He got away."

As the bad news echoed across the miles, I stared at the skeleton of the leaf-stripped tree beside me and tightened my grip on the burner phone.

"What do you mean, he got away? You told me this would be a piece of cake." A cloud of breath formed in front of my face, the frigid December air pricking my cheeks.

Silence on the other end of the line.

My hired gun must be miffed by my accusatory tone.

Tough.

I'd paid a premium price for his specialized skills, and I expected results—not screwups.

"He fought back." The man's voice was measured, but an undercurrent of annoyance tightened his words.

The irritation went both ways.

"Of course he fought back." I took a final drag on my cigarette, dug out one of the pieces of aluminum foil I always carried, and crushed the butt on the edge of the empty planter beside me. "He was in the army. I told you that."

"You said he was a medic—and that he's been out for several years."

"He was . . . and he has been."

"Then he does some serious workouts. I was fortunate to walk away with nothing worse than a bruised jaw."

"You should have done more homework."

"You didn't give me time."

That was true.

And the fast turnaround had cost me extra.

"You'll heal." I began to pace. If the man wanted sympathy, he was out of luck. "I want this finished before he goes to the police."

"If he was going to involve law enforcement, he'd have done so already . . . and I'd know about it."

That was probably also true—assuming the guy had all the connections he'd claimed.

Another reason I'd paid top dollar for the job.

"Where is he now?"

"Unknown. He's fallen off the radar. But I'll find him."

My stomach twisted into a hard knot, and I halted. "You think he realized he was set up?"

"His disappearing act would suggest that."

"How fast can you track him down?"

"Depends on whether his evasive abilities are as well-honed as his fighting skills."

I didn't like the sound of that.

"Our agreement called for this to be finished by the end of the week. Do I have to bring in someone else?"

"No. The job will get done—but from now on, I'm doing it my way."

I frowned. "What does that mean?"

"There are more creative methods of offing people than tossing them from a balcony or staging a robbery."

"It has to look like the death was an unfortunate consequence, not the goal."

"Understood."

"So what are you going to do?"

"Do you want details—or results?"

This guy had attitude with a capital A.

But as long as he earned his money, who cared?

"Fine. Let me know when it's over and I'll settle up."

"Count on it."

The line went dead.

I stabbed the end button and shoved the phone back into my pocket, quashing the tiny twinge of guilt nipping at my conscience.

Misplaced guilt.

After all, what choice did I have? Given what he knew, letting him live was too much of a risk.

Especially with the dream in sight.

The icy wind picked up, numbing my fingers.

I ought to get back inside. I had places to go, people to meet, things to do.

But I also needed another cigarette.

Bad.

I dug deep into the pocket of my coat and pulled out the pack of unfiltered Camels, along with the Bic. Shook out a coffin nail. Flipped the lighter against the tip. Inhaled slow and deep.

Yes, it was a nasty habit—but there was nothing like a nicotine rush.

And some days, a few stolen moments like these were the only downtime I got.

My regular cell began to vibrate, and I groped for it as I took another drag on the Camel.

Sighed as I glanced at the screen.

This break was going to be short-lived.

I put the cell to my ear. "Yes?"

"Did I catch you in the middle of something?"

"No." I stubbed out the cigarette on the piece of aluminum foil and folded up the whole mess. One of these days soon I'd have to quit for good. "What's up?"

"I wanted to confirm the details for this afternoon's meeting."

"Okay."

I half listened as I headed inside. I already knew the details . . . and the personalities . . . and the stakes. But this underling was just doing her job. Dotting the i's and crossing the t's. I couldn't hold her diligence against her—even if I had bigger issues on my mind.

Like an unfinished job.

But once this loose end was tied up, my goal would be within touching distance.

All I had to do was stay the course, follow the plan—and keep my eye on the prize.

1

There was blood on the ice.

Rick Jordan jolted to a stop, gaze riveted on the crimson spots blemishing the frosty ground, fingers tightening on the disposable cup of coffee he'd just nuked.

Could his eyes be playing tricks on him in the waning light of the December afternoon?

He leaned closer.

No.

His 20/20 vision hadn't failed him.

It was blood.

After all the gore he'd seen, it wasn't difficult to make a positive ID.

But with all the wildlife on the wooded acreage he called home, could it be from an animal?

As he peered at the ruby-colored stains, the hair on the back of his neck snapped to attention—and since metabolic cues had saved his hide on more Night Stalker missions than he cared to remember, ignoring them would be foolish.

The blood was human.

Giving the landscape a thorough, methodical sweep, he set

down the cup of java he'd picked up at the café during his supply run to town, balancing it on the uneven ground.

No movement other than the huge flakes that had begun to sift down from the leaden sky.

Apparently the blizzard warning issued this morning had been spot-on. Missouri would have a white Christmas.

Nothing wrong with a Currier and Ives–style holiday— except the flakes were rapidly covering the trail of splotches on the three-day-old ice crystals from Tuesday's sleet storm.

In minutes, they'd be impossible to track.

Continuing to scan his surroundings, he removed the compact Beretta from the concealed holster clipped to his belt. No reason to carry when the camp was full of kids and counselors, but wandering around unarmed in winter on 650 isolated, deserted acres?

Not happening.

He might never have needed a gun in the four years he'd called this rural Missouri acreage home, but it was better to risk overkill than be killed.

And while the camp had always been a peaceful refuge for him and the hundreds of kids who visited each season, his goosed adrenaline suggested that was about to change.

Pistol in hand, he followed the uneven trail of blood, only the muffled quack of a duck from the lake a hundred yards away breaking the stillness. No more than a few scarlet spots here and there dotted the frozen surface, but they were sufficient to keep him on course.

The trail ended at the canoe shed, which was closed up tight for the winter season.

Or it had been, before someone picked the padlock.

Shifting into military stealth mode, Rick edged next to the structure and put his ear to the door.

Silence.

Firming his grip on the Beretta, he yanked the wide door open and flattened his back against the wall, out of sight.

More silence.

If anyone was inside, they'd masked their surprise well.

Either that, or they weren't able to respond.

After thirty soundless seconds ticked by, Rick risked a peek around the edge of the door frame.

Nothing was amiss.

The racks of canoes looked the same as they had when he'd stacked them for the winter. The paddles were in their brackets, life vests stashed in their bins, fishing rods lined up against the wall like soldiers in formation.

And there was no blood inside, as far as he could tell after flipping on the light and making a quick circuit.

Nor was there anything to suggest someone had taken refuge in the structure.

A frigid gust of air swooped in through the open door, bringing with it an assault of snowflakes—but the arctic weather alone wasn't responsible for the shiver that snaked through him.

Where had the injured person gone?

Rick stepped outside again, ducked his head against the polar onslaught, and peered at the ground as he walked the area in a tight grid pattern.

There were no more red blots.

Even the original trail he'd followed had disappeared under a blanket of fresh powder.

Nothing remained to indicate anyone had ventured onto his property.

In fact, if he'd detoured to his computer after arriving home from town instead of indulging in a stroll to the dock while he finished his coffee, he would never have seen the blood. Nor would he have visited the canoe shed until he began prepping for the Saturday spring camps, a task that was weeks away.

Strange timing.

Providential, almost.

Yet what did it matter?

Whoever had broken into the outbuilding had done no harm or stolen anything. There was minimal blood, and the person had seemingly left of their own volition.

The incident might be a bit bizarre, but it wasn't a life or death situation, like the ones he'd faced in the Middle East.

Tugging up the collar of his coat, Rick returned to the shed and flipped off the light. Lock repairs would have to wait until the storm subsided—but the delay posed little risk. There wasn't much chance anyone would venture out in this weather to steal his lake equipment.

Best plan?

Go back inside and hunker down until the storm blew over. There was no reason to linger while the biting wind burrowed into every seam of his outerwear and the sky hurled icy BBs at his cheeks.

He turned away.

Took three steps.

Hesitated.

You're missing something, Jordan.

Hard as he tried to muffle the tiny voice in his head, it refused to be silenced.

Especially since he couldn't shake the feeling that his mysterious visitor had been more than a vagrant or a vandal who'd gotten cut on barbed wire or tripped on a rock and ended up with a bloody nose.

Heaving a sigh, he pivoted, tramped back to the shed, and opened the door again. Unless he did another walk-through, his keep-at-it-until-you-solve-the-puzzle gene wasn't going to shut up.

Back inside, he flicked the light switch and began a second loop, this one much slower.

Halfway through, he hit pay dirt.

The two small objects on the stern seat of one of the canoes, half tucked into the shadows, hadn't been there when he'd closed up the place for the winter.

Palming the items, he angled his hand toward the light.

Sucked in a breath.

The identity of his visitor was no longer a mystery.

Boomer had been here.

But . . . why had he shown up, unannounced, after all these years?

What had caused the blood?

Why had the man left?

Where had he gone?

Was he coming back?

Only one person could supply those answers—and he'd vanished.

Another blast of bitter air pummeled him, and Rick slid the two items into the pocket of his coat. After wrestling the door back into place, he slogged toward the cabin, head bent against the wind.

Halfway back, as he slowed to scoop up the cup of java balanced on the frozen ground, a vulture circled overhead, riding the wind currents in search of death.

Bad omen—if you were the superstitious type.

He wasn't.

Ignoring the macabre scavenger, he focused instead on the Christmas riddle that had arrived on his doorstep.

His visitor hadn't been some random stranger, but a person he'd once worked with every day.

A person who, under normal circumstances, would have contacted him to arrange a visit rather than show up out of the blue.

Meaning things were far from normal—and the man must need his help.

If I can ever do anything for you, all you have to do is pick up the phone or email me or knock on my door.

As the wind shrieked and ice pellets continued to sting his cheeks, the promise he'd made almost six years ago echoed through Rick's mind.

He'd meant every word of it then.

He still did.

It was the least he could do for the fellow soldier who'd saved his life . . . and almost lost his own in the process.

But to help a man, you first had to find him.

And with night falling, a blizzard approaching, and Christmas Eve mere hours away, that might be as difficult as a snatch 'n' grab mission in a Little Bird deep behind enemy lines.

* * * * *

"Come on . . . pick up . . . pick up."

As Jackson Dunn muttered the plea into the pay phone, he squinted at the parking lot of the truck stop through the frost-caked window. No suspicious activity that he could see.

But if there was no answer on this third try, he couldn't linger any longer. He'd have to hitch a ride back into St. Louis with one of the truckers, wait out the storm—and pray he'd eluded whoever had been tasked with silencing him.

"I'm sorry we can't take your call at the moment. Messages are retrieved every day during the off-season, so please leave your name and . . ."

Muttering an oath, Jackson slammed the handset back into the hook. Wiped an unsteady hand down his face. Filled his lungs with air.

He had to calm down. Think. Tearing out of Lexington with only a hastily packed overnight bag, his medical kit, a wallet containing less than two hundred dollars, and no clear plan hadn't been his smartest decision—but panic could muddle a man's thinking.

And driving around aimlessly for three days, holing up in out-of-the-way spots while he tried to figure out what to do, hadn't cleared his mind much.

Then he'd remembered Rick's promise—and his destination had become obvious.

The army captain was smart, honest, ethical, and trustworthy. He was also a clear thinker who would give sound advice.

Unfortunately, he hadn't been home.

Wincing, Jackson shifted to take more weight off his injured leg.

It was possible Rick had been out running errands ahead of the blizzard, though. He hadn't had any plans to travel for the holiday, according to his Christmas card. Waiting around in the shed for him to return had seemed like a reasonable option.

Until hypothermia had become an imminent concern—and those gunshots in the distance had gotten a little too close.

Maybe the volleys had been from hunters.

Maybe not.

Sticking around to find out, however, hadn't seemed like the best plan.

Jackson gave the greasy spoon another survey. As far as he could tell, no one had followed him here. He was safe . . . for now.

But hoofing it two miles to the camp and back from the small town where the cab had dropped him and later picked him up—a necessary precaution in case anyone was watching his rental car in St. Louis—had done a number on the superficial stab wound in his calf. Too bad he hadn't stocked the medical kit in his trunk with sutures.

He could also use a dose of Percocet.

Propping one shoulder against the wall for support, he looked down. The dark stain was barely visible on the denim of his black jeans, but he could feel the wetness.

The wound was bleeding again.

He'd have to duck into the bathroom, fix it as best he could with the remaining supplies he'd brought, and see if he could persuade one of the truckers to give him a lift back to the city. After he retrieved the rental car he'd picked up at the Lexington airport, he'd find a low-key place to stay and try calling the camp again.

If no one answered?

He'd have to consider leaving a message.

Not his first choice.

With the mess he was in, it would be safer for Rick if there were no voicemails linking the two of them. Putting the man at risk wasn't part of his game plan. A quick, under-the-radar visit to get his take on the situation and ask his advice—that's all he wanted.

In the meantime, he had to keep moving. His Visa purchases had left a trail, if anyone accessed his credit card records. Staying in one place too long would be dangerous.

Shoving his hands in his pockets, he limped toward the men's room and gave the diner another once-over.

None of the patrons were paying any attention to him.

Yet someone, somewhere, could be tracking his movements.

And it was possible they'd find him before he connected with Rick.

If that happened, he wasn't likely to escape again. They'd be ready for resistance on the next go-round.

Fear roiling his gut, he curled his fingers into tight balls and kept walking toward the men's room despite the sudden shakiness in his legs.

At least he'd left the most important items at the camp—and

once Rick discovered the open lock on the shed, he'd investigate
. . . and find them.

It would require effort to connect the dots, but the army
captain would do it. He was as sharp as they came.

He was also a man of honor who would keep the promise
he'd made to help if ever a need arose.

Hopefully, though, he wouldn't have to solve the puzzle alone.
If Rick picked up the next call, they could arrange an in-person
meeting and get all the facts on the table. And he might, if he'd
looked at his voicemail and realized someone was trying hard
to reach him.

Jackson pushed through the door to the empty restroom
and claimed a sink in the far corner. As soon as he applied a
fresh bandage, he'd head back to St. Louis, call the camp again,
and pray his good fortune held while he waited out the storm.

After all, escaping his attacker with only a minor wound had
been nothing short of a miracle.

But as he turned on the tap and hot water gushed out, burning
his fingers, he had a sinking feeling his luck was running out.

2

"Morning. How was your Christmas?" Heather Shields dropped her tea bag in the trash as the Phoenix Inc. office manager/receptionist entered the PI firm's kitchen through the back door.

"The weather outside was frightful—but inside was delightful." Grinning, Nikki Waters shrugged out of her electric-blue quilted jacket and headed toward the coat tree in the corner. "Zoe's at the perfect age for all the magic of Santa Claus, and it was great having Danny home from college."

As the woman hung up her coat, Heather eyed her ensemble. Christmas might be over in terms of the calendar, but Nikki's celebratory mood clearly wasn't. Her spiky platinum blonde hair still sported a red and green stripe, the earrings in her triple-pierced ears were holiday themed, and her green leggings dipped into pointy-toed elf boots. But the pièce de résistance was the giant LED-bedecked Christmas tree on her red tunic, centered under the word *JOY*.

It was vintage Nikki.

"Sounds like a wonderful family gathering." Heather hid her smile behind a sip of Earl Grey brew.

"It was." The woman helped herself to an herbal tea bag

from the stash she kept in the cabinet and filled a mug with water. "How was your day?"

"Quiet but pleasant." As usual. It was hard to create much of a party atmosphere with only two people.

"You know, you and your dad would have been welcome to join us. Though in hindsight, it was probably easier for you to shovel a path next door in that duplex the two of you share than trek across town."

"True. A blizzard is one thing, but sixteen inches in twelve hours? That's insane for St. Louis."

"Yep. It reminds me of the winter when Dev was trying to find his wife's missing sister. They weren't married at that point, but . . ." Her voice trailed off as James Devlin pushed through the back door, stomping the snow off his boots on the rug inside. "Speak of the devil."

He scowled at her. "What kind of greeting is that?"

"Hey—chill. It's just an old saying."

"Yeah?"

"Yeah."

"Pardon my skepticism." He shucked off his coat.

"Man. What happened to your Christmas spirit?"

"I've got plenty of spirit." He gave her a head-to-toe and shaded his eyes. "I just don't display it as . . . colorfully . . . as you do." He slipped his jacket off.

She arched an eyebrow. "I disagree. That red hair of yours is very Christmasy—as is your tendency to blush."

"I don't blush." Even as he denied it, his cheeks flushed.

Lips twitching, Heather took another sip of her tea.

Only Nikki could get a rise out of the cool-under-pressure ex-ATF agent. The banter between them was a stitch—even if it had taken her a while to realize the zingers they lobbed at each other were all show and masked a deep affection neither would ever admit.

"Right." Nikki smirked at him.

Dev turned his back on the office manager as he hung up his coat. "Who made the coffee?" He motioned to the full pot.

"I did. About twenty minutes ago." Heather leaned back against the counter.

"Thanks." He made a beeline for it. "I won't mention any names—but some people could learn by example."

Nikki sniffed and dunked her tea bag. "For the record, I get paid to manage the office, assist with data searches, and keep you guys in line. Barista isn't in my job description."

"It isn't in Heather's, either."

"She's nicer than me."

"No kidding."

Heather masked her laugh with a discreet cough.

Dev angled toward her as he poured his coffee. "So how long have you been here?"

"An hour."

"Seriously? The day after a long holiday weekend, you got here early?"

"I have a new client meeting this morning that required prep."

"Still . . ." He opened the fridge and inspected the empty shelves. Sighed. Shut the door. "You can stop trying to impress us, you know. After four months, we're well aware of your work ethic—and it's putting us all to shame."

"Not *all* of us." Nikki dropped her spent tea bag into the trash.

Dev shot her a disgruntled look. "Don't you have things to do? There are plenty of files in my office that need organizing."

"There are always plenty of files in your office that need organizing. However"—she held up a hand when he opened his mouth—"since we're in the midst of the twelve days of Christmas and I have plenty of holiday spirit left, I'll mosey in and survey the damage."

Dev waited until she sauntered out the door. "If there was a price on sass, Nikki would be a millionaire."

"I heard that." Her retort floated back down the hall.

"Good." As Dev called out his rejoinder, he winked and lowered his voice. "Truth is, we couldn't get along without her."

"I've figured that out." Nikki was not only the most organized person Heather had ever met, she was also a whiz at database searches and had an impressive knack for coaxing information out of reticent sources on the phone. "So how was your Christmas?"

"Hectic—but terrific. Laura went all out, and Erin was into everything. A typical two-year-old. Nikki's brother dropped in too, to see Laura's sister while they're both home from college. If Danny and Darcy stay together, Nikki and I could be in-laws." He chuckled. "Talk about sweet revenge for all the grief she's given me."

"Revenge?" Cal Burke pushed through the back door, bringing a gust of cold air with him, a few wayward flakes of snow clinging to his dark brown hair. "That sounds like a motive in one of our cases."

"We weren't discussing work."

"No?" Cal glanced at his watch. "Don't you think it's time we did?"

His tone was mild, his manner casual, but the ex–police detective and founder of Phoenix knew how to gently refocus his coworkers.

"Aye, aye, sir." Dev gave a jaunty salute. "But to be honest, I'd rather be in sunny Hawaii for two weeks of R & R like Connor and Kate. They picked a perfect window to ditch the Midwest. "

"Jealous?"

"Nah." Dev took a slug from his shamrock-bedecked mug. "He deserves one last carefree vacation before a new baby disrupts their lives. But I'm glad we have Heather now, or the two of us would be buried until he gets back."

"I agree that adding a fourth PI was a smart move." Cal sent her a smile and hung up his coat.

"Well . . . off to the salt mines." Dev strolled out, humming a vaguely familiar Gaelic melody.

"So are you ready to jump back into the fray?" Cal aimed the question her direction as he veered toward the coffeepot.

"Yes. In fifteen minutes I'm meeting with the client Colin Flynn sent our way last night. Do we get many referrals from the police?"

"More than you'd imagine, considering the reputation PIs have with law enforcement."

"Phoenix is different, though. Not many PI firms have investigators who've been ATF operatives, Secret Service agents, or police detectives."

"Agreed. It also pays to have friends—and former colleagues—at St. Louis County PD." He lifted the coffeepot. "Sorry I had to drop this one on you at the tail end of the holiday weekend."

"No worries. I know Dev's tied up with the insurance investigation and you're leaving town tomorrow on that executive security gig. I don't mind drawing the short straw—but I'm not certain our new client is too happy about it."

He stopped pouring. "What do you mean?"

"When we spoke by phone, he seemed a bit taken aback by my gender."

Faint furrows creased Cal's brow. "What did he say?"

"It wasn't so much what he said as how he said it. But I've been down this road in the past. Law enforcement isn't always the most welcoming profession for women."

"I know." Cal finished filling his mug. "If there's an issue, let me know and I'll reassure him your credentials are second to none."

"Thank you for the offer—but if I pick up any doubts during our meeting, I'm sure I can convince him I'm capable."

Cal grinned. "I'm sure you can too. Did he give you any hint what the case is about?"

"No. I ran him through the usual spiel about the scope of the work we do, and he assured me his case fell within our parameters. That was it."

"After you meet with him, bring me up to speed and we can decide if the job requires any additional resources."

"Will do."

As Cal left the kitchen, the phone in her office across the hall began to ring.

Probably Nikki letting her know her client had arrived.

But he was early—and she needed a few more minutes to sip her tea and psyche herself up to meet with a man who hadn't sounded at all convinced he trusted a woman to handle whatever issue he had.

Of course, it was possible she'd read too much into his inflection. Perhaps he was more rattled by whatever difficulty he was facing than by her gender.

However . . . after six years as a police officer and five as a detective, she'd run into her share of chauvinists. Not many, but enough to sensitize her to nuances.

Especially the last jerk.

Her phone continued to ring, and she struck off for her office, tucking those unpleasant memories back into cold storage—where they belonged.

She'd buy herself five minutes to finish her tea, then meet her new client . . . and find out if this post-Christmas week was going to be naughty or nice.

· · · · ·

O-kay.

If one of his two best friends in the world hadn't recommended this place, he'd be having a few second thoughts about his choice of PI firms.

From behind the magazine he was pretending to read in the

Phoenix Inc. reception area, Rick took another gander at the human Christmas tree with the punk-rocker hair, who was talking in low tones on the phone.

Not what he'd expected, in light of Colin's high praise for the firm's professionalism and skills.

But other than the glow-in-the-dark receptionist, the place *was* classy. A nubby Berber carpet covered the floor, the chairs were upholstered in soothing neutral shades, and the glass-topped coffee table was spotless. Not counting the receptionist's gaudy attire, accent color in the waiting area was provided by the artsy framed photos of landscapes and close-up nature images that graced the walls.

The firm's "Justice First" motto, displayed in brass lettering on a discreet rectangular plaque, was also reassuring.

And the credentials of the four PIs listed on the website were impressive.

The one disconnect was the woman who'd greeted him.

"Heather will be with you in a few minutes, Mr. Jordan. Are you certain I can't offer you coffee or tea?"

He hesitated.

Maybe an infusion of java would banish some of his fatigue—fallout from the four nights he'd tossed and turned since his unexpected visitor left a trail of blood on his property.

"I think I'll have a cup of coffee after all. Black is fine."

"Coming right up." She disappeared through the door behind her desk.

Stifling a yawn, he replaced the magazine on the coffee table, stood, and wandered over to the window. The quaint Kirkwood street had been plowed, but the snow-covered awnings and window boxes enhanced the Norman Rockwell feel of the close-in St. Louis suburb.

If his female best bud wasn't taking a few extra post-honeymoon days to settle into married life, he'd pop over a couple of streets for a visit after he finished here.

But he'd catch up with her and Colin at the Treehouse Gang's next biweekly Saturday breakfast in four days anyway, and—

A door clicked behind him, and he turned.

Blinked.

Instead of the walking Christmas tree, a woman who appeared to be in her early thirties stood on the threshold. Her skinny black slacks, silky white top, and burgundy blazer reeked of class—and professionalism.

Now *she* fit the image of the staff he'd expected to find here.

"Mr. Jordan?"

It was the same husky voice that had spoken to him on the phone last night.

"Yes." He crossed the carpet to join her, suddenly wishing he'd traded his worn jeans and thermal black bomber jacket for more polished attire.

"Heather Shields. Welcome to Phoenix Inc." She extended her hand.

He took her slender fingers and returned her firm squeeze. "Thanks."

"Let me show you back to my office."

He followed her through the door, taking a quick inventory of the space as they walked down the hall. The first two rooms were occupied by men. The next two were dark. One appeared to be an office, the other a conference area.

The receptionist met them at the door to the last office and handed him a sage-green ceramic mug bearing the Phoenix logo. "Black, as ordered."

"Thanks."

She retreated down the hall as Heather led him into her office. "Make yourself comfortable." She motioned toward a round table off to one side. "May I take your coat?"

"Not necessary. I'll drape it over the chair." He slipped his arms out of the sleeves, sat, and took a sip of the robust brew as she claimed the spot across from him. "Excellent coffee."

"I'm glad you like it. I'm not a fan myself, but my dad is. He taught me the finer points of brewing a decent cup."

"You made the coffee even though you don't drink it?" Interesting.

"I got here early. The guys consume it by the gallon, and it's a cold day." She shrugged.

"Lucky them. Most professional women wouldn't be caught dead doing coffee duty in an office." He hitched up one side of his mouth.

Her posture stiffened. "Our tasks here are gender neutral. We help each other out, and we all pitch in with whatever needs to be done since we're all equally capable."

Whoops.

He must have touched a nerve.

"Sorry. I didn't mean to imply otherwise."

Her hazel eyes studied him, her expression impossible to read.

The scrutiny was a touch disconcerting—but it did give him a chance to look at her too.

And Heather Shields was easy to look at, with her dark hair parted slightly off-center, the ends curving under where they brushed her shoulders. The style was a perfect frame for her classic oval face, emphasizing her model-like cheekbones, the graceful arch of her eyebrows, and her generous lips. As far as he could tell, her minimal makeup consisted of a hint of blush, a touch of lipstick, and a brush of mascara—unless those indecently long lashes were all hers.

Hard to be certain from this distance, but they sure—

"Let me be honest, Mr. Jordan." She folded her hands on the lined yellow legal pad in front of her, redirecting his attention to her words instead of her appearance. "When we talked yesterday, I sensed you might be concerned about a woman handling your case. If that's an issue, we should discuss it."

He stared at her.

What?

"Uh . . . no. It's not an issue." As he spoke, he replayed their phone conversation in his mind. As best he could recall, he hadn't said anything inappropriate. "Why would you think that?"

"In my business, I tune in to nuances. You seemed surprised when I introduced myself."

That was true—but not for the reason she assumed.

Better play this just right or those hackles he'd raised could turn into a wall.

"I'll admit the notion of a PI brings to mind characters like Sherlock Holmes, Mike Hammer, Philip Marlowe, and Sam Spade. I may have been a little thrown—but I have no issue with women in any role as long as they're capable. I reviewed the bios on the Phoenix website, and while no personalities were identified, all four of you appear to be experienced and qualified."

After a few moments of silence, her shoulders relaxed a mite.

"I'm one of the former police detectives. And *my* favorite fictional PI as a child was Nancy Drew."

"I was a Hardy Boys fan myself—but I think Nancy's books sold better."

"They did." Her tone was serious, but the tiny twinkle in her irises was a hopeful sign.

Better change the subject while he was ahead.

"If you were with County, I assume you know my detective friend who recommended Phoenix—Colin Flynn."

"We worked a few cases together. He's a good guy."

"Yeah. He is." Odd that Colin hadn't mentioned Heather during their phone conversation yesterday, when he'd passed on Phoenix's name.

Then again, if you were interrupting a man's first Christmas holiday with his bride of only eight months, some distraction could be forgiven.

Particularly in light of the romantic music that had been playing in the background.

"So before we talk about why you're here—do you have any other concerns or questions about working with Phoenix . . . or with me?"

She was back to that.

But a PI who didn't take anything for granted, who sought clarity and preferred clear communication, would be an asset on any case.

"No." He locked gazes with her. "I have a very close female friend who long ago eradicated any latent chauvinistic tendencies I may have had."

The corners of Heather's lips rose a hair, even as an emotion that resembled . . . disappointment? . . . flashed through her eyes, gone so fast it was possible he'd imagined it.

"Kudos to her." She picked up the dregs of her tea. "Let me give you our new-client paperwork to fill out while I get a refill, and then we can discuss your case."

As she walked over to her desk, a glint of light from the vicinity of her feet caught his attention.

Huh.

Heather Shields's manner might be all business, and her overall attire professional, but her black pumps sported impractical three-inch heels adorned with gold polka dots, and the flat bows on the front were "tied" with metallic knots.

The playful shoes seemed out of character. Frivolous, almost.

But they were also cute.

And very sexy.

Especially with her hot-pink-polished nails peeking through the open-toed front.

He tried without total success to ignore them as Heather returned to the table.

"I happen to like shoes. It's my one vice." She set the paperwork in front of him. "However, I wear much sturdier footwear for field work."

Shoot.

She'd noticed him gawking.

This woman's keen intuitive abilities would be a huge asset during an investigation, but they weren't working in his favor today.

Keep your response light and simple, Jordan.

"On the scale of vices, shoes are one of the least problematic."

"Unless you're Imelda Marcos." Her mouth flexed—suggesting she was more amused than annoyed by his interest . . . thank goodness. "I'll be back in a minute."

With that, she swiveled away and disappeared out the door, shutting it behind her.

In the silence that followed, Rick let out a slow breath.

That had been an intriguing—and unsettling—encounter.

He'd come here this morning to tap into the skills of a firm Colin said had strong credentials and a reputation for solving thorny cases that lacked sufficient evidence to interest law enforcement.

Heather Shields had plenty of the former, based on what he'd seen of her in the past few minutes, as well as the law enforcement citations, commendations, and diplomas arrayed on her walls.

No surprise there, knowing Colin's high regard for the company.

What he hadn't expected was the zing of adrenaline . . . attraction . . . testosterone . . . whatever . . . that had blindsided him the instant she walked into the lobby.

Which was totally inappropriate.

He was here for professional, not personal, reasons.

So before she came back through that door, he needed to rein in his pulse, corral his unruly hormones, and focus on the reason for his visit.

A missing man who'd left a trail of blood.

And if that mission wasn't sobering enough to shift his attention from the beautiful, captivating woman who'd walked into his life this Tuesday morning to more urgent matters?

He was in a boatload of trouble.

3

"Your new client is one hot dude."

As Nikki spoke behind her in the Phoenix kitchen, Heather concentrated on dunking a tea bag into the water she'd nuked—and suppressing the flush edging onto her cheeks.

Thank goodness she'd closed the door to her office across the hall, or her face would get even redder.

"He's a nice-looking guy." She managed a noncommittal tone—but Nikki was right. The photos she'd found on the net hadn't come close to capturing Rick Jordan's almost tangible masculinity or in-person charisma.

The other woman snorted as she moved beside her to retrieve another tea bag too. "Give credit where credit is due. The man is smoking. Does he have brains to go with the brawn?"

"I just met him." Heather turned away to ditch her tea bag . . . and give her blush another few seconds to subside. The brew wasn't going to be as strong as she liked—but she could tolerate weak tea better than a discussion about the man sitting in her office, who'd left her tingling from a mere handshake.

"So? You've got first-rate intuition." Nikki refilled her mug from the water dispenser in the fridge. "Is he just eye candy—or is there substance there?"

Based on what she'd read online this morning, there was plenty of substance.

But she wasn't about to discuss the man's attributes with Nikki while he was sitting a few feet away.

"Too soon to tell. Besides, what does it matter? A client is a client."

"Unless they become more. Ask your three fellow PIs about that."

She didn't have to. Nikki had given her the scoop on how all three had met their wives while investigating cases for them.

"I'm viewing him as a client. Nothing more." She walked toward the door.

"That's how it started with Cal, Dev, and Connor too."

"The odds of lightning striking twice—let alone four times—have to be astronomical. I wouldn't get carried away if I were you."

"Stranger things have happened." Grinning, Nikki lifted her mug toward the man across the hall. "And getting carried away by that guy would be worth dreaming about."

Keep moving, Heather.

"I need to get back to work."

"I would too, if I had a client who looked like yours."

Shaking her head, Heather crossed the hall. Nikki had a romantic streak as wide as the Mississippi, enhanced by the happily-ever-after she was living.

But since her own Mr. Right had been elusive for thirty-four years, Heather wasn't as convinced a chance encounter could lead to a fairy-tale ending.

Even if the attractive guy in her office could double for Prince Charming.

Erasing that inappropriate comparison from her mind, she opened the door and reentered.

Rick stood—and she came to an abrupt halt. "Are you leaving?"

Maybe the fee schedule in the new client packet had scared him off.

"No. I was . . ." He gave a sheepish shrug. "Sorry. I usually stand when a woman enters the room. It's a reflex at this point in my life. I didn't mean to offend you."

Good grief.

Thanks to her tendency to find gender slights where none were intended, the man felt obliged to apologize for being polite.

She had to fix this problem.

Fast.

"You didn't offend me—and I'm the one who should apologize. I've been misinterpreting cues and making inaccurate assumptions. My only excuse is that in my previous job, women weren't always viewed—or treated—as equals. On occasion I jump to wrong conclusions."

"Don't worry about it. I saw similar situations with women in the military. I can understand how being the target of that sort of bias could make a person wary."

"Thank you for being gracious." She retook her seat. "And thank you for being courteous. I didn't always experience that in my prior line of work. Your mother must have trained you well."

He sat more slowly, a shadow flitting across his eyes. "No. The friend I mentioned earlier taught me the social niceties." He pushed the single-page client information form across the table toward her but offered no additional information.

Drat.

Who was this female friend he obviously held in high esteem?

She picked up the sheet of paper and skimmed it, giving his left hand a surreptitious glance as she did so.

No ring.

Which didn't mean he wasn't married. Or living with someone. Or engaged.

A handsome, clean-cut, well-spoken guy like him would only be single by choice. Six-foot-plus, toned physique, precision-trimmed light brown hair, striking cobalt blue irises . . . Nikki's eye-candy description was spot-on.

But who cared?

This was, as she'd reminded their office manager, a business meeting.

Period.

"Did I miss a line?" He twined his lean fingers together on the table.

"No." She reined in her wayward thoughts and finished her scan. He'd supplied all the data required for the background check they ran on clients prior to accepting new cases.

Most clients.

For someone sent to them by a police detective, the Google search she'd done this morning should suffice.

"The landline I listed is for the camp. My personal and home phone is the cell number."

"Got it." She made a notation on the form. "Did you have a chance to review the fee schedule?"

"Yes. I think I'm in the wrong business." He flashed her a smile.

"People who've never used a firm like Phoenix are often surprised at the rates. If you want to reconsider, that's fine."

"No. I have to take a shot at this."

"Okay. Tell me how we can help you."

"I'm trying to locate an army acquaintance who may be in trouble. I called his landline, but it's out of service. I don't have a cell number."

"Why do you think he's in trouble?"

"Several reasons—including the blood I found on my property."

She raised her eyebrows. "Blood is never an encouraging sign. What are the other reasons?"

"Instinct . . . and the items he left behind."

Instinct wasn't always relevant. Not everyone's was sound in every situation—as her faulty conclusion about Rick's possible gender bias proved.

Hard evidence like blood and physical objects was far preferable.

"Before we talk about the items you found, could you back up and walk me through what happened?"

"Sure." He took a sip of coffee and set the mug aside. "This all began last Friday afternoon after I arrived home from town."

"Home being Camp Gideon?"

"Yes." He narrowed his eyes. "You ran background on me?"

"SOP for new clients, to ensure our services aren't being used for illegal purposes. However, the source of your referral is impeccable, so I just did some cursory internet browsing. You have a higher online profile than most people because of the camp. There's a wealth of material out there."

In fact, she'd read far more than necessary about the recreational facility for foster children located forty-five minutes west of St. Louis—and the ex–army pilot who'd traded combat missions for a humanitarian career.

Especially after she'd spotted a photo in one of the stories of a smiling Rick surrounded by a bunch of adorable, grinning kids clutching fishing poles.

No need to share all that, though.

He grimaced. "There's more out there about me than I'd like, to be honest—but press coverage generates donations, and we can always use those. The real story is the kids . . . and what the camp does for them."

The man was modest too.

Another checkmark in his plus column—if she was keeping score.

Which she wasn't.

"What happened after you got home?"

She listened to his trail-of-blood story, taking notes as he talked.

"During my second pass in the canoe shed, this is what I found." He withdrew a small key and a slightly bent medal from his pocket and set them on the table.

She leaned forward for a closer inspection. The medal was engraved with an image of Michael the archangel, but there were no distinguishing features on the key.

"Tell me the significance of both."

"I have no idea why this is important or what it's for." He indicated the key, then touched the medal. "This is a good luck charm given to me by a guy who was going home. He told me to continue the tradition and pass it on before I left too. It's gone through multiple hands."

"I take it you know who left these items."

"I'm 99.9 percent sure it was a guy named Jackson Dunn— better known as Boomer to the crew. He was the medic on our Chinook. I gave the medal to him after my last tour in the Middle East."

Helicopter pilot. Chinook. Middle East.

Phoenix's newest client may not have been an average GI Joe.

"What regiment?"

His eyes narrowed. "160th."

Hunch confirmed.

The man sitting across from her had been part of the elite special ops aviation unit that tackled nighttime attack, reconnaissance, and rescue/insertions missions at low altitude and fast speeds. A high-octane, high-risk, hero-making job.

"You were a Night Stalker." A tinge of awe crept into her voice.

He arched an eyebrow. "I'm impressed. The 160th wouldn't mean anything to most people."

"I have a friend who was in the army. I've heard my share of war stories and military minutiae."

His gaze flicked to her bare left hand.

Interesting.

Maybe she wasn't alone in feeling a tingle of electricity—and wondering about significant others.

Might that suggest his female acquaintance was merely a friend—or was she jumping to conclusions again?

Hard to tell.

But why not clear up any question that could be lingering in his mind about *her* marital status . . . even if this was strictly a business meeting?

"My friend works in Washington now. Once she got out of the service, she took a civilian job with the State Department."

Unless her imagination was working overtime, the emotion that sparked in his eyes was relief.

Yet his tone was measured when he spoke. "A fair number of people get government jobs after they muster out."

"You didn't. Running a camp for foster kids is about as far from military life as you can get."

He hitched up one side of his mouth. "We do have a mess hall, though—and our own version of reveille."

"But no helicopters."

"No."

"You don't miss flying?"

He shifted in his seat. "I haven't given up flying entirely."

She waited a few beats . . . but he didn't offer anything more.

Stop digging for personal information, Heather. The man's

here to find a missing friend, not play the background swap of the dating game.

Check.

She cleared her throat. "So tell me about Boomer. Have you been in touch recently?"

"No. I haven't seen him since I left the service five and a half years ago, but we always exchange Christmas cards. He lives in Lexington."

"Lexington." She cocked her head. "What kind of trouble could he be in that he'd come to you out of the blue from so far away, apparently injured, without any warning?"

"I haven't a clue—but I did tell him once that if he ever needed help, all he had to do was contact me and I'd give him whatever assistance I could."

"You two were that close?"

"No. I didn't hang out with him on the base between missions. But he put his life at risk once to save mine. Offering a helping hand was the least I could do."

There was a story there. One she wanted to hear.

But Rick's taut posture said it wasn't one he intended to share.

Let it go, Heather. You don't have to know those kinds of private details for this investigation.

Sound advice—even if she didn't want to hear it.

She forced herself to refocus on the reason for his visit. "Have you tried contacting any of his family members or mutual friends?"

"We don't have any mutual friends—or none that both of us have kept in touch with. After I was discharged, I left the military behind. And he doesn't have any family."

"Why wouldn't he pick up the phone and call you?"

"I don't know—but he may have tried to phone after he left the camp. There are four calls on the camp answering service from Friday. The area codes indicate three were made from nearby, one from St. Louis. There were no messages—but the timing is suspicious. I don't get many calls on the camp line in the winter. Most inquiries go to the director of operations during the off-season."

"Do you have the numbers from the calls that came in?"

"Yes. I jotted them down from caller ID." He retrieved a slip of paper from his coat and handed it to her.

The fourth digit of both numbers was a nine—common in pay phones in the area.

Also suspicious.

"I think these calls came from public phones. That, plus the timing you noted, adds credence to the notion that Boomer may have been trying to contact you."

"Strange that he didn't leave a message."

"Unless he's being tracked and is afraid to drop any clues that could indicate his whereabouts. The use of a pay phone would support that theory."

"Yeah." Rick picked up the bent medal again. "Colin wasn't convinced there was enough evidence to interest law enforcement in the case, but it seems to me there's plenty here to suggest Boomer has a big problem. You'd think he'd start with them, at least."

"I agree. So the fact he came to you may indicate he doesn't want the police involved."

"Won't they *get* involved if someone files a missing persons report, though?"

"You want the truth? The majority of adults who disappear choose to drop off the radar. In general, police don't give priority to a search unless there's clear evidence of foul play."

"Shouldn't blood on the ground raise antennas?"

"You said there wasn't a lot—and there could be a simple explanation for it. A nosebleed from the cold, a cut finger."

She folded her hands. "I agree with Colin. For now, I think you're handling this appropriately. Do you know where Boomer works?"

"The assembly line at the Ford truck plant."

"Really? With all his experience, I'm surprised he didn't stay in the medical field."

"Maybe he saw enough gore to last a lifetime. A lot of us did."

That was possible.

"Why don't you tell me everything you know about him?" She picked up her pen again.

He complied, but what he offered was sketchy at best.

"Sorry." Rick lifted one shoulder. "He didn't talk much about himself. Our exchanges were more the shoot-the-breeze variety on base, and there wasn't much conversation during missions."

"Are there any mutual acquaintances from your military days who may have kept in closer touch with him?"

"I have no idea—but I can give you the names of a few people who might know more about his background than I do. I don't have contact information for them, though."

"I can find that if you give me a few basics."

She jotted down the names of the three people he mentioned, along with their hometowns and a handful of details about their history.

"If I think of anyone else, I can give you a call or text you."

"That works." She picked up the business card she'd laid on the table while prepping for their meeting and handed it to him. "Let me do some preliminary digging. I may locate your friend with very little effort. If I don't, we can regroup. And give me a call if you hear from him in the meantime."

"Of course." He slipped the card into the pocket of his flannel shirt. "Do you require a retainer upfront? I can write a check." He reached for his jacket.

"No. Not necessary."

Actually, it was—in most cases.

But before she took any money from this man, a conversation with Cal and the other partners was in order. Rick hadn't asked for any special pricing consideration, but he wasn't getting rich running a nonprofit camp for foster kids. From what she'd read online this morning, it was more a labor of love than a moneymaker for him.

On top of all that, he was a veteran—and he had nothing to gain by pursuing this search for a friend who could be in danger. He was simply one ex-soldier honoring a promise to another.

As far as she was concerned, this case could qualify for one of the pro bono gigs Phoenix did on occasion—or at the very least they could offer him a discounted rate.

It was worth proposing, anyway.

"Are you certain?" His hand hovered inches from his jacket.

"Yes." She set her pen down and rose. "I'll walk you out."

He followed her back down the hall, slipping into his coat as they entered the reception area.

"How often will you give me updates?" He pulled out a pair of gloves.

"Once a day, minimum, at the beginning. In most cases like this, if you don't find the trail fast, the odds diminish. And we're already four days after the fact."

"I'll hope for positive news." He extended his hand.

She took it, and as her fingers disappeared in his, another jolt of electricity zipped through her.

When her breath hitched, his intense blue eyes studied her . . . which did nothing to restore normalcy to her respiration.

At least he wasn't a mind reader.

She hoped.

He released her hand at last and directed his attention toward the reception desk, where Nikki sat. "Nice to meet you."

"Likewise."

At their office manager's slightly amused inflection, Heather risked a peek at her.

Smug was the only way to describe her expression.

Oh, brother.

She did *not* need a matchmaker complicating her life.

Pivoting away, she walked to the front door and pulled it open. "Drive safe."

"Always. I'll look forward to hearing from you." He exited into the aftermath of the blizzard.

Much as she was tempted to watch him until he disappeared, Heather restrained herself.

Nikki would have a field day with that.

Instead, she secured the door and recrossed the reception area.

"He likes you."

At Nikki's breezy assessment, Heather halted. "How on earth did you arrive at that ridiculous conclusion?"

"It's all in the eyes." She tapped one candy-cane-striped fingernail beside her lashes. "They were drinking you in."

"Don't you think that may be a slight exaggeration?"

"No. And that good-bye handshake lasted longer than normal business protocol dictates." Nikki toed the button under her desk that released the security lock on the door to the offices. "For the record, the liking went both directions."

"I'm out of here."

Without giving the office manager a chance to respond, Heather escaped into the hallway, let the door click shut behind her—and sank back against it.

There was no way Nikki could know that Rick's presence had played havoc with her vital signs. The woman had barely seen them together.

Yet from everything Dev had told her, Nikki had a knack for intuiting matchups.

She'd done it with all three of the guys in the office, hadn't she?

But for now, Rick Jordan was a client—and as a condition of employment, she'd promised to abide by Phoenix's informal no-fraternizing rule. At the time, it had been no big deal. After all, she'd never dated anyone connected to work. It had always seemed like bad policy.

On the other hand, no one had ever crossed her path who'd generated such instant chemistry.

So if Nikki was right, and the attraction went both directions, working with her new client could prove to be challenging in ways that had everything to do with gender—but not at all for the reasons she'd expected.

4

"I don't know what else I can say to convince you to throw your hat in the ring, Brad. The party's behind you, financing is in the bag, and if a businessman with zero political experience can be elected to the highest office in the land, there's no reason you can't be governor. I realize this is a big decision, but we're only eight weeks away from the primary filing."

Phone to his ear, Brad Weston rose from his leather desk chair and faced the expanse of glass that offered a panoramic view of the historic cathedral and Gateway Arch on the St. Louis riverfront.

His unofficial campaign manager didn't have to remind him of the fast-approaching open season on filing. He thought about it every day—far more than was prudent, in light of the demands of his business.

But no matter how much pressure Chuck applied, he wasn't going to be rushed into a decision that could have long-lasting repercussions . . . and potentially unearth problems best left undisturbed.

Unless . . . or until . . . he was certain those problems weren't going to be an issue.

And he wasn't there yet.

"I know all that, Chuck, but I need more time. We're talking about a major lifestyle change—for me and for Lindsey. I'm not certain I want to walk away from my business yet, either."

"You have several excellent offers on the table for the business—at prices that will set you up for life. And your wife is 100 percent behind a run for the governor's office."

He couldn't dispute either of those facts.

The business he'd built over the past four years had flourished far beyond his wildest dreams. Who could have imagined his concept for small-group, shared senior living spaces as an alternate to large-scale independent living facilities would attract investors—and buyout offers—from coast to coast?

And while Lindsey would support whatever he decided, the notion of being the state's first lady did appeal to her.

"I'm not going to debate that, Chuck—but I'm not finished weighing the pros and cons."

"You said you were going to think about this over the holidays." A touch of impatience tightened the other man's voice.

"I did—but the holidays aren't over until January 2. I have seven more days." The door to his office opened, and his wife peeked around it. He motioned her in. "I have to run to a lunch meeting. I appreciate all you've done, but I have to be certain about this."

"Okay." The word was agreeable. The tone wasn't. "I'll chill until a week from today. But if you decide anything before then, let me know."

"I will. Otherwise, enjoy the New Year's celebrations."

"I'd enjoy them more if I knew you were on board for the race."

"I'll see if I can accommodate you. No promises, though. Give my best to Susan." He dropped the phone back into the handset and crossed the plush carpet to greet his wife. "Sorry.

The call took longer than I expected. How are you?" He kissed the cheek she offered.

"Fine—but hungry. I made a reservation at Kemoll's." She perched on the edge of his desk, displaying a shapely calf enhanced by the spike-heeled pumps she favored. "Was that Chuck?"

"Yes. Pressing for an answer."

"I thought you'd decided to go for it." She tipped her head, her long blonde mane perfectly—and professionally—mussed . . . as always.

Lindsey's beauty routine might cost him an arm and a leg—but he could afford it. And how could he complain when he woke up next to this beautiful woman each morning?

Besides, she'd given up her modeling/singing career to marry him. Indulging her was a joy. Yes, she'd benefited from the marriage in terms of her balance sheet—as his brother often reminded him during their infrequent calls—but having her for a wife made him the real winner.

And if she ever did occupy the governor's mansion, she'd be a spectacular first lady.

"I'm leaning that direction—but I keep having second thoughts."

"Brad." She stood and walked over to him, brushing a piece of lint off his suit jacket, the sultry scent of the pricey Dolce & Gabbana fragrance she favored invading his pores. "You'd be perfect for the job—and you know you want it."

Yeah, he did.

He wanted it so much he could taste it.

The whole notion of a kid with his background rising to the governor's mansion held an element of sweet revenge. Politics may not have been in his original plan, but now that the seed had been planted, he couldn't stop thinking about it. Success in that very public arena would constitute an in-your-face rebuke to all the people who'd never expected him to amount to anything.

Like his brother.

And his old man, if he were still around.

But there were risks to a dream like that.

"Honey?" Lindsey eased closer. "What's holding you back? You're a successful entrepreneur. You're personable. You're a decorated veteran, active in your church, generous to charity, and have no skeletons in your closet. You're a Boy Scout. Why not give it a shot?"

He kissed the corner of her crimson, flawlessly outlined mouth. Messing with her hair or makeup when she was planning to be seen in public was a no-no, as he'd learned early in their eighteen-month-old marriage.

Yet attention to appearances would serve her well in politics—and she made up for her public hands-off rule behind closed doors.

"Because politics doesn't provide any privacy—and I do have a skeleton." Or two.

If anyone dug deep enough, his Boy Scout image could crumble.

She waved a hand. "That's ancient history."

"Reporters can be tenacious."

"But there's no evidence to find, is there? You got rid of it, right?"

"Yes. Long ago."

"Then I don't see the issue. If anything was going to hit the fan, it would have happened already. Why would someone go public at this late date and implicate themselves? That would be stupid."

"True."

But blackmail could become a real possibility.

And that was a mess he didn't need.

"Brad—we all make mistakes. You're a fine, decent man, and Missourians would be lucky to have you for governor."

"I'm still considering the idea." Especially since one of the people who could have caused waves was no longer a threat.

"Well . . . if my vote counts, I say go for it."

She gave him the seductive smile he loved.

The one she'd aimed his way two years ago at the upscale bar he'd dropped into one night when the pressures of his mushrooming business and the dismal state of his personal life had been weighing him down.

"Your vote counts. Always." He brushed his lips across her forehead and twined his fingers with hers. "Let's go enjoy the best Italian food in St. Louis."

"I'm right behind you."

"Beside me."

She nudged him with her hip. "I like how you think. That must be why I married you."

"Was that the only reason?"

"There were a few others. I'll discuss them with you tonight at home." She winked and led him toward the door.

He followed without protest.

Too bad he couldn't skip the lunch, the afternoon of back-to-back meetings, and the fund-raising cocktail party he'd promised to drop in on after work—and go directly home.

To the woman who'd brought sunshine back to his life, who supported the idea of his candidacy despite the disruption it would cause in their lives—and who would relish the role of first lady.

He joined her in the elevator, and as they descended to the ground floor, he reached a decision.

If he felt comfortable by the end of the week that he could pull this off without having to worry about ghosts from his past coming back to haunt him, he'd toss his name in the ring for the party nomination for governor.

And hope no one ever discovered the Boy Scout candidate had an Achilles' heel . . . or two.

. . . . .

"Is that you, Heather?"

As her father called out from the kitchen, Heather stomped the snow off her boots in his foyer. "No. It's a burglar launching a sneak attack."

"Ha-ha."

A moment later, he appeared in the doorway of the short hall that led to the back of his half of the duplex, dish towel slung over his shoulder. "Your cheeks are red."

"It's fifteen degrees out, and the windchill is in the negative range."

"I know. That's why I stayed by the fireplace all day with my book." He motioned toward the living room, where flames from the gas logs added a warm glow to the space. "There are definite benefits to retirement."

She dispensed with her coat and shucked off her boots. "I hear you. But the roads aren't bad now. Are you going to your volunteer gig at the history museum in the morning?"

"Unless God dumps another batch of snow on us."

"The prediction is clear skies and warmer temperatures tomorrow. We may be in for a brief thaw."

"I'll take it. You hungry?"

"Do you have to ask?"

He chuckled. "Nope. You've always had a healthy appetite. Your mom did too—and she never gained an ounce."

At the hint of sorrow in his eyes, Heather's throat tightened.

Nineteen years may have passed since Nora Shields lost her battle with cancer, but not a day went by that her dad didn't mention her.

That was the kind of marriage she hoped to find someday.

One filled with deep, abiding love that endured beyond time and distance. Preferably with a handsome man who stirred her pulse.

An image of Rick Jordan materialized in her mind, and she frowned.

Her client was off-limits—and he might not be available anyway.

On top of that, she'd just met him this morning, and—

"Hey . . . kitten." Her dad closed the space between them and gently smoothed out her brow. "I didn't mean to make you sad about your mom. I'm sorry."

"It's okay, Dad." She forced up the corners of her lips. "I switched into work mode for a minute. These days, my thoughts of Mom are happy."

"Mine too. Somehow time softens the sorrow and puts the joyful memories center stage instead." He smiled at her, his bushy eyebrows lifting beneath his shock of white hair. "Now tell me about your day. Your expression a few moments ago makes me think it was a bit out of the ordinary."

"It was—but let's eat while I give you the scoop. What's for dinner?"

"Coq au vin."

"Yum." She linked arms with him as they strolled toward the kitchen. "You've become a fantastic chef in your retirement."

"I have to admit I've surprised myself. Who'd ever have guessed that a man who spent his career putting up drywall and hammering nails would learn to tell the difference between a spatula and a whisk?"

"You surprised me too, but I've eaten far better these past two years."

"Don't sell yourself short. You're a first-rate cook."

"Maybe—but I don't have time to labor over a gourmet dish like coq au vin every night."

"Those omelets and stir-frys you used to whip up before I

retired were fine. Also healthy. I put on a few pounds those first few months after I dived into the culinary arts."

"You and me both. Please tell me we're not having chocolate mousse for dessert."

"We're not. I agree with your suggestion that we restrict desserts to weekends or special occasions."

"Then let's dig into that coq au vin."

He dished it up while she got their drinks, and after a simple blessing he returned to the subject of her day.

"Now tell me what happened at the office. I expected the first day back after the holiday to be quiet."

"I did too, until my boss called last night."

She gave him a topline, leaving out names and details as she always did when she talked shop with him.

"So basically you have a missing persons case." He cut off another piece of his chicken. "One more somber than usual, with that trail of blood. Did you make any headway today?"

"A little." But Rick should be the first person to hear about that—in the morning, after she did more digging tonight.

"I know that look—and I won't ask for any more details on the case. Let's talk about your client instead. You said he and the missing man were in the service together?"

"Yes."

"How recently?"

"Five and a half years ago."

"In that case, I'm assuming he's on the young side."

"Depends on your definition of young. My personal scale keeps moving higher with every birthday that passes."

"Wait until you're my age. Give me a range on the guy—twenties, thirties, forties?"

"Thirties." In truth, she knew exactly how old he was, after running a bit more background on him once she had his social security number from the client contact form.

He was thirty-six.

And he'd never been married.

But single didn't mean available. He could be living with that female friend, or on the verge of getting engaged, or—

"Is he single?"

She refocused on her father, whose blue eyes had begun to twinkle.

Had he read her mind, or what?

"He's not married"—she gave her remaining chicken more attention than it deserved—"but he mentioned a woman friend in glowing terms."

"Doesn't mean they're involved. I consider Sandy a dear friend, but there's nothing romantic between us."

"There could be if you showed any interest along those lines. She's always inviting you places—and she's a nice woman."

"Yes, she is. But I'm a one-woman man. End of story. Your client may feel the same about the friend you mentioned. Nice woman, but not the one he wants to spend the rest of his life with."

This conversation had veered way offtrack.

"I can't debate that. We didn't discuss the matter." But that quick glance Rick had lasered at her left hand could suggest he didn't have any romantic leanings toward his female friend . . . or anyone else.

Or it may have been mere curiosity.

"You could find out."

Heather stopped eating. "Why would I do that?"

"You said yourself you're not getting any younger—and eligible men aren't as plentiful at your age as they were when you were twenty-five."

"Gee. Thanks for the encouraging words." She stabbed a bite of chicken.

"I'm just suggesting you should be open to opportunities—

unless this guy is a repulsive lowlife like some of the characters you met in your previous job."

"No." Not even close.

"There you go." Her dad waved his fork at her. "You were a detective. Don't you think this situation warrants further investigation?"

"You know . . . I'm beginning to suspect you're trying to marry me off so you won't have to cook for me anymore."

"You know better than that. To tell you the truth, I wouldn't mind cooking for three—plus a few smaller mouths. I'm not getting any younger, either. And I'd love to have a grandchild or two to spoil."

"You're as bad as our matchmaking office manager."

"Ah." His face lit up. "She thought this new client had potential too?"

"We have a no-fraternizing rule, Dad."

"Only while he's a client."

If she didn't know better, she'd swear he and Nikki had compared notes.

"Let's not get ahead of ourselves." She scooped up the last of her mashed potatoes, swirling them in the rich sauce.

He sighed and poked at a carrot. "I was hoping this new job would give you more time for a social life, but I haven't seen any evidence of that yet."

"I'm too busy learning the ropes. Next year, I'll dive into the social scene."

"How?"

She stopped eating. "What do you mean, how?"

"I mean, how are you planning to meet eligible men?"

Good question.

For a woman who didn't enjoy bars or the party scene, and whose friends were all married and immersed in family life, there weren't a huge number of options.

"Church is a possibility."

Her father snorted. "Not our church. The congregation is too small. The sole eligible man in your age range is Larry, and he seems to be a confirmed bachelor. Not that you'd be interested in him, anyway."

No, she wouldn't.

And it had nothing to do with the fact that the man looked like a stereotypical nerd, complete with thick glasses and puny physique. She wasn't so shallow that she'd write off a man based on his appearance. It was what was inside that mattered.

Unfortunately, Larry was as nerdy inside as out—and the man's conversational repertoire was limited to the weather and the latest gossip at the accounting firm where he worked.

She wanted a man who could converse on a wide range of topics, make her tingle with a mere touch, had a compassionate heart, and was trustworthy, honorable, and steadfast in times of trouble.

Of course . . . good looks wouldn't hurt, either.

Once again, an image of Rick flashed across her mind.

"Is this client of yours handsome?"

She stared at him. Strange how her father had an uncanny ability to pick up her thoughts—like her mom used to.

Perhaps Mom had passed that aptitude on to her husband, knowing a teenage girl would need guidance after the loss of her mother.

"Yes." She stood. "I'll load the dishwasher."

"Curious that you don't want to talk about this guy."

"There's nothing else to say."

"Uh-huh. So, would you like to stay for a while, play cards?"

And dodge more questions?

"Not tonight. I want to put in another hour or two of research."

"I rest my case about your lackluster social life." He finished his final bite of chicken and rose too. "You go ahead. I'll clean up. That suspense novel I'm reading can wait a few more minutes."

"The deal was that if you cook, I clean up."

"I'm waiving that obligation tonight."

She hesitated. It wasn't fair for her not to keep her end of their bargain—but truth be told, she didn't want to talk about Rick anymore, and she was anxious to follow up on a few more leads tonight.

"I'll agree on one condition. You let me fix dinner for us on New Year's Eve."

"You should be dining with a handsome guy that night."

An unexpected pang of yearning ricocheted through her, but she pasted on a grin and leaned over to kiss his cheek. "I will be."

"Pure flattery. However—I'll take it." Chuckling, he gave her a squeeze and followed her to the door.

"I'll call you later." She pulled her knit hat low over her ears and tugged on her gloves.

"Always appreciated. It's a blessing to have someone to say good night to."

"Amen to that. Talk to you later."

Turning up the collar of her coat, she followed the salted, shoveled path to her own front door and dived back into work before her sudden melancholy mood could take root.

Three hours later, stifling a yawn, she shut down her computer for the night. There would be a ton of information to share with Rick tomorrow—but sad to say, she was no closer to finding his friend than she had been when Phoenix's newest client walked out of their office this morning.

She wasn't giving up—but if she didn't find him soon, this would become a police matter.

Rising, she arched her back, then wandered into the kitchen to call her dad.

He answered on the second ring. "Let me guess. Your hour or two of work morphed into three."

"That can happen on a new case."

"Any luck?"

"I haven't tracked down my client's friend yet—but I've learned some interesting background."

"Will it help you find him?"

"Remains to be seen. How late are you staying up?"

"Until the end of the PBS special I tuned in to after I finished my book. How about you?"

"I'm brushing my teeth, washing my face, and going to bed."

"Sounds like a plan. Sweet dreams and stay warm on this cold night, sweetie."

"Same to you, Dad."

She slipped the cell back into the charger, her father's sign-off scrolling through her mind.

Sweet dreams and stay warm.

A dream about a certain ex–army officer would certainly qualify as sweet.

Or maybe spicy, if he contributed to the staying warm part of her dad's wish.

She quashed that fanciful notion at once.

This was ridiculous.

Not since her crush on the football hero in high school had she indulged in such romantic pipe dreams.

Nor was this the time to start.

The man was her client, and she had a job to do. Her total focus should be on solving the case he'd brought to Phoenix.

Squaring her shoulders, she marched toward the bathroom. She was *not* going to think about Rick Jordan again tonight. She would get ready for bed, pile extra blankets on to stay warm, and plan the menu for the New Year's Eve dinner she was going to make for her and her dad.

And she'd pray that if any sweetness infused her dreams, it would come from dessert possibilities for the holiday dinner versus the man Nikki had aptly dubbed eye candy.

5

As her cell began to trill from deep within her purse, Ellen Chambers let out a huff.

She did *not* want to field phone calls while maneuvering through the snarl of St. Louis rush-hour traffic on this Wednesday morning.

But with her boss out of town for the holidays and every crisis falling into her lap during his absence, there wasn't much choice.

Keeping one hand on the wheel and both eyes on the cars around her, she reached over to the passenger seat and groped through her bag until her fingers closed over the phone. Spared the screen a quick glance. Sucked in a breath.

What on earth . . . ?

Her heart stuttered, and her hand jerked on the wheel.

A loud, prolonged honk blared beside her, and she made a quick course correction as the other driver mouthed a word you didn't have to be a lip reader to understand.

She shifted her attention back to the cell, pulse pounding.

Why would Brad be calling her?

Unless . . . was it possible he'd come to his senses and—

The phone rang again, and she jabbed the talk button before it rolled to voicemail.

"Hello?" Safer not to assume it was him on the other end of the line.

"Ellen—good morning. Did I catch you at a bad time?"

It *was* him. That mellow voice was etched forever in her memory.

Her grip tightened on the phone. "Never. Although I *am* surprised."

"I'm sure you are—and I apologize for calling out of the blue like this. But I need to talk to you."

"Why?"

"I'd rather discuss it in person."

Fine by her.

"Do you want to drop by my place after work?"

"After work is fine, but I have to be discreet about the location. Why don't I pick up two coffees and meet you in a convenient parking lot?"

The traffic around her ground to a halt yet again, and she pressed on the brake, scowling.

He wanted to meet her in a parking lot?

What was wrong with Starbucks?

However . . . if he was thinking of running for governor, as the press had speculated, he'd have to be extra circumspect in his behavior. A whiff of scandal could derail his chances—and a rendezvous such as theirs could be fodder for the rumor mill.

But could this clandestine meeting mean he was having second thoughts about his hasty nuptials?

That would be welcome news.

If he was planning to dump the blonde floozy, maybe she could scrap the rest of the plans she'd been making.

"Ellen? Are you there?"

The cars began to move again, and she accelerated. "Yes. I can meet you. Where did you have in mind?"

"The parking lot at the office complex at Watson and Rott Road, across from Laumeier Park. In the middle, about seven thirty. There shouldn't be many cars left at that hour. Does that work for you?"

"Yes. I'll have a caramel latte."

"I remember. Are you driving the same car?"

"Yes."

"See you tonight."

He ended the call.

Ellen set the cell on the seat beside her, finger tapping a staccato rhythm on the wheel.

There was a slim possibility Brad had realized his impetuous marriage was a mistake—but it would be foolish to get her hopes up. He'd been totally infatuated with Lindsey from the moment he spotted her in that bar two years ago.

It had been so unfair.

Clenching the wheel, Ellen gritted her teeth. Hadn't she been there for him during those early days of his business, offering encouragement as he struggled with start-up issues and comforting him as he grappled with grief after the sudden death of his wife?

She was the one who'd helped him pull through that difficult period, as he'd often acknowledged. Not his trophy wife.

Cracking her window, she filled her lungs with fresh air—and corralled her emotions. She had to be logical about this. Face facts.

The truth was, part of the blame for the unfortunate outcome fell to her. She *had* been married—and Brad had never pretended that didn't bother him. If she'd moved a little faster on the divorce, he might never have ventured into that bar where Lindsey sang.

And she would have dumped David sooner—if Brad had ever mentioned the M-word.

Yet he'd been close to doing that. She'd felt it.

Until Lindsey entered the picture.

Ellen mashed her lips together and switched lanes.

The woman had obviously been out to get him from the beginning—and how could a mousy-haired accountant compete with a blonde model who moonlighted as a songstress?

Men were fickle like that.

David being a case in point, the jerk.

But Brad wasn't like David. He didn't bed-hop with abandon. He was a caring, kind, conscientious man who agonized over every flaw in his character, every mistake he made.

Which was foolish.

No one was perfect, as she'd assured him after he'd shared his secret shame with her in their early days together.

Pursing her lips, she flipped on her turn signal and edged toward the exit ramp.

Could that mistake be weighing on his mind, with the gubernatorial race looming? If he hadn't divulged that piece of history to his wife, he might just want to talk through his concerns with someone who knew about it.

But there was no reason to worry about that past blunder. Few people were privy to the details, and those in the know weren't going to talk.

Including her.

She'd tell him that if the subject came up.

On the other hand . . . the topic he wanted to discuss could be much more personal.

The corners of her mouth rose.

Maybe Brad had discovered that David was out of the picture now—and maybe . . . just maybe . . . he'd realized his beauty-queen bride had been one of his bigger mistakes.

That blunder, however, could be remedied.

And if he hadn't yet acknowledged that marrying Lindsey was an error in judgment?

That, too, could be fixed.

Because if Brad became governor—as he should—he would need a woman by his side who was able to contribute more to their relationship than a pretty face.

. . . . .

Cell chirping, Rick set the brake on his truck, skimmed the screen, and smiled.

A call from his favorite PI was a perfect way to launch this Wednesday.

After returning his greeting, Heather got straight to business. "If you have a few minutes, I can bring you up to speed on what I discovered after we met yesterday."

"I have more than a few minutes—and I'm in town running errands. Why don't you brief me in person?"

"Are you nearby?"

"I'm pulling into a parking spot at Kaldi's as we speak. I could come to you—or you could join me here."

As the impromptu invitation popped out, Rick frowned.

Since a cozy tête-a-tête with a beautiful woman hadn't been in his plans for the day, his subconscious must have taken over.

No surprise, considering how Heather had dominated his dreams last night.

As the silence lengthened, he curbed his disappointment.

Time for damage control.

"Sorry. During the off-season I keep fluid hours. I sometimes forget that not everyone has the flexibility to run out for coffee on a whim. We can do this by phone now, or I can swing by later if that's more convenient."

"To be honest, I'm salivating for a cup of Kaldi's fair-trade Earl Grey. It's a win-win whenever I go there—I get a wonderful cup of tea *and* support an ethically sourced product."

His spirits rebounded.

"My friend Kristin would applaud that sentiment. She runs a fair-trade shop a couple of blocks from your office." He turned off the engine.

Another beat of silence.

"Is this the friend you mentioned yesterday?" A note of caution wove through her voice.

"Yes."

"What's the name of the shop?"

"WorldCraft." He walked across the plaza to Kaldi's.

"I think I've driven by there."

"You should drop in sometime. She's done an incredible job with it."

He ought to tell her Kristin was *not* a romantic interest—and he would. In a few minutes. In person. So he could see her reaction.

"I'll have to do that. I can join you in fifteen minutes, unless that's too much of a delay."

"No. That works. I'll be waiting."

Once they said their good-byes, Rick ordered his own coffee, placed the order for her tea but told them not to make it until she arrived, and bought a Nutella scone and a piece of lemon pound cake.

It would be fun to see which the lady preferred—but he was betting on the chocolate.

By the time he returned to his seat and checked his email, Heather was coming through the door.

He rose as she approached. From the table he'd claimed near the back, he had plenty of opportunity to appreciate her leggings, black high-heeled boots with purple soles and purple stitching, and tweedy black-and-white wool poncho.

Yesterday's outfit had been 100 percent professional—except for the flirty shoes—but today's more casual attire was still all class.

She acknowledged him with a wave as she finished weaving through the tables. "Sorry I'm a few minutes late." She set a folder on the table. "Parking was a bear. I ended up on the next block. At least the weather's warmer today, so the walk wasn't bad."

"Parking's the one downside to this place."

"The only one." She pulled the poncho over her head in one smooth motion, shaking her hair back into place after it was off. "Let me grab a cup of tea."

"Already ordered. I'll get it for you. Go ahead and have a seat. I got pastries to snack on while we talk too." He nodded at the table.

"I noticed. I can see this meeting won't be good for my waistline."

That part of her anatomy wasn't visible today, thanks to the purple sweater that hit her mid-thigh—but he'd seen it yesterday, and it was in fine shape.

"You don't look like you have to worry about that."

"You sound like my dad." She sat, eyeing the sweet treats. "But that's because I *do* worry about it. However . . . I also like to eat. Helping you dispense with these will be my pleasure."

"All I ask is that you save me a few bites."

"I'll try—but you better hurry." She shot him a grin, her hazel eyes sparking with mischief. "My sweet tooth has a tendency to overpower my willpower."

His nerve endings began to buzz—and when the floor shifted beneath his feet, he groped for the back of the chair.

She tipped her head. "Everything okay?"

"Um . . . yeah. I'll be right back."

He escaped to the counter, struggling to regain his balance as he waited for her tea.

Of course he'd noticed Heather's beauty yesterday. That was the reason he'd tossed for a significant portion of the night.

That, and the tiny breath hitch that had stoked his libido as they shook hands while saying good-bye—clear evidence she'd noticed him too, despite her businesslike manner during their meeting.

But there was a different quality about her today. A sense of playfulness that made this get-together feel almost like a date.

Maybe it was the social setting.

Maybe it was her more casual attire.

Or maybe his imagination was working overtime and it was all wishful thinking.

"One Earl Grey tea." The barista set a disposable cup on the counter.

"Thanks." He turned and started toward the corner table.

"Since when do you drink tea?"

At the familiar voice, he stifled a groan.

Talk about bad timing.

Telling Heather about Kristin was one thing.

Telling Kristin about Heather was an altogether different story—and not on his agenda for today.

Conjuring up a smile, he swung back to find his friend watching him, her new husband beside her. "Welcome home. How was the honeymoon?"

"Blissful."

"I can see that." He gave her a hug and examined her face. She did, indeed, look the picture of contentment. "But where's the Caribbean tan?"

Grinning, Luke slipped his arm around her waist and tugged her close. "We didn't spend a lot of time outside."

"We did too." Kristin's cheeks grew pink as she gave her groom an affectionate jab with her elbow. "I used lots of sunscreen."

"Uh-huh." Rick didn't attempt to hide his amusement. "I'll have to hear all the details on Saturday—assuming we're still on."

"Of course we're on."

"It's New Year's Eve."

"Not until evening. I'll be home long before the celebrations begin."

"You okay with that?" He deferred to Luke.

"Her acceptance of my proposal was contingent on me cutting her loose for the Treehouse Gang's twice-a-month breakfasts. I'm fine with it—just like Colin's wife is."

"Thanks for that. Are you both still on vacation?"

"Yep. For five more glorious days. I may pop into the shop for a minute, but Alexa has it covered. And it's slow the week after Christmas anyway." Kristin examined the tea. "So what's with the Earl Grey?" She gave the shop a scan, as if searching for a clue.

In his peripheral vision, he saw Heather rise.

Blast.

"Hey. There's a former coworker of mine." Luke lifted his hand as she wound through the tables toward them.

No surprise that Kristin's detective husband would know Heather, even if his tenure with the St. Louis PD was far shorter than Colin's.

"Hello, Luke." Heather stopped a few feet from their threesome. "Nice to see you. I hear congratulations are in order."

"Yes. Thanks. This is my wife, Kristin."

The two women exchanged pleasantries, and when Heather turned to him, it was obvious she'd connected the dots and come to the obvious conclusion.

"This is the friend you mentioned."

"Yes."

"How are you liking the PI gig?" Luke eased aside as the order line grew.

"So far so good."

"You're a PI?" Kristin's eyebrows rose.

70

"Yes."

"And you two know each other?" She looked back and forth between Rick and Heather.

Rick transferred the hot tea from one hand to the other. "I'm working with her on a project."

"At a coffee shop?" Kristin squinted at him.

"Yes. A business meeting—and we should get back to it."

"No problem. We only emerged from our cave for a caffeine fix. We'll talk more Saturday."

Of that he had no doubt.

And by then, she'd have told Colin all the juicy details of this chance meeting.

It was going to be a jolly breakfast.

"The line's getting longer, Kristin. Let's join it or we'll be here all morning." Luke steered her toward it, calling a good-bye over his shoulder.

As the duo departed, Rick extended the cup of tea toward Heather. "I hope this hasn't cooled off too much."

"It'll be fine."

"Let me get a few extra napkins and I'll join you at the table."

She aimed a quizzical look his direction but headed back to their corner.

As she walked away, he retreated to the napkin dispenser. Exhaled. Rotated the kinks out of his neck.

His coffee date with Heather might not have gone quite as he'd expected up to this point, but there was one positive outcome.

Despite the grilling his two best friends would subject him to on Saturday, the untimely meeting with Kristin had given him the answer to a very important question.

Heather was glad the female friend he'd mentioned wasn't a rival.

The cues in her expression had been subtle—but they were obvious if you were watching for them.

And before today's meeting was over, he'd make certain she knew there was no one else in the shadows competing for his affection.

Why that was important in the midst of an investigation into a strange and troubling disappearance wasn't clear. After all, he and Heather were almost strangers.

But one thing he knew with absolute certainty.

They weren't going to be strangers for much longer if he had anything to say about it.

6

Heather took a sip of her perfect cup of tea, cut off a bite of the Nutella scone, and popped it in her mouth.

Mmm.

Also perfect.

That word fit the toned, handsome, ex–Night Stalker who was heading her way in the crowded coffee shop too.

Best of all, she didn't have to worry about his friend Kristin anymore.

His *married* friend.

Of course, there could be another woman in the wings. A guy like Rick wouldn't have to spend a single minute alone, based on the discreet—and not so discreet—glances being aimed his direction by the females at every table he passed.

But for the next few minutes, he was all hers . . . even if their relationship was strictly business.

For now.

"I could have made money on that one." He set the napkins on the table and took the chair across from her, indicating the scone with a grin. "I pegged you as a chocolate woman."

"Always my first choice—but I don't discriminate with

sweets." To illustrate, she cut off a bite of the pound cake too. "You better have some, or these will vanish before your eyes."

He did as she suggested, helping himself to a generous portion of each. "Sorry to delay our meeting. I knew Kristin frequented this place, but I thought she'd be holed up with her new husband until the weekend."

"No worries. I'm glad I got to meet her. Have you two known each other long?"

"Since I was twelve."

"Ah. Childhood friends."

"Yes. Colin Flynn and I teamed up with her in middle school."

That was a surprise. Boys that age didn't usually befriend girls.

"You weren't afraid of getting cooties?"

One side of his mouth hitched up. "There's a word I haven't heard in years. But no, that wasn't a concern. She was a kindred spirit."

"In what way?"

His lips flattened. "Let's just say we all shared less-than-ideal family situations."

Her first inclination was to ask more questions—but probing that topic wasn't relevant to today's get-together, and he might resent it.

Let it go, Heather. Change the subject.

"A troubled home life doesn't seem to have soured her on marriage. And Colin got married not long ago too." That ought to be a safe topic.

"Yes. I'm the last one standing."

"No interest in a trip to the altar?" As her query hung in the air between them, heat crept across her cheeks.

So much for not prying into the man's personal history.

"The interest is there." He locked gazes with her. "But the woman hasn't been."

74

She stared at him.

Not only had he answered her question, he seemed to be sending a message.

Like . . . the woman might be in the picture now—or a woman with potential, anyway.

Did he mean . . . her?

Come on, Heather. You met the man yesterday. Even Nikki, with her romantic heart and rose-colored glasses, would call that a leap.

"What about you?"

She blinked at his follow-up question. "Sorry?"

"I don't see a ring. Aren't you interested in a trip to the altar?"

"Oh." Scrambling for an excuse to break eye contact, she cut herself another piece of scone. The man's baby blues were much too discerning . . . and disconcerting. "Kind of the same story."

"I imagine your prior work with the PD could be intense and all-consuming. I know that's the case with Colin. He never had time for romance until the day Trish walked into his life. Or he walked into hers, to be precise."

"I guess that's how it happens sometimes." She bit into the scone and risked a peek at him.

"I guess so." He continued to look at her, his demeanor serious. Intense.

Oh, man.

She restrained the urge to fan herself.

"So . . . uh . . . let me bring you up to speed on what I've discovered in the past twenty-four hours." Her voice cracked.

Good grief.

She was acting like a schoolgirl in the throes of her first crush.

If Rick noticed her adolescent behavior, however, he gave no indication of it—thank heaven.

"Whenever you're ready." He picked up his coffee.

Focus, Heather.

Taking that advice to heart, she opened the folder in front of her. "I verified the source of the calls you got the afternoon Boomer visited the camp. They did originate from pay phones—three at a truck stop in Wentzville, the other in a mall in St. Louis. I also managed to get in touch with two of the three people who you said were mutual acquaintances overseas. One of them—Nathan—has kept in touch with Boomer on and off."

"That doesn't surprise me. He was always a social guy. Has he heard from him lately?"

"Not for several months. But during our phone conversation last night, he did pass on a few new pieces of information. Did you know Boomer had a drug problem after he left the service? Heroin, to be precise."

"No." Twin creases appeared on Rick's brow. "That's a disconnect. He wasn't into any of that kind of stuff when I knew him. He didn't even drink. In fact, he walked a wide circle around people who did."

"Nathan suggested he may have been battling PTSD."

"I never saw any evidence of that while he was on our crew."

"But he was in the army two years longer than you were. The stress could have taken a toll. Or there may have been a triggering incident."

"Possible, I suppose. And PTSD could also explain the drug issue."

"Nathan suggested that too. Last he heard, however, Boomer was clean." Heather sipped her tea. "I also asked about any romantic liaisons he may have had. As far as Nathan knew, there's no current relationship, but Boomer was involved overseas with an army specialist by the name of Beth Johnson near the end of his enlistment. Ring any bells?"

"No."

"She's out of the service, but Nathan didn't know where she lived or have any background that could help me locate her."

"Did you mention my name during your conversation?"

"No. Until we know what's going on, I'd rather not tell anyone more than we have to, given the lengths Boomer went to see you on the QT. I just said we were trying to locate him for a client, and referred him to our website to review our credentials."

"Do you think you can locate this Beth with so little to go on?"

"I'm going to try. One other piece of news. Boomer requested several unscheduled vacation days for a family emergency last week."

He arched an eyebrow. "Did his employer tell you that?"

"No. They told Nikki, our office manager/receptionist. She has a remarkable ability to finagle information out of people on the phone."

A beat passed.

"I didn't realize she assisted with cases."

Nor did he like it. The skepticism in his measured comment was subtle—but it was there.

Not unexpected. She'd been down this road with a couple of previous clients. Heck, Nikki had thrown *her* at their first meeting. Better set the record straight up front.

She folded her hands on the table. "Nikki is an incredible asset to our firm. She not only manages the office and keeps us all on track, but she's a whiz at database searches and phone pretexting—PI-speak for role-playing to get information, like undercover law enforcement operatives do."

His eyebrows peaked. "That surprises me."

"You're not alone." She gave him a quick smile. "There's far more to Nikki than first impressions might suggest. She became a street kid at fifteen after fleeing an abusive home. Despite the long odds against her, she managed to get her GED while working full-time, then won a scholarship to college. As soon as she was able, she rescued her kid brother from their toxic home environment by fighting for—and being awarded—custody."

A slight shift in his demeanor told her he was impressed. "That's quite a story. Most girls who are on the street at that age fall into prostitution . . . and worse."

"I know. I saw plenty of that during my law enforcement career. I think Nikki could have ended up in the same boat, except she met a minister in a homeless shelter who encouraged her—and convinced her she could overcome her background. In the end, her newfound faith gave her the foundation to survive and persevere."

"Lessons of the day—never underestimate the power of faith . . . and don't judge a book by its cover."

Heather grinned. "Well, I have to admit the Christmas tree outfit yesterday was a tad over the top. Her attire isn't usually that extreme. But she does have an abundance of holiday spirit."

"I'll drink to that." He lifted his cup and took a sip. "Did you—or Nikki—find anything else worthwhile?"

"Boomer's neighbor in the adjacent apartment last saw him a week ago Monday. His parking spot is also empty."

"Lexington can't be more than a few hours from here. Where was he before he got to my place?"

"It's a five-and-a-half-hour drive—and that's an excellent question. I'm working on it."

"Can you track his credit card purchases to see where he's been?"

"Not without pushing the legal limits—which we prefer not to do."

He swirled his coffee, faint furrows creasing his forehead. "So where does that leave us?"

"The old girlfriend may offer us a lead, if I can track her down. We've also been monitoring his social media sites . . . but there's been no activity for nine days. His last entry on

Facebook suggested he was looking forward to Christmas and planned to help serve dinner at a soup kitchen. I talked to the people there. He never showed."

"When is his leave up at work?"

"Tomorrow—and he hasn't tried to extend it."

"Do you think he'll show up?"

"No. Considering the distance he drove to see you, the blood on the ground, the four back-to-back phone calls after his visit, and the items he left behind at your place, I doubt he's going to stroll into work tomorrow as if nothing has happened."

"If he doesn't—what happens next?"

"I call law enforcement and inform them of our suspicions. I happen to know a detective in Lexington, and I've got lots of police connections here. That doesn't mean the case will get a ton of extra attention, for the reasons I explained yesterday. But at minimum, we can get a BOLO alert issued and put Boomer on their radar screen while I continue to dig."

"You think he may still be in this area?"

Heather took a sip of tea. Should she share her gut feeling . . . or hedge about her misgivings until she had more concrete evidence to support them?

"I won't hold you to your answer." The corners of Rick's mouth flexed up. "But you've spent a fair number of years at the detective game, and I'm betting your instincts are solid."

She hesitated—but only for a moment. The man was a former Night Stalker, who'd seen his share of ugly. He didn't have to be handled with kid gloves, like many clients.

"To be honest, I don't know where he is—but I'm worried that he hasn't tried to make contact again. After his concerted efforts to connect with you last week, I would have expected him to keep trying."

"If he could."

Their minds were tracking in the same direction.

"Yes."

"I don't feel warm and fuzzy about this, either." Rick swiped a wayward drop of coffee off the table with his finger. "Maybe the key he left is—pardon the pun—the key to the reason for his visit."

"I agree it must be significant. Yet it has no meaning to you."

"No."

"I showed it to the rest of the Phoenix folks in a staff meeting yesterday. The consensus was that it was for an old-style locker."

"Like the kind they used to have in schools?"

"And gyms. Was Boomer athletic? Would he have belonged to a health club?"

"He wasn't all that athletic in the Middle East. During off-duty hours, he preferred reading over working out. He grew up in Minnesota, and he hated the heat over there."

"He didn't exercise at all?" She took another bite of the lemon pound cake.

"Not much. He liked back-country hiking, but his favorite sport was ice skating—hockey, mostly, but I know he dabbled in speed skating too. Since there was more sand than ice around our forward operating base, he settled for an occasional jog on the treadmill and a few weight routines."

"Did he continue skating as an adult?"

"Yes. He said that was one of the things he missed most while he was overseas. Why?"

She finished her tea and set the empty cup on the table. "Now that you've mentioned skating, that key reminds me of the ones that used to be on the small lockers at the rinks I went to as a kid. The kind where you had to put a quarter in to make the key work when you wanted to retrieve your shoes."

"I imagine those sorts of lockers were used in numerous places in those days."

"True. However, given the meager information we have to

work with, I plan to investigate all possibilities. Once I'm back in the office, I'll identify the rinks in the Lexington area and run the key by them in case my hunch has merit. Especially any rinks that have been around for a while and may be using the old-style lockers. I'll also call the neighbor again tomorrow morning to see if Boomer's returned. If not, we'll verify with the plant that he's a no-show and I'll work my law enforcement contacts."

"You're putting substantial time and effort into this."

"I'm a 100 percent kind of woman."

A spark of heat flashed in his irises. "Nice to know."

She tugged at the cowl neckline of her suddenly too-warm sweater.

Time to switch subjects.

She flipped open the folder in front of her, withdrew a sheet of paper, and slid it across the table to him. "This is an updated rate schedule for our services."

He skimmed the document and shot her a puzzled look. "These prices are much lower than the ones on the other sheet you gave me."

"We discussed your case at our meeting yesterday and decided to extend a veterans' discount."

"Is that SOP?"

"No. It's a case-by-case call. In light of your military service, your current charitable endeavors, and your willingness to take on this search at no personal gain, we decided the case merited special consideration."

He rotated his cup in his fingers as several seconds ticked by. "In other words, this would be sort of like pro bono work that's done for charities."

"Not exactly—but similar."

"Did you make a pitch on my behalf?"

"Yes."

He tapped his almost-empty coffee cup against the table,

his expression neutral. "I can afford to pay the Phoenix bill, Heather."

Could he—or was pride overriding logic?

Even worse, had she offended him?

Hard to tell . . . but possible, despite her explanation that their discount rationale was about more than money.

Better take another stab at this.

"I didn't mean to imply you couldn't. That's why we're not offering to do the work for free. While Phoenix does take on an occasional pro bono case, this isn't one of those. However, it does have the potential to lead to a high-profile success story, which in turn could boost the image of the firm and increase business. So in addition to all the other reasons I mentioned for the reduced rate, there's a potential upside for our bottom line."

Amusement glinted in his eyes. "You offer a convincing argument—and I don't mean to sound ungrateful. I appreciate you going to bat for me."

"It was a business decision." To some degree.

"I'll tell you what. If you solve this and Phoenix ends up getting positive press, I'll accept the lower rates. Deal?" He held out his hand.

She'd rather he agree to the lower rates up front—but it was obvious that wasn't going to happen.

"Yes." She returned his firm grip, and the warmth of his strong fingers seeped into her pores.

The clasp went on longer than necessary . . . but he seemed as reluctant to end it as she was.

When at last his fingers loosened, she withdrew her hand and cleared her throat. "I, uh, think that's it for today." She stood and busied herself closing the folder and lifting her poncho off the back of her chair.

"You'll call later if you find anything worthwhile?"

"Yes." She slipped her head through the opening in the woven garment and picked up her purse. "Thanks for the tea and sweets."

"There's a bite of each left." He motioned toward the plates.

"I'll take one if you will."

"Sold. You pick first."

She chose the scone—as she knew he expected her to do.

He finished off the lemon confection in one bite. "I'll walk you out. I should get rolling with my errands."

Always the gentleman.

Nice.

"Thanks." She struck off for the door.

Once outside, he took her arm as the gusty wind pummeled them. "It's hard to believe a week ago we were preparing for a major winter storm. Today's almost balmy."

"I'll take it." She clutched her flapping poncho with her free hand.

"Not a winter person?"

"Definitely not. Give me sun and sand any day." She headed toward the street on the south side of the plaza.

"Ever think about relocating to a warmer climate?"

"No. I grew up in St. Louis. This is home. And my dad lives here."

"You two are close?"

"Very. I was an only child, and after my mom died when I was sixteen, we grew even tighter. Are you from St. Louis too?"

"Yes."

"Do you still have family here?"

He pulled a pair of shades from his jacket and slid them over his nose. "My mom's dead. I don't stay in touch with my father." He skirted an icy patch, keeping a firm grip on her arm. "Where's your car?"

She sneaked a peek at him.

The rigid set of his jaw said he wasn't going to expound on his family situation.

Drat.

The more she learned about this man, the more she wanted to know.

"There. The black Taurus." She waved toward the Phoenix-supplied vehicle, two cars down the street. Another perk of the job.

He walked with her to the door, waited until she slid behind the wheel, then backed up a step. "Thanks for meeting me. I hope it didn't disrupt your workday too much."

"No—and thanks for the tea and treats. Talk to you soon."

She started the engine, pulled out of the spot, and accelerated toward the corner.

At the stop sign, she checked her rearview mirror.

He was standing on the sidewalk now, hands buried in his pockets, watching her from behind those dark glasses that added to his mystery—and appeal.

As for his comment about disrupting her day?

She'd lied.

From the moment he'd invited her for coffee, he'd disrupted her day . . . in the pleasantest of ways.

But as she hung a right and drove toward the Phoenix office, she shifted mental gears. She had a job to do—and the number of days that had elapsed since Boomer tried to contact Rick wasn't giving her positive vibes. Unless her intuition was failing her, the man was in trouble, and speed was of the essence. She needed to make some headway on this case and find him fast.

If it wasn't already too late.

. . . . .

He wasn't supposed to call. Ever.

Frowning, I glared at the message on the phone I'd dug out of my gym bag and muttered a word I never used in public.

The reason for the contact was no mystery.

The man wanted his money.

But so far, I'd seen no proof he'd finished the latest job—and I wasn't about to take the word of a hired killer, no matter how many texts he'd sent assuring me it was done.

Still sweaty from my workout, I passed on a shower, picked up the bag, and left the locker room. I could return the call in the privacy of my car.

As I exited, I shaded my eyes against the glare of sun reflecting off the piles of snow in the parking lot. Blizzard one day, heat wave the next. Typical St. Louis.

I pulled out my sunglasses, slid behind the wheel, and punched in his number. This was going to be a short conversation. I had places to go this afternoon.

"You have an unpaid bill." No proprieties or civil greetings from this guy.

"I'm waiting for proof the job is done."

"As I said in my texts, your proof is weather contingent."

"I have no idea what that means."

"My method was rather creative this go-round. But in light of the current forecast, it shouldn't take long for proof to emerge. However . . . our agreement was payment upon completion of the job. The job was done last Saturday."

"How can I be certain of that? Your last attempt was a bust."

"I always finish my jobs—and I expect to be paid on completion." A hint of steel sharpened his voice.

If he knew who I was, his attitude would frighten me.

But he didn't.

Just like I didn't know his identity.

Amazing how you could contract anonymously for all sorts of services on the web these days.

Trouble was, if he was as smart as he seemed to be, he might be able to put two and two together and come up with a theory about who could be behind the hit—if I didn't pay him.

But I would.

As soon as I had proof.

"You know I'm good for the money. I paid you promptly after the first hit and I gave you half for this job up front. Did you find out why he was in St. Louis or who he saw, like I asked you to?"

"No."

"Did you try?" I dug through my gym bag for a cigarette.

"Yes. I exerted as much pressure as I could without leaving evidence that could jeopardize an accidental death ruling. He had a much higher tolerance for pain than your first target. She was happy to share a name after a little persuasion."

I lit the cigarette and took a puff.

Not the best news I'd heard today.

What if he'd met with someone, told them what he knew?

But even if he had, there was no evidence to support his story. As long as the original players had been silenced, anything that surfaced would be third-party hearsay. Easy to dismiss.

Nevertheless—it would be helpful to know what he'd done in St. Louis. Who he'd spoken to.

"Can you dig for that information if I pay you more?"

"Sorry. Not my area of expertise. I like jobs that are over and paid for fast. However . . . I understand your desire for verification. I'll see if I can speed that up, now that Mother Nature is cooperating. Watch for a text with proof. You know where to send the funds. If we don't talk again, it's been a pleasure."

A click sounded in my ear.

I punched the end button, dropped the phone back into my gym bag, and took another drag on the cigarette.

In all probability, the guy was telling the truth about completing the job. He was a pro, with excellent credentials.

I ought to assume it was over and relax.

But I couldn't.

Something didn't feel right.

I cracked the window and blew out the smoke. The tendrils wound toward the sky . . . dissipated . . . disappeared. Like they'd never been there.

That's how I wanted to feel about the people who could thwart my plans.

How I *should* feel, after all the effort I'd put into this.

Yet I couldn't shake the niggling worry that a loose end was out there somewhere.

And while I'd never been a big believer in intuition or the so-called sixth sense, I didn't discount them, either. On a few occasions, a prescient hunch had saved me a lot of grief.

Maybe this was one of those times.

Problem was, I had no idea how to pin down the source of my unease.

So until I did, I was going to keep my eyes open and my ear to the ground.

Because if there was another obstacle standing in my way, I'd find a way to deal with that too.

Just as cleanly and ruthlessly as I'd dealt with the others.

7

"Success. Your hunch paid off."

As Nikki strolled into her office, Heather swiveled away from her laptop. "Someone recognized the key?"

"Yep. I talked to the managers at both of the Lexington ice rinks and emailed them a jpeg. Here's the contact information for the guy who identified it." She set a slip of paper with the name of the rink and the manager's phone number on the desk.

"What was your story?"

"Distraught mother. My son went to several venues with lockers while visiting over Christmas, and since I don't want to send Grandma on a wild goose chase to retrieve his Kindle, I'm trying to pin down the location."

"Clever."

"Not one of my best—but it worked. What happens next with the key?"

"If I don't locate Boomer today, I see a road trip to Lexington in my future."

"You going solo?"

"It's not a two-person job."

"If you want company, I have a feeling your client might be willing to tag along."

Now wouldn't that be cozy?

Despite a sudden adrenaline rush at that notion, Heather maintained an impassive demeanor. "I'm sure he has plenty to do here."

"I bet he wouldn't mind delaying whatever's on his schedule."

"I wouldn't ask him to."

"He could volunteer."

"Put away your rose-colored glasses, Nikki."

"Why don't I loan them to you instead?"

"I don't need them." She rested her elbows on the arms of her chair and steepled her fingers. "Clients are off-limits."

"You met him for coffee."

"It was a business meeting."

"You could have asked him to come here."

Like she didn't know that.

"I didn't want to put him out—and I like the tea at Kaldi's."

"Uh-huh." Nikki sauntered back to the door. "If you want me to call anyone else, holler. I love exercising my acting chops."

From down the hall, Dev snorted.

"Hey." Nikki leaned out the door, eyes narrowed. "I heard that—and I'll remember it the next time you want me to make phone calls for one of *your* cases."

"I was sneezing." His explanation was laced with laughter.

"Try again." Nikki folded her arms, propped a shoulder against the door frame, and lowered her volume. "He's a piece of work."

"Excellent at his job, though." And a welcome change of topic from the personal turn their previous discussion had taken.

"True—and he gets points for being nice to Danny."

"He also brings you soy lattes."

"Bribery so I'll tackle that mess of files in his office." Nikki sniffed, but a twinkle glinted in her eyes as she pushed off from the door. "Give me a shout if you want any help."

"Thanks. I will." Heather swung back to her laptop, chuckling at the zingers Nikki and Dev exchanged as the office manager passed him on the way back to the reception area.

Their sparring added a healthy dose of spice to her days.

But so did the investigations she'd been working on during her brief tenure at Phoenix—especially this one.

And not just because the client was hot.

Cases didn't get much more intriguing than a bleeding man, desperate to see an old army buddy, who had disappeared without a trace.

Putting distracting thoughts of a road trip with Rick aside, Heather dived into a search for social media sites affiliated with women named Beth—or Elizabeth—Johnson.

She quickly found quite a few—Twitter, Facebook, Pinterest, LinkedIn, Instagram—but none for a woman in the appropriate age range who gave any indication she'd been in the army.

Odd.

Most people these days had a social media presence, and they often hinted at their background in a bio or their posts.

Turning to a general Google search, Heather found a bunch of Beth Johnsons.

Too many.

She tried a number of different search words in connection with the woman . . . army, Middle East, specialist, even Boomer's real name.

Also dead ends.

She started over, substituting Elizabeth for Beth.

As she scrolled through page after page, Heather sighed. At this rate, their sole clue in this case might be whatever was in the locker in Lexington. Unless that, like the key, was another enigmatic item neither of them would—

Six pages into her search, she froze. Sat up straighter. Leaned toward the screen.

This woman had potential.

She clicked on the article from the Lubbock, Texas, newspaper. Skimmed the short piece. Sank back in her chair.

It was possible the subject of the article wasn't the Beth Johnson who'd been Boomer's girlfriend—but her gut told her it was.

So she'd make a few calls, dig deeper, verify her intuition.

And if her suspicion was correct, this case had just taken another bizarre—and unsettling—turn.

■ ■ ■ ■ ■

She was here.

As Brad spotted Ellen's burgundy Accord among the sparse cars in the parking lot, his stomach clenched and he reduced his pressure on the gas pedal.

Maybe this was a bad idea.

Maybe he should do a U-turn, point his car toward home, and call her to say they didn't need to talk after all.

But they did.

She was a loose end—and loose ends were a liability if you'd set your sights on public life. All of them had to be tied up. Preferably in a neat, simple manner, with the least possible mess.

He pressed on the accelerator again.

Best case, a simple conversation would clear this up. Ellen was a reasonable woman, and she'd cared about him once. If she promised him the relationship they'd shared would remain known only to them . . . and if she appeared to be sincere in that assurance . . . he'd accept her word. She'd never done anything to suggest she was untrustworthy or had less than his best interests at heart.

In fact, if Lindsey hadn't come along, he might have married Ellen.

And likely lived to regret it.

He pulled into the empty spot on the passenger side of her car, retrieved the two drinks from the cup holders beside him, and gave the parking lot a sweep.

No one was about on this winter night.

Perfect.

As he stepped out of the car, her passenger door swung open.

Typical Ellen. Always thoughtful and accommodating. Always able to intuit his concerns, anticipate his needs.

Juggling the drinks, he slid inside, passed hers over, and closed the door, killing the dome light. "Thank you for doing this, Ellen."

It was difficult to see her features in the dim interior, but the glow from the streetlights scattered about the lot was sufficient to illuminate her tiny smile.

"*Dave.*"

He blinked. "What?"

"That's a line from the movie *Dave*. We used to play name that movie by tossing each other lines, remember?"

"Oh. Yeah. I do remember." But not until she'd reminded him. Those days felt like ancient history.

"Back to your thank-you—it's not necessary. You know I've always been at your beck and call." She sipped her latte. "What can I do for you tonight?"

He took a slug of his black coffee. "You may have heard I'm toying with a run for governor."

"Yes."

"I think I could have a shot at it."

"I do too."

"But I want to run on a platform of conservative values. Voters are sick of scandals and dishonesty and morally corrupt politicians."

"Yes, they are."

The car was too dim to read her expression, and it was impossible to tell from her inflection if she was getting his drift.

Better spell it out.

"Here's the thing, Ellen. I know our relationship is over, but it wasn't that long ago—and reporters will be sniffing around for any mud they can find to sling at me. Having an affair with a married woman might not raise eyebrows in the more liberal states, but Midwesterners aren't as lenient."

"No one knows about what we did except us, Brad."

"I realize that—and I don't plan to tell anyone. I was hoping you felt the same."

"Why would I sabotage you by talking about our relationship? I loved you . . . and you loved me, back then."

How to respond to that?

Yes, Ellen had been important to him—and he'd cared for her. A lot. She'd come along during a dark period in his life when he'd been desperate for comfort and encouragement.

But love?

No.

In hindsight, his feelings for her hadn't gone that deep.

Yet she was waiting for him to reciprocate her sentiments. He'd dealt with enough women to recognize a leading comment.

This required diplomacy.

"I don't think a married man should admit to that. It seems somehow dishonorable."

"Kind of like fooling around with a married woman."

"You know I always had reservations about that."

"Yes, I know." She took another sip of her latte. "I divorced David a year ago, by the way."

"I hadn't heard that."

"To tell you the truth, I wish I'd done it sooner. In time to give us a chance."

Another land mine.

"Rehashing the past isn't going to change it."

"That's true. I'm a firm believer in focusing on the future." She took another sip of her latte. "So how's married life?"

"Couldn't be better—and Lindsey's waiting for me at home as we speak. I can't linger too long."

"Of course not." Her voice hardened slightly.

She must still blame his wife for their breakup. But from his perspective, Lindsey had come into his life at the perfect moment. If she hadn't, he might have pushed Ellen to get a divorce and married her. Settled for less. Despite all of her fine qualities, the kind of spark he'd had with his first wife and Lindsey had never been there with the woman sitting beside him.

Another truth best left unspoken.

He shifted the coffee he didn't want from one hand to the other and posed the question he'd come to ask.

"So I can count on you to keep our secret between us?"

Ellen angled her head away, and the light illuminated her profile. She was pretty in a pleasant, homey sort of fashion—but more importantly, she was trustworthy. If she promised to remain mum, he would put his fears to rest.

About this risk, anyway.

She turned back to him, her face once again in shadows. "I don't plan to talk to anyone about what happened between us, Brad. You're a good man, and I wish you all the best. I always have. You deserve to be governor, and I won't do anything to damage your chances."

He let out a long, slow breath.

This was how he remembered Ellen. Kind, caring, generous. And what she'd just said was exactly what he'd hoped to hear.

"Thank you."

"My pleasure."

"Well . . ." He fumbled for the door handle.

"Good luck with the race."

"Thanks. I'll need it. Politics can be a nasty business."

"*Life* can be a nasty business."

"I can't argue with that. Thank you again for meeting me tonight—and enjoy the rest of your latte."

He slid out of her car, closed the door, and returned to his own vehicle.

Before he put his key in the ignition, she'd pulled away—without a backward look.

And that was what he had to do from now on too.

Aim for the governor's office . . . do whatever was necessary to get there . . . and never look back.

■ ■ ■ ■ ■

Two conversations with Heather in less than six hours.

This was his lucky day.

Smiling, Rick rose from the laptop in his home office, tapped the talk button, and strolled toward the picture window that offered a panoramic vista of the pine-rimmed lake under the full moon. "Long time no talk."

"Sorry to interrupt your day again, but I do have news. Are you in the middle of anything?"

"Camp paperwork. Your call gave me a welcome excuse to get up, stretch, and enjoy the view of my moonlit lake."

"Sounds lovely."

"It is. You'll have to see it sometime."

"I'd like that. I bet the photos on the website don't do it justice."

"No—and it's very different in winter. Quiet and peaceful. But I love it when the place is filled with energetic, enthusiastic kids too." *Get back to business, Jordan. The lady is busy. She didn't call you to shoot the breeze.* "So what did you find out?"

"I have two pieces of news. First, I managed to locate Boomer's former girlfriend."

Impressive.

"Did you speak to her?"

"No. That's not going to happen. She's dead."

As Rick digested that bombshell, an owl glided by, silhouetted against the moon—a nocturnal predator skilled in stealth, no doubt in search of an unsuspecting rodent for his evening meal.

"Do you have any details?"

"Yes. She died three weeks ago in Lubbock, Texas. The police report listed it as an accidental death from a fall off the balcony of her condo. The autopsy report hasn't been officially filed yet, but I was able to talk to one of the detectives there. Since those reports are public record in Texas, he was willing to share the findings. Her blood alcohol level was way over the limit."

"She was drunk?"

"Very."

Rick frowned. "That's a disconnect, given Boomer's aversion to alcohol. He didn't even touch beer while we were overseas—or associate with anyone who overindulged."

"I had the same thought. But it's possible her alcohol problem developed later, after she was home—like his drug issues did. The police had only one relative listed as a contact, a sister who lives in Connecticut. Apparently they've been estranged for years. I also spoke with her neighbors and her boss. She worked for a small construction company handling scheduling and logistics. No one was aware of any sort of substance abuse issues."

"Did you pass that on to the police?"

"Yes—but without any signs of foul play, I doubt they're going to expend much energy on further investigation."

"What's your take on the situation?"

"I'd be more inclined to accept their verdict if Boomer hadn't disappeared off the face of the earth."

"Me too."

"I plan to call Nathan back, see if he knows any more about their relationship, and when and where their paths may have crossed overseas. I also have news about the key."

He listened while she filled him in on the ice rink in Lexington.

Also impressive.

At her mention of a road trip, his ears perked up. "When are you going?"

"Tomorrow—assuming Boomer doesn't show up for work and his neighbor hasn't spotted him or his car. I'll stay overnight, poke around, and come back on Friday."

Rick mentally ran through his schedule for the next couple of days. There was nothing on it that couldn't be deferred.

And the prospect of thirty-six hours in Heather's company was too tempting to pass up.

"That's a long drive. Would you like some company?"

A few beats ticked by, and he exhaled.

She wasn't going to go for it.

It *had* been a long shot, and—

"I appreciate the offer, but I'm on the clock for this job. You aren't."

His spirits took an uptick.

She hadn't said no.

"I have a vested interest in the outcome, though—and my relationship with Boomer could come in handy if you're going to interview people who know him. They may be more willing to talk to a friend of his."

"You offer a convincing argument."

His lips twitched as she tossed his words from this morning back at him. "Is that a yes?"

"If you're certain you don't mind."

"Not in the least." Just the opposite.

"Okay. I plan to contact his neighbor again tonight and call his plant first thing in the morning. Once I confirm he hasn't shown up, I'll be ready to take off. You're about forty-five minutes out, right?"

"Yes. Could be longer at rush hour."

"I can call you as soon as I confirm he's a no-show. That could be as early as eight."

"I'll be packed and ready to drive in the minute I hear from you. Do you want me to do anything else?"

"No. I've got it covered. Talk to you tomorrow."

As they ended the call, Rick ambled into the kitchen for a soda before he went back to camp business, nerve endings thrumming.

Part of that physiological reaction was prompted by his concern about Boomer, and the mystery surrounding him.

What had happened to his army colleague?

Where was he now?

Why had he sought out an acquaintance he hadn't seen in almost six years?

Was the old girlfriend's unexpected death somehow related to Boomer's situation?

All those troubling questions were boosting his adrenaline.

But so was the thought of a road trip with the beautiful PI he'd hired to help him solve the mystery.

He couldn't think of a better way to wind down this year.

As for what they might find in the locker at that ice rink?

He could only pray that whatever it was would help them solve the puzzle Boomer had led him to five days ago with a trail of blood.

8

"Chuck? Sorry to call you so early, but I wanted to put you out of your misery. Lindsey and I discussed the race again last night, and we both agreed I should go for it." Brad extended his hand across the breakfast table.

Lindsey took it, squeezed his fingers—and exhaled.

Thank heaven the decision was made.

Brad might have been waffling about it for weeks, but the truth was, the governor's job was his for the taking. And there was no one better qualified than her husband to lead the state . . . or the nation.

If his political career followed the course she expected, the White House could be in their future.

"Sure, sure. I've got time this afternoon." He scrolled through the calendar on his cell while she sipped her orange juice. "Does two thirty work for you?" Catching her eye, he smiled and rubbed his thumb over the back of her hand. "Why?" The corners of his mouth flattened as he listened to Chuck. "I've already discussed that with you . . . I don't see a reason to do that . . . Fine. I'll consider it. See you this afternoon." He set his cell on the kitchen table.

"Is there a problem?" Rhetorical question, considering Brad's expression. But pushing was never smart. He'd tell her what she wanted to know in the end.

"No. I don't think so." He stirred cream into his coffee. "Chuck has a tendency to be overzealous about tamping down potential fires. He's more paranoid than I am—and that's saying a lot."

"Maybe all campaign managers are like that. It's not a bad trait, I guess, if it helps avoid glitches. Is there anything in particular he's worried about?" She scooped out a piece of her melon.

"Nothing you have to fret over." Brad waved aside the man's concerns, as if they were of no importance.

But she didn't buy that.

Her husband's protective instincts had been activated, meaning whatever Chuck had said related to her.

"Honey . . . didn't we promise to always be up-front with each other? To communicate and share? Tell me what he said. Please."

He frowned into his diluted coffee.

She waited in silence.

Finally he pressed a finger against the single crumb marring the pristine glass-topped table. Deposited it on his plate. "Chuck thinks the three of us should discuss your background this afternoon, decide on a few talking points."

She stared at him.

They were worried about *her* background?

She wasn't the one with the secret that could shatter this whole endeavor if it ever leaked out.

However . . . only she and Brad knew about that.

Her history, on the other hand, was out there waiting to be discovered for anyone who wanted to dig deep.

"Hey." He reached over and touched her cheek. "This is no

big deal. No one's going to hold your upbringing against you. In fact, you could be a role model for how to overcome a terrible family situation."

"I'd rather not revisit those early years at all. I told you that."

"I understand—and I'm not saying you have to. But we do have to decide how we want to spin this for the media."

"I thought we agreed that I'd offer a few generic comments, then say I've put that difficult life behind me and no longer talk about it."

"We did—and I'm on board with that plan. But why not discuss it with Chuck, tell him our position, get him on our side? He can develop a bio that skims over the details and makes it clear your early family life is an off-limits subject. In any case, all the players are gone except for your half brother, and you lost touch with him long ago."

That was true.

It was also the reason she wanted to leave her ugly past in the past. Just thinking about those terrible days knotted her stomach.

At the same time, sticking your head in the sand didn't make difficulties go away. The media had an appetite for the kind of juicy details she could provide—if she was inclined to capitalize on her hard-luck story. And if doing so would help Brad claim the governor's seat, she'd suck it up and do it.

But her husband could win this election on his own merits—and she didn't want public sympathy. Nor did she want to be the poster child for a worthwhile cause related to her history.

The first-lady role was prize enough for her.

Still . . . she needed to cooperate with Brad's campaign manager. Talking with the man could do no harm.

"All right. Shall I meet you there at two?"

He twined his fingers with hers and gave her a warm smile. "Have I told you lately that I love you?"

"Every day." She lifted his hand and kissed his fingers. "But don't ever stop."

"I don't intend to. I know I'm the luckiest man in the world—and I'll never forget that."

After a quick kiss, they went back to their breakfast and moved on to less intense topics—but as Lindsey finished her toast and wiped a linen napkin across her lips, her husband's comment about luck replayed in her mind.

He might be the luckiest man in the world—but she was the one who'd hit the jackpot the day he'd walked into that bar and swept her into a life that was the stuff of fantasies.

She would never forget *that*—and no matter what challenges lay between them and the governor's mansion, she would stand by his side and do her part to earn the title of first lady.

. . . . .

"Eat lunch, or head straight for the locker?" As they approached the highway exit for Lexington, Heather glanced at her passenger.

Rick continued to thumb in a message on his cell. "One sec."

She flipped on her blinker and stifled a sigh.

So much for the lively conversation she'd hoped they'd have en route. Thanks to a crisis with the septic system at the camp, he'd spent the majority of the trip texting, emailing, and talking on the phone with contractors and his director of operations.

"Sorry about this." He set the phone on his leg and sent her an apologetic look. "If I'd known the minor sewer backup last night was going to mushroom into a major issue, I would have bailed."

"I'm used to working alone—and I don't mind quiet. Did you get everything resolved?"

"Joyce is going to go out there to meet with a couple of contractors this afternoon. She's a whiz at handling the day-to-day operations of the facility. I'm just glad this didn't happen while camp was in session. That would have been a colossal mess." He slid the phone into his pocket. "Did I hear you mention lunch?"

"I asked which you preferred to do first—eat or check out the locker?"

"My stomach votes eat . . . but my curiosity trumps my appetite. What about you?"

"The locker gets my vote." She flipped on her turn signal again, following the directions from the GPS on her phone. "While you were dealing with your crisis, I heard from my PD contact here. The BOLO alert that was issued paid off. Boomer's car was found in a parking garage at the airport."

Rick's brow puckered. "He flew to St. Louis?"

"Maybe. The police are reviewing passenger manifests to see if his name shows up. They'll also be checking with the car rental companies, in case he just switched vehicles."

"Why are they suddenly interested in searching for him?"

"There was blood in the car. On the driver's side."

"That's consistent with what we know." The puckers deepened. "Am I going to be getting a phone call for a police interview?"

"Could happen—but the presence of blood doesn't constitute a crime scene. We may have more answers before they zero in on you . . . *if* they do. Also, his car's been in the lot since a week ago Monday."

"If he flew into St. Louis then, why did he wait until Friday to contact me?"

"I'm thinking he rented a car at the airport here and drove somewhere else for a few days first."

"Where?"

"I have no idea." Heather motioned ahead of her. "There's our destination."

The ice rink loomed less than a block away.

"Did you alert the rink manager we were coming?"

"No reason to. The locker area should be accessible. It is at most rinks."

"You sound like you've spent a fair amount of time on the ice."

"I was a recreational figure skater in my younger days." She swung into the parking lot, claimed a space, and set the brake. "Let's hope our long drive yields something useful."

Once inside, it took only a few minutes to locate the locker that matched the number on Boomer's key. Like the ones she remembered from her childhood, the cubbyhole was sized to accommodate no more than a pair of shoes and a few personal items.

"I feel a little like I used to at the critical point on a mission in the Middle East." Rick inspected the locker.

She retrieved the key from her purse and held it out to him. "You do the honors."

He took it from her, inserted it, and twisted.

As he opened the door, they both leaned forward to peer inside.

A memory stick lay in the shadowy center.

There was nothing else inside.

"I don't know what I expected—but that isn't it." Rick stared at the data storage device.

"Me neither. However, good things can come in small packages. Let's plug this into my laptop and see what's on it."

Heather slipped on a pair of latex gloves, extracted the item, and deposited it in a ziplock bag.

"You carry gloves and bags with you?" Rick raised an eyebrow.

"Standard detective gear—and most of the same supplies come in handy as a PI. Let's see what we have." She hurried toward the exit.

He followed her to the car, opened her door, and slid into the passenger seat as she booted up her laptop.

"Well . . . here goes." She stuck the flash drive into a port. Clicked on the icon.

The stick contained one item—an Excel spreadsheet.

Heather opened it.

Rick leaned closer to examine the document that appeared on her screen, his breath a puff of warmth against her cheek.

Focus on what's in front of you, Heather.

She forced herself to ignore the faint woodsy, masculine scent that was invading her personal space and scrutinized the information.

The entries on each line were dated with the day and month. No years.

The abbreviations throughout the document meant nothing to her.

The various sets of initials with each entry could represent anything—or anyone.

The dollar amounts on each line were small.

She hadn't a clue what any of it meant.

"Does any of this . . ." Her voice trailed off as she turned her head and found Rick inches away, his broad shoulder brushing hers, his gaze riveted on the screen.

Keep those lungs inflating and deflating, Heather.

She cleared her throat and tried again. "Does any of this mean anything to you?" Somehow she managed to keep her voice from squeaking.

He looked at her . . . and she almost drowned in his blue irises.

It didn't help when his Adam's apple bobbed—as if he was affected by their close proximity too.

He backed up a few inches, lending credence to her suspicion. "No."

She moistened her lips and redirected her attention to the screen. "Not the best news I've had. It's Greek to me, but I was hoping the fact that Boomer came to you with this meant you'd be able to decipher it." She closed the document and right-clicked on properties. "It's not new. This was created six-plus years ago and last worked on a little more than four years ago."

"While Boomer was overseas."

"Right." She saved the document to her computer, pulled out the flash drive, dropped it back into the plastic bag, and peeled off her latex gloves. "I wonder if this could have any connection to Beth Johnson, given her recent death under circumstances that seem dubious in light of what's been going on."

"That thought crossed my mind."

"I definitely think another conversation with Nathan is in order. I tried to call him last night but never connected. A conference call with you on the line may be more productive, anyway. If you're in on the discussion, it may trigger a memory that slipped his mind during our first chat."

"I'm fine with that."

"I also want to talk to Boomer's neighbors, see if any of them can offer any leads or insights in person that they weren't willing to share by phone. I made an appointment with the director of the food kitchen where he volunteers too."

"Speaking of food—I think that should be our next stop."

"Agreed. There's a local sandwich shop nearby that gets high marks on TripAdvisor. Does that work for you?" She put the car in gear and backed out of the parking spot.

"You researched lunch spots?"

She flashed him a grin. "Absolutely. I don't like to waste calories on bad food."

"Did you consult TripAdvisor on the hotel too?"

"Of course. I don't like surprises."

"Remind me to hire you as the travel agent for my next trip."

"Are you on the road a lot?" She pulled onto the main road and accelerated.

"No. I did as much work travel as I ever want to in the military, and it's not much fun to vacation alone."

"No single friends who could go with you?"

"Not anymore. What do you do on vacation?"

She gave an unladylike snort. "What's a vacation?"

"You never take time off?"

"Not much. Police work is intense. My dad and I have taken a few trips together, but mostly I hang out at home if I have a few days off. I'm hoping this job will give me more downtime."

"Is that the reason you changed careers?"

"It was a factor." But not the biggest one. And talking about the end of her detective career wasn't on the agenda for this trip. "There's the lunch place." She pointed down the street. "My taste buds are all set for their pastrami sandwich. Reviewers raved about it."

Thankfully, Rick didn't ask any follow-up questions about her prior career.

But the subject could come up again during this trip. They'd be spending hours together.

And if it did, she might be tempted to share a few of the details—if he opened up about his family history . . . and told her why he'd gone from being a Night Stalker to running a camp for foster kids . . . and dropped a hint or two that he was interested in moving their relationship from professional to personal once this case wrapped up.

For now, though, she'd pull up Boomer's document again while they ate and hope that, between the two of them, they could spot a nugget of information that would give them a clue to follow.

Because if they didn't . . . and if none of the interviews she had planned for the remainder of their stay panned out . . . and if Boomer never resurfaced . . . the reason for his visit to Rick's camp on that cold, snowy day almost a week ago could forever remain a mystery.

9

"Where you at, girl? Don't you hide from me. You know it'll be worse if I have to come a-lookin' for you."

From the tiny spot she'd squeezed herself into behind the logs in the woodshed, Ruby June cringed as her pa bellowed from the back door of the hovel they'd called home for all of her ten years.

He was probably spun out on the latest batch of meth he and Ma had cooked. The whole house stunk like cat pee from it. Same as a bunch of people's houses did here in the Missouri Bootheel, once you got off the main roads.

"Ruby June, you're tryin' my patience! Get out here!"

She peeked through a tiny opening in the pile of logs.

Pa was walking back and forth, jeans flapping around his scrawny legs, waving a willow switch.

Tears brimmed on her lower lashes.

If he found her, she'd be going to school again tomorrow with red welts on her back. The ones that hurt whenever she leaned back in her desk.

But she couldn't complain to nobody.

The one time she'd ratted on her pa, after her teacher asked *about the marks on her legs, the state had sent a man in a fancy suit to the house to talk to him and Ma.*

And she'd paid for that. Her back ached just thinking about that whipping.

After that day, her pa was careful not to switch her anyplace anyone could—

Her heart skittered.

He'd stopped walking and was staring straight toward her.

No!

He couldn't have seen her behind all these logs. And she'd never hid here before. Why would he think to look here?

His eyes got meaner than a spittin' cat's, and he whipped the switch in the air.

She cringed.

Please, God, don't let him find me. Please!

But God must not have heard her, 'cause Pa started toward the shed.

Whimpering, she tucked herself tight into the darkest corner and kept praying—up to the second his shadow fell across the logs and he leaned over the top to glare down at her.

He flicked the switch again, and she flinched.

"I told you to come out, girl." He leaned closer, his rotting teeth as crooked and black as the mouth of a charred jack-o'-lantern. "You're a piece of filthy . . ."

She wrapped her arms around herself and tried to block out the ugly words he hurled at her.

When the tirade ended, he snatched her arm and yanked her from her hiding place.

"No! Please, don't hurt me, Pa! Please don't . . ."

"Lindsey! Relax, sweetheart. You're fine."

Expelling a shuddering sob, she jerked her eyelids open. Sucked in a deep breath. Went limp.

It was okay.

She was safe.

The arms holding her were gentle. The voice soothing. The face above her filled with compassion rather than contempt.

"Sorry." She lifted a trembling hand and massaged her temple. "D-did I disturb you?"

"I heard you while I was coming up the steps. It sounded like a bad one."

"Yes." Brad knew all about her nightmares. If she could have kept them secret, she would have—but you couldn't control your subconscious while you were asleep.

"Migraine?"

"Yes."

"I'll get you a pill."

She closed her eyes, and the bed jiggled as he stood—which didn't help the nausea that always accompanied the searing headaches.

He was back fast with the medicine and a glass of water. The bed dipped again as he sat. "I'm sorry, sweetheart. Today's meeting with Chuck brought this on, didn't it?"

"I guess so." She swallowed the pill with a gulp of water, handed him the glass, and sank back onto the pillow.

"He agreed to abide by the rules we set down."

"I know. Talking about my past just brought it all back."

"I'm sorry to put you through this. I know how bad your childhood was."

No, he didn't. She'd shared a lot—but not everything. What was the point? It would only upset him.

"I'll be better after I rest for a bit."

"It's not too late for us to change our decision, you know."

"No." That was the last thing she wanted to do. Brad was meant to be governor—and perhaps more. "Give me a couple of hours and I'll be back on my feet."

"Are you certain? Your peace of mind is more important to me than the job in Jeff City."

"I appreciate that—but I'm not going to let memories from my past stand in the way of your future."

He hesitated . . . but at last he stood. "You're an extraordinary woman, you know that?"

"You're prejudiced."

"No. It's true." He touched her hand. "Call if you want anything. And if you're up to it later, I'll run out and pick up dinner for us. How does that sound?"

"Perfect. Thank you for taking such good care of me."

"Nothing but the best for Missouri's future first lady." He bent to press a tender kiss to her forehead. "I'll be in the den, going over a few reports."

"You work long hours."

"They'll get longer if we move to Jeff City."

"But you'll love it."

He smiled. "Yeah. I think I will. Try to rest."

She watched him leave . . . then closed her eyes, willing the migraine to subside as she silently cursed the man who'd dominated her existence for sixteen long years. Until her beauty and intelligence gave her the tools she needed to break free and create a new and better life—and a new identity.

If only she could erase all those memories.

But that was a foolish, impossible wish. Every painful one would follow her until the day she died.

However . . . she didn't have to let them control her. The nightmares were subsiding. Slower than she'd like, but there'd been steady progress. The last one had been months ago, and without today's meeting, it was unlikely they would have reared their ugly head again.

As long as Chuck kept his promise and deflected any queries about her past, she'd lick the migraines once and for all.

But even if she didn't—she wasn't going to let them impact her ability to be an outstanding first lady. She may have come from nothing, but she'd excel at that job. Just like Brad had excelled with his business—and would end up as governor—despite his own less-than-perfect background.

They were both self-made people who had triumphed over the odds.

And together, they'd continue to show the world that there were no limits to what an ambitious, aggressive, determined person could achieve.

No matter the obstacles that had to be overcome.

■ ■ ■ ■ ■

Their road trip had not gone as well as Heather had hoped.

The faint, parallel furrows above her nose, the strain at the corners of her mouth, the slight tautness in her features—maybe no one else would notice those subtle signs of tension, but they were obvious to Rick.

And understandable.

The interviews with Boomer's neighbors had yielded zilch, and while the director of the food kitchen had sung the man's praises, he'd offered nothing helpful. Unless the last neighbor—on their schedule for tomorrow morning—shared some new information, their trip would yield nothing but an indecipherable Excel document.

"I'd like to try Nathan once more before we call it a day." Heather opened the trunk of her car and leaned in for her overnight bag.

He beat her to it.

"I've got this." He picked up her bag and slung his duffle over his shoulder. "I'm fine with another call to Nathan tonight—and with letting him know I initiated the search."

But that could also be a bust. The man either wasn't retrieving messages or was ignoring Heather's attempts to contact him.

"Let's check in, take a few minutes to get settled, then find a quiet spot to do a conference call." She started across the hotel parking lot, toward the lobby.

He fell in beside her as a bus rumbled up to the covered entrance. The instant it stopped, the doors opened, and a crowd of loud, laughing, college-age young people poured out.

Heather groaned. "And I was hoping for a peaceful night's sleep."

"They may calm down later."

"I wouldn't place any bets on that." She wove through several clusters of revelers to get to the front door. "Must be a group getting a jump on New Year's Eve. So much for any hope of finding a quiet place to make our call. We may end up back in the car."

"Or we could call from one of our rooms."

Her tiny hesitation before she reached for the door would be apparent only to someone watching her carefully.

Like him.

"That may work." She pushed through, with an assist from him.

But the notion made her nervous—no doubt for the same reason it was setting his nerve endings on fire.

The electricity between them was almost palpable.

However . . . they were both adults. This was a business trip, and they needed to make a private phone call. A hotel room was the most convenient place to do that. There would be nothing personal about this get-together.

Unfortunately.

Can that train of thought, Jordan. It's not your style—and it would be wise to reassure the lady of that.

"There's the registration desk." Heather motioned toward it and began walking that direction.

"Hang on a minute."

She pivoted toward him. "Doubts about this hotel?"

"No. I just want to be certain we're on the same page with the hotel room idea. In case you have any concerns, I'm viewing this as a business meeting. For the record, I practice the values my faith teaches—including the ones related to relationships with women. Call me old-fashioned—and most of my acquaintances have—but that's the code I live by."

She blinked. "That's . . . direct."

"It's also honest."

"I appreciate that." She took a deep breath. "And as long as we're being candid . . . I feel the same way."

As her comment sank in, it warmed him to his core.

When had he last met a beautiful woman his age who hadn't succumbed to the temptations and looser morals the media tended to depict as a normal part of adult life?

Maybe never.

Whatever the outcome of this case, he'd owe Boomer a huge debt of gratitude not only for saving his life years ago but for bringing Heather into it now.

"Can I tell you I'm glad to hear that?"

She smiled. "If I can tell you the same."

"You know . . . I think this could be the beginning of a beautiful friendship—or more."

A faint flush spread over her cheeks. "I like the sound of that . . . after this case is over. I don't mix business and pleasure. Company—and personal—policy."

"Understood."

The front door opened, and the younger folks began to stream in.

She motioned toward the registration desk. "We better hurry or we'll be in line for an hour."

"At the very least." He took her arm and hurried her across the lobby.

Once they had their room assignments, he walked her to her door.

As she inserted the electronic key, she spoke over her shoulder. "I'll join you in your room in fifteen or twenty minutes."

"That works. In the meantime, why don't you email me the Excel document? I want to give it another going-over tonight."

"You got it. See you soon." She slipped through her door.

Shifting his compact duffle into a more comfortable position, he returned to the elevator and rode up two floors.

Hopefully this visit to Lexington would provide a lead or two on Boomer's disappearance—but even if it didn't, the trip had been productive.

Because while he might not yet know the whereabouts of his old army colleague or understand the cryptic document the man had led them to, he *had* gleaned important information—about Heather.

Enough to know that once this case wrapped up and Boomer's mystery no longer required his attention, he was going to focus on the lovely PI who'd walked into his life—and made this a Christmas to remember.

· · · · ·

Heather leaned toward the mirror in the hotel bathroom, touched up her mascara, fished out her lipstick—and frowned at her reflection.

If she wanted Rick to abide by the keep-things-professional rule she'd laid down in the lobby ten minutes ago, she shouldn't be going to all this effort for a conference call.

She added more lipstick anyway.

After all, meticulous grooming was part of being a polished professional.

Nice try, Heather.

She made a face at her image and dropped the lipstick back in her makeup case.

Fine.

It was possible she had ulterior motives.

But laboring over minor decisions like this was silly. They both understood the ground rules, and they were adult enough to honor them.

At least she hoped they were.

Yet when Rick answered her knock a handful of minutes later, it was apparent he too had freshened up—for her. The five o'clock shadow on his jaw was gone, and he'd slapped on a tad more aftershave.

Her pulse stuttered as the enticing aroma enveloped her.

"Welcome to my humble abode." He ushered her in.

"Thanks." Gripping her phone, she crossed the threshold into a room that was a carbon copy of hers, with a desk in one corner and an upholstered chair beside it. "Shall we sit there?" She skirted the bottom of the bed as she spoke.

"I'm right behind you."

She took the straight-backed desk chair, leaving the cushioned seat for him.

"This could be a short visit, if the call rolls to voicemail again." She scrolled down the screen on her cell to Nathan's number. "I was hoping for more from this trip."

"We have one last neighbor to talk to in the morning."

"I'm not too optimistic that will yield anything useful. She wasn't very forthcoming on the phone—and no one we've chatted with here has offered a single insight into Boomer's personal life."

"He was always on the quiet side. Almost to the point of being a loner. I'm not surprised he still keeps to himself."

She tapped in Nathan's number and put the phone to her ear. "Doesn't make him easy to track down, though." One ring. "I've got Nikki working the plant angle, trying to identify a coworker or two. He may have had a friend at work." Two rings. "If she doesn't come up with a name, we should be able to head home by ten tomorrow." Three rings. "I think it's going to roll again—"

"Hello."

"Nathan?" She sat up straighter.

"Yes."

"Heather Shields. We talked a few days ago, about Boomer."

"I remember. And I got your messages, but I've been crazy busy. Did you find him?"

"Not yet. This is proving to be a challenge. I'd like to put you on speaker so my client can participate in our conversation. He's an army colleague of yours. Rick Jordan."

"Rick's the one looking for Boomer? Sure, put him on."

Heather pressed the speaker button, set the cell on the desk, and nodded to Rick.

"Hey, Nate. It's been a while." Rick leaned forward and rested his forearm on the desk.

"Like almost six years. How are you, man?"

"Doing okay. Or I was, until Boomer paid me a visit when I wasn't home, then disappeared."

"You worried about him?"

"Yeah. For several reasons related to that visit, I'm thinking he may be in trouble."

"Bummer. But it makes sense that he'd go to you if he needed help."

Twin creases appeared on Rick's brow. "Why is that?"

"Are you kidding me? He thought you walked on water after the Black Hawk extraction you did in Raqqa. That was epic. I wasn't surprised he was willing to risk life and limb to get to you after the Chinook crash. Every guy on the crew would have done the same if he hadn't gone out there first."

Rick glanced at her, a slight ruddiness tinting his cheeks. "We all had each other's backs."

"Not like you did. Boomer told me once you were the bravest and most trustworthy person he ever met. If he was in trouble, I can see why he'd think of you."

Rick's flush deepened, and he shifted in his seat.

Her client was modest too.

Another admirable quality.

Much as Heather would have liked to pursue this line of discussion, she ought to get them back on track—and save Rick any further embarrassment.

"Nathan, we wondered if you could tell us any more about the woman Boomer was involved with overseas. Beth Johnson."

"I'm afraid I don't know much. He only mentioned her a few times. He met her after he transferred to a desk job near the end of his enlistment."

"Where was that job?"

Nathan rattled off a name that meant nothing to her.

"A forward operating base near the Afghanistan/Pakistan border." Rick answered her unasked question.

"I wish I could help you track this Beth down." Nathan exhaled, his frustration clear. "But Boomer could be tight-lipped about personal information."

Heather looked at Rick.

He shrugged as he pulled out his cell, leaving the decision about how much to reveal to her.

"Actually . . . I did track her down." She propped her elbow on the desk, beside the cell. "She died three weeks ago after falling from the balcony of her condo. The death was ruled accidental."

"Holy sh—" Nathan cleared his throat. "Sorry—but that's a shocker. Especially on the heels of Boomer's disappearance."

"We agree. That's why we were hoping you could offer a few more facts that might give us a lead we could follow."

"Nate—do you know who Beth or Boomer worked for at that forward operating base?" Rick asked.

"I have no idea who Boomer's boss was, but he didn't like the major Beth reported to."

"Why?"

"I don't know. Maybe he was hitting on her. And a specialist is pretty much at the mercy of someone that high up the food chain."

"Do you have any idea what the guy's name was? Even a first name would help."

As Rick lobbed the questions, Heather sat back. She had no clue why he was pursuing this, but she knew him well enough to be comfortable he had sound reasons.

A few beats of silence passed.

"I'm digging deep here, but I think it was West—or a variation of that. I've always used this mnemonic technique to remember names, and I tied this guy's name to the Wild West. The way Boomer described him, he sounded like one of those old-time sheriffs who ran the town his way. A weird memory system, I know . . . but why argue with success?"

"That's very helpful. I'll work my contacts, see if I can find the full name now that we have more information to go on." Rick transferred his attention to her and raised his eyebrows.

"I think that's it for tonight, Nathan." Heather rejoined the conversation. "Thanks for all your help."

"Happy to assist. If I think of anything else that could be useful, I'll give you a call or shoot you a text."

"I'd appreciate that."

"Take care, buddy." Rick sat back in his chair.

"You too."

Heather ended the call and slipped the phone back into her

pocket. "I'd wager you found that conversation more instructive than I did."

"Interesting, anyway." He crossed his ankle over his knee. "Some of those forward operating bases did have elements of the Wild West. A ton of questionable stuff went on. Too much for the CID to corral."

If Rick thought the army's Criminal Investigative Command might be interested in their investigation, that moved this case to a whole new level.

"Are you thinking the Excel spreadsheet could be proof of some crime?"

"That's one theory. If it is, Beth may have given it to Boomer for safekeeping since they were romantically involved."

"Why wouldn't she contact CID herself?"

"She could have been afraid of retribution. Or she may have been involved in an illegal scheme, and the evidence was a bargaining chip. Or she might have been worried about being made the scapegoat should whatever was going on come to light, and this document would prove others were also involved."

Heather cocked her head. "It's a plausible scenario—except why wouldn't Boomer just go to the authorities with this once Beth died?"

"Assuming he knew she died."

"True. But I have a feeling he did—and that her death may have been the impetus for his trip."

"The same thought occurred to me. Maybe he sidestepped law enforcement because he was involved in the scheme too—or was afraid he'd be in hot water for remaining silent all these years."

Heather expelled a breath. "You realize we could be jumping to all kinds of conclusions on the basis of pure speculation. All we know for sure is that Boomer's missing, Beth is dead, and we have a document that's currently indecipherable and therefore of marginal use."

"I'm going to put out a few feelers tonight to my army colleagues and see if we can get any more intel on the setup at the operating base where Boomer and Beth were stationed. That could yield some useful data."

"None of this is helping us find Boomer, though—and that's why you hired Phoenix." Heather rose. "Let's hope the last neighbor on our list tomorrow morning has information pertinent to that investigation."

"I'll second that." He stood too. "If you're ready, I'll walk you back to your room."

"Thanks—but not necessary." A group passed by in the hall, talking and laughing loudly, and she rolled her eyes. "Sorry about this. Some negatives are beyond the scope of TripAdvisor."

"Don't worry about it. I learned to sleep anywhere under any circumstances. But in light of the party atmosphere here, I'll sleep *better* if I know you're locked in for the night."

"That sounds like an excuse my dad would use."

"Trust me. My feelings are *not* paternal."

He locked gazes with her, and her lungs short-circuited.

Whew.

With a wink, he swept a hand toward the door. "Shall we?"

He followed her out, and they dodged more party groups as they traversed the hallways. At her room, he left her with a simple "sleep well."

But as she clicked the door shut and strolled toward the vanity, she had serious doubts that would happen.

The puzzling missing persons case Cal had dropped into her lap three days ago was growing more complicated by the hour.

The hotel was noisy, and she hadn't honed her sleep skills in battlefield conditions.

Plus, the most appealing man she'd ever met was preparing for bed two floors up—and despite the distance between them, she could feel the sizzle.

That was not a recipe for a sound night's sleep.

So until she got too tired to prop her eyelids open, she'd boot up her laptop and focus on trying to figure out what was in Boomer's spreadsheet that was important enough to make people die—and disappear.

10

Everything was going to be fine.

Brad sipped the espresso he'd picked up on the way to his office and reread the Lubbock newspaper article displayed on his computer screen. The two people who knew what he'd done in the Middle East and who could have caused him a problem if they were willing to put their own necks on the line were no longer a risk. He may not have mentioned that to Lindsey when they'd discussed the gubernatorial race decision on Wednesday night, but the neutralized threat was the real reason he'd finally agreed to throw his hat into the race. That, and Lindsey's continued assurance that she was up to the campaign and accompanying scrutiny, despite the migraines that were plaguing her again.

His desk phone rang, and he closed his browser. Swiveled toward the expanse of polished walnut. Scowled at the digital display.

A phone call from his older brother was about the only thing that could cast a cloud on his day.

But if he became governor, maybe the fraternal gloating would finally come to an end.

He picked up the phone. "Hi, Brian."

"Morning, bro. How's life in St. Loo these days?"

Despite his jovial, shoot-the-breeze tone, his college-football-hero sibling hadn't contacted him to chew the fat. There was always a purpose behind his sporadic phone calls.

"I'm fine. What do you need?" Why beat around the bush?

"Hey, can't a guy call to see how his brother and his brother's trophy wife are?"

Brad bit back the retort that sprang to his lips. He was done letting Brian bait him.

"You always have a reason for calling." Even if it was only to yank his chain.

Silence.

Brad stopped perusing the day's appointments on his calendar as the seconds ticked by.

Strange.

Usually Brian came back with a smart-aleck response in the next breath.

"I, uh, do have a small favor to ask."

Brad's antennas went up.

That, too, was different.

"What is it?"

"You know my company was acquired by an overseas operation a few months back."

"Yes."

"Well . . . I got the old pink slip today. The new outfit's rightsizing to streamline and avoid redundancy. Their term, not mine. But rightsizing or downsizing, a bunch of us lower-level peons got the boot. To make matters worse, Marie's hours at the restaurant got cut too."

More silence.

Brad waited Brian out.

If his brother thought he was going to offer sympathy—or more concrete help—he'd be twiddling his thumbs all day.

Finally Brian broke the awkward stillness. "So, uh, money's kind of tight around here, and the bills are piling up. The mortgage company is giving us major grief. I know you've raked in a few bucks with that geriatric venture of yours, and I wondered if you'd be willing to give me a loan until I can find a new job. With interest, of course."

Brad rocked back in his leather chair, the corners of his mouth flexing.

How about that?

The runt of the family . . . the son their sports-crazed father had ridiculed for his lack of athletic ability . . . had ended up being the real success in the Weston clan.

Too bad his father hadn't lived to see the flourishing start-up his wimpy son had created . . . or the posh condo he occupied with his gorgeous wife . . . or witness him being sworn in as governor.

But lording it over Brian was almost as satisfying—especially now that he'd come begging for money.

"How much cash are we talking about?"

The sum his brother quoted was a pittance relative to the bank balance in the fun money account he'd set up for Lindsey, let alone his net worth. He could write a check for it today and never miss a dime.

That would be too easy, though.

Why not make Brian sweat a little first?

"I'll have to run some numbers, discuss it with Lindsey. Can I get back to you in a few days?"

"Uh . . . yeah. Sure." His brother exhaled. "It's just that we have to come up with the money pretty fast."

"Understood."

"Okay. Thanks. Whatever you can do. Listen . . . we ought to get together one of these days. It's been too long. Our door is always open."

Brad barely restrained a snort.

Like he'd ever want to traipse up to the wilds of Idaho to visit his sibling.

He didn't acknowledge—or reciprocate—the invitation.

At last his brother spoke again. "I guess I'll wait to hear from you."

"Watch your email. I have to run to a meeting."

"Got it. Happy New Year."

Brad dropped the handset into its cradle without responding and leaned back in his chair.

All through their growing-up years, his goofball brother had sailed through life with more brawn than brains, their father's golden boy. Brian's college football scholarship had been valued by their old man far more than the academic one his younger son had received.

It hadn't been fair.

The taste of injustice bitter on his tongue, Brad stood and walked over to the window that offered a view of the Mississippi River framed through the Gateway Arch.

No matter how many classes he'd aced or awards and honors he'd won, his dad had been more interested in his oldest son's *Sports Illustrated* ranking than his smarter son's grade point average.

It shouldn't still bother him, and he should be past having to prove himself.

But it did—and he wasn't.

Maybe selling his company for millions of dollars and winning the governor's race would banish forever the inferiority complex he'd carried for forty-eight years.

Even if the road to those successes had involved a few choices that burdened him with guilt he would carry to his grave.

. . . . .

"Let's hope this pans out." Heather glanced at the address she'd scribbled in her notebook and motioned toward the first-floor apartment to the right of Boomer's unit. "That's the one."

"After you."

Rick followed her up the path to the no-frills building and gave her another surreptitious scan. Despite the large cup of tea she'd downed during a fast breakfast at the coffee shop in the lobby, the smudges under her lower lashes hadn't faded.

Since the revelry in the hotel that had awakened even him a few times until the place quieted down about three in the morning, she probably hadn't clocked more than three or four uninterrupted hours of shut-eye.

If she didn't accept his offer to share the driving on the return trip to St. Louis, he might have to strong-arm her. She needed to catch up on her z's.

The door opened as they approached the unit, and a wiry, gray-haired woman peered at them over the top of her glasses.

"Ms. Reynolds?" Heather managed to summon up a weary smile.

"Yes. You're the PI?"

"That's right. Heather Shields. And this is Boom . . . Jackson's . . . army friend I told you about on the phone. Rick Jordan."

After giving them each a thorough once-over, she drew back and pulled the door wide. "I like people who are prompt. It's a sign of respect . . . and good breeding. Make yourselves comfortable." She waved them toward a modest, clutter-free living room.

Heather bypassed an upholstered chair with a knitting bag beside it and sat on the couch. Rick claimed a seat beside her.

"Would either of you care for coffee?"

"I never pass up caffeine." Rick smiled at the woman.

"I'm fine, thank you." Heather did her best to smother a yawn.

The older woman gave her a keen scrutiny. "Would you prefer tea?"

"I don't want to put you to any trouble."

The woman waved her comment aside. "I like a cup of tea myself every afternoon. I have an electric kettle that boils the water in a jiffy. You two entertain each other while I'm gone."

She bustled out of the room, and a few moments later the muffled sound of running water came from the back of the apartment.

"I'm hoping another cup of tea will help clear the fog from my brain." Heather sighed. "Did you really sleep through all that noise last night?"

"Most of it."

"I wish I had your technique."

"It wasn't worth the price I paid to acquire it."

He frowned as the admission slipped out.

Odd.

In general, he didn't reference his military experience. Comments like that invited questions he'd never been inclined to answer.

Fortunately, Pauline Reynolds saved him by returning with a tray that held two mugs and a plate of what appeared to be homemade coffee cake.

"The tea will be ready in sixty seconds. In the meantime, help yourself to my cinnamon streusel loaf."

"This is very kind of you." Heather moved aside a Monet art book on the coffee table to clear space for the tray.

"Nonsense. Jackson is a fine man, and I expect he chose friends of a similar bent. I understand this is a job for you," she addressed Heather, "but I can see in your face that you care about finding him. And you, young man"—she turned to him—"must be fond of my neighbor to go to all this effort to help him. Let me get the tea, and we'll chat."

She returned to the kitchen.

"This may be a productive meeting after all. She seems co-operative." Rick sipped his coffee and eyed the cake.

"Go ahead and take a piece. I am." Heather selected one of the slices and set it on a napkin in her lap. "I agree she appears to be willing to talk. Whether she knows anything useful remains to be seen."

"Here we are." The woman hustled back into the room, deposited a mug in front of Heather, and settled into the upholstered chair. "I'm assuming you haven't heard anything from Jackson."

"No." Heather took a careful sip of the steaming tea. "And to be honest, we're running out of leads to follow. As I explained on the phone, we know he was on Rick's property the day before Christmas Eve, but we have no idea where he went after that."

The woman's brow crinkled as she picked up her mug. "I knew that bad feeling I had when he called a week ago Wednesday wasn't my imagination."

Rick's ears perked up.

Boomer had called Pauline?

He leaned forward. "What did he say?"

"That he'd had a run-in with a knife-wielding robber. My! Can you imagine?" She placed a hand on her chest. "I asked if he was hurt, but he brushed that off. I also asked if he'd called the police, but he said the situation was complicated. He was agitated and in a huge hurry."

Heather set her mug down, her eyes sharp and alert. Apparently Pauline's news had been more effective than caffeine in chasing away her fatigue.

"Why did he call you?"

"He wanted me to feed his cat and change the litter box. He said he'd be gone for a few days."

"Did he say where he was going?"

"No."

"Have you heard from him since?"

"No."

"Ms. Reynolds"—Heather moved her coffee cake aside and folded her hands in her lap—"when we spoke on the phone, you didn't mention any of this."

"Of course not! I don't talk to strangers about my friends—and I didn't want to add to whatever problems Jackson already has."

"But you're talking to us now," Rick pointed out.

"Because you came all the way from St. Louis to try to find him. That tells me you care. And I can also see you're good people. You can't judge a person's character until you meet face-to-face."

"Is there anything else Jackson told you that could give us a clue about why he might be in trouble?" Heather jumped back in.

"No. He was the quiet sort. An upright, churchgoing, kind man."

"Did he ever mention the name Beth Johnson?" Rick set his coffee on the table, next to Heather's tea.

"No. Who is she?"

"A woman he was involved with while he was in the army. She died recently—in Texas."

"Ah." Pauline bobbed her head. "That must be the friend Jackson was so upset about. Not long ago, he told me someone he knew had died in an accident. He was distraught and . . . I don't know quite how to describe it . . . nervous, maybe? Though that doesn't seem to fit, does it?"

Rick looked at Heather. From her expression, it was clear their thoughts were tracking the same direction.

It fit better than Pauline could ever imagine—if Boomer suspected Beth's death was no accident and the perpetrator might come gunning for him next.

"Did he ever mention the names of any other acquaintances he kept in touch with?" Heather asked.

"No. I don't believe he had a large circle of friends. He lived here for two years before we said more than hello to each other. I don't know if he would ever have started talking to me if I hadn't taken him a plate of fresh-baked cookies one Christmas Eve and a bag of treats for Rosie. That's his cat. In fact"—she twisted her wrist—"I have to run over there and feed her. She expects me every morning promptly at nine."

"You have a key to his apartment?" Rick raised an eyebrow.

"Yes. For emergencies. We exchanged keys months ago. Would you like to come along after you finish your snack? Perhaps you'll spot a clue that will help you in your search."

"Yes." Heather polished off her cake in two large bites and downed the rest of her tea.

He did the same.

"Let me get the key in the kitchen."

While the woman was gone, Heather leaned closer to him. "This one stop made the whole trip worthwhile—and who knows what we may spot in Boomer's apartment? One word of warning—don't touch anything."

"Hands in pockets. Got it."

They followed Pauline to the adjacent unit, where a meowing tabby greeted them at the door.

"Hello there, Rosie. I bet you're hungry—and lonesome." Pauline scooped up the cat and hustled toward the back. "Feel free to look around. I thought Jackson would be back days ago, and the fact he isn't is making me nervous."

She disappeared into the kitchen, and Heather motioned to the right side of the living room—a bland space except for several framed photos that appeared to have been taken while Boomer was in the army. "I doubt we'll have more than a few minutes. Why don't you take that side and I'll take the left?

Snap a shot of anything that could be helpful." She dug out her cell as she spoke.

Rick did the same and began a slow circuit of the room, snapping photos of the photos—but nothing else stood out.

When they met in the dining nook, she nodded toward the bedroom. "Let's do a fast circuit in there."

There was nothing of any interest in the room, other than a computer that might contain useful information if they knew the log-in—and a printout of the article from the Texas paper about Beth's death.

"Identity of the woman he was talking about to Pauline confirmed." Heather snapped a photo of the article. "Let me check out the bathroom."

She was back in less than a minute.

"Find anything?"

"Toothbrush and razor are there, as are all the other usual toiletries."

"Suggesting a fast exit?"

"Bingo." She led the way back to the living room. "Did you have a chance to put out any feelers to your army contacts, see if you could find out who Beth reported to at the forward operating base?"

"I sent several emails. No responses yet."

Pauline rejoined them. "Rosie's a happy camper for now. As well she should be, with that expensive food Jackson feeds her. That is one pampered cat." She made a sweeping motion around the room. "Do you two want a few more minutes here?"

"No." Heather slipped her phone back into her pocket. "We have to get on the road to St. Louis."

"Smart move. That should put you ahead of the snow."

"What snow?" Rick followed the two of them out of the apartment.

"According to the weather report I heard on the radio this

morning, another blizzard is predicted for the weekend." The woman locked the door behind them.

"News to me." He looked at Heather.

"Me too. I was only concerned about driving conditions yesterday and today."

"I think the front was quite unexpected. A change in the wind or some such development." Boomer's neighbor inspected the blue sky. "You'd never know it today, though. It's almost balmy out here—but I'll take this weather for as long as I can get it. These old bones are already tired of winter." She refocused on them. "Is there anything else I can do for you?"

"No—but thank you for talking with us." Heather extended her hand. "You've been a great help. If you happen to hear from Jackson, I'd appreciate a call."

"You'll be the first to know. You drive safe going home." She shook hands with him too and walked back toward her own unit.

"That was worthwhile." Rick fell in beside Heather as she started toward her car.

"Very. You don't give a key or entrust your pet to someone who's a mere acquaintance. Boomer must have liked and trusted Pauline. If she hasn't heard from him, I doubt anyone has." She dug through her purse as they approached her Taurus.

"I agree." He watched as she pulled out her keys—the cue for his driving offer. "I have a proposition for you. Why don't you let me take the wheel for the first part of the trip while you log a couple of hours of sleep? I'm rested and fresh, and at the risk of putting my foot in my mouth, you have faint shadows here"—he tapped under his lower lash—"that suggest you're short on beauty sleep. Not that you need sleep to be beautiful . . . but fatigue can drain the brain as well as the body."

Her lips tipped up. "Very diplomatic. And while my tea infusion helped, I must admit I'm not one of those people who can function at optimal levels on four or five hours of sleep. I accept."

"And here I thought I might have to twist your arm."

"Your suggestion makes sense—and you'll find I'm a very logical woman." She handed him the keys. "We can switch places at the Illinois border . . . although I expect I'll wake up long before that."

Except she didn't.

Heather fell into such a deep sleep that Rick leaned close a few times during the drive to verify she was breathing.

Either she was a world-class snoozer if conditions were conducive to slumber—or she was totally exhausted.

Only as they crossed the Mississippi into St. Louis and a police car zoomed by with sirens screaming did she rouse.

When she caught sight of the Arch, her jaw dropped. "I slept all the way from Lexington?"

"Yep."

"Why didn't you wake me?" She shoved her hair back and sat up straighter.

"You were out cold. Besides, you drove the first leg of the trip."

"But you hired *me*. You shouldn't have to be a long-distance chauffeur."

"I didn't mind. It gave me a chance to enjoy the view."

"The route isn't that scenic."

"It was scenic *inside* the car." He grinned as a becoming flush spread over her cheeks. "Sorry. I couldn't resist."

"Do you flirt like this with all the girls?"

He dropped all pretense of teasing. "No."

Her flush deepened, and instead of responding, she pulled out her phone, dipped her head, and began scrolling through messages.

Once they cleared the bridge and he picked up speed, he gestured toward the ear buds dangling from his own cell phone. "I've been listening to music—and the weather forecasts. It appears Boomer's friend was right. There's a major storm barreling our direction. ETA is Sunday morning."

"I'm glad most of the New Year's Eve revelers will be home before it hits."

"Do you have big plans for the evening?"

She set her phone on her leg. "Nothing exciting. My dad and I are going to share a gourmet meal. What are you doing?"

"Dinner with Colin and his wife, then back to the camp."

"A quiet night for you too."

"Yeah." Unfortunately.

Spending New Year's Eve with the woman beside him would be much more exciting.

But there was always next year—a thought that gave his spirits a sizeable boost.

Her phone began to vibrate, and after she skimmed the screen, she shot him an apologetic look. "Sorry. I have to take this. It's my boss."

For the remainder of the short drive to her duplex, she was occupied with the call, which revolved around a surveillance gig.

The conversation didn't wind down until they pulled into her driveway.

"Sorry again." She stowed her phone as he set the brake.

"No problem. This is a workday for you." He released the trunk catch and met her at the back of the car. "I'll call you as soon as I hear from my army contacts."

"And I'm going to rattle the cages of my law enforcement acquaintances again about Boomer, now that we have more reasons to be suspicious."

"Whoever has news first calls. Deal?"

"Deal."

"Well . . ." He dug out his keys.

Leave, Jordan. You're done here.

Yet he lingered.

And Heather didn't appear to be in any rush to go inside, either.

Until the door in the adjacent unit opened and an older man emerged. He hesitated, then lifted a hand in greeting and continued down the walk toward the mailbox.

"That's my dad."

Rick did a double take. "You live with your dad?"

"No. He owns the duplex, and I rent the second unit. But we eat dinner together most nights. He's a talented cook." She waved the older man over as he turned from the mailbox. "I'll introduce you."

Rick took a quick inventory of his jeans and windbreaker.

Not how he would have dressed for a first meeting with the father of a woman who had serious possibilities.

But he was stuck.

At least the older man was garbed in similar attire.

As her father joined them and Heather did the introductions, Rick returned the man's firm grip and locked on to his shrewd blue eyes.

"Nice to meet you, Rick. Thanks for going with Heather on her road trip. Call me old-fashioned, but I slept better knowing she had a companion."

"It was my pleasure."

"Yes. I can see that."

Plus a whole lot more, based on the twinkle in the older man's irises.

And that was fine by him.

Her father would find out about his interest in Heather very soon anyway.

After chatting for another minute, Rick said his good-byes and walked to his truck.

Father and daughter were standing where he'd left them as he pulled away from the curb with a wave and headed to the camp—and the septic tank issue awaiting him.

He grimaced.

Dealing with a backed-up sewer was *not* how he'd expected to end this year.

But if things played out as he hoped, next year might wind down on a much sweeter note.

. . . . .

"Happy New Year, Ellen. Any plans for the weekend?"

Forcing a smile, Ellen angled toward her administrative assistant, who was slipping her coat on at the door to her office. "Nothing special. With the boss gone, I'll probably be here both days."

The woman wrinkled her nose. "It's not fair that he gets to dump all the work on you while he and his family jet off to Switzerland to ski."

"He's the boss. And life isn't always fair. On the bright side—I have a job with a steady paycheck. Not everyone is so lucky."

"You're my role model, you know." The woman leaned a shoulder against the door frame. "Despite dealing with a divorce and a demanding job that eats into your personal time, you never complain. What's your secret?"

"Always expect tomorrow to be better than today."

"You should have that framed." The woman straightened up. "Try to work in a little fun this weekend."

"I'll do my best."

She waved her assistant off and leaned back in her chair. As usual, she was the last one at the firm. But that was fine. She didn't have anything—or anyone—to go home to these days.

That, however, was about to change . . . assuming everything went according to plan.

And there was no reason to think it wouldn't.

She was a numbers person. Logic was her strong suit. She knew how to dot i's and cross t's. She'd done her homework and lined up qualified professionals to handle the jobs that had to be done.

All she had to do was sit back and wait for the players to report in.

Coffee mug in hand, she strolled down the hall to the deserted kitchenette. Another hour or two, she'd call it a night.

But by nine tomorrow morning, she'd be back at her desk, even if it was Saturday . . . and New Year's Eve . . . and a day off for most people.

Down the road, however? Different story.

If all went well, she wouldn't be working next holiday season.

Nor would she be alone.

She rinsed out her cup, dumping the dregs from her coffee down the drain, the corners of her mouth lifting.

Next Christmas, she'd be with Brad.

It had been obvious during their brief rendezvous in the parking lot that he still cared for her, despite his careful language. He was simply too honorable to admit it now that Lindsey was a noose around his neck. Brad wasn't the type of man who would be unfaithful to a wife in word or deed. It was no wonder he'd been conflicted during *their* affair. He may have been a widower, but she'd been married—and that had gone against his moral values.

The very values that would make him a wonderful governor.

That was why she was doing everything she could to help him achieve his dream—and be the best governor he could be.

With the best wife he could have.

That was what you did for people you loved.

Whatever it took.

However long it took.

But at last the pieces were falling into place—and the goal was in sight. Soon this would be over.

And Brad's happily-ever-after—along with her own—would be assured.

11

"Mmm. Smells delish in here—and it's snug and warm too."

"Morning, Dad." Heather pulled the front door wider and took his arm. "Come on in. The wind is picking up."

"That it is." Her father handed her a covered bowl and shrugged out of his coat. "Here's my contribution to our New Year's Eve dinner. Thought I'd bring the dough for the rolls over and let it do a slow rise in your refrigerator. What're we having tonight?"

"A new recipe—bacon-wrapped pork tenderloin medallions. But what you're smelling is the almond torte in the oven."

"Yum. One of my favorites."

"I know. Help yourself to coffee and stay awhile."

"I don't want to interrupt your cooking—unless you could use two extra hands?"

"Nope. This dinner's on me, except for your homemade rolls—which are gratefully accepted. And you're not interrupting."

"Sold." He followed her into the kitchen and pulled a mug from the cabinet while she slid the bowl into the fridge.

"You working today?" He waved his mug toward her laptop on the table.

"Sort of. I'm trying to decipher a puzzle."

"Related to the current case?"

"Yes. Our trip to Lexington yielded a document that's a mystery to both of us."

He filled his mug and wandered over to her computer. "Your friend seems like a nice young man."

"He's a client, not a friend."

"Bet he'd like to be more."

She didn't respond.

Thankfully, her father dropped the subject and nodded to the computer. "Mind if I take a gander?"

"Help yourself."

He sat and studied the screen while she peeled potatoes. There wasn't much chance he'd have any insights about the spreadsheet, but if it diverted his attention from matchmaking, he was welcome to have a go at it.

"Any idea where this came from?" Her dad squinted at the gibberish on the screen.

"We think it's from an army base in the Middle East."

He pursed his lips. "Kind of looks like a tracking document of some sort. Accounts receivable, maybe."

She stopped peeling. "Why do you say that?"

"It reminds me of the scheduling spreadsheets our office manager, Fred, used to work on. He always had one like this up on his screen when I stopped by his desk. It was mumbo jumbo to me—and I can't make heads nor tails of this—but it has a similar appearance."

"I'll have to run that theory by Rick, see if it triggers any ideas with him."

"What's he doing this evening?"

They were back to that.

"Having dinner with friends, then going home."

"He's ringing in the new year alone?" Her dad frowned.

"I assume so."

"Kind of lonely."

Yes, it was.

But if Rick had wanted a date, he'd have had no trouble finding one.

Heck, any of those women who'd been ogling him at Kaldi's on Wednesday would have been more than happy to sing "Auld Lang Syne" in his company.

"I expect he's doing what he wants to do." She went back to peeling potatoes.

"Or he may not have had a better offer."

She arched an eyebrow at him. "Last I heard, those kinds of offers usually come from the man."

"Boy, are you behind the times." Her father finished off his coffee and stood. "These days, anybody can do the asking."

"Not my style."

"I thought you were a liberated woman? Shoot, you've been competing with men in a man's world your whole career. You were always adamant about equal abilities being given equal opportunity—and you're as capable of inviting a man out as vice versa."

Her fingers faltered for a second, but she quickly resumed peeling. "I'm liberated in the workplace, but I prefer the man to do the asking for dates."

"That could be the reason you're single."

"Dad!" She scowled at him.

"Hey . . ." He lifted his hands, palms forward. "Just sayin'. You could always make a New Year's resolution to ask someone out once a month. You said you wanted to beef up your social life."

"We also discussed the difficulty of finding suitable eligible men."

"Honey . . . if you'd open your eyes, you'd realize there's one on your doorstep."

"He's a client."

"Not forever. And he's interested."

Oh, brother.

"When are you coming back to work on the rolls?"

"Changing the subject, hmm?" He strolled toward the sink to rinse his cup. "Very telling."

"You didn't answer my question."

"No—but you answered mine." He chuckled and winked at her. "I'll be back in five or six hours to punch down the dough. Give me a call if you want a hand with anything before that."

"Will do."

He wandered into the living room to retrieve his coat, and she joined him at the door.

"You know I only want the best for you, don't you?" He tugged on his gloves.

"I know." She gave him a hug.

"And that young man appears to fit that description."

She huffed out a breath. "How can you say that? You've spoken with him for all of . . . what? Two minutes?"

"A man's handshake and eye contact speak volumes. He gets an A for both."

"I'll keep that in mind."

"If I were you, I'd do more than that. See you this afternoon." With a lift of his hand, he slipped out into the icy air.

Heather locked the door behind him and returned to the kitchen, pausing in front of the computer to survey the Excel spreadsheet.

Her dad could be wrong about the document—but he was definitely right about Rick.

As far as she could tell, her client *was* the best.

So once this case wrapped up, if Rick didn't initiate the pursuing, she might follow her dad's advice and become as assertive in her social life as she'd always been in her career.

And pray for better results.

∎ ∎ ∎ ∎ ∎

This was going to be fun.

Not.

Rick hesitated outside the restaurant, burrowing into the collar of his coat as a gust of frigid wind whipped past.

For once he wasn't looking forward to the every-other-Saturday Treehouse Gang breakfast.

Because today, Colin and Kristin would be all over him.

Kristin, mostly.

But Colin wouldn't be far behind.

Delaying his entrance, however, wasn't going to make this any easier—and it was warmer inside.

He pushed through the door and homed in on the far corner table where the three of them usually congregated.

Kristin lifted a hand in greeting and elbowed Colin, who stopped perusing the menu to offer a wave too.

He was on.

Rick threaded through the New Year's Eve midmorning breakfast crowd and slid into the empty seat at the table.

"You're late." Kristin broke off a bite of the huge cinnamon roll that was part of her standard order.

"Sorry. Traffic was bad."

But not bad enough to make him tardy. If he hadn't sat in his truck for five minutes in the parking lot psyching himself up for this encounter, he'd have been punctual, as usual.

Not that he was going to admit his cowardice.

"I was hoping you'd bring your friend." Kristin smirked at him.

Here it came.

Play it cool, Jordan.

"What friend would that be?"

Kristin snorted and elbowed Colin. "I told you he'd blow me off."

Colin grinned and took a swig of his juice. "I heard you had a cozy meeting at Kaldi's with a hot chick on Wednesday."

Rick willed the heat on his neck to stay below his collar. "She—and her firm—are doing some work for me. The firm *you* recommended."

"You knew about this?" Kristin's hand froze halfway to her mouth, a trickle of gooey icing dripping off the piece of cinnamon roll as she sent Colin an accusatory glance.

"I didn't know who Cal would assign to the case. And"— Colin held up a hand as she started to speak—"I don't know any details. I didn't ask."

"*Some* of us are more discreet than others." Rick directed his comment to Kristin.

"Hmph." She swiped up another renegade drop of icing with a finger and sucked it off.

Carmen, bless her heart, came to take their order—and Rick stretched his out so long his friends began to discuss the weather.

Maybe . . . if fate was kind . . . they'd move on to other topics and leave him in peace for the rest of the meal.

He finally finished making his selections and handed his menu back to the waitress.

"So is there anything you can—or want to—tell us about this case of yours? I was tied up the day you called, or I'd have asked more then." Colin adopted his detective demeanor and linked his fingers on the table.

Also not a topic he wanted to discuss in detail—but at least his male friend was more interested in the case than the woman investigating it.

"Like I told you on the phone, an army colleague is missing."

"Any leads?"

"A few more than we had in the beginning." He filled them in on the discoveries of the past couple of days.

Kristin stared at him. "You went on an overnight trip with this woman to Lexington?"

"We had separate hotel rooms."

"I assumed that. But . . . you spent two days following her around while she was doing a job you were paying her to do?"

Put like that . . . it did sound a little suspicious.

He flicked a few crumbs off the table. Straightened his silverware. "It's slow at the camp in the winter—and I thought it might help during interviews if a friend of Boomer's was along. So . . . any ideas yet for your summer youth show?"

Her eyes widened. "Whoa. This is more serious than I thought if you're bringing up the show just to change the subject. I have to drag you two kicking and screaming into my pet project every summer."

"It's too early to talk about the show." Colin shot him a disgruntled look but aimed the comment at Kristin.

"It's never too early to think about it, though. I may even tackle a musical this go-round. *Peter Pan* is a possibility. Or *Cinderella. Annie* would be fun too."

Colin groaned. "Straight plays are bad enough—now you want to throw music into the mix?"

"What? You don't like music?" Kristin broke off another bite of her cinnamon roll.

"I like it fine. But it's going to complicate the sound setup."

"You can handle it. I have absolute faith in your technical abilities. And remember—it's for a very worthwhile cause. It builds kids' self-esteem in a safe, faith-based environment."

"Yeah, yeah, I've heard the spiel." He waved her off as Carmen set a plate of food in front of him.

Rick was no more anxious than his detective buddy to think

about the annual summer activity Kristin always roped them into, but if it kept the conversation away from Heather, he'd be willing to start talking about set construction today.

While Colin skewered him with a narrow-eyed look and dived into his omelet, Rick peppered her with questions about the show. And when that topic waned, she was more than happy to gush over her honeymoon and reminisce about the wedding.

By the time the bill arrived, Rick was as exhausted as the day he'd taken part in a marathon dodgeball tournament as a kid.

As she gave her lips one more swipe and laid her napkin on the table, Kristin leaned toward him. "By the way . . . in case you think you pulled one over on me, forget it. I have lots more questions about your PI."

Great.

"I'd love to hang around and listen in, but I have to run." Colin dug a few bills out of his wallet. "Trish wasn't feeling great this morning, and I don't want to leave her alone for too long."

"Why didn't you tell us that sooner? Or bail?" Kristin's brow puckered. "Sickness is an acceptable excuse for canceling."

"She insisted I come—but I don't want to linger."

"Listen . . . why don't I take a rain check on tonight's dinner?" Rick counted out his money and tossed it on top of Colin's. "If Trish is feeling under the weather, she shouldn't have to worry about entertaining a guest."

"Let me see how she is after I get home. I'll call you."

"You could always join us for dinner if the deal with Colin and Trish falls through," Kristin offered.

He snorted. "Are you kidding? You guys are on your honeymoon."

"The tail end. Luke won't mind." Her reassurance was half-hearted at best.

"Right." He slid his wallet back into his pocket. "I prefer to stay in your husband's good graces—but I appreciate the offer.

Besides, it might be better if I get home earlier, with the snow and ice they're predicting."

"That's not supposed to arrive until tomorrow." Kristin caught her lower lip between her teeth. "I don't want you spending New Year's Eve alone."

"Thanks for that thought—but I'll be fine. I'm in the middle of a suspense novel that will keep me entertained into the wee hours if I want to stay up and watch the clock turn over."

"Let's not jump the gun. Trish may be fine by now." Colin stood. "You guys staying awhile?"

And endure more grilling from Kristin?

Forget it.

"I'm not." Rick rose. "I have errands to run."

"And I have a new husband waiting at home." Kristin got to her feet too. "We can walk out together—and pick up the questioning next year." She elbowed him.

He ignored her.

The instant they stepped through the door, Kristin shuddered and burrowed into her coat. "Brrrrr. I'm missing that sunny, tropical beach already."

"Oh, I bet you can find a way to warm up right here in St. Louis." Colin waggled his eyebrows. "One of the benefits to marriage in colder climes, if you haven't figured that out already."

"I think I'll have to explore that concept further. ASAP." The corners of her mouth rose. "See you guys around."

"Count on it." Rick returned her hug, slapped Colin on the back, and headed for his truck—while his two best friends in the world headed home for warmth and cuddles.

Neither of those activities were in his plans for today.

Nor had he anticipated them being part of his life anytime in the immediate future.

And he'd made his peace with that—more or less.

Or he had until his best friends had taken back-to-back walks down the aisle, leaving him the odd man out. The guy poised to be the unmarried, adopted uncle of his friends' kids.

He unlocked his truck and climbed up behind the wheel, giving Colin a wave as his friend drove by, eager to get home to his wife.

Not like the old days, when the three of them sometimes took in a movie or played Frisbee in the park after breakfast.

Oh, Kristin and Colin both went out of their way to stay in touch and remain tight.

But it wasn't the same.

It wasn't like having a family of his own.

A familiar wave of melancholy rolled over him as he put the truck in gear and steered it toward the exit—yet for the first time since his fellow Treehouse Gang members met their future spouses, he didn't feel quite as down about his single state as usual after one of their breakfasts.

Thanks to Heather.

Maybe he was letting himself get carried away about the dark-haired PI with the vibrant, intelligent hazel eyes—but why not ring in the new year with hope in his heart?

And God willing, perhaps the woman he'd hired to find Boomer would solve not only that mystery but also the case of the lonely ex–Night Stalker.

■ ■ ■ ■ ■

Payment due.

I checked the time.

The pithy text message had come in on my burner phone an hour ago—and there was a PDF attached.

This had to be the proof I'd asked for from my hired gun.

Leaving the phone on the desk, I crossed to the door.

No one should be around at this hour, but it didn't hurt to verify that.

A quick sweep of the hall confirmed I was alone.

I closed the door.

Locked it.

Returned to the desk and opened the file.

The proof wasn't what I'd expected—but it was definitive.

No reputable news outlet would report a name in a story like this until they were certain of the identity.

Jackson Dunn was dead.

I sauntered to the other side of the room, dug out my secret stash of cigarettes, and lit one. Sucked in a lungful of nicotine. Blew the noxious fumes toward the ceiling.

I should stop this secret smoking.

No—I should stop smoking, period.

And maybe I'd finally find the willpower to do that as the stress I'd been living with for weeks began to abate.

I wandered over to the window. The leaden skies didn't bode well for weather on this New Year's Eve, but I wasn't going far. I'd be fine.

I took another puff, waiting for the feel-good dopamine rush.

But it wasn't as strong as usual today.

And why should it be? No chemical was powerful enough to instill a feeling of happiness in a person responsible for taking lives.

Tamping down a flicker of revulsion, I dug out a piece of aluminum foil and stubbed the glowing tip of the cigarette in it. Folded the edges over and crimped them. Tucked it in my pocket for later disposal—after I took care of one final piece of business.

I returned to the desk and picked up the phone. With a few strokes, I transferred the amount due to the man I'd hired, depleting yet again the balance in the offshore account I'd set up for this operation.

There would be no more impediments to Jefferson City.

I opened the door to the hall. This phone had served its purpose—and I knew the perfect place to ditch it. An object like this was best discarded in water.

Deep water.

I pulled out my car keys and twisted my wrist. Four o'clock. I could take care of this chore before darkness fell. Then I'd prepare to usher in the new year.

Not exactly feeling guilt-free—but conventional wisdom had it right.

Politics was a dirty business.

12

Why on earth had she suggested that Rick come over?

Heather blew out a breath and went back to arranging sliced almonds around the rim of tonight's dessert.

Whatever news he'd received from his army contact could have been conveyed during their earlier phone conversation.

But it was too late now. He'd accepted her impulsive invitation and would be arriving any—

A musical ding-dong echoed through the rooms, and she jerked, scattering a dozen almonds across the floor.

Real smooth, Heather. So cool and composed.

She snatched up the nuts, tossed them into the garbage, whipped off her apron, and dashed toward the foyer.

Remember—this is a business meeting. Be professional.

Check.

But the slow smile Rick gave her as she opened the door was much, much warmer than any she'd ever received from a client.

Doing her best to put the brakes on her galloping pulse, she pulled the door wide. "Come in."

"Am I interrupting anything?" He crossed the threshold,

bringing with him the crisp, invigorating scent of a cold winter day.

"I'm in between dinner preparations. Your timing is perfect."

"I bet you just finished the cake."

She closed the door and turned to him. "How did you know that?"

He reached over and brushed his index finger down her cheek.

As her lungs stalled, he displayed a glob of chocolate on the tip of his finger.

Then he licked it off with a wicked grin.

Oh.

My.

Word.

She fumbled for the edge of the hall table.

Held on tight.

"If this icing is any indication, the cook knows how to satisfy a person's sweet tooth."

O-kay.

That statement could be interpreted in a couple of ways.

One of them very delicious.

Stop it, Heather! Get your mind on business.

"So, uh"—she cleared her throat—"would you like a cup of coffee while you tell me what you learned from your army contact?"

Based on the mischievous glint in his baby blues, he knew exactly the effect he was having on her.

Thank goodness he didn't comment on it.

"Coffee would hit the spot—but I thought you were a tea drinker."

"I am, but I made a pot earlier for my dad."

"Is he here?" A glimmer of . . . disappointment? . . . flickered in his eyes.

"Not at the moment . . . but his dinner rolls are." She led

him back to the kitchen. "They require several stages, and he decided to do the final steps here rather than transport them when they're ready to bake. Yeast doesn't like cold weather."

"You learn something new every day."

"I hope about more than baking. Help yourself." She handed him a mug and indicated the coffee maker.

"Definitely more than baking." He moved to the counter. "Like I told you on the phone, I got an email from an acquaintance who knew someone stationed at the same base as Boomer and Beth while they were there. He introduced us via email, and I sent the guy a few questions, along with a request for any other information that could be pertinent. Some intriguing data came back."

"You have my full attention." She slid her laptop aside, motioned him to the table, and sat. "Tell me everything."

"First—can I say that looks like an incredible cake?" He stared at the almond torte as he claimed a chair.

"Thanks. It's an old family favorite."

"I can see why." He gave the cake one last, lingering perusal before shifting his attention back to her. "My contact didn't know Beth, but he was able to track down the name of her boss by sending a note to a few friends at the base. It was a Major Brad Weston."

"Brad Weston." She scrolled through her mind until the familiar name clicked into place. "There's a businessman named Brad Weston here in St. Louis who's been in the press lately. They're speculating he's going to run for governor."

"It appears to be more than speculation. I heard a news story earlier today that he's called a press conference for Tuesday morning."

"Could he be the same Brad Weston who was Beth's boss?"

"I wondered that too. I googled his background and discovered the governor wannabe was a decorated army major who served in the Middle East before launching a successful senior housing concept that's rumored to be attracting buyout offers valued in the tens of millions of dollars."

"Wow." Heather sank back in her chair. "It all fits. Do you think Boomer might have contacted him during those days he was MIA?"

"I suppose it's possible—but Nathan said Boomer didn't like him. Why would he seek him out?"

"Well . . . he was upset about Beth's death, and the Excel document dates from their tenure at the forward operating base." Heather tapped her finger against the table. "Depending on what it represents, he may have suspected that a certain person or persons had a hand in Beth's so-called accident. Maybe he thought Weston knew their whereabouts—or had relevant information he might be willing to share."

"Could be. You want to take another stab at the spreadsheet together, see if anything new jumps out at us?"

"I'm game." She positioned her laptop so they could both view the screen and called up the document. "You know, I had this open while my dad was here earlier, and he said it reminded him of the tracking forms the office manager at his company used to work on."

Rick leaned closer for a better view. "It could be some sort of logistical record. But there's not much detail to work with. Even the dollar amounts are nebulous." He indicated one entry for $7.5. "I think we can assume this represents more than $7.50—but how much more?"

"I'll concede there's very little to go on—but quite a few of the initials appear over and over again." She pointed them out. "They could represent people or places . . . but in either case, it might suggest the keeper of this document was doing a steady business with regular customers."

"I agree." He touched his pocket, then pulled out his cell and skimmed the screen. "Sorry. I have to answer this. Give me a minute?" He rose.

"Sure. Don't rush on my account."

As he stepped into the adjacent living room, she pulled the pork medallions out of the refrigerator and turned them over in the marinade.

She didn't *try* to listen to his side of the conversation while she worked, but despite his low pitch, every word drifted into the kitchen.

"Hey, Colin . . . Bummer . . . Listen, don't worry about it. Tell her I hope she recovers fast . . . No, I've got plenty of food in the freezer at home—but I'll be happy to come another night. Trish is a superb cook . . . Don't give it another thought . . . Yeah, you too. Talk to you next week."

Sounded like Colin's wife had gotten sick, nixing their dinner plans.

Meaning he'd not only be ringing in the new year alone, he'd be pulling who-knows-what out of his freezer and eating dinner by himself.

Heather surveyed the medallions. The recipe served four.

All the sides did too.

There was plenty of food to accommodate an extra guest.

And while she and her dad may have planned a quiet father/daughter New Year's Eve celebration, she had no doubt he'd welcome a third guest.

Especially if that guest was the man in the next room.

No—the *client* in the next room.

At the nudge from her conscience, she huffed and slid the pan of pork tenderloins back into the fridge.

Asking Rick to dinner would definitely bend Phoenix's no-fraternizing rule. But her dad would be here too. And it *was* New Year's Eve. No one should be alone on a holiday except by choice. Inviting him to stay would be a considerate gesture—wouldn't it?

Yes.

It would.

And that was exactly how she'd explain it to the Phoenix crew if the subject ever came up—while sending a silent prayer heavenward that they wouldn't recognize her explanation for the flimsy excuse it was.

. . . . .

Phone in hand, Rick took a moment to survey Heather's comfortable, uncluttered living room. The gray and blue palette created a restful ambiance, and accents like a needlepoint pillow and fluffy throw draped over the arm of a chair gave the place a homey feel.

Her holiday touches added warmth too. Gas logs flickered below a mantel draped with a pine-bough garland laced with white twinkle lights, and a Christmas tree in one corner was topped with an illuminated angel and hung with shimmering tinsel.

A definite step up from his bare-bones bachelor-quarters cabin at the camp, where his sole Christmas decoration consisted of a simple crèche given to him long ago by the man who'd kindled in him the light of faith.

The food here was better too.

All that awaited him at home was a frozen dinner—and a nuked meal would be nothing like the gourmet feast Heather was preparing.

But he had no excuse to linger now that he'd passed on the message from his army contact.

Sighing, he stowed his phone.

Oh well. He'd spent worse New Year's Eves.

If he finished his novel, he could always study the spreadsheet again. Maybe he'd spot a detail or two that would offer a clue about the significance of the document.

It was better than moping around feeling sorry for himself.

After one more sweep of the cozy room, he returned to the kitchen, psyching himself up to say good-bye.

Heather offered him a tentative smile as he entered.

Like she was nervous.

His antennas went up.

"I want you to know I wasn't eavesdropping—but I couldn't help overhearing parts of your conversation. It sounds like your New Year's Eve plans have fallen through."

"Yeah. Colin's wife came down with the flu. I had a late breakfast with him and Kristin this morning, and he told us she wasn't feeling well. So it's not a total surprise."

Heather's jaw dropped. "Kristin met the two of you for breakfast during her honeymoon?"

"The honeymoon is winding down—and our every-other Saturday breakfast date is sacrosanct. Their spouses had to accept that in writing before Colin and Kristin would agree to marry them." When Heather's eyes widened, he grinned. "Just kidding. But we do take our friendship seriously."

"I can see that." She pulled a bowl of jumbo shrimp out of the fridge and began threading them on bamboo skewers.

His mouth started to water.

As if reading his mind, she spoke again. "Lemon-garlic shrimp—our appetizer."

"Sounds delicious." A definite understatement.

"They are. Perfect for a special occasion dinner." She retrieved a bottle of olive oil from a cabinet and made a project out of twisting off the cap. "You know . . . I have plenty of food for tonight. Now that your plans have changed, you'd be welcome to join us for dinner." The invitation came out a bit breathless.

No wonder. She was stretching her company rules big-time by asking him to dinner.

Which only sweetened the invitation.

In fact, her willingness to go out on a limb for him was the best gift he'd received this holiday season.

But she didn't have to worry about anything getting out of hand. Even if her dad wasn't around to play chaperone, he'd respect her commitment to maintain a professional distance while his case was active.

"Sorry. I shouldn't have put you on the spot." She sent him a sidelong glance, a faint pink tinge coloring her cheeks. "I know this is last minute, and—"

"I accept." No way was he letting her retract her offer. "I'd be honored to join you and your father. And from what I'm seeing in this kitchen, I'm sure the food will be second only to the company."

"You may want to reserve judgment on that. I'm trying a new recipe for the entrée. It could be awful."

"I have a feeling it will be spectacular. But if I stay, you have to let me help. I'm not much into cooking, but I'm excellent at table-setting and cleanup, as Kristin can attest. She gives me dish duty when I eat at her place."

"I don't like to put guests to work."

"If I don't work, I don't stay." Hopefully she'd cave and he wouldn't have to make good on that threat.

"You drive a hard bargain." Her lips quirked.

"I prefer to think of myself as a man who knows what he wants—and goes after it." He let a beat pass while she digested that statement . . . and its broader implications. "You could ask Kristin about that too. Or Colin."

She blinked . . . averted her gaze . . . and began chopping up garlic. "I'll, uh, find a job for you to do. In the meantime, help yourself to more coffee."

"Thanks." He ambled over to the counter to refill his mug.

She began peeling another clove of garlic. "So tell me how the three of you teamed up. I know you said you were kindred spirits—but isn't it kind of unusual for twelve-year-old boys to befriend a girl?"

"Yes." He leaned back against the counter. "But she had a treehouse—and we wanted in."

"Ah." Heather gave a low, throaty chuckle that spiked his adrenaline. "The truth comes out."

"What can I say? Boys and treehouses go together. We called ourselves the Treehouse Gang, and the name's stuck."

"Cute. Did you have a secret password, or an oath signed in blood?" She tossed the garlic into the olive oil.

"No. Kristin wouldn't have gone for the blood thing. But we did have a code."

"Like a secret password?"

"Not that kind of code. More like a standard to live by. We all pledged to do our part to make the world a better place when we grew up."

"Admirable." She stopped stirring the mixture to look at him.

He shrugged. "It seemed like a noble idea to three kids who'd had too many tough knocks."

"And you all followed through."

"Yeah." He took a sip of his coffee. "I think we were all born with the honor-your-promises gene."

"Nice to know." The corners of her mouth lifted for a moment before she went back to stirring. "You mentioned once that the three of you shared less-than-ideal family situations too."

Rick hesitated.

Her tone was casual, and he suspected she wouldn't push if he acknowledged her comment and changed the subject as he usually did when background questions arose.

Yet today he wanted to offer more.

"Yes, we did." He held on tight to the mug. "Colin's parents divorced after his younger brother died in a hit-and-run accident, and he spent the rest of his childhood shuttling back and forth between the two of them. Kristin's parents are still together, but for most of her life they were too absorbed in their careers to have any time for an unplanned addition to the family. She had no material wants, but she lived in emotional poverty."

Heather stopping squeezing juice from a lemon into the concoction she was making, distress etching her features. "How sad for both of them."

She didn't say anything else, but he knew she was waiting for him to tell her his story.

His stomach knotted.

He'd never shared the details of his traumatic childhood with anyone but Colin and Kristin—and even they didn't know everything.

Strangely enough, though, he wanted to tell Heather some of it. The bare bones, anyway.

But better test the waters first. See how receptive she was to hearing a few of the ugly details.

"My story is worse than theirs. It might not be the best subject to discuss on a festive occasion like New Year's Eve."

"The festivities won't begin for a while. And in my previous line of work, I saw the worst humanity has to offer. I have a high tolerance for bad scenes."

That was probably true.

Why not gloss over the nastiest parts and give her the condensed version?

"My mother was killed in a domestic violence incident when I was six. My father went to prison with a life sentence." He kept his inflection flat, excising every ounce of emotion. "I spent the rest of my childhood in the foster system. Some of the families I was placed with were better than others, but despite the state's screening process, too many were more interested in the monthly stipend than in parenting."

"Wow." She set the depleted lemon on the counter and faced him. "I can't begin to imagine how awful that must have been."

"It wasn't *Leave It to Beaver*."

Not even close.

"Did your dad ever . . . was he . . ." She bit her lower lip.

She didn't have to utter the question for him to hear it.

"Yeah." His voice scratched, and he swallowed. Set his coffee down. Gripped the edge of the counter behind him. "He got his jollies beating up on both me and my mom—and making our lives as miserable as possible in every way he could."

Sympathy and compassion softened her features, and she took a step toward him. Stopped. Gripped her hands together in front of her. "With that kind of history, how did you become such a high-achiever? Most kids from backgrounds like yours don't end up being Night Stalkers—or heroes."

"I'm not a hero."

"You are according to Nathan."

He dismissed the comment with a wave. "I was just a guy doing his job. But you're right about how most kids with my history turn out. I was lucky. One of the families I lived with for a while went to church every Sunday, and they hooked me up with a youth group. The summer I was ten, I went to a summer camp the church sponsored and met a young minister. He helped me realize I was worthy of love and that I could rise above all the badness in my life if I kept my focus on God."

"And now you're paying back that gift with the camp you founded for foster kids."

Warmth crept up his neck at the soft gleam of admiration in her eyes. "I wanted to do more in my post-military career than make money, and I had no interest in a desk job. The camp was a natural fit."

"I can see how it would be. Did you stay in touch with the minister?"

"Yes. He has a church in Kentucky now. We talk every few weeks and try to get together once a year. He came up last summer and spent a week at the camp, working with the kids."

"I bet he's proud of all you've accomplished."

A blast of "Joy to the World" erupted from her cell on the counter, saving him from having to come up with a response.

"Sorry. My seasonal ringtone." She wiped her hands on a towel and picked it up. Frowned. "Give me a sec." She punched the talk button. "Hey, Jack. You must have pulled the short straw to end up with a holiday shift . . . Yeah, I hear you. There was always a crime spike here too. What's up?"

The silence stretched so long that Rick glanced over at her as he topped off his coffee.

Twin furrows had appeared on her brow.

Deep ones.

At last she spoke. "I do have a few questions. Let me grab a paper and pen. Can you hold a sec?" She pressed a button on the phone. "This could take a few minutes. Make yourself comfortable and I'll be right back."

Without giving him a chance to reply, she disappeared down the hall.

A few seconds later, a door quietly clicked shut.

Hmm.

There was a pad of paper and two pens at the end of the counter. She could have taken the call here.

Translation? She didn't want him to hear her side of the conversation.

Her reference to a crime spike must mean she was talking to one of her police contacts—and as far as he knew, her only recent discussions with law enforcement had been related to Boomer's disappearance.

A spiral of tension began to coil in the pit of his stomach, and he forced himself to take a deep breath.

He couldn't hear a word being said behind the closed door down the hall, but he knew one thing with absolute certainty.

When Heather emerged, she'd be bearing bad news.

13

Heather jabbed the end button. Closed her eyes. Filled her lungs with chocolate-infused air.

But even the sweet scent wafting through the rooms couldn't chase away the sour taste in her mouth.

Failing Rick—and Boomer—was not how her current case was supposed to play out.

One shoulder propped against the wall, she kneaded the bridge of her nose. There was no way to sugarcoat the news she had to deliver, and delaying her return to the kitchen wasn't going to soften the blow.

Might as well get it over with.

She pushed off from the wall, straightened her shoulders, and opened the door to the hall.

Rick was waiting in the kitchen where she'd left him, but the slight tautness in his posture spoke volumes.

He'd already figured out the phone call was related to his friend—and that the news wasn't good.

Those sharp Night Stalker instincts of his didn't miss much.

"You have an update on Boomer." His voice was steady. Controlled.

At least his direct approach saved her having to lead up to the subject.

"Yes."

After scrutinizing her, he pulled out a chair at the table. "You look like you should sit."

Did she?

Maybe.

But he was the client. She ought to be focused on *his* needs.

Yet despite all the gore she'd seen during her law enforcement career, her stomach flip-flopped again as the conversation she'd had in the bedroom replayed in her mind.

He took her arm, urging her toward the chair—and she gave up the fight.

Rick claimed the adjacent seat and watched her in silence.

Just tell him, Heather.

She swallowed. "That was my Lexington PD contact. Boomer's been found."

A muscle in Rick's jaw ticced. "He's dead, isn't he?"

"Yes. I'm sorry."

Rick remained motionless, but his irises darkened like the sea during a storm. "Tell me what happened."

"He was found by a hiker yesterday in the Daniel Boone National Forest, about sixty miles south of Lexington. The medical examiner is doing an autopsy as we speak, but cause of death appears to be either a heroin overdose or hypothermia. His coat was several yards away from the body, and a syringe with traces of the drug was beside him."

"Was there any sign of a struggle?"

That had been her first question too. His death so close on the heels of Beth's demise seemed too coincidental—and convenient.

"It was difficult to tell. It appears he'd been there since the snowstorm over Christmas . . . and that area is known for abundant wildlife"—she swallowed—"including feral hogs."

Rick's face lost a few shades of color.

He'd obviously called up the same gruesome image she had.

Feral hogs weren't known for being choosy about their food source—and a body that couldn't fight back was easy pickings.

Rick cleared his throat. "Do they have a definite ID?"

"Yes. His driver's license was on him, and they verified the ID with a fingerprint match. Boomer's name has already appeared in a news story or two online, thanks to the hiker's loose lips. My contact promised to let me know as soon as the medical examiner determines cause of death, but all indications point to it being classified as accidental rather than homicide."

"Like Beth's."

"Yes."

"This isn't sitting well." His mouth flattened into a grim line.

"With me either."

He stood and began to pace. "What would it take to get the police interested in pursuing this?"

"Evidence to suggest foul play."

"We have the flash drive. Whatever's on there could be a motive."

"But we haven't been able to decipher it—and we've given it more attention than the police will."

"I'm betting it means something important enough to get two people killed."

"I won't dispute that. This whole scenario reeks."

He stuck his fists on his hips. "Are you willing to stay on the case?"

"The case you hired me for is over. Boomer's been found."

"I want to find out why he died."

"That's a different kind of investigation—and it could take far more time."

"I'm willing to pay for it. I don't expect Phoenix to give me a discount rate on a case I'm undertaking to satisfy my curiosity."

"And to find justice for Boomer and Beth." Heather stood too. "Let me text my boss, get his take. It's the kind of puzzle he likes to tackle—and it may still end up being one of those cases that boosts the reputation and visibility of Phoenix. That could qualify it for a lower rate."

"If it doesn't, I'd still like you to take it on."

"Let me talk to Cal. Now that the scope has broadened considerably, he'll want the entire staff to weigh in on this." She picked up her cell and thumbed in a message.

As she finished, a knock sounded on the front door.

Rick's eyebrows rose. "Let me guess. Your dad's arrived to work on his contribution to your dinner."

"That would be a safe bet. Why don't you make yourself comfortable in the living room and I'll join you in a minute? It's always better to give my dad space when he's in culinary mode."

Or inclined to play matchmaker.

"Works for me." He followed her to the hall, veering off toward the living room while she continued to the foyer.

Heather opened the door and stepped out into the cold before her dad could enter. "We have company."

"I noticed his truck." Eyes twinkling, he tipped his head toward the vehicle parked on the street. "Am I interrupting anything?"

"A business meeting."

He gave her a disgusted snort. "If that's the best you can do on New Year's Eve, I suppose *I'll* have to liven up this party." He nudged her aside and pushed the door open.

She grabbed his arm. "Define liven up."

"I'm still working out the particulars."

"Dad."

He ignored her cautionary tone. "You're going to catch pneumonia if you stand around out here. How long is your friend staying?"

Hedging on the truth would get her nowhere. Besides, her dad would soon find out Rick would be joining them for dinner.

"My *client's* plans for the evening fell through, so I invited him to stay and eat with us rather than go home to a frozen dinner." She brushed past him into the warmth of the house. "It seemed like the considerate thing to do."

He followed her in but didn't say a word.

When she risked a peek at him, he was grinning.

Mashing her lips together, she scowled at him. "What?"

"I was just admiring your . . . considerate . . . gesture." He winked. "I'll go tackle that dough as soon as I pop in and say hello to our guest." After shrugging out of his coat, he handed it to her to hang in the closet.

That must mean he was staying awhile.

Drat.

While she stowed his coat, she listened in as the two men exchanged a few pleasantries . . . but she waited to join Rick until her dad continued on to the kitchen.

"Your phone's vibrating on the counter." Her dad called out the news before she got three steps into the living room.

"Slight detour." She switched direction as she spoke to Rick. "I'll be right back. That could be Cal responding to my text."

She joined her dad in the kitchen and checked the new message.

Yep. It was from Cal.

She scanned his succinct reply.

Interesting development. Let's discuss in Tuesday's staff meeting.

The exact response she'd expected.

But she had no doubt the other three PIs would be supportive about tackling a case that had taken unexpected and intriguing turns.

"Work call?" Her dad had already punched the dough down and was forming it into rolls.

"Yes."

"Related to your client's missing persons case?"

"The person isn't missing anymore. His body was found yesterday." She gave him the topline.

"You don't think this was an accident, do you?" He scrutinized her.

"No."

"You going to continue investigating?"

"Depends on the consensus at the office."

"How's your friend taking the news?"

She let the friend reference pass. Her corrections didn't appear to be sinking in anyway.

"He's not happy—and he's not convinced it was an accident, either."

"You think that document you showed me from the flash drive is the key to all this?"

"I don't know if it's the key, but I think it's significant."

"So what's next?"

"I'm going to discuss that with Rick now—and the Phoenix crew on Tuesday."

"Have at it." He waved her toward the living room with a flour-dusted hand. "But once you finish your business, you may want to switch out of work mode for the rest of the evening."

"I'll take that under advisement."

But in truth, she'd already decided how to play the remainder of this day.

Once she wrapped up their business discussion, she'd shift her mind-set from work to fun. There was no reason she couldn't enjoy the next few hours. With her dad rounding out their threesome, it wasn't as if her willpower would be put to the test. Nothing could happen, no matter her—or Rick's—inclinations . . . although the downer news could put a damper on romantic leanings anyway.

Nevertheless, she was going to do her best to relax and enjoy welcoming the new year with the handsomest, most appealing man she'd ever met.

It was the safest possible pseudo-date imaginable, with no risk of a midnight kiss on this New Year's Eve.

Much as she might want one.

. . . . .

This was the best New Year's Eve of her life.

Lindsey took a judicious sip of the champagne their host had pressed into her hand and surveyed the elegant Ladue living room that was larger than the house where she'd spent her childhood. A jazz quartet played on one side as the fifty-plus tux-clad men and jewel-bedecked women chatted in clusters and helped themselves to the hors d'oeuvres the waitstaff was passing on silver trays.

This was the life she'd always dreamed of leading—and now it was hers forever.

Thanks to Brad, God bless him.

She searched the crowd for her husband. Spied him huddled in one corner with Chuck, a prominent state political operative, and their host—one of St. Louis's high-roller businessmen.

All three of those men knew about—and supported—Brad's ambitions.

And soon, all of the other movers and shakers in this room would have the inside scoop too. Giving potential supporters with deep pockets a heads-up about the announcement Brad would be making on Tuesday morning was smart.

Their host slapped her husband on the back, disengaged from the group, and walked over to the leader of the jazz ensemble. After a brief exchange between the two men, the musicians wound down the current song and gave him the floor.

He faced his guests and held up his hand to quiet the chitchat. Only after a hush fell over the room did he speak.

"I want to thank all of you for joining me and my wife tonight as we say good-bye to the old year and welcome in the new. We don't know most of what the next twelve months will hold, but I'm privileged tonight to tip you off to a piece of news that will soon be public. Next Tuesday, one of my guests this evening—a man many of you know—will be announcing his candidacy for governor of our great Show Me state. Please join me in welcoming Brad Weston."

As the room erupted in applause, Brad emerged from the crowd, shaking hands along the way to the front. When he got there, he smiled her direction and motioned her to join him.

Throat tightening, Lindsey wove through the crowd and took her place next to her husband, squeezing his hand as he linked his fingers with hers.

This was the first of many moments in the spotlight she'd been waiting to savor.

Brad spoke for several minutes, his comments articulate and funny, touching and patriotic, by turns. His polished, congenial tone was perfect, as the rapt expressions on the partygoers attested.

Her husband was a born politician.

The thunderous applause at the end, the swarm of people engulfing them with congratulations and promises of support, proved that—and made it clear he was destined for high places.

Like the governor's mansion.

But there was no reason his aspirations had to be constrained by state borders.

He might not realize that yet, but he would.

She'd make sure of that.

After all, it was the duty of a wife to look out for her husband's best interests. To help him be all he could be.

And there wasn't a single obstacle standing in the way of Brad achieving his full potential except too-small thinking.

A bad habit of his, thanks to a father who had always demeaned him for marching to the beat of a different drummer than his brother.

She, however, was thinking big enough for both of them.

So when the time came for him to spread his wings and move on to bigger arenas, she'd convince him he was worthy of the job and up to the task—then do everything in her power to support him.

As she had since the day they'd met.

14

"Well, kiddos, I'm ready to call it a night."

As her father rose from the kitchen table where they'd spent the past two hours playing a killer game of Scrabble, Heather gaped at him. "It's only eleven thirty."

"I know, but I'm getting sleepy."

"You always stay up to ring in the new year." She sent him a narrow-eyed look. His ploy was obvious—to her, anyway. He wanted to give the two young people—as he'd kept referring to her and Rick during the evening—a chance to get cozy.

Not happening.

Not while this case was active.

But it was far easier to resist the hunk of temptation sitting beside her with a third party present.

Alone, on New Year's Eve at midnight, with fireworks illuminating the dark sky and bells ringing?

Much more difficult.

And her dad knew that.

He crossed to the counter and set down his cup. "I'm older than I was last year. Midnight's getting too late for me."

Ha.

She wasn't buying that for a minute.

Her dad was as vigorous and energetic as he'd ever been.

Rick hesitated . . . looked from her father to her . . . and stood. "I should probably take off too. I've got a long drive back to the camp and—" He stopped. Tipped his ear toward the window. Frowned. "Is that what I think it is?"

The distinctive ping of sleet against glass intensified even as he posed the question.

"Uh-oh. Sounds like the winter storm rolled in early." Her dad took off toward the front door, she and Rick on his heels as he pulled it open.

The sheen illuminated by the streetlamps and her porch light spoke volumes—every paved surface was already glazed with ice.

"This wasn't supposed to arrive until morning." Heather watched as a car inched down the street, fishtailing despite its slow speed.

"Couldn't pick a worse night for an ice storm." Her dad shook his head and closed the door. "Given all the people at parties who are drinking too much, this is a recipe for disaster."

Brow pinched, Rick walked toward the coat closet. "I better leave before this gets any worse."

"It's already worse. The freezing rain must have kicked in a while back for the roads to be a skating rink already. The sleet's just the latest development." Her dad squinted . . . then brightened. "Hey. I have an idea. Why don't you use my guest room tonight?"

Rick paused at the closet and cast a questioning glance her direction.

Her cue.

"Stay, Rick. It's not worth risking life and limb to get home unless you have to be there tonight for some reason."

One beat passed.

Two.

"Okay. I don't mind driving in snow, but ice is tricky. Thank you for the offer."

"Happy to put my guest room to use. Heather can give you her key when you're ready to leave. It's the first door on the right, down the hall. I'll put out towels for you in the bath next door."

"Why don't I walk over with you now? We can hold each other up." Rick flashed her dad a grin.

He waved aside the suggestion. "I'll cut across the lawn. The grass won't be slippery." Without waiting for a reply, he bustled over to the closet and pulled out his coat.

Rick shifted toward her again.

He was waiting for her to make the call about whether he should linger.

Let him go, Heather. It will be safer.

But different words tumbled out of her mouth. "I plan to watch the clock turn over at midnight. You're welcome to stay if you like."

Well, shoot.

Her heart was sabotaging her brain.

"Thanks. I'll do that."

No hesitation on *his* part.

Which did nothing to calm the sudden flurry of butterflies in her stomach.

After kissing her dad good-bye with a promise to join them in the morning for their usual New Year's waffles and soufflé casserole, she stayed on the stoop as he rounded the bushes and flicked his porch light to let her know he'd arrived safely at his door.

"Sorry you got stranded." Heather retreated to the warmth of the hall, suppressing a shiver as a gust of frigid air followed her in.

Rick gave her a swift once-over—and shoved his fingers in

his pockets. "No worries. It's been an enjoyable evening, and I'm not sorry to extend it for another half hour."

"Shall we sit by the fire until midnight?"

"Sounds perfect to me."

"Could I interest you in a cup of hot chocolate to finish off the evening?"

"What? No champagne?" He grinned.

"Can I be honest? The bubbles tickle my nose and I don't like the taste. Hot chocolate suits me better."

"Sold."

"Give me five minutes."

"Can I help?"

"No way. You did all the dishes. You're done working for the night. This won't take long."

She dashed to the kitchen and made the hot chocolate at record speed, adding a dollop of whipped cream to the top of each mug.

As she picked them up to carry them into the living room, the strains of "Unforgettable" wafted in from the Pandora station she'd tuned in to earlier.

Appropriate.

This evening would be one she'd long remember.

And it wasn't over yet.

As a delicious tingle raced up her spine, she huffed out a breath.

How ridiculous was that?

In twenty minutes, Rick would walk out the door and New Year's Eve would be over.

Nothing was going to happen between now and then.

She wouldn't let it.

Still . . . a girl could dream, couldn't she?

Snorting at such a silly fancy, she returned to the living room to find Rick perusing her bookshelf.

As if sensing her presence, he swiveled around. "You have eclectic taste in literature."

"True—but I don't read much of anything anymore. Most of those titles date back to my pre-career days, when I had the leisure to indulge in books." She set the mugs of cocoa on the coffee table. "Here's the key to my dad's place." She held it out.

"Maybe more reading time will be another benefit of your change in career." He strolled over and took the key, his lean, strong fingers brushing hers—and leaving a trail of heat in their wake.

She resisted the urge to fan herself.

He joined her on the couch, sitting a respectable distance away—but close enough for the subtle scent of his aftershave to invade her pores.

She tugged at the neckline of her sweater.

As the silence lengthened, he tilted his head . . . like he was waiting for a response to his last comment.

Whatever *that* had been.

She scrambled to reconstruct their conversation in her mind.

Books . . . reading . . . ah. Time for both now that she'd changed careers. That was it.

"It would be great to make a dent in my TBR list." She picked up her hot chocolate.

"I'll drink to that." He hoisted his mug and settled back on the cushions. "Tell me about your career as a police detective."

Somehow she managed to hang on to her smile even as her stomach morphed into a macramé factory.

Since that was *not* a subject she wanted to talk about tonight, diversionary tactics were in order.

She took a sip of her favorite comfort beverage and tried for a teasing tone. "I might—if you tell me about your career as a Night Stalker."

"Most of what I did was classified."

Exactly what she'd expected him to say.

Thank you, God!

"Well . . ." She shrugged. "So much for that."

"I did tell you about my childhood."

He *would* bring that up.

And he *had* shared more personal background with her than she'd shared with him.

Better change tactics.

"There isn't much to tell. Police work is police work. And compared to your army experiences, it was boring for the most part." Maybe he'd be satisfied with that.

He studied her. "You have unhappy memories from that career, don't you?"

She inhaled slowly, watching the whipped cream on top of her drink deflate.

How did the man always manage to see straight into her heart?

Was she that transparent—or did he have razor-sharp intuition?

She took another careful sip of the chocolaty beverage, buying herself a few seconds to compose an answer. "I expect every job has its share of unhappy memories."

A spasm of pain whipped across his face, so swift she almost missed it. "Yeah."

Wonderful.

Now she'd reminded him of negatives in *his* past.

This was turning out to be a jolly welcome-the-new-year party.

"I bet you never had to deal with gender-related discrimination, though."

Her spontaneous comment was meant to distract him from his own distressing memories—but why, oh why, had she opened that can of worms?

"You alluded to that at our first meeting." His eyes thinned.

She lifted one shoulder and tried for nonchalance. "It's not uncommon in fields that have been traditional male enclaves. I expected that when I joined the force—and I dealt with it."

"How?"

"By doing the job as well or better than my male counterparts did."

"The pressure of constantly having to prove yourself must have gotten old."

"Yes." Another reason she'd left.

But not the main one.

The primary motivation for her departure was one she'd never shared with anyone.

Including her dad.

"How did you get interested in law enforcement?"

At least that was a safer topic.

"I think I was born with the Don Quixote gene. The whole romantic notion of tilting at windmills in the name of justice appealed to me. I considered going into law, but being confined inside all day didn't appeal to me. So I went with the enforcement side of the equation."

"I bet you were excellent at it."

She was . . . up until the day fear undermined her ability to do her job—and almost cost a colleague his life.

Her fingers began to tremble, and she set her mug down as the contents sloshed near the edge.

Of course Rick noticed.

He placed his own mug beside hers and angled her direction, hands clasped between his knees. "You want to talk about whatever baggage is still causing the shakes?"

She stared at the flickering flames in the fireplace as his gentle question echoed in her heart.

Did she?

Dredging up that painful incident hadn't been on her agenda for New Year's Eve.

In fact, it hadn't been on her agenda for *life*.

But in light of his caring, sympathetic demeanor, a simple no would be too abrupt—leaving her two choices.

She could go back to the gender issue and share a couple of the snide comments her jerk of a boss had thrown out . . . or she could tell him the real reason she'd lost confidence in herself.

Strangely enough, it took her mere seconds to make her choice.

Because if her vibes about this man were accurate, he was destined to be much more than a client in the not-too-distant future.

And if they were going to get involved, it was only fair to alert him to the flaws in her character—and the painful secret she harbored.

If she could dig deep and muster up the courage to tell him.

■ ■ ■ ■ ■

He'd pushed too hard.

Her rigid posture and the pulse throbbing in the hollow of her throat sent a clear message.

Heather was on the verge of shutting down.

That wasn't how Rick wanted this New Year's Eve to end.

Time to backpedal.

He hitched up one side of his mouth. "You know . . . my army buddies used to give me grief about my tendency to ask too many questions. You'd think I'd have learned my lesson. Sorry for probing. I understand wanting to keep painful incidents private."

She knitted her fingers together in her lap and offered him the ghost of a smile. "Funny. I was just about to spill my guts." Her tone was light—but her eyes were sober. Searching. Trying to gauge whether she should reveal her secrets to him after all.

Huh.

He must have read her body language wrong.

Course correction.

"In that case . . . I take back my apology. Because I *am* interested in whatever happened to you."

She dipped her chin and focused on her clamped knuckles. "There was an incident near the end of my tenure that left a bad taste in some people's mouth—including mine."

"It must have been traumatic, if it can still tie you up in knots." Better to comment than interrogate. Too many questions could give her cold feet.

"It was." She drew in a lungful of air. Slowly released it. "One of my colleagues and I were tracking down a suspect in a drug-ring case. We went to his last known address. He wasn't there—but several other bad actors were. None of them were receptive to our presence . . . or our questions."

Rick tried to imagine the woman beside him walking into such a volatile, dangerous setting.

Squelched the images strobing through his mind of all the things that could have gone wrong.

They were too terrifying.

"I take it the encounter didn't go well." He did his best to maintain a conversational manner despite the roiling in his stomach.

"No. The situation deteriorated fast. We went outside to call for backup, and as we walked toward our car, one of the players came out and started yelling obscenities at us. His rage was almost palpable. We didn't stop, but I kept him in my sights while my colleague pulled out his phone to call headquarters." She uncrimped her fingers and flexed her white knuckles.

The temptation to fold her hand into his was strong.

Too strong.

He picked up his mug and wrapped his fingers around it to keep them out of trouble.

When she continued, her voice wasn't quite as steady. "All at once, the guy reached inside his jacket. My gut told me he was going for a gun. I drew my Sig. There was only a split second to make a choice—wait and see . . . or t-take him out."

He swallowed at the all-too-familiar nightmare scenario. During his Night Stalker days, lives had often hung in the balance during missions, and an error in judgment could be a death sentence. The weight of responsibility had been horrendous, the pressure mind-bending, the consequences—

"I made the wrong choice."

Heather's whispered admission was like a punch in the gut.

He had to call up every ounce of his willpower to hang on to the mug when all he wanted to do was pull her into his arms. Hold her. Comfort her.

"What happened?" There were several possible tragic outcomes in the situation she'd described.

"While I hesitated, he whipped out a gun and used it before I got off a shot." She looked at him, her hazel irises awash with tears. "I took him down—but my colleague was already critically wounded."

He stifled the word that sprang to the tip of his tongue. An incident like that could leave permanent scars—deep ones if the other person died.

"Did your partner survive?"

"Yes—no thanks to me."

"Did he blame you?"

"No. But it was a bad mistake. *I* blamed me."

"Heather . . . it was a high-stress situation. Easy to misread. I think you're being too hard on yourself. If you'd made a different call, you could have ended up shooting an unarmed man."

"That was the problem." Anguish seared her eyes. "I was afraid of doing exactly that—and for all the wrong reasons. Law enforcement is under intense scrutiny these days. Patrol officers and detectives have to analyze every move. I hesitated because I was worried about the consequences of overreacting—disciplinary action, being fired, lawsuits. None of those concerns should have been on my mind at that moment."

He wasn't going to dispute that.

However . . . the scrutiny she'd mentioned was very real for law enforcement—and it wasn't hard to see how that could color a person's judgment. Slow their reflexes. Make them doubt their instincts.

Thank heaven he'd never had to worry much about red tape in the heat of battle—or public backlash over mistakes.

"Did your higher-ups think you made a mistake?"

She exhaled, and her shoulders drooped. "No. There were no professional repercussions. I was put on administrative leave—normal protocol after a shooting incident—but I was cleared of any fault."

"Yet that incident convinced you to leave law enforcement."

"Yes. I may have been absolved of guilt officially, but I know I should have pulled the trigger sooner. *Would* have pulled it if I'd trusted my gut. Instead, I second-guessed myself. And cops or detectives whose fear of the personal consequences of a mistake make them falter are a danger to their colleagues and put their own life on the line."

There was no rebuttal to that.

She was right.

And her decision to leave spoke volumes about her character.

"I'm not going to argue with your rationale for walking away. I think it's sound. I also think you made a smart—and honorable—choice."

She searched his face, her expression skeptical. "But a man almost died because of me."

"Heather . . . factoring in all the pressures you mentioned, don't you think a fair number of your colleagues could have faltered for the same reason in a similar situation? You're human. Flawed, like we all are. But I'm confident you did the best you were capable of under the circumstances. That's all anyone—including God—can ask."

Her eyes began to shimmer again. "Thank you for saying that."

"It's the truth—and I doubt I'm the first to point it out. I'm sure your father was supportive."

She picked a piece of fuzz off the couch. "I've never told him the details of that story. I've never told *anyone* outside law enforcement that story."

Pressure built in his throat as the implications of her admissions registered. "In that case, it's my turn to thank *you*. I'm honored by your trust. And can I be honest? For selfish reasons, I'm glad you left that high-risk life behind."

"So am I. I like PI work, and the Phoenix crew is stellar. They all treat me as an equal. There are a few things I miss about being a detective—but my sergeant isn't one of them." She grimaced.

"He was one of the chauvinists?"

"The worst one. His wife never worked outside the home, and he thought women's contributions to society should be limited to baking and babies."

"Did he actually say that?"

"No—but actions speak louder than words. One Christmas, he gave me an apron."

He cringed. "Ouch."

"Yeah. But I learned to let that kind of garbage roll off my back. Most of the guys were—" She cocked her ear, then checked her watch. "Oh my gosh! It's midnight!" She vaulted to her feet and dashed toward the closet.

He stood. "What are you doing?"

"Oh." She froze, hand on her coat, while a faint flush crept across her cheeks. "Dad and I always go outside at midnight to listen to the bells and whistles and watch for fireworks. When I was younger, we also threw homemade confetti—which we were still cleaning up in June." She offered him a self-conscious smile and sent a yearning glance toward the door as the volume of the din increased. "Sorry. It's a silly custom. No sane person would stand on the porch in freezing weather just to listen to a bunch of noise."

"I think it's a charming custom—and traditions should always be honored." He crossed the room in a few long strides and pulled his own coat off the hanger. "Let's go."

"Seriously?" She was already shoving her arms into the sleeves of her coat.

"I wouldn't kid about a New Year's Eve tradition." He donned his own jacket and took her arm. "Let's hurry or we'll miss the show."

They stepped outside, into a wonderland of glistening ice, in time to catch a short burst of fireworks and listen to the cacophony of banging pots, blowing horns, and muted shouts of "Happy New Year."

If Heather noticed the biting nip of the glacial wind, she gave no indication of it as she lifted a luminous face toward the inky sky. Only her red cheeks and frosty breath suggested she wasn't immune to the cold.

The arctic air didn't bother him in the least, either. Not with her standing close beside him, filling his heart with warmth.

But all too soon, the revelry died down.

"Some years, the racket goes on for ten minutes. The cold must be forcing people inside." She sighed and tucked her hands under her arms as she scanned the frozen scene. "I guess the celebrations are over."

"Oh, I don't know. *I* think they're just beginning."

She sent him a cautious look. "What do you m-mean?"

He wasn't certain if the catch in her voice was due to the cold or a sudden case of nerves—but she had no reason to worry. He wasn't going to overstep.

Not much, anyway.

He simply wanted to ensure they launched the new year on the right note—and the message he was about to send should do the trick.

"We should toast the new year." He turned toward her.

"We don't have any champagne."

"I can think of something more intoxicating." He grasped her arms in a gentle clasp. "Happy New Year, Heather. Here's to the next twelve months—may they be filled with possibilities."

Before she could balk, he leaned down and brushed a kiss over her forehead.

Her breath hitched as he straightened up—and this time he had no doubt about the cause.

"Sleep well." With a squeeze of her fingers, he plunged into the darkness and traversed the brittle, ice-encrusted grass to her father's unit.

Removing himself as fast as possible from temptation.

When he looked back, she was standing motionless where he'd left her, watching him, fingers pressed to her lips.

Like the simple kiss had shaken her world.

He could relate.

And if all went as he expected, that kiss would be the first of many in this new year.

15

Why was someone calling her at . . . Heather squinted at the clock on her nightstand . . . eight in the morning on New Year's Day?

Usually she and her dad didn't eat breakfast until at least nine.

Of course, any other year, she'd be up by now.

But she'd never spent a New Year's Eve night tossing after a surprise kiss and an alluring toast that had—as Rick predicted—been far more intoxicating than champagne.

Now that she was awake, however, she intended to join him next door ASAP.

She grabbed her phone, skimmed caller ID, and sat up. "Morning, Dad."

"Happy New Year. Did I wake you?"

"Uh . . . I was about to get up."

"Sorry to disturb your beauty sleep. I thought you'd be wide awake and primping for breakfast."

She ignored his insinuation. "When are we eating?"

"Nine o'clock. I heard Rick come in not long after midnight, so I didn't think that would be too early. I guess you two didn't make a late night of it."

"No."

"Pity."

She ignored that too as she stood. "I'll be over in fifteen minutes."

"Don't hurry on my account—or your friend's. He took off early."

"What?" She tried to stem the tsunami of disappointment that swept over her. "Didn't you invite him to stay for breakfast?"

"Of course I did. I left a note on the pillow in the guest bedroom. He left me one in return, on the kitchen counter. That man moves like a shadow. I didn't hear a sound this morning— and you know I'm a light sleeper."

"What did he say?"

"A work issue came up that required his immediate attention. He wrote a very gracious thank-you for my hospitality, and asked me to have you call his cell."

She rummaged around in her closet for her oldest, most comfortable jeans. No reason to dress up for breakfast after all.

"I'll give him a ring as soon as we hang up. Expect me in ten minutes." It wouldn't take long to get ready, since no primping was involved.

"Don't rush the conversation with your friend on my account. We're not eating for almost an hour."

"Okay. See you soon." She sat back on the edge of the bed and tapped in Rick's speed dial number.

A work issue on New Year's Day.

The septic tank again?

She wrinkled her nose.

Not the pleasantest kind of news to wake up to on a holiday.

Three rings in, Rick picked up and wished her Happy New

Year—although she could barely hear his greeting over the sound of voices and . . . engines?

"The same to you—but you may have to talk louder. It's hard to hear with all the background noise."

"I know. I'm walking to a quieter place as we speak. Give me a minute."

As she waited, the din diminished—but wherever he was, there was a lot of activity.

Much more than a septic problem should entail.

Curious.

"Sorry to leave without any warning this morning." Rick came through loud and clear now. "I take it your dad got my note."

"Yes. Are you at the camp?"

"No." A beat ticked by. "Do you remember asking me not long after we met if I missed flying?"

"Yes." That early conversation was etched in her memory. "You said you haven't given it up entirely."

"As a matter of fact . . . I haven't given it up at all. I don't fly much in the summer, but during the camp's off-season I spend most of my free hours in the air."

"For work . . . or fun?"

"Work. I fly for a charter company out of Spirit Airport, and I train pilots for an aviation search and rescue firm. I'm also on call with the Highway Patrol when they need a pilot experienced in fast-rope tactical insertions, difficult short-haul rescues—or anything that requires precision flying. They're responsible for my early exit this morning."

She might not know what a fast-rope tactical insertion or short-haul rescue was, but apparently her ex–Night Stalker client was still piloting dicey—and dangerous—missions.

A spurt of adrenaline jacked up her pulse.

"Is it safe to fly in this kind of weather?" She darted over to the window and lifted a slat in the blinds. The sleet had stopped, but it was a sheet of ice out there.

"Safer than driving. Getting to the hangar was the hard part. The rest will be easy."

Was that true—or was he trying to downplay the hazards?

"What kind of job are you doing for them today?"

"Rescue. A couple of hikers got surprised by the early arrival of last night's storm. In their rush to get out of the backcountry, one of them slipped and fell into a ravine. His buddy made it out and gave us the location, but in these conditions a land rescue would take too long. Besides, the ravine is dangerous to descend on foot in any weather, let alone after an ice storm. We're going to pick up the injured friend and deliver him to an ambulance that will be waiting on the main road, a mile or two away."

"You make it sound simple."

"Not simple—but I've been on far riskier missions. And no one will be shooting at us on this one. That's always a plus."

He was trying to position a dramatic helicopter rescue in frozen terrain as no big deal.

And it may not be—to him.

But it was miles outside her comfort zone.

Better get used to it, though. If she and Rick became a couple after this case was over, there would be frequent moments like this in her future.

"Be careful."

"Always."

"I'm sorry you'll miss breakfast."

"No sorrier than I am. Maybe your dad will invite me again." The background noise picked up again.

"I think that could be arranged." She turned her back on the frozen landscape. "Would you text me later? I'll feel better if I know you're home safe and sound."

"I'll be happy to." Now the noise was almost drowning him out. "I have to run. You caught me as we were about to take off."

He'd delayed his liftoff to talk to her?

Sweet.

"I'll be waiting to hear from you."

He said something else, but his words were drowned out by what sounded like the *thwump* of rotor blades. Then the line went dead.

Heather slowly lowered the phone from her ear, her lips curving up.

It was mind-boggling how life could change in the blink of an eye.

One week ago, she hadn't even known Rick Jordan.

Yet already she was beginning to think he could be The One—and unless her intuition was off, he was thinking the same.

Funny.

She'd never been the impetuous type.

All her life, she'd preferred to take her time and methodically gather as much evidence as possible before making up her mind about anything.

But despite their short acquaintance, she'd amassed a fair amount of intel about Rick. And every scrap of it led to the same conclusion.

The ex–Night Stalker who ran a camp for foster kids, cared about his friends, and flew rescue missions was the real deal.

So unless some less-flattering piece of data surfaced, she was all in on this relationship—as soon as they figured out why two people had died under mysterious circumstances . . . and what a perplexing flash drive had to do with their demise.

. . . . .

The press conference had gone well.

Even better than he'd expected.

While Chuck made a few closing comments and the cameras clicked off, Brad scanned the company conference room, homing in on Lindsey. She was talking with one of the reporters, but she glanced at him, as if she'd sensed his gaze.

He gave her a thumbs-up.

They'd have much to celebrate tonight.

That was why he'd made dinner reservations at Tony's. A momentous day like this deserved to be celebrated in high style.

A few reporters latched on to him, and another twenty minutes passed before Chuck managed to clear the room.

"Fabulous job." He beamed at the two of them as Lindsey joined him. "You had them eating out of your hand. There wasn't a single hardball question."

"There will be."

"I know . . . but if we can get the press on our side up front, they'll be more receptive to your answers. You want to debrief now, or let the dust settle and talk tomorrow?"

"Tomorrow."

"Works for me. I have a bunch of follow-ups to do." He held up a sheaf of business cards to illustrate. "I'll give you a call later to set it up. Lindsey." He dipped his head toward her.

As Chuck headed for the door, Brad took his wife's hand. "Shall we adjourn to my office? It's more private there."

"Why, Mr. Weston—why on earth would you need privacy?" She batted her eyelashes and gave a soft laugh.

"I'll demonstrate after we get there." He winked and tugged her toward the door.

When they reached his outer office, his administrative assistant swiveled toward them. "Several messages came in during the press conference. I put them on your desk."

"Thanks." He kept walking.

Once inside his private domain, he closed the door and turned

Lindsey in his arms. "You look exquisite today. Every person in that room could picture you as the first lady."

"I'm mainly interested in being *your* first lady." She wrapped her arms around his neck.

"You've got that job for life."

He kissed her, holding nothing back, and for once she seemed not to care if he mussed her hair, despite their date at Tony's this evening.

When at last he drew back, he swept a hand toward the conference table off to the side. "I ordered a light lunch for us."

She smiled as she surveyed the picnic basket in the center of the polished surface, a wine bottle in a cooler beside it. "You're such a romantic."

"Only with you. Give me a minute to freshen up and we'll see what's inside that basket."

He returned as fast as he could and found her perched on the edge of his desk, a message slip in her hand, brow furrowed.

"What's wrong?" He crossed the room to join her.

"I wandered over to enjoy the view and noticed your stack of messages. This one was on top." She held it out to him.

Her frown deepened.

A niggle of unease snaked down his spine.

He took the slip of paper and read the name and message.

Heather Shields from Phoenix Inc.

A PI firm.

The woman wanted to meet with him to discuss a case she was working on that involved someone from his days at the forward operating base where he'd spent the final two years of his service.

A cold knot formed in his stomach.

"Do you think this could have anything to do with the . . . situation . . . you told me about before we got married?" Lindsey's mouth was tight. Like she was worried.

She wasn't as worried as he was, though.

But he couldn't let her see that.

This was his problem, and he'd have to handle it.

"I don't see how it could be." He set the message on top of the pile, feigning indifference. "There's no one left who knows about that. A roadside bomb took out the contractor who was involved, and the other party died in an accident not long ago."

"You never told me that."

"I didn't think it was relevant—and I only heard about it by chance. There's no one else who knew anything about what was going on."

"Are you going to talk with this woman?"

"I don't know."

She touched his arm. "May I make a suggestion?"

"You never have to ask that question. Your input is always welcome."

"It couldn't hurt to see what she has to say. You could be right, and whatever she's working on may have nothing to do with the situation in which you were involved. But wouldn't it be better to confirm that rather than wonder—and worry?"

He covered her hand with his. As usual, she'd offered sound advice.

His brother might think of her as nothing but a trophy wife with more beauty than brains, but that was his mistake.

"Excellent counsel. After lunch, I'll give her a ring and see what this is all about. Now let's put aside petty worries and enjoy our food."

For the next forty-five minutes, while his administrative assistant handled his calls and they ate a leisurely meal, he tried to follow his own advice.

But it was impossible not to worry.

Even though all the players were gone and no longer a threat . . . even though the statute of limitations was on the cusp of expiring . . . even though there was virtually no chance he was in any danger of exposure . . . he couldn't shake the feeling that the rosy future he'd envisioned as he launched his gubernatorial bid two hours ago was about to come crashing down around him.

. . . . .

For a kid from a blue-collar background, Brad Weston had done very well for himself.

As she waited in the outer office for the man to see her, Heather took an inventory of the posh space.

Hardwood floors were covered by what appeared to be a high-end Persian carpet with an intricate border. A large crystal sculpture rested on a pedestal—Lalique, perhaps. Fresh flowers adorned the coffee table.

All the trappings of wealth and success were on display.

The senior housing business must be booming.

And if stellar entrepreneurship was how Weston had acquired this kind of luxury, kudos for him. Self-made men were to be admired.

But where had he obtained the funds to launch his start-up?

Based on her research after the Phoenix partners had given her the go-ahead to proceed with this investigation, he hadn't bankrolled his venture from family wealth.

And he sure hadn't gotten rich being a major in the army.

Unless he was making money on the side.

Unless he was the key to the flash drive Boomer had left in that locker at the Lexington ice rink.

His willingness to see her within hours of her call suggested he was very cooperative . . . very curious . . . or very nervous.

It would be instructive to watch his responses to her questions and try to determine which descriptor fit him best.

The phone on his assistant's desk trilled, and after a brief exchange, she stood. "Mr. Weston is ready to see you. He does have a dinner engagement this evening, so please be aware his time is limited. He announced his candidacy for governor this morning, and he's been busy fielding calls from the press all day. But he did want to accommodate you ASAP."

"I appreciate that—and I don't plan to delay his dinner." Heather rose and followed the woman into the man's office.

As she entered, he circled around from behind his desk to greet her, hand extended. "Ms. Shields, Brad Weston. Please, have a seat." He motioned toward a sitting area off to the side furnished with plush chairs and a settee. "May I offer you a beverage?"

"No, thank you." She took one of the chairs, and he sat in an adjacent seat.

"You mentioned in your message that you're investigating a case connected to my years in the Middle East. I must admit, I'm intrigued. Tell me how I can help you."

She opened her notebook. "Do you recall a woman by the name of Beth Johnson?"

His eyebrows peaked. "Now there's a name from the past. Yes. Beth reported to me at the forward operating base where I was stationed near the end of my army career."

"Did you know she died a few weeks ago?"

He blinked. "Good heavens. She was a young woman. What happened to her?"

If he was faking surprise, he was doing a stellar job of it.

"She fell over the railing of her condo balcony. It was ruled accidental."

He scrutinized her. "*Ruled* accidental—not *was* accidental. Are you suggesting there was more to her death than that?"

The man was sharp.

"Let's just say I'm not convinced the police report is accurate. Did you know a man by the name of Jackson Dunn, who was also at the base while you were there? He went by the nickname Boomer."

Forehead puckering, he slowly shook his head. "No. That name doesn't ring any bells. How is he connected to whatever you're investigating?"

"He and Beth were involved in a romantic relationship while they were at the base. I believe they kept their liaison under wraps."

"That would have been in their best interest. But as I said, I didn't know him. And I only knew Beth through our work association. I didn't pry into her private life." He glanced at his watch. "What exactly are you investigating, Ms. Shields?"

"The nature of my investigation has changed over the course of the past week. Initially, my client asked me to find Mr. Dunn."

"Did you?"

"No. A hiker did. He turned up dead on a hiking trail three days ago in Kentucky."

Weston blinked. "Another accident?"

"So the authorities seem to think."

"You're not buying that, either?"

"I don't like coincidences."

"But . . . why would anyone wish these people harm?"

"I believe the motive is related to the flash drive Mr. Dunn left behind for my client to find."

He went absolutely still. "What was on it?"

Heather extracted a sheet of paper from the folder she'd brought with her and handed it to him. "I printed out one of the pages. They're all similar."

After a brief hesitation, he took it.

As he skimmed the document, some of the color leached from his complexion. "Do you know what this is?" The sheet quivered as he posed the question, and he lowered it to his lap.

"I was hoping you could help me with that."

He skimmed it again. "It appears to be a code of sorts—but it means nothing to me. I'm sorry." He started to hand it back.

"Why don't you keep it? Perhaps some notation on there will prompt an idea. The document does date from your tenure in the Middle East."

"I'll be happy to do that—but don't get your hopes up. This bears no resemblance to any of the official paperwork I dealt with at the base."

"May I ask what your job was there?"

"I was in charge of the trucking operation."

"What did that entail?"

"Fuel distribution. We were the supply point for surrounding bases."

"What did Beth do?"

"She recorded fuel deliveries and escorted trucks past the gate. It was a basic clerical position." He looked at his watch again. "I wish I could be of more help, but I haven't kept in touch with Beth, I never met her friend, and this"—he lifted the sheet—"is a mystery to me."

The man was smooth. Only the tiny tremor in his fingers and the slight loss of color in his face suggested he might know more than he was sharing.

But he'd told her his story, and she suspected he was going to stick to it.

Time to change tactics—and topics.

She closed her notebook to suggest the official interview was over. "I appreciate you squeezing me in today, considering the announcement you made earlier. I imagine your life is about to get much busier."

"True—but I can't think of anything more satisfying than serving the people of Missouri as their governor."

"I agree it's an important job. But from what I've read, you've done an enormous amount of worthwhile work with this company too. Your senior housing concept is very innovative."

"Thank you. I've been gratified by the reception."

"How did you come up with the idea?"

"Observation, for the most part." He leaned back and crossed an ankle over a knee, lowering his guard—as she'd hoped. "I had a few friends with family members in traditional assisted living and senior facilities, and even the nicest ones tend to be large and impersonal. I thought there was a niche for a business model that featured smaller-scale developments—and also an opportunity to make significant money, to be honest."

"Naturally. This *is* a business." She gave him an agreeable smile. "May I ask how you launched this? It was an untried concept."

"Yes, it was—but I was convinced that if I could get a few units up and running, future developments would sell themselves."

"And you were right." She tucked her notebook in the crook of her arm, as if she was preparing to stand, and kept her tone conversational. "So many ideas like that die on the shelf, though. I'm certain it's difficult to raise funds for that kind of investment. You don't come from wealth, as far as I could determine."

His shoulders tensed a hair. "No. Very blue collar. But my late wife had a fair amount of money, and I was always frugal with my pennies. I managed to save enough to pull it off." He checked his watch again and stood. "Did my assistant tell you I had a dinner engagement?"

He didn't like her questions about his funding source.

Another red flag.

"Yes." She rose. "Thank you for seeing me on such a busy day. If you happen to spot anything on the document I gave you, I'd appreciate a call." She handed him a card.

"As I said, I doubt that will happen. It's just a jumble of

dollar amounts and initials. I expect only the person who put it together will be able to decipher it. Trying to decode it may be a waste of time."

"Well, as long as my client is willing to fund the investigation, I imagine we'll stick with it. Enjoy your evening."

He shook the hand she extended, accompanied her to the door, and wished her good luck.

But as she left his suite of offices behind and walked toward the elevator, his parting comment wasn't registering as sincere.

Meaning that after she gave Rick an update on their meeting, she'd be spending the next few days immersed in research on the new gubernatorial candidate.

Because unless she was way off her game, Brad Weston knew far more about the activities at that forward operating base— and the contents of that flash drive—than he'd shared with her.

16

"I have news. Call me."

Frowning, I skimmed the text from my PI on my new burner phone while keeping one eye on the traffic.

I could wait to contact him until I finished my errands on this blustery Thursday noon hour—or I could pull into the nearest parking lot and get an update now.

No contest.

At this stage of the game, my patience was wearing thin.

Flipping on my turn signal, I hung a right into a fast-food outlet and claimed a parking spot near the back, past the extended line at the drive-through window.

Seconds later, I had my guy on the line. "What's up?"

"First . . . happy New Year, and thank you for extending our association."

"I didn't call to exchange pleasantries. What do you have?"

"Sorry to waste your time." Tone cooling, he got down to business.

I listened in silence while he recounted the new data he'd dug up.

Gritted my teeth.

The expanding list of players in this drama was *not* comforting—nor did it bode well for the seamless operation I'd anticipated.

"Did you find out the name of Heather Shields's client?"

"Yes. Rick Jordan."

"I assume he lives in the area?"

"Correct. An army vet who runs a camp for foster kids in the county."

I didn't care what he did.

All I cared about was making sure he and the woman PI didn't create any waves.

Since the press conference, the media had been gushing about the latest development in the governor's race, generating tons of positive publicity.

But reporters were fickle.

If they sensed any sort of scandal, they'd be all over it like maggots on a corpse.

And if they dug deep enough . . . if that PI or her ex-army client planted any seeds of doubt with the press . . . the resulting coverage could deep-six the fledgling campaign.

"Stay on this. I want to know where these two go, who they see, what they do."

"I'll have to bring a couple of colleagues on board if you want that kind of coverage."

"Do it."

I had the money.

It wasn't how I'd prefer to use it, but if the data I was buying kept this thing from going south, it would be worth every penny.

"You're the boss."

"I'll expect reports twice a day."

"No problem."

I jabbed the end button. Stowed the phone. Glared at the overflowing dumpster outside my window.

The two newest players could complicate everything.

What if the PI and Jordan managed to piece together what had gone on at that forward operating base?

What if they were able to definitively identify the people who'd been involved?

They had to be stopped before this went any further.

I was in too deep—and far too close to my goal—to allow any potential risk to jeopardize the future I'd planned.

If this gumshoe and her client didn't give this up fast, there would be no option.

Another accident—or two—would have to be arranged.

.....

"Sorry I couldn't get into town sooner." Juggling a takeout tray from Kaldi's, Rick stood as Heather entered the reception area at Phoenix Inc. and walked over to him. "One flying job after another came in. I've been on the go for the past four days."

"No worries. I've kept you in the loop by phone—but it will be nice to catch up in person."

"I agree." In his peripheral vision, he caught Nikki giving the two of them an inquisitive appraisal.

Apparently Heather did too, because she angled away from the office manager and motioned toward the door that led to the offices. "Let's continue our discussion back here."

The door clicked as they approached, and as he reached past her to push it open, a subtle, floral fragrance swirled around him.

He inhaled.

Slowly.

"I'd offer coffee, but I see you already made a beverage run." She motioned to the tray in his hands as they walked down the hall.

He forced himself to refocus. "Tea for the lady, an Americano for me"—he plucked a bag from between the cups—"and a Nutella scone to share."

"You know the way to this PI's heart." She motioned to the round conference table as they entered her office.

"I'm working on it, anyway. I like the outfit." He scanned her tailored gray slacks, plum-colored sweater, and black flats with saucy purple and hot pink striped bows on top.

"Thanks." She sat, opened the bag, and broke off a piece of scone. "You sound like you've been crazy busy."

"Yes. Two corporate charters dropped into my lap after the Highway Patrol job. But in between I've been sending out more emails to my contacts, based on our conversations since your meeting with Weston. What have you been up to?"

"I've been doing more research. Online for the most part, but I also called a CID contact at Fort Leonard Wood, who provided some helpful information. I worked with him a few years ago on a case that overlapped our jurisdictions."

"You've been busy too."

"Very—and it's paid off." She opened a folder on the table and flipped through her notes. "I want to run a theory by you."

"Shoot."

"My CID contact verified that Weston oversaw the distribution of thousands of gallons of petroleum a day. I researched that topic and discovered there's rampant corruption at several of those forward operating bases. One of the most pervasive crimes is selling US military fuel to locals and pocketing the proceeds. The CID investigator said the fuel oversight system at many of those bases is less than optimal. Remember Nathan's term—the Wild West?"

"Yes. I think we're tracking the same direction. Oversight *is* loose. I heard plenty of rumors about graft and fraud while I was deployed there—and petroleum is a hot commodity. My contacts confirmed that."

"My CID investigator did too." She consulted her notes again. "According to him, civilian Pentagon contractors usually distribute the fuel, and the supply trucks are often driven by locals who are under contract with bases. At a major facility like the one where Beth and Weston were stationed, they'd be sending fuel to twenty or thirty nearby bases."

"I think I can pick it up from there. As the recorder of fuel deliveries, all Beth had to do was order the trucks to transport more than was needed, then file a fake shipping record with a bogus amount. Once the truck left her base, it would rendezvous with buyers in a designated location. Cash would change hands, a lighter truck would continue on its way—and the proceeds would be divided among those involved."

She raised her cup of tea in salute. "Give the man a gold star."

"And you're thinking Weston may have been part of the scheme."

"Someone at a higher level would have had to be involved to make it work. But I'm amazed no one noticed what was going on."

"You wouldn't be if you'd ever been in the Middle East. Corruption in that culture is common—and in all likelihood only two or three people on the base were keeping track of where the fuel went after it left. Was your CID guy interested in helping us? An army insider could open doors."

"I wish." She sighed. "I broached that idea, but he didn't bite. He sounded slammed."

"That doesn't surprise me. From what I understand, CID doesn't have the manpower to investigate all of the bribery, fraud, kickbacks, and petty theft that goes on over there. They tend to concentrate on the larger cases."

"And I expect the players know that, which is why get-rich-quick schemes with low risk can be tempting."

"Plus, it's often hard to muster the evidence to bring a case to trial."

"The flash drive could be evidence." She pulled out a printed copy of the Excel document.

"Did you tell that to your contact?"

"Yes—but in its present undecipherable form, it isn't of much use to him. He did promise to send me a list of the bases in the area, along with the names of everyone who had been involved in the fuel operation during Weston's tenure. He thought that might help us determine whether the document supports our theory."

"It's worth a shot."

"Let me see if his email came in while we've been talking." She rose, broke off another piece of the scone, and popped it in her mouth as she moved behind her desk to retrieve her cell.

"I have a hard copy of the document from the flash drive too." Rick opened the folder he'd brought with him.

"Perfect. We can spread everything out." She tapped her screen and smiled. "Yes! He came through." A few keystrokes on her laptop, and her printer began to hum. After snagging the sheets it spit out, she rejoined him and passed over a copy.

"Let's hope four eyes are better than two on this." He took another sip of his Americano and scrutinized the Excel document and the new CID information side by side.

It didn't take him long to spot a number of connections.

"Did you—"

"Look at—"

He grinned at her. "Our brains must be in sync. You first."

"The first initials of the bases Weston supplied match up with quite a few of the initials in the second column on the spreadsheet."

"That jumped out at me too. Also . . . did you notice how three different letters of the alphabet appear with each entry, followed by dollar amounts—and separated by slashes?" He pointed them out. "I was thinking the letters stood for a place, but now I'm wondering if they represent three different people. If someone who worked for a Pentagon contractor was in the mix, these could represent the three people involved in the scam, followed by the amounts they received for each shipment."

Heather wrinkled her brow. "But none of the initials match the two suspected players. How do M, S, and C fit in?"

He offered her the only explanation he could come up with. "Maybe he used titles to keep it as anonymous as possible, so no one could be identified if this ever saw the light of day. Major . . . specialist . . . contractor."

"That's a bit of a stretch—but it does fit."

"Do you think your CID contact would give you the name of the contractor employee over there at the time—assuming there was one?"

"It can't hurt to ask." She picked up her cell and thumbed in a text. "He's been very responsive. Let's hope that pattern continues. After what happened to Beth and Boomer, it may be worth tracking this guy down if he exists. A conversation could be illuminating."

"True." He took a bite of the scone and gave the Excel document another perusal. "You know . . . if these dollar amounts represent thousands of dollars—or more . . . the M person made a heap of money out of this."

"Yeah. He got the bulk of each transaction. S came out on the short end."

"Consistent with Beth's rank, if that's what the initials represent. But before we get too far down this road, let's talk motive."

"Greed is the obvious one for the contractor employee and Beth—unless she was coerced or intimidated into participating by her boss. But Weston?" She shook her head. "I don't think that fits."

"Why not?"

"On the surface, he appears to be a decent man with lofty ambitions—as his charitable and entrepreneurial ventures suggest. However . . . he needed funding to launch his business."

"And it didn't sound as if he liked your questions on that topic during your meeting."

"No, he didn't. If he *was* the mastermind behind a fraud scheme overseas, I think he simply saw it as an opportunity to get the necessary seed money."

Rick leaned back in his chair, cradling his coffee cup in his hands. "I could buy that. A low-risk enterprise that many consider a victimless crime would be an easy way to bankroll cash relatively guilt-free. Which leads me to a disconnect. Pilfering petroleum is on a different scale than killing people."

"I know. I'm struggling with that too. From everything Nikki and I could find, Weston's led an otherwise exemplary and honorable life. He was awarded several medals during his years in the service. Despite losing his wife to an embolism days after returning home, he followed his dream to create his company. He's active in his church, on the board of several charitable ventures, and participates in the Big Brothers program."

"He sounds like a Boy Scout."

She took a sip of her tea, watching him over the rim. "Can you think of a more perfect cover for a murderer?"

He arched an eyebrow. "You're a cynic."

"No—a realist. You can't imagine the stuff I've seen."

Yeah, he could.

But he didn't want to.

"Did you run any background on Beth?"

"Nikki's doing that as we speak. One thing we already found is that she bought a very upscale condo on a receptionist's salary."

"The pieces are fitting."

"I know. And isn't it odd that both Beth and Boomer—two of the four people who may have known what was going on over there—died not long before Weston announced his run for governor? As if someone wanted to eliminate anyone who could derail his political—" Her phone began to vibrate on the table, and she picked it up. "My CID contact."

Rick filched another piece of the scone while Heather did more listening than talking. But in the end, she jotted a name on the notepad in front of her.

Paul Schmitz.

When she ended the call, he motioned toward the paper. "The Pentagon contractor employee?"

"Yes." She folded her hands on the table. "But he's not going to be of any help to us. He died a month after Weston's enlistment was up. A roadside bomb."

So much for talking to the third person in their theoretical ring.

"I think we can rule out foul play with that death—at least the kind that could be initiated by our person of interest."

"Agreed."

"If Schmitz, Weston, and Beth *were* our three players—and Beth was discreet about her relationship with Boomer—how did the perpetrator find out about him?"

Forehead furrowed, Heather straightened the papers in her file until they were in precise alignment. "Well . . . assuming Beth's fall wasn't an accident, the killer may have been instructed to ask a few questions—and press for answers. The mastermind behind this would want to know if she'd told anyone about the operation in the Middle East."

"Weston doesn't sound like the type who'd be into strong-arming."

"I won't argue with that. Besides, he has a solid alibi for that night."

"You asked?"

"I didn't have to. While I was digging into his background, I found a story about him attending a charity gala here in St. Louis the night she died, complete with pictures."

Rick did the math.

"You think this may have been a paid job?"

"That would be my guess—no matter who the mastermind is. An amateur would be less skilled at staging a murder to read as an accident."

This was getting more sinister by the day.

"What happens next?" He took a sip of coffee.

"I'm going to have another conversation with the investigator at Fort Leonard Wood. See if he can verify that shipments left the base on the dates in the Excel document during the two-year window Weston was there."

"I can't imagine he'd object to providing that information."

"Me either. I also think—in light of everything we've learned—another visit with our aspiring governor is in order. A fishing expedition more than anything. Turning up the heat can often lead people to make mistakes, let information slip."

"Assuming he'll see you again."

"If he's our man, he will. He'll want to appear cooperative. As if he has nothing to hide."

He hiked up one side of his mouth. "You've been down this road a few times."

"Yeah. Too many." She cast a covetous glance toward the last morsel of scone. "You want that?"

"It's all yours."

She didn't argue.

After washing it down with a final swig of tea, she closed her file. "What's on your schedule for the next few days?"

"Camp business tomorrow, followed by a road trip."

"Work related?"

"No." He exhaled. "I'm going to Boomer's funeral in Louisville."

Her features softened. "When is it?"

"Saturday. The police department gave me the name of the funeral home that picked up the body once the coroner released it, and I called them for the details."

"We could have done that for you. Saved you some red tape."

"There wasn't much hassle."

"Who made the arrangements?"

"The funeral director told me Boomer left detailed instructions for a service."

Heather tilted her head. "Isn't that unusual for someone so young?"

"Not if you have no family—and not if you've seen battle. The latter gives you a new perspective on the unpredictability of life—and death." He pressed a finger against a stray crumb on the table. "I don't know how many people will show up, but I have to be there. It's the least I can do after—" The last word rasped, and he swallowed.

"He saved your life, didn't he?" Her voice was quiet. Filled with empathy. "In the Chinook crash Nathan mentioned."

"Yeah." He swallowed, the metallic taste of fear once again as vivid on his tongue as it had been that terrible night. "I would have died if he hadn't dived into the fray to get to me. And he paid the price with injuries of his own."

"It must have been a horrendous crash."

She didn't say or ask anything else . . . but he knew she hoped he'd share more—as she had shared the story of the traumatic shooting at the end of her law enforcement career.

If you want this relationship to go anywhere, tell her the story, Jordan. Let her know you trust her with the bad parts of your life as well as the good.

That was true—in principle.

But putting it into practice?

Much harder.

He swirled his coffee and drained his cup—but the dregs were bitter.

And there was nothing left of the sweet scone to offset the caustic flavor.

He set the cup down as the silence lengthened.

Just do it, Jordan.

Dropping one hand to his lap, he balled his fingers. "I haven't talked much about the incident."

"It's hard to put painful events into words."

And she wasn't asking him to.

That wasn't her style.

But he also knew a woman like Heather wouldn't be happy in a relationship with a man who wasn't willing to let her all the way in.

"You positive you want to get into this now?" Maybe she'd let him off the hook.

"Is there ever a good time to talk about unpleasant memories?"

So much for a reprieve.

After a few beats ticked by, she picked up her cup and started to rise. "There may be better times than others, though."

"Wait." He grabbed her hand. Letting this moment slip by would be a mistake. He knew that as surely as he knew that once he told her the story that haunted his dreams, he would cross a line he'd never crossed with anyone.

"It's okay, Rick."

No. It wasn't. He needed to suck it up and be honest with

her. "If you can spare a few more minutes, I'll tell you what happened."

She searched his face, then slowly sank back into her chair. "I have all morning."

"It won't take that long. I'll give you the abbreviated version." As abbreviated as possible.

"Any version is fine."

Shoring up his resolve, he filled his lungs and plunged in. "We were supposed to extract some troops trapped behind enemy lines. Those kinds of operations are risky under the best conditions, but everything that could go wrong did go wrong that night. Bad weather, mechanical issues, poor communication." His fingers began to tremble, and he linked them together. Tight. "We made it to the pickup point, but less than twenty feet from the ground, an RPG got us."

A bead of sweat broke out on his upper lip, and he swiped it away. He ought to be able to handle this better after all these years.

She rested her hand on top of his clenched fingers.

"Sorry." His apology came out hoarse. Shaky.

"Don't be." Her eyes were warm. Sympathetic. Filled with compassion . . . and a deeper emotion that stirred his heart.

He swallowed and forced himself to continue. "We went down hard. Our people on the ground opened fire to give us a chance to get out and take cover. I sent a distress signal back to the base while everyone else escaped—but when I tried to follow them, I got clipped."

She sucked in a breath. "As in shot?"

"Yeah." Just thinking about those eternal minutes lying injured and unprotected beside the downed Chinook, certain he was going to die, twisted his gut. "Boomer began to creep toward me. I waved him back, yelled at him to take cover. But despite his own injuries, he somehow managed to drag me behind several large rocks and slap a hemostatic dressing on the wound. If he hadn't, I'd have bled out. The bullet had nicked my femoral artery."

"How did *anyone* get out of that situation alive?" Her voice was hushed.

"With the additional personnel from my crew providing backup, the ground troops were able to hold their own until another rescue mission could be launched."

"How long ago did all this happen?"

"Six years. My enlistment was almost up, and I'd been debating whether to re-up. While I was recovering, I decided my injury was a sign to stop pushing my luck and to get out." He wadded up the bag that had held the scone. "Before I came home, I gave Boomer the medal he left at my place, along with a promise that if he ever needed anything, all he had to do was call."

"Instead, he showed up unannounced."

"Yeah—and I wasn't there to help him. If I had been, he might still be alive."

"Or you both could be dead." Her features hardened slightly. "I learned to face reality early in my law enforcement career. The friends and families of crime victims often lament over what-ifs and if-onlys. The truth is, no one can see the future except God. All we can do is make the best choice we're capable of with the information we have in the present." Her eyes clouded. "And sometimes we make mistakes."

Like she had.

She didn't have to say that for him to see her regret.

He repositioned his hand to twine his fingers with hers. "If we're exchanging philosophies, here's mine: Living in the past doesn't change it. The key is to learn from our mistakes and move on."

Her lips twisted. "Point taken. But you didn't make a mistake with Boomer. You had no idea he was going to show up—and you've done everything in your power since then to help him. There's no reason for you to have any regrets."

"Still—I'd feel better if we could figure out what's on the flash drive . . . and what happened to him and Beth. If it was foul play, as we suspect, I'd like justice to be served for both of them."

"We're getting closer to those answers—and I'll work this case hard until you tell me to stop." She tugged her fingers free and gathered up a few crumbs from the table in front of her. "How long are you staying in Lexington?"

Her posture remained relaxed, but a subtle undercurrent of tension put him on alert. "I'm leaving tomorrow late afternoon and coming home after the service, which is at ten on Saturday."

"Would you like some company?"

He tried to mask his surprise at the unexpected offer.

Was she offering to accompany him for personal—or work—reasons?

If it was the latter and those hours were billable, the trip would add significantly to his bill. And while he had the funds to hire a private investigator, paying just to have her company would be an expensive luxury.

As if she'd read his mind, she spoke again. "This is off the clock."

A ripple of warmth swelled in his core and radiated throughout his body. "I accept—with pleasure. I can pick you up about three, unless you have to finish out the workday."

"Three is fine. Swing by my duplex."

Meaning she didn't want to advertise to her colleagues that she was heading out of town with a client on a nonbillable trip.

"Got it."

"I'm sure you do." She flashed him a smile. "But who knows? Maybe we'll learn a helpful piece of information at the service.

The people who attend will be Boomer's closest acquaintances, and we can talk to them afterward. It could be productive."

True—but that wasn't the reason she was going.

And she knew he knew that.

He gathered up his papers, closed his folder, and stood. "I should let you get back to work."

"The next item on my to-do list is a call to Weston." She rose too. "I'd like to talk to him again before we leave. Now that we have more information about the workings of the fuel operation at his base, I want to rattle his cage. Imply we know more than we actually do. If he's got anything to hide, that should spook him."

A sudden hum of unease thrummed in his fingertips. "Spooked criminals with a lot to lose can be dangerous—and two people associated with this have already died."

"I know. I'll be on guard—and carrying—until this case wraps up."

That didn't ease his mind much.

But Heather had dealt with plenty of people who had murder on their mind during her years in law enforcement.

He needed to let her do the job he'd hired her for.

"Okay." He tried to mask his worry.

"I'll walk you to the lobby."

She led him down the hall but remained by the inner door once she released the lock and pushed it open. "I'll let you know what happens—or doesn't happen—with Weston. Expect a call from me later today."

"I'll look forward to it."

He nodded to the office manager, who'd ditched her holiday attire for a psychedelic patterned long sweater over hot pink leggings and changed the red and green streak in her hair to purple.

She gave him a cheery smile. "Be safe out there."

"That's the plan."

Literally.

As soon as he got back to the camp, he was going to get his compact Beretta out of the gun safe.

And until this case was over, Heather wasn't the only one who was going to be carrying.

17

That had not gone well.

As the door shut behind Heather Shields, Brad sank onto the edge of his desk and fished out his handkerchief. Mopped his brow.

The PI and her client might not have absolute proof he had anything to do with the document on Jackson Dunn's flash drive, but the two of them had pretty much nailed the operation.

If they persisted—and found his fingerprints on any piece of it—he was hosed.

And they would if they dug deep. Traced his income sources in the first couple of years after he'd launched his business.

The offshore accounts helped—and the trail leading to his personal finances was concealed—but it was there.

However . . . it would take time to uncover it, and the five-year statute of limitations on the crime was running out.

Even if he snuck past that, though, his all-American hero image would be forever tarnished should an investigation be made public.

If that happened, he could kiss the statehouse good-bye.

He rose and began to pace.

It had been a mistake to succumb to the temptation of easy money, let the stories of get-rich-quick-with-low-risk schemes persuade him to cross a line he'd never before crossed.

But how else would he have found the financing to underwrite his dream? Venture capitalists didn't fund untried concepts proposed by people without track records, and angel investors were hard to come by.

Still . . . if he had it to do again, he'd make a different choice.

It was too late for that, though. He had to deal with the current reality. Decide what he was going to do if the PI and her client amassed sufficient evidence to take this to law enforcement—or CID.

A knock sounded, and he spun toward the closed door. "Yes?"

His assistant stuck her head in. "Chuck's on your landline. He said he's been trying to reach you on your cell."

"Thanks. I'll pick it up."

He returned to his desk as she retreated, took a steadying breath, and greeted his campaign manager.

"Finally. I've been trying to get ahold of you for the past hour." Frustration scored Chuck's words.

"I was in a meeting. My cell was off, and I forwarded my landline to my assistant. What's up?"

"I've been lining up appointments with key legislators for you next week. It's important to get face time with them at the beginning of the session, and in light of all the positive press you've generated, they were happy to work you into their schedules. I've set up meetings for Wednesday through Friday next week. Do you have a minute to go over them?"

"Can we do this later?" Brad massaged his forehead. The dull throbbing that had begun halfway through his meeting with Heather Shields was escalating to a raging headache.

"I have to confirm the appointments ASAP or they won't hold the slots." Now Chuck sounded annoyed. "You're going to have to give this race priority if you want to build and sustain momentum."

"Fine." Brad eased into his chair, trying not to jar his head. "I'm listening."

While the man rattled off names and topics, he leaned back and closed his eyes. Whatever his campaign manager set up was fine.

Assuming there *was* a campaign by next week.

He started to sweat again.

There were ways to handle this situation—but none of them were pleasant. And he wasn't going to make a mistake by rushing decisions, jumping to conclusions.

Best case, the PI would run into a wall and her client would cut off funding.

If that didn't happen, he'd have to—

". . . work with your schedule?"

He only caught the last part of Chuck's question, but he could guess the rest.

"I'll rearrange my commitments to accommodate the trip. Email me a detailed itinerary, with background on all the players."

"Will do. Any preferences on transportation or hotel?"

"No. You know Jeff City better than I do. I trust your judgment."

"As soon as I confirm everything, I'll let you know. Would Lindsey want to come along?"

"Is there any reason she should be there?" Asking her to cancel her Wednesday yoga class or Friday morning hair and manicure appointments would be tricky. Both were high priority for her.

"Not unless I can set up a dinner with the secretary of state and his wife. Her presence would be useful for a quasi social event like that. She could just come for the evening if that pans out. Other than that, you'll be in back-to-back meetings."

"Let me run it by her tonight."

"No later. We're cutting this close already. Call me as soon as you have an answer."

As Chuck broke the connection, Brad opened his desk drawer and rummaged around in the back for the bottle of aspirin he kept on hand but rarely used. Opened the top.

Most of the pills were disintegrating from the repeated jostling.

He could relate.

But he had to hold it together until he had an inkling of how the PI's investigation was proceeding.

Hopefully, it would die soon.

Before he had to take drastic action.

. . . . .

Including his pastor, only eight people came to Boomer's simple graveside service.

Not a very notable end for a man who'd served his country and saved countless lives.

Throat tightening, Heather huddled deeper into her coat on the gray Saturday morning and glanced at Rick as they stood side by side near the casket.

The stoic set of his jaw told her their thoughts were once again in sync.

As if sensing her scrutiny, he looked down at her—and she tucked her arm through his. A sign of support . . . and more.

Eyes warming, he covered her gloved hand with his, squeezed gently, then transferred his attention back to the minister.

While the cleric wound down, Heather gave the group another discreet perusal. It had been helpful of the man to ask each of the mourners to explain how they were acquainted with Boomer. She already knew a bit about Pauline Reynolds and the director of the food kitchen, but the wild cards were two of Boomer's coworkers and an ice rink employee.

She needed to corner them for a quick conversation.

After reciting the twenty-third psalm, the minister closed his book.

"Jackson's neighbor Pauline has provided homemade pastries, which are set up in the main building at the cemetery entrance. I invite you all to stop for a few minutes to take advantage of her hospitality, warm up with a cup of coffee, and share remembrances of Jackson. May our brother rest in peace."

Following a murmured amen from the group, the minister stepped away from the casket.

Heather leaned closer to Rick. "I want to talk to the coworkers and rink guy."

"I had a feeling you would."

"If you could find out whether the rink guy is going to stop for coffee, I'll do the same with the other two. If he's not, try to detain him."

"Got it."

As the crowd began to disperse, she hurried toward Boomer's colleagues.

"Excuse me . . . I believe you worked with Jackson."

The thirtysomething guy and fiftyish man turned to her.

"Yes." The older of the duo spoke for both of them.

"May I ask if you're going to stop for coffee?"

"No. We both have family events today."

"In that case, could you spare a few minutes here?" She gave them a cursory explanation of the reason for her request, and passed each a business card.

"Sure. We can hang out for a few minutes." This from the younger guy as he pocketed her card.

They didn't rush her—but neither offered anything she didn't already know. Though the older man was Boomer's boss and the younger guy had worked side by side on the assembly line with the ex-medic, neither knew many details about his life.

"I wish we could help you more." Boomer's line partner gave her an apologetic shrug. "But Jackson was quiet and kept to himself. He'd talk about sports and the headlines of the day, but never anything personal. The only thing he ever opened up about was his cat."

Another gust of wind blew past, and Heather flipped up the collar of her coat. "Okay. Thank you both for talking with me."

She shook their hands and swiveled around to find Rick walking toward her.

The rink guy was nowhere to be seen.

"Did we lose him?" She scanned the area. Other than the gravediggers waiting off to the side—and a solitary figure near a black car a hundred yards away, one hand resting on top of a gravestone, head bent as if in prayer—the place was deserted.

"No. He said he was going to stop for coffee. I thought you could talk to him there, where it's warmer."

Heather tried to mask her dismay. The guy might have said he was planning to have coffee—but he could also keep on driving.

Rick held out a slip of paper.

"What's this?" She took it.

"His name and contact information. I got it in case he changed his mind about stopping."

She exhaled. "You'd make an excellent detective."

"Not my forte. Solving the mystery of a troubled kid at camp is more my speed. You ready to go?"

"Yes."

He took her arm as they crossed the uneven turf toward his car, the frozen grass crunching under their feet.

True to his word, the rink guy was guzzling coffee and chowing down on Pauline's sweets when they entered the room hosting the subdued reception.

"You want to do this together or go solo?" Rick stopped

inside the door as Pauline lifted her hand in greeting and walked toward them.

"If you could run interference"—she nodded toward the woman—"I'd like to try and get him alone."

"Done."

He moved forward to greet the older woman while Heather veered off.

The rink guy appeared to be in his early twenties and was open and responsive—but he knew less about Boomer than the man's coworkers did.

"Did he ever say anything at all about his private life? Mention anyone who was special to him?" Stifling a sigh, she closed her notebook and unbuttoned her coat in the too-warm room.

"No. We just shot the breeze. Only once did he say anything kind of personal. I told him my brother was in the Marines in the Middle East, and he said I should watch out for him after he came home because the junk that goes on over there can mess with your mind. I got the feeling he might have had PTSD."

Further confirmation that Boomer had borne more than physical scars from his deployments.

"How did you get to know him?"

"He came to the rink a couple nights a week and every weekend. He was a real good skater."

This was going nowhere.

After thanking him, she rejoined Rick.

"Any luck?"

She shook her head. "Nathan knows more about him than any of these people."

"Like I said, he was always a loner—but the PTSD could have exacerbated that trait." He lifted his cup. "Would you like some? There's no tea in sight."

"I'm fine. What did Pauline have to say?" She glanced at the older woman, who was talking to the minister across the room.

"That Boomer's lawyer had been in touch with her, and that Boomer wanted her to donate his belongings to the charities of her choice."

"Wow. He really *was* alone."

"Yeah. Hearing a story like that makes me grateful for old friends . . . and new." He captured her gaze—and an arc of electricity zipped between them as Boomer's neighbor moved toward them.

"So did you decide to take me up on my offer?"

Pauline's question registered somewhere in the recesses of her mind, but Heather couldn't get her brain to engage as she stared at Rick.

"I, uh, haven't told her about that yet." Her client seemed to be having difficulty forming a coherent thought too.

Wrenching her attention away from him, Heather focused on the older woman. "Told me what?"

"That the two of you are welcome to take another look through Jackson's apartment, in case you missed anything help-ful on the first pass."

She blinked.

Seriously?

Who knew what they might uncover if they had the chance to do a more thorough search?

Her spirits picked up. "Thank you. We accept."

"If there's anything useful, feel free to take it." Pauline leaned closer and lowered her volume. "To tell you the truth, I'm not certain I buy the official version of what happened to Jackson. From what he told me about how he prepped for solo hikes, he was always careful—and I never saw any evidence of drug use while he was my neighbor, no matter what the police found near his body. You two seem committed to uncovering the truth, and I'll be happy to help in any way I can."

"Do you mind if we take his laptop?" That had the potential

to yield gold, and extracting everything it held could require Nikki's hands-on expertise. "I'll be happy to ship it back after we're through."

Pauline waved the offer aside. "Take it. Once you're finished, you can wipe the hard drive and donate it. That will be one less item for me to deal with."

"What will you do with Rosie?" Rick tossed his empty coffee cup in the trash can beside him.

Relevant question. Boomer had loved that cat.

And it said a great deal about Rick that he'd cared enough to ask.

"I've already adopted her. She always did take a fancy to me. Jackson said so himself."

"I think he'd like that." Heather touched the older woman's arm.

"I believe he would." Pauline sniffed and pulled a key from her shoulder bag. "Stay as long as you like at his place. I should be home before you finish. I don't think this little get-together is going to last long."

No, it wasn't.

No one had even taken off their coat.

"Do you want any cake?" Rick directed the question to her as he motioned toward the table.

"Please, let me get a piece for you. I expected this would be a sparse crowd, but I still made far too much." Pauline hurried off.

Heather rebuttoned her coat. "Free rein at Boomer's place could be a godsend."

"Let's hope so. Otherwise, I'm not certain where we go next."

Neither was she.

But giving up wasn't her style, as any of her former detective colleagues would attest.

Especially when there was a high probability that two accidental deaths hadn't been accidental at all.

. . . . .

"Morning, sweetheart. Is the migraine better?"

As Brad rose from the table in the breakfast nook where he'd been sipping his Saturday coffee and reading the paper, Lindsey leaned over for a kiss. "Much. Sorry I was out of commission last night when you got home from the office."

He touched her cheek, faint creases marring his brow. "I worry that my political ambitions have brought these on. You haven't had any for months until the past few days."

That was true—but it wasn't his ambitions that had triggered the headaches.

It was the things that could *derail* his ambitions.

"Stress of any kind can bring them on, Brad—positive or negative." She gave him an encouraging smile as she took her place at the table. "And I'm excited about your run for governor. After we get past this initial flurry of media interest, I'm sure my headaches will go away."

"What if they don't? Your welfare is my primary concern. Besides"—he folded the paper and set it carefully beside him— "there could be other . . . glitches ahead."

Her pulse spiked. "In relation to the Middle East situation?"

"Yes."

"When I asked about that PI's second visit, you said everything was fine."

"You weren't up to a discussion last night."

"Does that mean everything isn't fine?" She poured herself a glass of juice, reining in her panic.

"Let's just say I'm . . . concerned." His Adam's apple bobbed. "She and her client have a copy of a document I destroyed long ago."

A cold knot formed in her stomach. "What kind of document?" If they had proof of Brad's involvement in the scheme, disaster could be imminent.

He exhaled. "You know how methodical I am. I even track mileage on my car."

"Are you telling me you tracked the transactions over there? On paper?"

"For all intents and purposes. I kept the document on a flash drive in my desk."

"Did anyone know about it?"

"My assistant may have. She came into my office once while I was updating it. I suppose she could have made a copy while I was out."

"The one who died not long ago?"

"Yes."

The juice she'd sipped continued to curdle in her stomach. "Is your name on the document?"

"No! Of course not. Only obscure initials. The spreadsheet itself is innocuous. But this PI and her client figured out what it meant. Now I'm concerned they may delve into my finances."

"Will they be able to trace the funds?"

"It would be difficult—but not impossible for someone who's committed to digging."

Frowning, she straightened her silverware. "Why would they care about something that happened almost five years ago?"

"I don't know."

Her brain shifted into high gear. "If your assistant was involved overseas with that Dunn guy the PI told you about in your first meeting, their deaths could have raised questions. Maybe this private investigator and her client suspect a nefarious plot."

"You think they think I killed her?" He gave her an incredulous look.

Rightly so.

The man was a decorated war hero, for heaven's sake.

"That does sound ridiculous, doesn't it? No one would give such a preposterous theory any credibility."

"Let's hope not. To be honest, I'm more concerned about the financial risk. A trail exists if they're determined to uncover it."

"But as you said, it's hard to find. And unless this PI's client has deep pockets, why would he fund that sort of investigation—especially with the statute of limitations running out?"

"All valid points." He poured her coffee.

She forced up the corners of her mouth and added a dash of cream to the dark brew. "I think we're worrying about this too much. I have a feeling it's all going to blow over soon. In the meantime, we should concentrate on your campaign."

"Speaking of the campaign—Chuck wants to know whether you'd be up for a dinner with the secretary of state and his wife, if he can arrange it. I'll be in Jeff City for meetings the latter part of next week, and you could come down just for the dinner."

"I'd be delighted to join you. Friday night would be best. I'll have a fresh manicure and do." She fluttered her fingers and patted her hair.

"I'll tell him that." He pulled out his phone. "Would you excuse me for a moment while I call him? I promised to let him know as soon as we had a chance to discuss it."

"By all means."

As her husband placed the call, Lindsey sipped her coffee and watched a squirrel scamper along the ground outside the bay window, an acorn in its mouth. Retrieved from a secret, buried stash, no doubt.

But some secrets should stay buried.

Pressing her lips together, she wadded up the napkin in her lap. It wasn't fair for this PI and her client to be stirring up a hornet's nest about a minor discretion from years ago that had hurt no one. Why would they want to ruin a good man's future?

As for any suspicions they harbored that Brad had been involved in the death of his assistant or the woman's friend?

Ludicrous.

Brad Weston was the finest, most accomplished man she'd ever met. He could no more be involved in murder than he could stop trying to rid himself of the inferiority complex that had been his father's dismal legacy.

Despite that dreadful inheritance, however, he was destined for—and deserved—accolades and adulation.

She might not have as much to offer as he did, but a polished, articulate, glamorous wife would be an asset—and if a bit of the adulation filtered back to her from his coattails, she wouldn't complain. Her early life hadn't been a bed of roses, either. She deserved better too.

"We're confirmed for Friday night with the secretary of state and his wife." Brad set his cell on the table beside him. "Chuck will be in touch about timing and transportation."

"Perfect." She laid her hand on his. "Now let's put all the unpleasantness about that PI out of our mind and enjoy our breakfast. Everything's going to be fine."

"I hope you're right."

"I am. I can feel it."

He touched her hand. "In that case . . . I'll bow to your intuition and try not to worry."

They went back to eating, and he did seem less disturbed.

Good.

Because he didn't have to worry.

He really didn't.

They'd come too far down this road for anything to go wrong.

18

"Nada, except this"—Heather lifted Boomer's laptop—"and this." She waved a sheet of passwords they'd found in the man's desk during their search of his apartment.

"Maybe the answers to our questions are in there." Rick replaced the last book he'd riffled through from the bookcase.

"I like your optimism."

He gave her a wry smile. "Sometimes, on a hazardous mission, that was our biggest asset. You ready to head back?"

"Yes. I'd rather not do the last part of the drive in the dark."

"No worries if we do. Night travel is my specialty." He flashed her a grin. "Let me return the key to Pauline and I'll meet you at the truck."

They parted outside the door, Heather following the walkway to the parking area while he veered off toward the adjacent unit.

After exchanging the key for two of the coffee cakes the older woman had lugged home from the cemetery, he hustled toward the truck, giving the apartment complex Boomer had called home a sweep.

It wasn't bad—but it wasn't first class. A few of the gutters were sagging. Several dead bushes needed to be replaced. The parking lot hadn't been resurfaced in far too long.

The medic who'd saved his life had deserved better.

He also deserved justice for what was more and more seeming to be a malevolent end.

Hopefully, with the help of the woman waiting beside his truck, he could provide the man with that much, at least.

A blast of cold air whooshed past, and he frowned.

Why was Heather standing outside in this biting wind? Hadn't he unlocked the doors?

Pressing the autolock again, he picked up his pace.

She shifted toward him. "The door was already open."

"Why didn't you get in?"

"I was distracted." Without further explanation, she grasped the handle and hoisted herself up to the seat.

He handed her the cakes. "Leftovers. Pauline insisted I take them."

By the time he'd circled around to the driver's side and started the engine, she'd stowed the cakes and laptop on the back seat and was buckling her seat belt.

He put the truck in gear. "Do you want to have lunch here, or stop en route?"

"The latter. The piece of cake I ate at the cemetery will hold me for a while." She flipped down her visor and peered into the built-in mirror.

Rick grinned at her as he exited the lot and accelerated toward the highway. "If you're worried about being windblown, don't. The mussed look suits you."

"Trust me, I'm not that vain. My interest in the mirror is work-related."

"What does that mean?"

She continued to watch the reflection. "I think we've got a tail."

"What!" He squinted into the rearview mirror.

"I saw a black Chrysler at the cemetery, and there was a car of the same make in the apartment parking lot. It followed us out, and it's staying several cars back. It also has dark windows—standard in vehicles used for surveillance."

A thread of tension snaked down his spine.

That was a twist he hadn't seen coming.

"Not the best news I've had today."

"I agree. But we *have* been asking questions that could make a guilty person nervous."

"Aside from you and me, though, only two people are aware of what we found on that flash drive."

"That we know of. In terms of the two people you mentioned, I don't think my CID contact is having us followed."

"That leaves Weston."

"Uh-huh—and based on the subtle cues I picked up during our meeting yesterday, the man is very worried. Everything points to him being our guy, despite his otherwise pristine record."

"Desperate people can do desperate things."

"True. And once someone crosses the line to the dark side, they can find themselves getting in deeper and deeper. The challenge is proving it."

"If he made any significant money from a petroleum scheme in the Middle East, there has to be a paper trail."

"There should be—but if he was savvy about how he set up the transfers, it could be buried deep. Too deep for me to find. It would take law enforcement's clout to amass that kind of evidence. I can't get a subpoena for his financial records."

"Then where does that leave us?"

"On the Middle East scheme, I think our best option is for me to put together a document detailing our findings and our theory and present it to my contact at CID. The statute of limitations on fraud is five years—if that's the charge the authorities decide to pursue—so the clock is ticking. Unless CID wants to be aggressive and try to find sufficient evidence for the authorities to file charges fast, he won't be prosecuted."

Rick tightened his grip on the wheel.

More bad news.

However . . . given the timing of Boomer's visit to the camp, so close on the heels of Beth's death, his military colleague likely had a more serious accusation than fraud in mind.

"There's no statute of limitations on murder, is there?"

"No." Heather sounded as grim as he felt.

"In that case, I vote we give what we have on the Middle East situation to CID and concentrate our efforts on the bigger crime—or crimes. I suspect Beth's death, along with the violent robbery Boomer never reported, are the reasons he came to me for help . . . or direction . . . or justice . . . or whatever. I don't want to give this up."

"I didn't think you would." Her voice was warmer now—and when he glanced over, her eyes were too. "A man who lives by a code of honor would want to see this through."

Heat flooding his cheeks, he refocused on the road. "That was years ago. I was a kid."

"It stuck." Thankfully, she continued without embarrassing him further. "I'll tell you what. Let me see what I can find on Boomer's laptop. I'll pull Nikki in if I need any forensic magic. Between the two of us, we may be able to uncover a tidbit or two that will help us determine with more certainty whether the accidental death ruling he and Beth got deserves to be revisited."

"Is it legal to access his email?"

"A little iffy—but since he authorized Pauline to dispose of everything in his apartment . . . and she gave us permission to do a search and take whatever we found . . . and the passwords were in plain sight in the desk drawer . . . I'm considering that sufficient permission."

"Works for me." He swung onto the highway entrance ramp and watched the rearview mirror. Two cars back, the black Chrysler made the same turn. "In the meantime . . . what do we do about our shadow?"

"I'm going to have one of the Phoenix guys join the parade once we get closer to town, see if he can ID the car." She pulled out her cell and tapped in a number, offering her boss an abbreviated explanation for the Lexington trip before making her request. The conversation was over in less than a minute.

"Are we covered?"

"Yes." She stowed her cell. "He'll let me know who's going to take this, and I'll call with a location about thirty minutes out."

"If you want to catch some z's during the drive, feel free. I can keep tabs on our friend."

"Not necessary this trip. In the absence of revelers at the hotel last night, I slept fine. But thanks for offering. Besides, four eyes on our tail are better than two."

"You think he knows you've spotted him?"

"I doubt it." She checked her mirror again. "He's not doing anything special to lay low. Just the usual keep-a-few-cars-between-me-and-the-subject protocol."

And he continued that pattern for the next three hours, claiming a parking spot at an adjacent restaurant during their fast-food lunch stop.

As they finished their meal, Heather picked up her cell and skimmed the screen. "Text from Cal. Dev's going to do the honors. I'll alert him to our approach forty miles east of St. Louis."

"Let's hope our tail doesn't spot him."

"A former ATF undercover agent?" She hiked up an eyebrow. "I don't think we have to worry."

Not about that, perhaps.

But as he pulled back into traffic and steered the truck toward St. Louis, it was hard to shake the apprehension coiling in his gut.

Heather had said she wanted to rattle cages, and it appeared she'd succeeded.

Problem was, animals in rattled cages were prone to bite.

And people who felt cornered could do much worse.

. . . . .

"Home sweet home." As Rick hung a left onto her street, Heather's cell began to vibrate.

"And Dev is ready with an update." She put the phone to her ear. "What do you have?"

"Car is registered to a Jason Barnes."

She narrowed her eyes. "Why is that name familiar?"

"He's one of our competitors. Someone may have mentioned him in a staff meeting."

"A PI following a PI. That's different. What do you know about him?"

"He's at the higher end of the fee scale and takes sleaze cases we wouldn't touch. Scuttlebutt is he's not above bending the rules, and that he leans toward a liberal interpretation of privacy laws. You want me to stick with him once your client drops you off?"

"Yes. Just long enough to see if he continues to follow Rick. I'll wait to hear from you." She pressed the end button.

"Someone hired a PI to follow us?" Rick parked, set the brake, and angled toward her, twin creases denting his brow.

"So it would appear. An expensive one."

"He can't be worth his fee if you spotted him."

"I was a police detective, remember? I've had plenty of experience on the other side of surveillance, unlike most of his clients. I know what to watch for."

He blew out a breath. "I'm not liking this."

Neither was she.

But worrying about it wasn't going to change the reality.

"To give this a positive spin, forewarned is forearmed—in a literal sense. I assume you have a concealed carry permit?"

"I've been putting it to use since we met in your office Thursday."

That didn't surprise her.

"I'd recommend you continue to do so."

"That's my plan. I presume it's yours too."

"Count on it." She snagged Boomer's laptop from the back seat and opened her door.

"I'll get your bag."

He slid from behind the wheel and retrieved her overnight case from the rear of the truck. After looping the strap over his shoulder, he leaned into the back seat for the coffee cakes.

"Wait. I don't need both of those."

"And I don't need the calories. Share them with your office mates."

There was no reason to refuse. With Cal and Dev in the loop about the tail, everyone at Phoenix would hear about her weekend trip anyway. "Thanks. Dev does have a sweet tooth."

"Then give him one as a thank-you for disrupting his Saturday."

"Not a bad idea. That will win me brownie points." And it might mitigate the teasing she was bound to get from her red-haired colleague about her unofficial weekend trip with a client.

Rick followed her into the foyer, closing the door behind them with his foot.

She set the laptop down and reached for the cakes he was balancing in each hand.

"Uh-uh." He pivoted away, keeping a firm grip on them.

"Change your mind about giving them up?" Smiling, she propped her hands on her hips.

"No. They're my safety equipment."

She tilted her head, trying to interpret the roguish glint in his eyes. "I think you're going to have to explain that."

"I need to keep my hands occupied so I can do this safely." He leaned over and pressed his lips against hers.

Her heart stuttered.

One second ticked by.

Two.

Three.

"I know that was pushing the boundaries." Rick's words were a puff of warmth against her cheek as he backed off a mere inch. "But I'm past the forehead thing. All I can say is, this case better get solved fast because I don't know how long my admirable restraint is going to last."

With that, he handed her the cakes, set her overnight case on the floor, and slipped through the door with a wink.

Her lungs took their sweet time kicking back in, and when she finally crossed to the window, he was driving away.

Two minutes later, she was still staring after him as her cell began to vibrate.

After fumbling the cakes, she set them down and groped for her phone.

It was Dev.

"Hi." Her greeting rasped, and she cleared her throat. "Are you, uh, still on the tail?"

"Yeah. I just turned onto the main drag." A beat ticked by. "You okay?"

"Sure. Why?"

"You sound out of breath."

No kidding.

"I was, uh, carrying my suitcase into the bedroom." She snatched up her bag and hurried down the hall to take the edge off the lie.

"Uh-huh." There was no missing the amusement in his tone. She ignored it.

"So why did you call?" She dumped her bag on her bed.

"Did you notice that the black car didn't follow him?"

She would have—if she'd been paying attention to her job instead of floating in blissful oblivion on the cloud of Rick's kiss.

"There's nothing wrong with my observation skills." A hedge . . . but if she was lucky he wouldn't call her on it. "So why did you leave?"

"A second tail followed your client when he left."

"What?"

"You had two tails for the past fifteen minutes. I wasn't 100 percent certain about the second one until the last half mile. If you have a piece of paper, I'll give you the plate number and you can run it."

She zipped into the kitchen and grabbed a pen. "Ready."

As he recited the numbers and letters, as well as the vehicle make and model, she jotted them down. "Thanks. I'll get right on this."

"You may want to let your friend . . . um . . . client know he still has a shadow."

She didn't miss his intentional slip.

Great.

She better be prepared for some heavy-duty ribbing from Dev and inquisitive looks from Cal come Monday.

Unless everyone was too busy welcoming Connor back from vacation.

If only.

"I'll give him a call."

"You want me to continue following him?"

"Not necessary. I have what I need to get an ID."

"Roger. I'm peeling off as we speak."

"Thanks for doing this, Dev."

"Happy to help. See you Monday."

He ended the call, and Heather pulled her laptop out of its case. As soon as she ran the plates on the second car and researched the owner, she'd alert Rick to the latest development.

Then she was going to dig into Boomer's computer and see if it held any clues that would help them convince her CID contact to take on the petroleum case—or perhaps even point them to the culprit in what could be a double murder.

■ ■ ■ ■ ■

Ellen leaned back in the chair at her kitchen table, stretched, and examined the columns of numbers on the month-end statement displayed on her laptop screen.

Why not call it a night and pick up tomorrow? It wasn't as if she had anywhere to go on Sunday mornings. Not like in the old days, when she'd reserved that slot for worship instead of work. For putting her trust in the Almighty and believing he'd watch out for her.

She snorted.

What a waste that had been.

All her fervent prayers and diligent church attendance hadn't stopped David from being a philanderer.

Nor had they stopped Brad from falling for a floozy.

That was why she'd washed her hands of God.

These days, she was the master of her own destiny. She called the shots. She would determine her future instead of—

From deep within her purse, a phone began to vibrate.

Not her usual cell.

Pulse accelerating, she rooted through the contents until her fingers closed over her pay-by-the-minute phone.

She flipped it open and pressed it to her ear. "Yes?"

"I have the additional information you wanted."

"Let me find a pen." She vaulted to her feet and dashed to the counter. Rummaged through a drawer. "Ready."

242

As the voice on the other end spoke, she jotted detailed notes. The man's tone, as always, was pleasant. Professional. Matter-of-fact.

"Thanks." She set the pen down.

"Always happy to be of service."

Of course he was.

He charged enough.

Closing the phone, she returned to the table and sank into her chair, rereading the notes she'd taken.

They confirmed the pattern she'd been monitoring.

But now that Brad had officially launched his campaign, it would be harder to predict what might happen next.

That was why she had to act before schedules got too crazy.

She closed the spreadsheet and opened her calendar. Scanned her notes again.

Wednesday would work.

She could be ready to wrap this up in four days, and there was no reason to delay. Why not get the messiness behind her?

A sudden wave of panic rippled through her, and she took a slow, deep breath.

Don't be nervous. You've thought this through, and your plan is in everyone's best interest.

Well . . . almost everyone's.

Certainly in Brad's.

And Brad was all that mattered.

If she had any qualms as the day got closer, that's what she had to remember. Nothing must stand in the way of his ambition—or the future she envisioned for him.

And for her.

19

A ringing phone late at night was never a positive omen.

As Heather groped for her cell, she peered at the bedside clock.

Two twelve on Sunday morning?

Bad news for sure.

When her father's cell number came into focus on the screen, she bolted upright, every vestige of sleep vanishing as she put the phone to her ear. "Dad? What's wrong?"

Silence.

"Dad?" She shot to her feet, untangling her legs from the blanket.

"I-I'm sick. I n-need you." The thready plea was barely audible.

Her heart began to pound. "I'm coming. Hang on."

Fighting back panic, she yanked on her jeans, exchanged her flannel sleep shirt for a tee, and dashed toward the foyer.

Please, Lord, let this be a false alarm, like the heart scare last year that turned out to be indigestion.

Fingers shaking, she deactivated her security system, pulled the door open, and braced for a blast of cold air.

It hit her in the face, as she expected.

But the punch in the stomach came out of nowhere.

Gasping in pain, she doubled over.

Before she could catch her breath, someone shoved her back, twisted her arm behind her, and kicked the door shut.

Reeling, she bit back a word she never used.

Despite all her dealings with the dregs of society in her previous job, she'd fallen for one of the oldest tricks in the book.

A fake distress call.

The intruder had used a phone spoofing service to display her father's phone number on her caller ID.

How stupid could she be?

"Let's make this easy, okay? Just give me the laptop."

As the bass voice spoke close to her ear, her rattled brain assembled the pieces.

Someone was strong-arming her to get Boomer's laptop.

And after spending hours last night poring over it, she knew who had the most to lose if the correspondence she'd found between the ex-medic and his former girlfriend ever saw the light of day.

None other than Major Brad Weston.

Giving away that evidence—circumstantial though it might be—wasn't in her plans.

She had to buy herself a few moments to figure out how to get control of this situation.

"Why do you want my laptop?"

The guy switched grips with lightning speed, pinning her arms behind her with one hand while exerting pressure on her windpipe with the other. Cutting off her air supply.

She tried every self-defense trick she knew to free herself, but her assailant's grip was like steel.

Black spots began strobing in front of her eyes.

"Don't act stupid. You know I'm here for the laptop you

brought back from Lexington. Give it to me, and I'll leave as quiet as I came."

He loosened his grip a fraction, and she sucked in a wisp of air. "I-I don't have it anymore."

"That's a lie." The vise on her throat tightened again. "You haven't left here since you got home. I'll give you five seconds to think about whether you want to cooperate. Then this is going to get nasty."

Her vision began to fade—but the object that appeared inches in front of her face registered clearly.

A blade, glinting in the dim light.

Stomach churning, she froze.

This situation was going downhill fast.

And much as she wanted to solve Rick's case and nail the mastermind behind Beth's and Boomer's demise, she didn't want to die doing it.

There had to be a way out of this.

Brain firing on all cylinders, she latched on to the plan beginning to gel in her mind. "Fine." She wheezed out her reply. "A l-laptop isn't worth dying for."

The pressure on her windpipe eased. "Now you're being smart."

"It's in the laundry room. By the back door."

Actually . . . it wasn't.

But the keypad for her security system was—and it would take no more than three seconds to punch in the emergency code that would alert 911 to dispatch a police cruiser.

Assuming she could grab the hammer in the detergent cabinet where she kept her meager supply of tools and disable this guy long enough to send a distress signal.

The intruder pushed her ahead of him, toward the rear of the duplex, keeping the knife pressed against her carotid artery.

At the doorway to the laundry room, he stopped. "Where is it?"

"In the cabinet on the left."

He propelled her forward again without loosening his grip.

Heart banging against her rib cage, she psyched herself up for the skirmish to come.

With the hammer in hand, she had a fighting chance. All she had to do was inflict sufficient damage to gain the advantage.

While this guy was stronger than she was, there was a chance she could subdue him. Her self-defense skills might be a bit rusty, but with the element of surprise on her side, the hammer in hand, and the application of appropriate leverage, she could fell him.

Maybe.

But she had nothing to lose by trying.

He may have said he'd leave quietly once he had the computer, but two people had already died. If he'd been involved in those so-called accidents, it was doubtful he'd have any compunction about killing again.

And the truth was, that could be his plan, no matter what she did.

She swallowed past the fear congealing in her throat as he stopped at the cabinet.

Under the circumstances, her odds were fifty/fifty at best.

But if this went south, at least there would be no possibility of an accidental death ruling.

She would fight to the very end—and leave plenty of evidence to indicate that.

"Get it." He stopped in front of the cabinet.

Nerves vibrating, she filled her lungs . . . opened the door . . . seized the hammer . . . and twisted around.

He muttered an oath, and she swung as hard as she could.

Metal connected with bone and flesh, and he yowled in pain as the knife clattered to the floor.

Just beyond her reach.

She lunged toward it—but he caught her arm, his fingers like an iron clamp.

Once again, she swung the hammer.

He grasped her wrist, intercepting the blow.

Squeezed.

The hammer fell to the floor.

With her arms incapacitated, she had only one weapon left.

Summoning up every ounce of her strength, she kicked. Hard.

More curses rained down on her ears.

He released one of her arms, but before she could put it to use, he delivered a bone-jarring punch to her jaw.

Her head snapped back.

Three feet away, the knife faded in and out of her misty vision.

She made a final feeble attempt to dive for it, but he yanked her back and threw her against the washer.

Moaning, she crumpled to the floor.

As the world spun around her, a distinctive rip registered in her brain.

Duct tape.

An instant later, he whipped her arms behind her and secured her wrists. Pushed her flat on the floor. Sat on her legs and bound her ankles.

At last, he picked up the knife.

She stiffened.

He crouched beside her, a black ski mask hiding his identity, his dark irises glittering in the dim light as he pressed the knife to her throat. "Last chance."

Heather stared at the intruder. She could refuse to tell him where the computer was, but what would that accomplish? He'd find it within minutes.

Maybe, if she cooperated, he wouldn't kill her.

After all, this guy's approach was nothing like the methods

used to finish off Beth or Boomer. He was making no attempt to set up an accidental death scenario.

It was possible all he really wanted was the laptop.

Wishful thinking, perhaps—but she was out of options.

"In the office. First door on the left, down the hall. It's in a case on the floor."

"Better." He ripped off another piece of duct tape and slapped it over her mouth. "Don't move a muscle."

The man made no noise as he retrieved the computer. But the red light on her security system remained on for five minutes—meaning he was still moving about.

Then it turned green.

Heather stayed where she was, gaze riveted to the keypad.

The minutes inched by. How many, she had no idea.

But at last, after what felt like an eternity, she allowed herself to accept the miraculous truth.

He'd left.

And she was alive.

Vision blurring again, she choked back a sob and gave thanks.

Only after that silent prayer did she think about immediate next steps.

Namely, freeing herself from the duct tape . . . calling the police . . . and putting ice on her throbbing jaw.

＊＊＊＊＊

A ringing phone late at night was never a positive omen.

Rick groped for his cell, squinting at the clock on his bedside table.

Four twenty on Sunday morning?

Bad news for sure.

He snatched up the phone and skimmed caller ID.

Colin?

His pulse took a leap.

Only a major issue with one of the Treehouse Gang would prompt a call from him at this hour.

He jabbed the talk button. "What's wrong?"

"I'm fine. So is Kristin."

His friend knew him well.

"Then what's with the call?" Frowning, he tuned in to the static crackle in the background. It sounded like a police radio. "Are you working tonight?"

"Yeah. Listen . . ." Colin dropped his voice. "I'm going out on a limb by calling you. If you're ever asked, this never happened. But I figured you'd want to know sooner rather than later."

"Know what? What's going on?" He stood and strode toward his closet, the buzz in his nerve endings sending a clear message—there would be no more sleep this night.

"I can't give you any details. Those have to come from Heather. I'd suggest you call her."

"Now?" Balancing the phone between his neck and shoulder, he shoved his feet into his jeans.

"Yes. She's up."

His mouth went dry. "Is she okay?"

"More or less. She's one tough lady." A radio blared in the background. "I gotta go. Heather can fill you in."

The line went dead.

Rick pulled on a sweatshirt and shoved his bare feet into the nearest pair of shoes. As he barreled out the door to his truck, he tapped in her speed dial number.

Four rings in, it rolled to voicemail.

Gritting his teeth, he started the engine, sped down the drive to the main road, and tried a hands-free call.

After three rings, she answered.

"Rick? Why are you calling me at thish hour?"

Had it not been for Colin's tip-off that there'd been trouble, he'd attribute her slight slur to being awakened from a deep sleep.

But in light of his friend's comments, she hadn't been sleeping anytime recently.

Her words were slurred because she was hurt.

"What happened? Are you all right?"

"How did you know *anything* happened?"

"Call it telepathy. Now tell me—"

"Did Colin call you?"

Expelling a breath, he raked his fingers through his hair. "Heather. Talk to me."

"I was going to call you in the morning."

"It *is* morning. What's going on?"

A beat ticked by.

"Someone paid me a visit around two. He was after a certain laptop."

Rick squeezed the wheel and held on tight. "Give me the details."

She complied, her voice steady, her tone matter-of-fact.

Yet the content of her bare-bones account curdled his stomach.

Someone had muscled his way into her place, physically subdued her, and taken Boomer's laptop.

What she didn't mention was that she could have ended up as dead as Beth and the ex-medic.

She had to know that as well as he did.

And she seemed to be handling it far better.

"What did he do to you?"

"Got the upper hand, I'm shorry to shay." She sounded disgusted.

"I want specifics."

"Shoved me around a little. Put a roll of duct tape to use. I'm fine. A few sore muscles, a tender jaw . . . I'll be back in fighting form by tomorrow."

Colin wouldn't have called him if that were true.

"I'll feel better after I verify that myself."

"Are you coming into town later?"

"More like sooner. Expect me in about thirty minutes." Unless he got pulled over by a cop for speeding.

"You're already on the road?"

"Yes." He checked his rearview mirror. If the second tail Heather had alerted him to last night was back there, the PI was keeping his distance.

"Rick . . . that isn't necessary."

"Yes, it is."

"But it's the middle of the night."

"An exaggeration."

"Look . . . why don't you turn around and get a few more hours of sleep?"

"You really think I'm going to sleep after all this?"

"You could try."

"Heather . . . if the situation was reversed, what would *you* do?"

Silence.

"I rest my case. See you soon."

Pressing harder on the accelerator, he raced through the night and tried to control the panic squeezing his windpipe.

Heather's life had been spared this go-round, but the violent turn in their investigation didn't bode well for the future—especially if Boomer's laptop held incriminating evidence.

Since he and Heather were the only living people who'd had access to it—and it was doubtful the mastermind behind this would want to leave any loose ends lying around—that put them in the bull's-eye.

However . . . if the two of them backed off—and the computer contained nothing of value—the target plastered on their backs might fall off.

As far as he was concerned, it was time to retreat.

Putting himself in a risky position was one thing.

But if it came down to a choice between justice for his army buddy or jeopardizing the life of the woman who was fast stealing his heart?

No contest.

The trick would be convincing a certain tenacious PI with a strong justice gene to throw in the towel on a missing persons case that had morphed into fraud and two likely murders.

Because unless he'd read Heather very wrong, that was going to be a hard sell.

20

"The next shift has arrived."

As her father motioned toward the front of the house, Heather set her makeshift icepack on the kitchen table and smoothed her hair back. She'd done as much as she could to disguise the damage, but there was no hiding her swollen jaw. It had been far too tender to mask with makeup.

At least the long-sleeved turtleneck top she'd changed into covered most of the bruises and abrasions.

The exchange in the foyer between Rick and his Treehouse Gang buddy, Colin, was quiet but audible.

". . . lucky you didn't get a ticket."

"I have a friend who could have fixed it." Rick's distinctive baritone was a tad rough around the edges. "Where is she?"

"In the kitchen."

"You leaving?"

"Yes. We're done here for tonight."

The conversation continued at a more muted level. Either Rick had followed Colin out or they'd lowered their voices.

Her father rose. "I think I'll try to catch a couple more hours of shut-eye."

"Sorry about disturbing your sleep." She stood gingerly, bracing herself on the table. Every square inch of her body hurt.

"I'm just glad you're okay." His irises began to shimmer, and he took her hand. "I'd offer a hug, but I don't want to hurt you." He squeezed her fingers instead.

She squeezed back. "I think I'm going to pass on church today, but call me when you get home."

"I'll do that. You try to rest—and let me know if you need anything." Footsteps sounded in the hall, and his lips twitched. "Although I expect someone else will be more than happy to lend a hand if you do."

A moment later, Rick appeared in the doorway, his complexion a few shades paler than usual, features taut.

"Did you fly?" She tried to smile, but it hurt too much.

He gave her a rapid sweep, and a muscle ticced in his cheek. "Not literally. Morning, Bill." His attention remained on her as he greeted her dad.

"Morning. I'm going home—but I know I'm leaving Heather in good hands."

"Count on it."

"Talk to you later, sweetie." Her father pulled his coat off the back of the chair and disappeared down the hall. Less than thirty seconds later, a soft click confirmed his departure.

Rick walked toward her—and didn't stop until he was inches away.

At such close proximity, she could see the fine lines radiating from the corners of his eyes and the creases bracketing his mouth.

Pressure built behind her eyes.

Since her mom died, no one but her dad had ever worried about her like this.

She touched his cheek. "Thank you for coming."

His Adam's apple bobbed. "I'd kiss you, but I'm afraid it might cause more pain than pleasure."

Sad but true.

"Can I have a rain check?"

"Always." He pulled out her chair. "Let's sit."

Gripping the edge of the table, she lowered herself stiffly onto the seat, trying not to wince.

"Do you need anything before I join you?" He angled a chair toward her.

"No." Everything she needed was standing within touching distance.

He sat, scrutinizing her. "Tell me how you feel."

"Not as bad as I did a couple of hours ago."

"How's the neck?"

Her hand fluttered to her throat.

How much had Colin told him?

"It's not too bad."

"Then you won't mind if I take a look." He leaned forward, gently folded down the high neck of her sweater—and sucked in a breath.

The same reaction she'd had after getting her first glimpse of the black-and-blue finger marks splayed on her skin.

In silence, he took her hand and tugged up the sleeve of her sweater.

The raw areas where she'd rubbed her wrists against the corner of the cabinet door to loosen the end of the tape were also puffy and turning purple.

Rick swallowed. "You ought to be in bed."

"I'll rest after you leave."

"You may not want to wait that long."

"How long are you staying?"

"Until you throw me out."

That would be never, if she had her druthers—but she didn't

256

require a babysitter. And making Rick sit around all day and keep her company wasn't fair . . . especially when she wasn't up to socializing.

"I'll tell you what. Why don't I fill you in on what I found on Boomer's laptop, then you can go home while I go back to bed?"

"Are you up to talking?"

No, she wasn't. Her aching throat hurt with every syllable she uttered.

But someone other than her needed to know what the laptop contained.

"I can manage a short conversation." She picked up her mug of honey-laced tea and took a tiny sip, forcing herself to swallow past the pain.

"Heather . . ." He covered her hand with his. "We can do this later."

"No. I want to tell you now. I stayed up late going through all the documents I could find, but the real payoff was in his email exchanges with Beth."

"They were in touch?"

"On and off. It was obvious Boomer still cared about her and wanted to get back together. Beth didn't. She was determined to build a new life, with no reminders from her military career. But he checked in with her periodically. In one of their final email conversations, he asked her what she wanted him to do with the flash drive she'd given him at the forward operating base."

"What did she say?"

"That she doubted she'd need it, because a person who was considering running for political office wouldn't want to stir up a hornet's nest that could implicate himself. She called it her insurance policy in case someone got nervous and tried to pin the whole rap on her, and said it had outlived its usefulness."

Rick leaned back and folded his arms. "That ought to be enough to get your CID contact interested in the case."

"Except I don't have the laptop anymore. He can't take this forward without hard evidence."

"We have the Excel document—and there has to be more if he's willing to dig."

"That will take time he may not have with the clock ticking on the statute of limitations—but I intend to call him Monday morning and discuss it." She took another sip of tea. "That wasn't the only helpful information I found. In one of her last emails, Beth told Boomer that she thought someone might be watching her, and that she was freaked out."

His gaze sharpened. "How long ago was that?"

"A week before she died."

He let out a soft whistle. "Confirmation that Boomer had grounds to be suspicious about her death."

"Yes. And there's more. They also had a recent back-and-forth about his drug problem. He assured her he was clean—and had been for more than a year. Her reply was that drugs . . . and alcohol . . . were a bad scene—which was why she'd never wanted any part of them."

"That shoots major holes in the accidental death theories for both of them. Did you tell any of this to Colin?"

"All I said was that the stolen laptop was associated with a case I was working on. I'll pass on what I learned to the appropriate authorities in Lubbock and Lexington—but there's no guarantee they'll reopen the investigations without hard proof."

He touched his pocket and pulled out his phone. Skimmed the screen. "Give me a sec. It's the Highway Patrol."

Rising, he greeted the caller and walked a few steps away.

A wave of fatigue swept over her, so strong she had to muster every ounce of her willpower to fight the urge to lay her head on the table.

Rick's soft conversation was mere background noise until one of his questions penetrated the fog swirling around in her brain.

"When do you need me?"

She tuned in.

"I'm dealing with an emergency of my own at the moment." Ten seconds ticked by, and he wiped a hand down his face. "I appreciate the confidence, and I'd like to help. How long has the teen been missing?"

While Rick went back into listening mode, Heather struggled to her feet.

The Highway Patrol must need him to assist with a search—and she wasn't about to stand in his way. She was safe. The poor young person wandering around lost was a higher priority.

"Rick." She touched his arm.

"Hold for a minute." He pressed the mute button on his cell and turned to her.

"Go. I'll be fine. I want to sleep anyway."

He hesitated. "Are you sure? They can get another pilot if they have to."

"But not someone as skilled as you. Don't say no because of me. I don't want the guilt trip."

After a brief hesitation, he put the cell back to his ear. "I'll be there in less than half an hour." Stowing the phone, he leaned down and gave her one of those forehead-brush kisses.

"I thought you said you were past that."

"Don't tempt me." His eyes darkened—and he slowly exhaled before continuing. "I'm going to wait on the porch until I hear your security system beeping. Promise me you won't open the door for anyone except me or your father."

"Don't worry. I won't make that mistake again."

He carefully twined his fingers with hers and walked to the door.

On the threshold, he stopped. "I hate to go."

No more than she hated for him to go.

But duty called.

"Phone me after you finish?"

"I'll text first so I don't wake you. You can call me if you're up. We have to talk about our strategy going forward."

She tipped her head. "I thought we discussed that yesterday, during the drive back from Lexington?"

"That was before this." He swept a hand over her.

"But we have more reason than ever to believe our theory is correct."

"I know—and the person who authorized tonight's break-in will know that too after they delve into Boomer's laptop. That makes the two of us targets."

"So?" The throbbing in the lower half of her face intensified, and she willed herself to remain upright. "I imagine we've both been in that position in our previous lives. We'll just have to proceed with extra caution. Besides, after tonight I have a personal interest in seeing justice done."

"Do you think the police will be able to identify the intruder?"

"Doubtful. He was covered head-to-toe and wore gloves. He didn't leave fingerprints, and I doubt they found any other trace evidence. At this hour, it's also unlikely the neighbors were up to witness anything. However . . . that doesn't mean *we* have to give up."

"What if I want to?"

"What if I don't?"

"Then I may have to fire you."

She blinked. "You can't be serious."

"Do I look serious?" He crossed his arms, jaw taut, expression grim.

Yeah. He did.

She huffed out a breath. "Did anyone ever tell you you're stubborn?"

"I've been called much worse than that. Set the alarm."

With that, he exited onto the porch and shut the door behind him.

After arming the security system, Heather watched through the window as he disappeared into the darkness.

His truck came to life half a minute later, the engine clearly audible in the early morning stillness.

At last she limped toward her room, took two more painkillers, and eased into bed.

In her exhausted state, sleep wasn't long in coming.

But as she drifted off, one last thought strobed through her mind.

She wasn't a quitter.

Neither was Rick.

The only reason he wanted to back off of this investigation was to protect her.

So during their next conversation, her number one job would be to convince him to stick with this until justice was served for Boomer . . . for Beth . . . for the United States government . . . and for her.

■ ■ ■ ■ ■

"There's been some excitement."

Burner phone pressed tight against my ear, I closed the bathroom door and turned on the water to mask our conversation.

"This better be important. I told you I'd initiate the calls from now on unless it was an emergency."

"My news should qualify." His tone cooled. "There was a break-in last night at one of the subject's homes."

"Which one?"

Rhetorical question.

I knew all about the robbery.

I'd orchestrated it.

"The woman's."

"Do you have any details?"

"Not many. I had to keep my distance once the cops and paramedics started showing up."

I frowned.

The retrieval wasn't supposed to involve injuries.

You couldn't trust anyone to follow instructions anymore—no matter how much you paid them.

"Why were paramedics there?"

"I assume the woman was hurt. Our other subject showed up about three hours later."

"Is he still there?"

"No—and neither am I."

I stared at my reflection in the vanity mirror. "What does that mean?"

"It means we're no longer working your case."

"Why not?"

"We don't mind pushing the limits of the law, but we don't break it. Providing information to a client who intends to use it to perpetrate illegal acts is way outside even our generous boundaries."

"You think I was behind that robbery?"

"Let's not play games. I saw the intruder leave. He was carrying a laptop in a case. A case that matched the one our subjects removed from the apartment in Lexington. Who else knew about that but you?"

If this guy thought I was going to admit I had anything to do with the robbery, he was crazy.

"That's ridiculous."

"Maybe. But a client who insists on anonymity is always a red flag. We only took this on because you were willing to pay a premium. However, no amount of money is worth going to jail for."

As he recited the balance due and ended the call, I exhaled.

I'd pay the bill. They'd done what I'd asked, and I didn't want any trouble.

At least I didn't require their services anymore. I had all the information necessary to decide on next steps.

Or I would, once I got my hands on the laptop.

The next order of business.

Any minute, the man I'd hired should be calling to confirm he'd deposited it at the drop point.

If there was nothing on it, this could all be over.

If it contained incriminating evidence?

I was ready to take the necessary action. One phone call would get the ball rolling. I already had the perfect person lined up to do the job.

The cell began to vibrate in my hand.

I answered it at once.

"The job is done. I've left the merchandise for pickup." The male voice was slightly distorted.

"I told you I didn't want any injuries."

"The injuries were on both sides. She fought back."

If he wanted sympathy, he'd have to find it elsewhere.

"Why didn't you disable the security system like we discussed and retrieve the laptop and a few other items while she was sleeping? You said stealth robberies were your specialty."

"Her system was more sophisticated than I expected. The easiest way to get in and out fast was to have *her* disable it and tell me where the laptop was."

I froze. "You told her you were after the laptop?"

"Yeah. She'd have figured it out anyway, even if I'd taken a few other items."

True.

But the police would likely have classified it as a general robbery versus one targeting a specific item.

Now they might be more receptive to any claims she made.

"You didn't follow instructions." Anger began to simmer in my gut.

"I did the best I could under the circumstances." He didn't sound happy, either.

It wasn't good enough.

But it was too late to change the outcome. The damage was done.

All I could do at this stage was focus on the future.

"Our association is over."

"It's been a pleasure." Sarcasm underscored his saccharin sign-off.

I jabbed the end button and shoved the cell into my pocket.

My contracted thief was history—but the person waiting in the wings was ready to make his debut as soon as I gave the word.

Whether I hired him depended on what was on that computer, and I'd know that soon. My expertise and experience might be in other areas, but I had computer skills few people knew about.

It shouldn't take me long to hack into Jackson Dunn's documents and emails.

Then I'd wipe the hard drive, remove and destroy it, and dispose of the whole mess as I'd disposed of my previous burner phone.

If the PI's client was fortunate, there would be nothing on there to link any specific person to any specific crime.

Should that not be the case, the funding for the case was going to have to dry up.

Fast.

No firm worked for free.

And even if that woman PI passed on the information she had to law enforcement, police were overburdened these days dealing with new crimes. Reopening a closed case in the absence of hard evidence wouldn't be a top priority.

Nor would my plan to cut the funding for the case raise any

red flags with law enforcement. That demise, too, would appear to be an accident.

One requiring very specialized skills.

No worries there.

My guy was well-prepared to carry out the task I had in mind.

After all, who could be better equipped to take down a helicopter from apparent mechanical failure than an aircraft mechanic who'd crossed over to the dark side?

21

"You look like you were hit by a truck."

As Nikki delivered that pithy assessment from the hall, Heather made a face. Or tried to. But her jaw didn't cooperate. "Good morning to you too."

The Phoenix office manager pushed through the half-closed door and marched in. "You should have stayed home."

No kidding.

She not only *looked* as if she'd had a close encounter with a truck, she *felt* like it.

But there was work to be done—and decisions to be made if Rick followed through on his threat to pull out of the case.

That was why she'd asked Cal to schedule a staff meeting first thing this morning to discuss the situation.

"I may go home early."

Nikki gave an unladylike snort. "That'll be the day. Anyway, the gang's all here. Dev's already devouring the coffee cake you put in the conference room."

"I'll be right in."

"You want more tea?" She motioned to the empty mug on the desk.

"I can get it."

"I could use a refill myself." Nikki picked up the mug and cocked her ear toward the adjacent office as a faint ring sounded. "That must be the call Cal's been waiting for. Don't rush. He said if it came in he had to take it, and that he might be a few minutes late."

"In that case, I'll answer a couple more emails first."

And try to summon up the energy to stand and make the short walk down the hall.

How ironic that during all her years with the PD, she'd never sustained injuries this extensive.

And she'd thought working at Phoenix would give her a quieter, gentler career. That she'd left her previous high-risk life—as Rick had termed it—behind.

Go figure.

After dealing with several more emails, she struggled to her feet, splayed her fingers on the edge of the desk, and sucked a breath through her teeth. Her jaw ached like the dickens, but that punch in the stomach had also done a number on her. Every expansion and contraction of her lungs hurt, and walking upright was a challenge.

Maybe she should have followed the paramedic's advice and gone to the hospital for a more thorough exam.

Maybe she still would if she didn't improve fast.

In the meantime, she'd muscle through the day. Tomorrow she could reevaluate.

By the time she got to the conference room, the other three PIs were seated around the table.

"Welcome back, Connor. I didn't hear you come in." She summoned up a smile for the clean-cut, dark-haired ex–Secret Service agent. "How was the trip?"

"Wonderful—but too short. You were on the phone earlier, or I'd have stuck my head in to say hi." He gave her a quick head-to-toe, rose, and pulled out an empty chair. "You better sit."

"Thanks." She eased into it.

"Aren't you the gallant one today." Dev grinned and lifted his shamrock-bedecked mug toward his colleague.

"You may want to take a few notes." Nikki breezed in with the two teas and set one in front of her.

"Since when do you get other people coffee—or tea?" Dev sent the woman a peeved look.

"I've been known to fetch beverages on occasion."

"Not for me."

"If you ever show up in Heather's condition, I might."

"I don't think I want a coffee delivery bad enough to get that beat up." He helped himself to another piece of Pauline's coffee cake. "This is great, by the way. Almost as good as the caramel pecan stollen from McArthur's."

"High praise, coming from him," Nikki told Heather. "That stollen is his favorite artery-clogging food."

"I'm glad you like it." She fidgeted, trying without success to find a more comfortable position.

"For the record, I concur with Dev's assessment." Connor took a second piece too.

"I'll add my vote to the tally too." The napkin in front of Cal contained only crumbs.

Nikki gave the male members of the firm an exasperated sweep. "No offense to Heather's offering, but you three have atrocious eating habits. You're going to pay the price someday for all the sugar you ingest."

"We'll die happy, though." Dev sent her an unrepentant smirk.

Lips twitching, Cal wadded up his napkin. "Now that we've all boosted our glucose into the danger level, let's talk about Heather's case." He shifted his attention to her. "I gave everyone a cursory overview, but why don't you fill them in on the details of what happened over the weekend? Then you can bring us up to speed on the status of the case—or, more accurately, cases. The original assignment has mushroomed into a much bigger deal than we anticipated."

Heather complied, ending with her call last night to Rick.

"Despite his threat to fire me—us—I think we should stick with this. That's why I asked for this staff meeting. If he backs off, going forward the work will be on our dime. But I can't see letting a murderer walk away. Not until we run out of leads."

Twin creases dented Connor's brow. "I know investigative work is expensive, but why would Jordan lose interest now, when it appears the missing man he wanted us to find was likely murdered? If he was concerned enough to spend money to find him, wouldn't he want us to do our best to identify his killer?"

In the silence that followed, Dev, Cal, and Nikki all looked at her. Dev's eyes glinted with amusement, Cal's demeanor was serious, and Nikki wore a smug expression.

Connor might have been out of the loop while he was on vacation, but the rest of the staff members knew—or suspected—the answer to his question.

At least they were giving her a chance to explain.

And since her colleagues would soon find out that a romance with her client was brewing, it would be best to be honest.

"During the course of the investigation, Rick and I have developed a . . . rapport." She chose her words with care, striving for a businesslike tone. "I've maintained a professional relationship with him throughout, but I believe it will develop into more than that after this case is over. I think he's worried about my safety and is getting cold feet."

"Well put." Dev hitched up one side of his mouth and lifted his mug again. "And we've all been there."

"Some more discreetly than others—without mentioning names." Nikki pinned him with a pointed stare.

"Hey. I was 100 percent professional while I searched for Laura's sister. Ask her."

"I may do that someday." Nikki picked up a stray crumb from the coffee cake and popped it in her mouth. "Of course, she's prejudiced in your favor now that you somehow convinced her to say 'I do.' Talk about a miracle." She rolled her eyes.

Heather choked back a laugh. The banter between those two was always a stitch. "I can't speak to Dev's situation, but I can assure you I haven't mixed business and pleasure on this case."

Not much, anyway.

After all, could she help it that merely being in Rick's company was pleasurable?

As for those kisses—*he'd* initiated them.

Her answer must have satisfied Cal. "Based on what happened Sunday morning, our client's safety concerns are obviously valid. In light of that, how would you like to proceed?" He directed the question to her.

It was typical of Cal to defer to the lead on a case—but in the end, this would be a group call. And she'd abide by the consensus, difficult as it would be to let this go if that was the decision.

"Given the statute of limitations issue—and our inability to access the suspect's financial records—I recommend turning what we have over to my contact at CID."

"That makes sense. Anyone disagree?" Cal scanned the head shakes around the table. "Let's go with that. What about the apparent murders?"

"A conversation with law enforcement in those jurisdictions would be my first step, but unless they plan to aggressively follow up—which is doubtful due to workload demands and the lack of hard evidence—I'd like to continue to devote time to those two cases even if Rick pulls his support."

Cal rolled his pen between his fingers. "As a former homicide detective, I'm not inclined to let anyone get away with murder, either—and based on what you've uncovered, there's sufficient circumstantial evidence to suggest those two deaths were not accidental. Anyone else?"

"I say we go for it." Connor drained his mug, as if he anticipated a rapid conclusion to the meeting.

"Count me in," Dev said.

"I'll help in whatever way I can." Nikki flicked a crumb off the sleeve of Dev's sweater before he could mash it into the fibers as usual.

"I believe we have a consensus. Go ahead and continue to pursue this, Heather. If more hands are required, don't hesitate to pull one or more of us in."

The tension in her shoulders dissolved.

This was the exact outcome she'd hoped for—and it was one of the things she most enjoyed about working at Phoenix. While they always had each other's backs, Cal trusted each of them to pursue their cases as they thought best. However she chose to investigate this, the whole team would be behind her.

"Thanks."

He rose, signaling the end of the meeting. "Make it a short day."

"I'll try."

The three men filed out, but Nikki lingered. "I wonder how Rick is going to feel about the firm's decision to pursue this whether he's in or out?"

She didn't have to wonder.

She knew.

"He won't be happy."

"You realize that's a positive sign."

Yeah, she did.

But delivering the news wasn't going to be easy.

"If he gets mad, though, our relationship could be over before it begins."

"I don't think that's going to happen. He'd be crazy to walk away from someone like you."

"I hope that's true."

"My track record here is flawless." Winking, Nikki reached around and patted herself on the back. Then she grew more somber. "But be careful until this is resolved."

"That's my plan."

Heather followed her out, a niggle of unease quivering through her as she returned to her office.

By now whoever had authorized the laptop snatch must have discovered the incriminating content. If they were smart, they'd already disposed of the evidence.

But Rick was right.

They would be worried that she—and in all likelihood he—had also found Boomer's emails and that the two of them could pose a considerable threat.

Meaning the target on their backs wasn't going away anytime soon, whether they dropped the investigation or not.

Not being the operative word.

Perhaps her calls to the Lexington and Lubbock PDs and her conversation with CID would spur those groups into action.

But even if they all agreed to follow up on the information she supplied, she was going to dig deeper on the two murders. Beth and Boomer deserved justice.

Whatever it took.

No matter the risk.

· · · · ·

Gaze fixed on the horizon, Rick lowered the collective on the Bell 407 helicopter, adjusting for ground effect to maintain a steady descent rate as he approached touchdown.

Hovering just above the landing pad, he felt one skid make contact—but only someone sensitized to the subtle sensation would notice. His corporate passengers certainly didn't. They were too busy gathering up their briefcases and stowing their laptops.

He balanced for a few seconds, lowering the collective a tad as he put a bit more skid on the ground and adjusted the cyclic to compensate for drift. No pitch or roll on his watch.

It was another whisper-soft landing.

One of the passengers touched his arm and pointed at his watch. "I have a two o'clock meeting."

"Give me a minute to shut down." He rolled down the RPMs.

The guy didn't seem too happy about having to sit on the tarmac—but Rick was as anxious as his passengers to end this flight so he could check texts and voicemails. The Phoenix staff meeting should be over, and if his prayers had been answered, they'd voted to let the case go.

Just thinking about Heather's close call yesterday had kept him tossing most of the night.

If she insisted on continuing with the investigation, however—and Phoenix blessed the effort—he'd have to implement Plan B.

Whatever that was.

He closed the throttle, completed the shutdown routine, and removed his headset as the main rotor blades slowed . . . and stopped.

After opening the door, he stepped out and extended a hand to the two suit-clad businessmen. "Thanks for flying with us."

They beat a hasty retreat, and Rick turned the aircraft over to the charter company mechanic. After tucking himself into a quiet corner in the hangar, he pulled out his cell.

Heather had texted *and* called.

He pressed her speed dial number and propped a shoulder against the wall.

She answered halfway into the first ring. "How was the flight?"

"Smooth. Simple. Easy money. How was the meeting?"

"Also smooth and simple. Not as profitable as your morning."

"What does that mean?"

"We're going to stick with the investigation whether we're paid or not. Letting someone get away with murder doesn't sit well with any of us."

He closed his eyes.

Not what he'd wanted to hear.

But he had to admire her—and Phoenix—for their commitment to finding the truth.

"I'm not happy about that—for personal reasons."

"I know. You've been clear about your feelings. But I can't walk away from this, Rick. I'm not wired that way—and I don't think you are, either."

That was true.

If Heather weren't at risk, he'd be all over this.

"I'm not—but I don't want you hurt any worse than you already are."

"I'll be careful."

"That's no guarantee you'll be safe."

"Life doesn't come with guarantees." Her voice had taken on a determined edge.

She wasn't going to budge.

Rick raked his fingers through his hair.

Let it go, Jordan. Pushing her to compromise her principles is wrong. She needs support, not pressure.

Yeah, yeah.

But backing off was hard.

He took a deep breath, willing his pulse to slow. "I won't argue with that. Tell me how you're feeling."

"Hanging in. Cal insisted I go home at noon and rest, so I'm getting ready to lie down as we speak. I do have one piece of news, even if you don't want to be our client anymore."

"I've reconsidered my position. I'm still in." If she was going to stay on this, he had to be part of it.

"Cal will be glad to hear that—and I am too. For different reasons."

The warmth in her tone didn't banish his misgivings . . . but it made them more palatable. "What's the news?"

"It appears I've lost my tail. Have you spotted yours today?"

"No. I haven't seen either of the cars that followed us on Saturday—but I don't have your eye for detecting a shadow. I assumed I'd missed them or they'd changed vehicles."

"I don't think so. I took a rather odd route on the drive home, and I'd lay money no one was on my tail."

Rick frowned, watching the mechanic run the Bell through a standard post-flight check. "Why would the person behind this stop the surveillance?"

"I've been pondering that." A squeak came over the line, like the give of a mattress. "It's possible that despite what's on Boomer's computer, the perpetrator has decided we're no longer a threat. It isn't as if any names were mentioned in the emails."

"Or they could have sufficient information on our comings and goings to implement whatever plan they have in mind for us. If Weston is our guy, the stakes in this game are high. He may not want to take any chances with potential loose ends."

"That's why I'm not letting my guard down. You shouldn't, either."

"I'm still putting my concealed carry permit to use." The owner of the aviation company waved at him from across the hangar, and he lifted a hand in acknowledgment. "I have to run. I think another job may have come in. It's feast or famine with this flying gig. Worse right now with the other first-string pilot on vacation."

"But you love every minute of it. Your eyes lit up when you

were telling me about that search and rescue course you'll be teaching next month."

He hiked up one side of his mouth. The types of helicopters he flew now were child's play compared to the Chinooks and Black Hawks and Little Birds from his Night Stalker days, but the adrenaline rush at liftoff was always the same.

"Yeah. I do. So what's your next step?"

"I've already been in touch with CID and the PDs in Lexington and Lubbock. I saved the good news for last. Thanks to everything we've discovered, my contact at Fort Leonard Wood is going to try to muster enough substantive evidence to get a subpoena for Weston's financial records."

"That *is* good news." If they couldn't get Weston on a murder charge, maybe CID could nail him for fraud—or another equally serious crime.

"In terms of Beth and Boomer, I want to dig deeper into Weston's background. Talk to a couple of former employees from the early days of his start-up."

"Why?"

"Ex-employees often know inside information about their employer—and they have nothing to lose by sharing it. If there are any cracks in his armor, we may be able to exploit them to smoke him out on the murder cases. It could go nowhere . . . but I've seen the technique work."

"What if it doesn't?"

"I'll touch base with Beth's neighbors. The detective on the case would have talked to them about what they saw the night she died, but I want to delve deeper."

The lady was thorough.

"Busy week. Any time to give me an in-person update, since I'm funding this effort?"

"The investigation has broadened far beyond your original scope. Cal won't expect you to pay for my hours on Beth's case."

"We'll work it out. The cases are connected." He strolled toward the owner's office. "You didn't answer my question."

"I thought you were going to be in the air all week."

"I don't have anything booked yet on Friday. We could discuss the case over dinner. Or if I end up flying that day, Kaldi's on Saturday is an option. Doesn't matter to me where we meet, as long as you're there." Women like Heather didn't come along every day—and he wanted no doubt in her mind about his intentions.

"Ditto. And either one works for me."

He smiled. "Easy sell."

"Smooth talker."

His smile morphed into a chuckle. "I'll call you again tomorrow. Let me know if anything interesting turns up before that."

They said their good-byes, and he picked up his pace as he crossed the hangar.

The risks Heather was taking with this investigation were troubling—but the case wasn't going to last forever. Within the next few days she'd either uncover useful information or hit a dead end.

As long as she'd insisted on pursuing this, the best outcome would be a fast resolution that nailed the perpetrator—and removed the danger.

That's what he'd pray for.

Because the longer this dragged on, the more perilous it would become.

Maybe no one was on their tail anymore . . . maybe the emails that had convinced the two of them they were on track with all their theories were gone . . . but that didn't mean the mastermind had written off the threat he and Heather posed.

And if Heather continued to make waves, those storm clouds massing along the western horizon on this January afternoon might be an omen of more than impending nasty weather from Mother Nature.

. . . . .

It was worse than I'd expected.

As Jackson Dunn's laptop finished shutting down, I rummaged in the drawer for my stash of cigarettes. Slid two in my pocket, along with a book of matches. Stowed the laptop and its case in my gym bag, beside the miniature screwdriver and hammer I'd already tucked inside.

Destruction and disposal were my priority.

Meaning that on this warmer-than-average January Monday, I'd be making a short drive to a secluded lake.

After I placed a critical call.

Taking a deep breath, I pulled out the slip of paper containing the ten-digit number, tapped it into my burner phone, and began to pace.

Too bad it had come to this. I'd never wanted so many people to get hurt.

But even though the correspondence between Dunn and his female friend hadn't contained any names, there was sufficient detail to pique the interest of law enforcement.

And it would certainly have energized the woman PI and her client. Unless the funding ran out, she'd continue to poke her nose into shadowy areas best left undisturbed.

It was time for Phoenix Inc. to lose a client.

My mechanic-for-hire answered after five rings, and I got straight to the point. Why waste social niceties on paid help?

"I'm ready to pull the trigger—rhetorically speaking. How soon can you move?"

"I've already done the homework. I was waiting for a green light from you."

"You have it. But remember—this has to be ruled accidental."

"Understood. There are several methods I can use that will read as mechanical failure."

"What about security at the facility?"

"Easy to circumvent. Small businesses like Palmer Aviation don't spend big bucks on fancy systems. It's a perimeter setup, and the staff is lean. I'll slip in through an open hangar door, hide till they close for the night, take care of my business, and slip out in the morning. Piece of cake."

"How will you know which helicopter to . . . work on?"

"They post a list of the flights on a bulletin board in the office, including pilot names and assigned aircraft. Easy to see through the office window with binoculars. I have one question. Passengers aren't identified on those printouts. Only the number of people traveling. Some outbound flights are pickups, and in that case the pilot is alone. Do you want me to wait for one of those?"

I stopped pacing. "Is anything like that on the board now?"

"No."

Frowning, I stared out the window at the barren branches of a massive maple tree. Killing innocent people had never been part of the plan.

But every day that passed increased the risk. Who knew what else that PI might uncover if I dallied?

If there were other passengers, I'd have to live with the guilt. View them as collateral damage, like the military did when innocent people were killed.

"Don't wait."

"You're the boss."

"How fast can you get it done?"

"Before the end of the week. The other main pilot is on vacation, so our target will be picking up most or all of the flights."

"How do you know that?"

"The owner's wife was more than happy to discuss the available pilot's credentials when talking by phone with a potential customer."

The guy sounded buttoned up.

This operation should be smooth and easy.

"Keep me updated. I'll wire the rest of the money once the job is finished."

"You'll hear from me soon."

The line went dead.

Pressing the end button, I picked up my gym bag. I was a creature of habit who maintained a strict schedule—but a person was entitled to take a break in the middle of the day on occasion to work off stress . . . and shed a little weight.

At least that would be my story if anyone asked about this unscheduled trip to the gym.

And if the weight I was shedding consisted of an incriminating laptop—no one but me need ever know that.

22

He wasn't going to show.

Heather checked her watch again . . . sighed . . . and picked up her purse from the ledge next to the fireside table she'd claimed at Panera.

Sources didn't always follow through on agreed-upon meetings, but Weston's former employee had sounded sincere during their phone conversation.

Oh well.

She dug through her purse for her keys. As soon as she got back to the office, she'd call the other two ex-employees on her list and—

"Ms. Shields?"

Heather lifted her head.

Yes!

Adam Bennett had come through after all.

She rose and extended her hand. "That's me. Thank you for coming."

"Sorry I'm late. Traffic was a bear."

"Don't worry about it. Would you like a drink or some food?"

"No thanks. I'll get a sandwich to go after we're finished." He claimed the empty chair at the table as she retook her seat, giving her bruised jaw a discreet perusal. "In the interest of transparency, I want you to know I googled your firm before I returned your call. You can't take any chances in this crazy world we live in."

"You're preaching to the choir."

"However . . . I'm glad you told me you'd be wearing purple, since the Phoenix site didn't include any photos of the PIs."

"In our business, we do a lot of surveillance and undercover work. It's better if we remain anonymous."

"Makes sense." He linked his fingers on the table. "You said you wanted to talk about Brad Weston. What would you like to know—and why would you like to know it?"

"Let me answer the latter part of your question first. While I was working on a missing persons assignment, Weston's name came up. After further investigation, he appears to be integral to our case, which has morphed into quite a different—and much more complicated—situation than we anticipated."

"Have you found the missing person?"

"Yes." She sipped her tea. Best to say as little as possible about that. "But Weston is still on our radar because of other information that came to light. As a result, we're digging deeper into his background. I thought it might be productive to talk with a few people who knew him during the start-up phase of his business. As I said on the phone, your name was mentioned in a newspaper article I found on Google."

"I'll help you out if I can."

She ran through her list of questions, but none of Adam's answers raised any red flags. Weston sounded like he'd been a perfect boss, fair and generous with his employees.

"May I ask why you left the company?" She'd promised to keep the man no longer than thirty minutes, and that mark was approaching.

"A better offer. More money, more responsibility, and a more impressive title. But to tell you the truth, I wish I'd stayed. If I'd known the company was going to take off and end up attracting buyout offers, I'd have turned down the other job. Although I suppose I may have ended up hunting for another position anyway if Brad wins the governor race and sells the business."

"Speaking of the race—did he have any political ambitions while you were with the firm?"

"Not that I know of. He worked insane hours. The man ate, lived, slept, and breathed the company. I know he believed in the concept, but I also think grief was part of the reason he poured himself into the job. You knew he lost his wife suddenly not long after he left the army, right?"

"Yes."

"To be honest, I think work saved him in those early years. He had difficulty adjusting after she died."

"That's understandable." She closed her notebook. All Adam had done was confirm what they already knew about the man's character and history. "I appreciate your willingness to meet with me today."

If the other two employees offered no new insights, either, she may have to take a different tack and talk to Beth's neighbors.

Adam pulled out his keys, faint creases denting his brow. "May I ask you a question about your case?"

"Yes—but I can't promise I'll be able to answer. Clients expect us to keep our findings confidential."

"I respect that. I just wondered if your investigation involves Brad's . . . personal life?"

A subtle nuance in his inflection raised her antennas.

"Define personal."

He shifted in his seat. "You know . . . relationship stuff."

"If you're asking me whether his love life is a focus of our investigation, the answer is no. However . . . it's possible a relationship could be pertinent to the larger case."

"Does that case involve criminal activity?"

"Yes. We're in the process of trying to figure out how—or if—your former boss fits into it." A slight stretch of the truth, since they'd already pegged him as their prime suspect in both the fuel scheme and murder cases.

"Did you happen to get that"—he indicated her jaw and tapped his own—"while investigating this case?"

There was no reason not to answer his question.

"Yes. It's taken a violent turn. I got caught in some crossfire."

He took a breath. "Well . . . I don't see how this will help you . . . but I'll share one other piece of information if you promise not to go public with it."

"I won't leak it to the press, if that's what you mean. Or contact law enforcement—unless what you're about to tell me involves an illegal activity."

"Not illegal . . . but of questionable morality. In light of Brad's squeaky-clean image and traditional values platform for the governor's race, this could hurt him if it got out. And I'm not 100 percent certain what I saw was what I thought it was. This is just an observation."

"Understood." She opened her notebook again.

"Three years ago, not long after I left the company, I was at a corporate retreat with my new firm at a resort in the Ozarks. One night, while I was walking to the dining room, I spotted Brad through the trees having dinner with a woman on the terrace of one of the more secluded cabins."

"Did you recognize her?"

"No, and there was never any scuttlebutt around the office that he was dating anyone. I tried not to jump to conclusions about what I saw, but the body language suggested they were having more than a business discussion—if you know what I mean."

"I get the drift. But why would that be an issue in terms of

Weston's image? I'm not saying I approve, but lots of single people take weekend trips together."

"That's the problem. The next day, while I was in the gift shop at the resort, the woman he'd had dinner with made a purchase. After running her credit card, the clerk thanked her by name for her business. Turns out I knew her husband."

As the implications of Adam's revelation sank in, Heather tried to maintain a neutral expression.

Boy Scout Weston had had an affair with a married woman.

That was a brand-new piece to add to the puzzle.

How—or if—it fit in, she had no idea.

But it was worth further investigation.

As the silence grew, Adam spoke again. "Look . . . I'm not judging him, okay? I know he missed his wife—and loneliness can tempt people to do things they would never consider doing under normal circumstances."

"That's true." She picked up her pen. "Would you mind sharing the woman's name?"

"Ellen Chambers."

She jotted it down. "Do you keep in touch with Weston?"

"No. Our relationship was strictly business. I haven't spoken to him since I left the company."

"I won't keep you from your lunch any longer. But if you happen to think of anything else that could be of interest, please give me a call." She passed him one of her cards.

"I'll do that." He stood and extended his hand. "Good luck with the case."

She returned his firm shake. "Thank you."

While he joined the line forming at the order counter, she slipped her notebook into her purse, put on her coat, and left the eatery, still digesting this new twist.

Of course, the fact that Weston had taken a married lover might be insignificant to their case. The indiscretion had occurred after his activities at the forward operating base and before the murders.

However . . . it did confirm that the morally upright image he presented to the world wasn't altogether accurate.

And a conversation with the woman who may have been privy to the man's most intimate secrets could yield a bountiful harvest.

Especially if he'd dumped her.

A woman scorned could be a font of information.

Heather pressed the autolock release and quickened her pace as much as her sore muscles allowed, her pulse picking up. This might go nowhere—but the hum in her nerve endings said otherwise. And after the disastrous shooting incident, she'd vowed to never again discount her instincts.

Which meant that the next order of business was in-depth research on Ellen Chambers—followed by a spur-of-the-moment visit that would give the woman no opportunity to contact Weston first, on the off-chance they'd remained in touch.

And if she was lucky, perhaps their chat would lead to the break she needed to pin a murder charge on the person who'd killed Beth and Boomer.

. . . . .

The spaghetti bolognese she'd picked up from Pasta House smelled delicious, but her appetite was nonexistent.

Maybe by next week, after this was all over, she'd be hungry again.

Assuming everything went as planned.

Stomach churning, Ellen closed the takeout container and pushed it aside.

She had to stop worrying.

There was no reason to think there would be any hitches. She'd used professionals where necessary, done plenty of research on her own, and mapped out the whole operation. No one outshined her when it came to nailing down details.

Yet there were always unknowns. You couldn't plan for every contingency, no matter how hard you tried.

Like the front that seemed to be moving in. If the sleet that had begun bouncing off her windshield on the drive home was any indication, the winter storm the meteorologists had been dithering about had decided to roar into town.

Weather like that could disrupt everyone's normal activities—and require a change in timing. This could drag on another week or—

Ding-dong.

She jerked as the doorbell echoed through her condo.

Who on earth could that be?

Not an invited guest, that was for sure. She hadn't socialized since the divorce.

Slipping out of her shoes, she tiptoed down the hall toward the foyer.

Ding-dong.

She frowned.

Whoever was on her porch was persistent.

Sidling up to the door, she peeked through the peephole.

An attractive, thirtysomething woman was standing on the other side.

She didn't come across as a salesperson, but she did look professional—despite the slight discoloration on her jaw that seemed to belong more on someone who'd been in a bar fight.

It couldn't hurt to see what she wanted.

Ellen twisted the lock and pulled the door open.

"Good evening." The woman smiled at her. "I hope I'm not disturbing your dinner."

"No. I've only been home for a few minutes. How can I help you?"

Her caller extended a card. "I'm Heather Shields with Phoenix Inc., a private investigation firm. I was hoping you'd be willing to answer a few questions for me about a case that involves someone you used to know. Brad Weston."

Ellen gaped at the card, shock numbing her brain.

How did this woman know there was a connection between her and Brad? She'd never mentioned his name to a soul—and Brad wouldn't have told anyone about her, either.

A ripple of panic lapped at the edges of her composure.

"Why do you think I know Brad?"

The PI's expression remained pleasant. Composed. "The person who passed along your name saw you together."

They'd been spotted during one of their discreet trysts?

Bad news.

"I'm sorry . . . I have a busy schedule this evening." She started to close the door.

"I won't delay you long—and I'd be happy to explain more about the case if you could spare a few minutes."

Ellen hesitated.

She wasn't going to tell this woman anything—but it might be wise to listen to what she had to say.

Forewarned was forearmed, as conventional wisdom said.

She opened the door. "All right. I can give you ten minutes."

"Thank you." Heather crossed the threshold.

"We can talk in the living room." Ellen motioned to her left as she closed the door and led the way into the room, claiming an upholstered chair. "Why don't you tell me what this is about and what you want from me?"

Heather pulled a notebook from her purse. "A couple of weeks ago, we were hired to find a missing person. In the course of our investigation, Brad Weston's name came up. Since then, the case has become more complex. We're now dealing with a number of crimes—including one that involves theft."

"You think Brad was involved in criminal activity?" She did her best to appear shocked.

"At this point, we aren't jumping to any conclusions. We're simply gathering information."

"Have you talked to him?"

"Yes."

"You've gone to the source. I don't know how much else I can offer. And I haven't seen him in a long while."

"But you were acquainted with him once, in the not-too-distant past. Well acquainted."

It wasn't a question.

Heather Shields knew she and Brad had had an affair. She could see it in the woman's face.

Her heart began to thump.

This didn't make sense. The two of them had always been scrupulously careful and discreet about their meetings, and they'd indulged in no untoward behavior on the rare occasions they'd ventured out in public.

She tucked her feet under her, forcing her taut shoulders to relax. "May I ask how you knew Brad and I were acquainted?"

"The information came from a reputable source who wishes to remain anonymous."

Ellen narrowed her eyes. "Have you been talking to my ex-husband?" It was possible David had had her followed during their marriage. As if he'd been in any position to throw stones, the jerk.

"As I said, my source is confidential. Would you mind telling me why you and Weston broke up?"

Still fuming about her ex, she tossed off an answer. "He met his current wife."

The instant the words spilled out, her stomach knotted.

Her unexpected visitor had tricked her into confirming that she and Brad had been romantically involved.

She choked back a curse.

"That must have been hard for you." The PI oozed sympathy.

Get your act together, Ellen. Keep it pleasant. Don't let her see you're upset. And don't fall for any more tricks.

"Not really." She forced up the corners of her mouth, keeping her tone nonchalant. "Our relationship filled a need for both of us at that stage of our lives, but circumstances change. Our parting was cordial."

"What can you tell me about his character?"

"Brad Weston is the finest man I ever met—principled, intelligent, compassionate, conscientious, hardworking." About this, at least, she could be honest. "He'd be a wonderful governor."

"So you don't think he would ever be involved in anything illegal?"

"No." Her gaze didn't waver as she answered the question. Despite what this woman and her cohorts might suspect about Brad's activities overseas, there was no hard proof linking him to any crime.

On top of that, the statute of limitations was due to expire soon—and then he'd be home-free.

This woman would get nothing further from her.

As if she sensed that, Heather closed her notebook, picked up her purse, and stood. "I appreciate your help."

She rose too. "I'm not certain what it is you're investigating, but if you're trying to connect Brad to any illegal activity, it's a lost cause. A man with skeletons in his closet would have to be crazy to set his sights on the governor's office—and Brad's not crazy."

"Thanks for that input."

Ellen walked the woman to the foyer, closed and locked the door behind her, and sank back against the wall.

This was not good.

Particularly in light of her imminent plans.

Now that she was on the PI's radar, the risk was higher.

Yet she was only a peripheral player in Phoenix's investigation. She hadn't been involved in the activities at that forward operating base. The woman had just wanted to pick her brain about Brad, no doubt hoping a dumped girlfriend would be out for revenge and willing to spill any dirt she knew.

But it hadn't played out like that. All of the comments she'd offered about Brad had been positive.

Heather Shields was probably sorry she'd wasted her time.

Nonetheless, it was clear the woman wasn't going to back off on her investigation. Law enforcement might never be able to prosecute Brad, but a political opponent could use such allegations to his or her advantage if they leaked out.

However . . . in the absence of definitive proof, a reputable PI firm wouldn't risk a slander charge. And they had nothing substantive to back up such claims.

This was contained.

Pushing off from the wall, she returned to the kitchen and lifted the lid on her dinner.

Wrinkled her nose.

The red sauce looked like blood.

Stomach flipping, she closed the container and eyed her laptop.

Work was always an effective distraction, and there was no lack of that in January, with all the year-end numbers to crunch. She could spend the rest of the evening occupying her mind with that.

And taking comfort in the fact that the payoff for all her hard work and planning was mere days away.

▪ ▪ ▪ ▪ ▪

"We may have a change in plans."

Cell to his ear, Brad walked over to the window as Chuck

delivered the news. "Weather related?" He moved aside the drape and peered out. The flagstones on the back terrace were glistening.

"Yeah. The sleet is expected to continue all night. Unless the road crews can work magic by morning, we may have to cancel tomorrow's lunch and afternoon meetings." He blew out a breath. "If we reschedule, you'll have to plan another trip down there next week."

"I've already got a full plate. Two potential buyers are flying in to discuss a deal."

"I don't want to put this off too long." Chuck's exasperation came over the line loud and clear. "We're getting a late start as it is."

"Why don't we touch base in the morning? If the sleet stops earlier than they're predicting, the drive could be doable."

"Let's keep that as an option. I'm also working on a backup plan. In either case, be ready to go on a moment's notice. Is Lindsey still on for dinner Friday night with the secretary of state?"

"Yes."

"Okay. We can't let the weather derail that one. I'll call you early tomorrow."

After they said their good-byes, Brad keyed in his wife's number.

She answered at once. "I was about to call you. It's no fun being snowed in—or iced in—alone."

"I agree. I miss you already. But it's safer for you to stay at the hotel overnight. The roads are already treacherous. How was the meeting?" He scrolled through his brain trying to recall which charity event she was in the midst of helping plan. Came up blank.

"Productive. The facility is lovely, and the hotel manager and his wife are contributors, so he threw in a few extras for the gala. What's the status of your trip to Jeff City tomorrow?"

"I just talked to Chuck." He relayed the highlights of the call. "The first event is a noon luncheon. Thanks to the weather, we'd have to double the normal travel time. That would mean a seven thirty or eight departure. If the weather forecast is accurate and the sleet doesn't let up, that's not in the cards. But Chuck wants to leave as soon as it's safe. I'll call you tomorrow with an updated schedule."

"If the roads aren't clear in the morning, I may hang out here until I have to leave for my yoga class rather than swing by the house first."

"That would be safer. You're closer to the studio than you are to home—but I'd rather you skip the class and stay put if there's any question about the roads."

"I'm sure they'll be fine by lunchtime—and you know I can't live without my yoga session."

A slight exaggeration—but that hour-and-a-half workout every week *was* important to her. Since the day they'd met, she'd never missed a class unless they were out of town.

"Well, be careful—and enjoy yourself. I'll have Chuck call you to confirm your travel arrangements for Friday's dinner."

"I still can't believe we're having dinner with the secretary of state." There was a touch of awe in her voice. "Who'd have guessed anything like that would ever happen, given our backgrounds?"

"I know. I wonder what my father would say if he was alive?"

"I wonder what *both* our fathers would say?"

Probably nothing positive.

"At this stage, it doesn't matter. We've both overcome our upbringings." Except for the inferiority complex he'd never been able to fully shake and the migraines that plagued his wife on occasion. "Best of all, we have each other."

"If you were here, we could toast to that."

"I'll make up for it in person."

"Hold that thought. Sleep well, Brad."

"The bed will feel empty without you."

"I'll make up for *that* in Jeff City."

"And I'll hold *that* thought."

Smiling, he slid the cell back into his pocket and wandered over to the gas logs burning in the fireplace. Just hearing Lindsey's voice could—

His phone began to vibrate again.

Brad's smile broadened.

Maybe she was missing him as much as he missed her and wanted to continue their chat.

But when he scanned caller ID, his lips flattened.

Why was Ellen contacting him?

He hesitated for a second, but finally pressed the talk button and greeted her.

"I'm sorry to bother you, Brad. Do you have a minute?"

No.

Not for her.

Their chapter was closed and he wanted it behind him.

However . . . Ellen had never been reckless. If she was calling him, there must be an important reason.

Better hear what she had to say.

"I can talk for a few minutes."

"I thought you'd want to know about a visitor I had this evening. A PI named Heather Shields. She said she's spoken with you."

The bottom dropped out of his stomach.

How had the PI connected him to Ellen?

"I've met with her. She has suspicions about the situation I discussed with you from my army days. Did she know about us?"

"Yes. That's why I called. I assumed you'd want to know."

His lungs locked, and he closed his eyes. "How did she find out?"

"She wouldn't reveal her source. But our liaison isn't relevant to the other situation, so I don't see why she'd tell anyone about it. In case it leaks, though, I wanted to assure you the information didn't come from me. I wouldn't do that to you. And for the record, all my comments about you were positive."

"I appreciate that." But it wouldn't help him if his opposition got wind of their affair and created a smear campaign.

Nor would it help his marriage.

He'd been faithful to his first wife, and he'd never strayed with Lindsey, either—but would she believe that?

His head began to pound.

It was beginning to feel as if his run for governor had been doomed from the beginning.

"Brad?"

"I'm here." He bolted toward the bathroom in search of aspirin. "Thank you for letting me know about this."

"I've always looked out for your best interests."

"I know. Take care of yourself, Ellen."

"That's my plan. Good night, Brad."

Shoving the phone back into his pocket, he lengthened his stride. He had to tame the throbbing in his temples.

But that wasn't going to fix his bigger predicament.

He kneaded his forehead as he hurried through the silent house.

Why did there have to be another glitch just when he thought he had everything under control?

Of course, if the Phoenix investigation ended, Heather Shields would have no reason to tell anyone about the affair.

And that would happen.

Soon.

She didn't have one speck of hard evidence that would interest law enforcement, other than the flash drive. And the coded spreadsheet it held could never be traced to him. The overworked CID wasn't going to waste time and manpower on an exhaustive search of his finances without more to go on.

In the meantime, he could only hope the ice storm that was bringing the city to a standstill would also put a temporary halt to an investigation that had the potential to shatter all the careful plans he'd made for a shining future untainted by the past.

23

Surveillance was boring.

Heather adjusted the small fan unit that was plugged into the lighter of her Taurus, aiming it toward the front window. The optional heat element did a better job defogging the glass than keeping her warm, and she wanted a clear view of Ellen's condo.

Shifting into a more comfortable position, she gave the parking lot another slow scan. Very few people were stirring on this cold Wednesday morning. At least the short, turtle-pace drive to Ellen's place on almost empty roads hadn't been that taxing.

And since she wasn't in top fighting form after her struggles with the intruder on Sunday morning, sitting in a car wasn't such a bad task for this workday.

Her phone began to vibrate, and she pulled it out of her pocket. Smiled as she put it to her ear. "Good morning."

"Morning." Rick's warm baritone chased some of the chill from the car. "Sorry I didn't return your call last night. By the time I slipped and slid home from the hangar and took care of a generator glitch at the camp, it was too late to phone you. And I was too busy trying to keep my tires on the pavement during the drive to take any calls en route. How are you feeling?"

"Better every day. The bruises are fading." Even if the aches weren't.

"You should have taken a few days off."

"I'll think about that after we wrap up this case. You want an update on my meeting with Ellen? That's why I called last night."

"I'm all ears."

She relayed their conversation. "Bottom line, I went expecting her to be a bitter ex, but all she did was sing Weston's praises. I picked up zero animosity. Just the opposite."

"Some breakups are amicable."

"True—but this one was friendly in the extreme. Her feelings toward the man were verging on passionate. And there were strange vibes radiating from her. That's why I'm sitting outside her condo on surveillance duty as we speak."

"In this weather?"

"I'm armed with hot chocolate and a plug-in heater that's doing its best to keep me warm and toasty."

"Too bad I'm not there. I could find other ways to do that."

At his husky tone, a delicious tingle ran through her. "Are you flirting with me, Rick Jordan?"

"Guilty as charged. But at this distance, it's all words. No action."

"Could I get a sample of that action in person soon?"

"Done. So has anything happened there?"

"No. She's laying low. I assume her office closed today, along with 95 percent of schools and businesses in the metro area. Doesn't mean she's not in touch with Weston, though. I can't shake the feeling she's somehow involved in this."

"How long are you going to watch her?"

"Cal suggested forty-eight hours. One of the guys will spell me later this afternoon. If the surveillance ends up being a bust, I'm going to contact the other two former Weston employees I tracked down and see if they have anything to offer."

"And if they don't?"

"I'll schedule a trip to Lubbock and poke around, talk to Beth's neighbors. Very few crimes are unsolvable if you ask the right questions and look in the right places."

"If there's any evidence to be found, I'm betting you'll find it."

"Thanks for the vote of confidence. Now tell me what's going on with you."

"After yesterday afternoon's flight got scrubbed, I stayed at the hangar to catch up on paperwork. Hence the trek home in the ice. I had a flight scheduled for this morning, but the customers canceled late yesterday after they heard the forecast."

"Does that mean you have a free day?"

"Maybe not. While we've been talking, a call came in from Palmer Aviation. Could be a reschedule from yesterday—or a new job."

"Can you fly in this?" She inspected the gray sky. The sleet was tapering off, but there was a quarter-inch-thick layer of ice on every exposed surface.

"Yes, as long as no freezing rain or sleet is falling and there's no forecast for either. I flew in those kinds of conditions on a few occasions in the Middle East when I had no choice, but in general helicopters don't like ice. How are the roads at the moment?"

"Not great, but the salt trucks made another pass a few minutes ago. If the sleet doesn't kick in again, the highways should be in better shape in another hour or two. I wouldn't recommend any long-distance driving until later this afternoon, though."

"No worries. Any significant miles I log today will be in the air."

The front door of Ellen's condo opened, and she picked up her binoculars. "Hold a sec."

The woman was bundled up head-to-toe with hat, gloves, long coat, and neck warmer. If she hadn't come out of the front door of her condo, Heather would have been hard-pressed to identify her.

"My subject is on the move. Maybe she's going in to work after all. I have to run."

"Be careful."

"Always. Talk to you soon."

She waited while Ellen scraped the ice from the window, slid into her car, and backed out—then gave her a lengthy lead before following. In view of the sparse traffic, it wouldn't be difficult to keep her in sight. Besides, if the woman was going to her office, Heather had already mapped out that route.

But she wasn't.

While Ellen did get on the highway, she went west instead of east.

Curious.

Heather swung onto the on ramp behind her.

If she wasn't going to work, what was so important that she felt compelled to venture out on a day most St. Louisans were staying safe and warm at home?

. . . . .

Rick pushed through the door to the business office of Palmer Aviation and greeted the owner's wife.

"Morning." Sue Palmer smiled at him from behind her desk in the reception area. "The boss is waiting for you in his office. Sorry about the last-minute call."

"No problem. I'll pick up the paperwork on my way out to the hangar."

"It's all ready for you."

Naturally.

Sue was the dynamo who maintained the flying schedules,

monitored the maintenance records, did the bookkeeping, answered the phones, greeted customers—and served as all-around girl Friday.

Her husband and business partner would be lost without her.

But Harvey knew helicopters—and he'd still be flying if an eye ailment hadn't grounded him forever eighteen months ago.

When he reached the office, the man looked up from a desk piled high with stacks of papers, wearing his usual frazzled expression. "Hey, Rick. You got here fast."

"If departure is at one thirty, I'll need every minute I have for the preflight check. Is the mechanical inspection finished?"

"Done yesterday. Before the canceled flight."

"That works. What's today's gig?"

"A drop-off in Jeff City. Two passengers. They intended to drive, but had to scrap those plans due to the weather. The tentative booking came in last night. Sounds like they have to be there for a midafternoon meeting at the capitol."

"Political honchos?"

"Aspiring honchos. Brad Weston, who's running for governor, and his campaign manager."

Rick stared at him. "Seriously?"

"Yeah." The man peered at him over the top of his glasses. "You know the guy?"

"No." *Regroup, Jordan.* "But I've heard about him. He has an impressive résumé."

Harvey shrugged. "You've hauled around bigger wigs than him."

Yes—but none whom he suspected of fraud . . . and murder.

Since Harvey seemed to expect a response, Rick kick-started his brain. "Never anyone with his army background, though. It's possible we may have mutual acquaintances from our years in the Middle East."

"I wouldn't count on him being too chummy. He and his manager will probably be huddled together the whole trip discussing strategy."

"True. Any special instructions?"

"Just bring my Bell back in one piece. According to the National Weather Service, you've got about a five-hour window before another wave of ice hits."

"I know. I checked. Believe me, I don't intend to linger. I'm estimating ground time in the five-minute range."

"If you can stick to that, you'll be home with a couple hours to spare."

"That's the plan. I'll stop in after I get back." With a mock salute, he exited the office and pulled out his cell, tapping in Heather's number as he walked back to the reception area.

She answered on the first ring. "I didn't expect to hear from you this soon." The background noise indicated she had him on hands-free.

"I have news. Guess who I'm ferrying to Jeff City in half an hour?"

"A celebrity?"

"No. Not yet, anyway. But he will be if he becomes governor."

A beat ticked by.

"Brad Weston is your passenger?"

"Him and his campaign manager."

"What's the story?"

She listened as he filled her in, waiting until he finished to speak. "What a weird coincidence."

"Agreed."

"I'll be curious to hear your impressions."

"I'll pass them along later. I was going to suggest dinner, but the meteorologists are predicting another wave of ice tonight."

"Drat."

"Is that an expression of displeasure over the return of bad weather or disappointment about dinner?"

"What do you think?"

"I'll go with the latter. It's better for my ego." His lips curved at her snicker. "Any activity at Ellen's place?"

"Uh-huh. I followed her to a gas station, a drive-through Starbucks, and a strip mall in West County—where we're now sitting."

"She hasn't left her car?"

"Not yet."

"Odd."

"Tell me about it. Stay tuned for an update."

"Be careful."

"Likewise."

"Considering the road conditions, I'll be safer in the air than you are on the ground."

"I'll take your word for that. I hate to admit this, but flying has always freaked me out a little."

"Ever been up in a helicopter?"

"No."

"Whole different ball game."

"Yeah—and even scarier. If the rotors give out, or the engine stops, don't you drop like a rock?"

"No. That's a common misconception. In general, a well-trained pilot can land a helicopter except in the most catastrophic of conditions." Like an RPG hitting a Chinook.

He swallowed past the acrid taste on his tongue.

As if she'd read his mind, Heather spoke again, her voice softer and more personal. "For the record, I'd go up with you anytime—and feel totally safe and secure."

"Thanks. I appreciate that." He took the paperwork Sue held out as he passed and continued to the hangar. "I have to run, but if Ellen leads you anywhere surprising, text me—

although I won't be responding to messages until I get back here around four."

"Why don't you call me once you're on the ground? Even if I don't have any news, we can chat."

"Deal. Talk to you then."

Rick stowed his cell and picked up a clipboard containing the preflight checklist. After all his years of flying, he could do the routine in his sleep.

But Palmer Aviation prided itself on thoroughness and safety, and no flight left without a written report on file from the mechanic and the pilot. An admirable practice—and one of the reasons he'd agreed to work for them, despite their small size.

He hadn't lied to Heather. In the hands of an experienced pilot, flying in a well-maintained helicopter *was* safe. The pilots who got into trouble were often the ones who took chances or got sloppy.

He did neither.

Meaning the short flight to Jeff City and back should be a piece of cake.

. . . . .

Lindsey Weston was a creature of habit.

That had made planning a breeze.

Ellen hunkered down in her car, keeping one eye on the door to the yoga studio while she felt in her pocket again for the subcompact Glock she'd purchased after the divorce. It was small—but adequate for this job.

Not that she planned to use it. The weapon was a bluff. A coercion tactic. But Lindsey didn't know that. So she'd do what any reasonable person would do if a gun was pointed at them. She'd follow instructions to the letter.

At least she better.

Because pulling the trigger would ruin everything.

Despite the chill in the cold car, Ellen began to sweat. Tremors rippled through her fingers. Panic squeezed her lungs.

No!

A case of nerves could be a disaster.

If she didn't remain calm and in control, she might blow this.

And she couldn't let that happen.

Not after all her work and planning.

She groped in another pocket until her fingers closed over the photo of her and Brad she always carried. Pulled it out. Focused on the face of the man she loved with every fiber of her being.

The quality was marginal, since it had been snapped on the fly, but it was the only one she had of them. Brad had never wanted to take any photos, skittish as he was about evidence. But after a few glasses of wine, he'd posed for this selfie the weekend they'd gone to the Ozarks.

Merely looking at the two of them together calmed her. Helped her concentrate on her goal.

Her breathing evened out.

The outcome she wanted wouldn't be immediate, but once Lindsey was out of the picture, Brad would eventually realize his hasty marriage to a floozy who'd only been after his wealth had been a mistake.

And once that happened, she'd be ready to step back into the role of confidante and lover she'd played during the traumatic early start-up days of his company, when he'd been struggling to get a foothold in the market *and* cope with the loss of his wife.

He'd loved her back then.

He could love her again.

It might take months for that to happen. Perhaps as long as a year.

But she was a patient woman.

Especially when the payoff would change her whole life—and his—for the better.

Forever.

· · · · ·

Yawning, Heather hit a few keys on her laptop and ran the plates from another car parked near Ellen's. No reason to think any of the empty vehicles were related to the woman's reason for being here—but you never knew. And it passed the time.

Of course, it was possible Weston's ex-girlfriend was meeting a friend for lunch at the small café a few storefronts down. Her motivation for sitting in a cold car on a half-empty parking lot might not be in the least nefarious.

Except she'd been here forty-five minutes.

And something still felt out of kilter about the woman.

Heather jotted down the name next to the license plate in her notebook and moved on to the next car—a Mercedes sedan. An S 550 model, unless she was mistaken. Super nice wheels, with a tab of close to a hundred grand. That driver had some—

She froze.

Gaped at the screen.

The car was registered to Lindsey Weston.

That couldn't be a coincidence.

Heather's brain shifted into high gear.

Did Ellen and Lindsey know each other?

If so, why were they meeting clandestinely?

Could they somehow be involved in the crimes she was investigating?

Before she could sort through the unexpected development, Lindsey emerged from the yoga studio, gaze fixed on her phone as she strolled toward the Mercedes.

Ellen opened the door of her car.

Heather snatched up her binoculars as the woman got out from behind the wheel and walked toward Weston's wife.

The columns on the arcade of the upscale mall interfered with her line of sight, but if luck was with her the two women would meet in an open area that would allow her to observe their exchange.

And depending on what happened next, she might have to place a call to Cal and alert him to stand by in case she needed more eyes on this job.

24

It had been an excellent yoga class.

Not to mention a much-needed hour and a half of chilling out after the adrenaline-pumping call she'd received a few minutes before it started.

Lindsey filled her lungs with the cold air. Exhaled.

Today was the day.

Yes!

Soon life should begin to settle down.

She walked toward her car, scrolling through her messages. The follow-ups from the committee meeting at the hotel yesterday could wait. The one from Chuck was probably about travel plans for Friday. She could read that after she got in the car.

The two from Brad had top priority.

Her finger hovered over the first one, a smile curving her lips. How her world had changed the day he'd wandered into the bar where she was singing. Overnight she'd gone from a lonely, eking-out-a-living existence to a loving relationship and a life of luxury.

And once he was elected governor . . . once he had exposure on the national stage . . . it wouldn't take long for the party

powers-that-be to realize Brad Weston had tremendous potential. That there was no office too high for him to—

"Hello, Lindsey."

She looked up.

The woman who'd greeted her stood six feet away, bundled
up for arctic weather even though it wasn't *that* cold outside.

And why was she wearing sunglasses on such a gray day?

She squinted, but it was difficult to get a read on her identity
with most of her face covered. The voice wasn't familiar, either.

"I'm sorry . . . do we know each other?"

"You've never met me—but I know all about you." The
woman moved closer.

Too close.

Lindsey retreated a step.

The woman kept coming.

A ripple of unease skittered through her.

"Excuse me." She tried to edge around the stranger.

"Don't be in such a rush to end our conversation." She shifted
her muffler to reveal a small pistol.

Lindsey's breath hitched. "What . . . what do you want?"

"I want you to take a little trip with me."

"Where?"

"You'll find out soon."

"Who *are* you?"

"You can call me Ellen."

The name meant nothing to her.

"Look . . . if you want money, you can have my purse. And
my jewelry." She had to stall until someone left the studio—or
exited one of the stores—and saw she was in trouble.

Except class attendance had been sparse, and half of the
businesses in the mall were closed because of the ice storm.

"I don't want your money. Let's go." The woman nodded
toward the Mercedes, a few yards away.

Lindsey's stomach clenched.

Getting in her car with this crazy person would be a mistake.

But if she didn't comply, the woman might shoot her here on the sidewalk.

"It doesn't matter to me when you die. If you want to end it here, that's fine." Ellen's tone was matter-of-fact. Unemotional.

Yet the words sent a chill through Lindsey.

She'd said *when* you die, not *if* you die.

This woman was planning to kill her—either now or later.

If that was the intended outcome, later was obviously a better choice. The more time she bought herself, the more chance she had of outsmarting or overpowering the woman.

Unless . . . could the stranger be bluffing? Shooting someone in broad daylight would—

As if sensing her thoughts, Ellen's hand twitched, and the gun moved an inch closer to her.

Lindsey's heart stuttered. "Fine. I'll g-go with you."

"A wise choice."

The woman fell in beside her, pressing the gun against her kidney.

One tiny flick of a finger, and she would die in this parking lot.

A bead of sweat began to trickle down her temple.

"Continue to the passenger side and open the door." The woman spoke close to her ear.

She did as instructed, glancing at her cell as she dropped it into her purse.

If she could respond to Brad's message, send some sort of coded SOS—

"Move."

The pressure against her side increased.

Maybe . . . maybe she could tell this woman Brad was expecting a response. That if she didn't text him back, he'd be worried and call the police.

It was a long shot—but it was the only idea her muddled brain could formulate.

Fingers trembling, she opened the door and slid into the car.

The woman leaned down, into her face. "Move behind the wheel."

It wasn't easy to scoot over the console in her bulky winter clothes, but she managed it. What choice did she have, with a gun aimed at her?

The woman got into the passenger seat and shut the door, the pistol never wavering. "Get your pills out of your purse."

Lindsey blinked. "What?"

"Get out your migraine medicine."

"I don't . . . how did you . . . what is . . . ?" Her mind was reeling so fast she couldn't manage to form a coherent sentence.

"Going through a person's trash and following them around can yield all kinds of helpful information. You like expensive white wine. Gourmet to Go is one of your favorite takeout places. You get migraines. And you never, ever miss your yoga class."

An icy knot formed in the pit of Lindsey's stomach. "You've been watching me?"

"No. My PI has. Get the medicine out."

What?

A PI had been following her around?

This was surreal.

"I-I don't carry it with me."

"If you don't want to take your own, I brought pills with me. Canadian pharmacies are very obliging." She dug into the pocket of her coat and produced a bottle.

Containing who knew what.

It would be better to take the medicine she had with her. She knew what was in *her* bottle.

"I'll use mine." Lindsey opened her purse and rooted through the contents for the container. Pulled it out.

"Take three tablets."

Three?

Her usual dose was one—and even that made her groggy.

"I won't be able to drive. I'll be too sleepy."

"We aren't going far."

Fingers trembling, she shook out three of the oval orange pills. "I can't take them without water."

"I'm sure you have a bottle in your yoga bag."

In silence, she withdrew the half-empty container. Unscrewed the cap. Hesitated.

"Take them. Three pills won't kill you." The woman's voice was cold.

Lindsey swallowed them one at a time.

"You're very good at following directions. Start the car."

"Where are we going?"

Silence.

"Listen . . . my husband has texted me at least twice. He knows my yoga class is over, and I always return his messages ASAP. If I don't answer him, he'll be alarmed. He could call the police. He's an important man, and he can get fast action."

"I know all about your husband."

At the woman's odd inflection, Lindsey narrowed her eyes. "What do you mean?"

The twist of Ellen's lips didn't remotely resemble a smile. "We were close—until you came along. Start the car."

As she stuck the key in the ignition and put the car in gear, Lindsey tried to process the implications of that comment.

Had Brad ever mentioned a woman by the name of Ellen? Or *any* woman with whom he might have had a relationship after his wife died?

No.

Could her abductor be lying?

But what would be the point?

"Turn right out of the parking lot."

Lindsey forced herself to focus on the situation at hand. She could think about the other issue later.

If there *was* a later.

"Why won't you tell me where we're going?"

"You'll know when we get there. Just follow my directions."

"Why are you doing this?"

No response.

Lindsey tightened her grip on the wheel and cast a sidelong glance toward the passenger seat.

The gun was still aimed at her.

Whatever Ellen had in mind, this wasn't going to be a long ride. She'd already said they weren't traveling far.

So she better think of a strategy to outwit her.

Fast.

Or all her dreams of taking Jeff City—and Washington DC—by storm with the man she loved . . . of proving to the world she and her husband were somebodies . . . were going to be as dead as she was.

·····

"Even though you didn't have a clear view of what happened on the sidewalk, what's your take?"

Cell on hands-free, Heather followed Lindsey's car out of the parking lot as she responded to Cal's clipped question. "The whole scenario is suspicious. The fact they both got in on the passenger side suggests coercion. I definitely need a second set of eyes on this. Also, can someone dig into Lindsey's past? I did basic research after Weston entered the picture, but nothing raised any red flags."

"I'll get Nikki on it. As soon as I wrap up a couple of things here, I'll head out. Where are you now?"

"Eastbound on Clayton Road."

"I'll call you for an update from my car."

The cell went dead.

Brow knitted, Heather kept the Mercedes in sight, matching her speed to the sedan's. Although the columns at the mall had hidden most of the interaction between the two women, Lindsey's shocked expression once she'd come into view had been telling.

Either Ellen had a weapon, or the woman had somehow convinced Weston's wife to go with her.

The entry on the passenger side suggested a weapon.

Lindsey passed a slow-moving SUV. She could always call one of her colleagues at County and ask them to have a patrol officer pull the car over on some pretext. See if he or she spotted anything amiss while they filled out a field interview report.

But if Ellen had a gun . . . if she was tottering on the edge of a meltdown . . . she could end up shooting Lindsey *and* the officer.

Not a palatable outcome.

The best plan might be to follow the car, see where it was going. By then Cal shouldn't be too far behind, and between the two of them they ought to be able to handle this.

Unless the situation went south very suddenly, very fast.

Like the day she and her partner had gone to interview the suspect in the drug-ring case.

Her knuckles whitened on the wheel.

She couldn't let this degenerate to that point.

As soon as Cal was en route, they'd discuss strategy. Determine the best approach to intercept the duo a few cars ahead of her.

She would not let this end badly for any innocent party.

Not again.

. . . . .

"Brad . . . we have to leave."

"I know." He pressed the end button on his cell and turned

to his campaign manager. "But Lindsey isn't answering, and the yoga class is over. Maybe she had an accident."

"Or maybe she's concentrating on driving. The roads are full of slick spots."

Brad raked his fingers through his hair. Chuck could be right . . . but he had an unsettling feeling that the explanation for her silence was more ominous.

"Gentlemen . . . we're ready to go." Rick Jordan joined them.

"Come on, Brad." Chuck took his arm. "You can call her later."

"Can you give me five more minutes?" He directed the question to the pilot.

"No longer. I have to get back before the next front moves in. If you'd like to cancel, I can have the owner—"

"No." Chuck squeezed Brad's arm. "We're going. We'll be on board in five minutes."

With a dip of his head, Jordan strode toward the door of the hangar.

"This isn't like her, Chuck." Brad pulled his arm free.

"Isn't it possible she met a friend and got caught up in a conversation? We're only going to be a short flight away in the unlikely event you have to get back for any reason."

That was true—and yes, he was being overprotective. But he'd already lost one wife. He couldn't go through that again.

"I'll keep trying. If she doesn't answer in five minutes, we'll leave."

He called again at the two-minute mark, while Chuck paced.

Repeated the drill at three minutes.

Again at four minutes.

No response.

He'd delayed their departure as much as he could, based on the arms-crossed, wide-legged stance and let's-get-this-show-on-the-road demeanor of the pilot waiting beside the helicopter outside the hangar.

He resorted to another text.

Taking off now. Text or leave a message ASAP. Worried about you. Will call as soon as I land.

Chuck stopped in front of him. "Any luck?"

"No." He slid the cell into his pocket. "I'll try her again after we land."

"I bet everything is fine. Let's go." He motioned toward the briefcase in Brad's hand as they began walking toward the helicopter. "During the flight, you may want to reread the material I prepared for these meetings. It doesn't hurt to remember a few personal tidbits too. Number of children, hobbies, spouses' names. You'll earn brownie points with these people by taking an interest in more than their support."

"Got it."

Yet as they boarded the aircraft and buckled in, the only spouse he cared about at the moment was his own.

For despite his campaign manager's reassurances, he couldn't quash the worry that all was not right in his wife's world.

· · · · ·

Ellen and Lindsey were traveling in the direction of Weston's house—and the closer they got, the more certain Heather was that the cushy, five-acre estate Lindsey called home, which backed up to a large, wooded county park, was their destination.

Why would Ellen want to go there?

Her cell chimed, and she answered without taking her gaze off the car a hundred yards ahead of her. Now that they were deep into residential territory, she had to drop back or risk being spotted.

"Heather, it's Cal. I'm en route to your last position. What's the status?"

She gave him her current location. "We're closing in on Weston's house. If that's where they're going, I can't follow them in by car." She tried to call up an image of the aerial photo of the place she'd googled while digging up background on the man. "I seem to recall quite a few pine and spruce trees that could provide cover if I decide to go in on foot."

"I'm not certain what that would accomplish if they go in the house."

As usual, the Phoenix chief was the voice of reason.

She blew out a breath. "Me, neither."

"However . . . she doesn't know me. I could drive in and ring the bell. If no one answers, we could bring in law enforcement."

"But if Ellen does have a weapon, she could use it if she feels cornered."

"My showing up at the door shouldn't make her panic. I can come up with a credible pretense. If I get bad vibes, we'll turn this over to law enforcement ASAP. We can't force our way in."

"Yeah." The inability to invoke probable cause as an excuse to take action was one of the downsides of being a PI.

"Why don't we touch base as soon as the destination is confirmed and go from there?"

"That works. Expect a call shortly. What's your ETA?"

"Ten minutes, unless ice on the side roads slows me down."

"They're a bit precarious. Passable but slow. Talk to you soon."

Three minutes later, the Mercedes's right-turn signal began to blink as the car approached the entrance to the Weston property.

Her hunch had been correct.

She called Cal back and gave him the news. "I'm going to pass the drive and park on the side of the road wherever I can find a spot. We can discuss strategy after you get here."

"That will be soon—but road conditions are slowing me down a bit. I'll watch for your car."

Heather continued along the narrow, two-lane road, slowing as she passed the entrance to the Weston house. The Mercedes was creeping toward a stone bridge on the icy drive. As best she could recall from the aerial photography, the arched structure spanned a ten- or twelve-foot-deep ravine containing a creek that emptied into a lake in the adjacent park.

The vehicle was already somewhat obscured by the abundant evergreen trees that dotted the property and lined the road. And once it crossed that bridge and followed the curving drive toward the house, it would be totally hidden from view.

People in this part of town liked their privacy.

Which wasn't helping her do her job.

They might have to go with Cal's plan in the end. He was a stranger to them and should be able to ring the bell on a plausible pretense without arousing suspicion.

In the meantime, she had to find a spot to wedge her car on the skinny shoulder and hope—

She jammed her foot on the brake as the Mercedes picked up speed on the slick road . . . rolled onto the bridge . . . and crashed into the side.

What the . . . ?

Keep going, Heather. The impact wasn't hard enough to cause injuries, and if you stop here, they'll see you.

She transferred her foot to the gas pedal and swerved into a cluster of pine trees that would hide her car from the view of anyone on the bridge.

Snagging her binoculars, she slid from behind the wheel and blended into the branches of the trees, using the abundant boughs as cover. As soon as she was in a position to see the bridge, she put the binoculars to use.

The two women were outside the car, talking or arguing. Impossible to tell which from this distance.

Then Ellen lifted her arm.

Heather zoomed in on her hand.

It was difficult to make a definitive call given her angle and the distance, but it looked like she could be holding a pistol.

Her pulse sped up.

Whatever was going to happen might go down before Cal could get here.

She had to move in.

Pulling out her Sig, she surveyed the terrain. If she stayed in the shadows and hugged the trees, she ought to be able to get close enough to hear their conversation and figure out what was going on.

And she had to do it quickly, even if every muscle in her aching body was protesting loudly.

Because when a person had a gun, and you already had bad vibes about them, the situation could turn lethal in a heartbeat.

As she'd learned to her regret.

25

Harvey had been right.

His two passengers had no interest in chitchatting with their pilot—or with each other.

Not that the noisy cockpit of a helicopter was conducive to conversation anyway.

As Rick cleared his takeoff with the tower—ten minutes behind schedule—Weston continued to riffle through documents while his campaign manager made notes on a tablet.

Too bad the two of them weren't interacting more. It was hard to get a bead on a silent man whose head was down.

Maybe as they got closer to their destination, the men would begin to converse and he could pick up some vibes that would give him a few clues about Weston's character.

He opened the throttle to increase the speed of the rotor, scanning the instruments. RPMs were nominal, pressures and temperature gauges were in green, altimeter was set.

The helicopter was good to go.

Slowly pulling up on the collective, he depressed the left foot pedal, keeping tabs on the torquemeter as the skids left the pavement.

He hovered about five feet off the ground for a moment, then nudged the cyclic forward and raised the collective a bit. The nose tipped down and they began to move parallel to the ground.

At eighteen knots, he eased up on the left pedal and continued to gradually apply forward cyclic during the climb-out until he reached cruise speed.

A textbook takeoff.

If the rest of the flight went this smoothly, he might be back faster than he expected. And if the weather, by chance, didn't turn bad, it was possible he and Heather could meet for dinner after all.

As he continued to climb toward his cruising altitude, the corners of his mouth rose.

A cozy meal for two would be a perfect end to this gray winter.

And as long as Weston was occupied with political activities in Jeff City, maybe life in St. Louis would be calm and quiet for a few days.

. . . . .

A gust of polar wind whipped past, and a shiver rippled through Lindsey.

"Don't worry. You won't be cold much longer." Ellen gave her a smile laced with malice.

A wave of dizziness swept over her, and Lindsey groped for the edge of the car door.

The pills were kicking in.

No!

She had to get control of this situation before fog muddled her brain.

Her cell chimed again with another text, and she grabbed that excuse to distract the woman.

"I'm sure that's my husband again." She motioned toward

her purse. "I'm telling you, he's going to call the police if I don't answer."

Ellen took off her sunglasses and scrutinized her for several seconds. "Fine. Toss your purse over to me." The gun held steady.

Gripping the door, Lindsey leaned in and withdrew her bag. If she got an opening, she could throw it at the woman and—

"Don't even think about it." Ellen's tone was as icy as the weather. "Toss it low and slow."

Scratch that idea.

But she might be able to rush the woman once she was occupied with the phone.

That was the only option left—whatever the outcome.

Because every nerve in her body was screaming at her that she was almost out of time.

She did as the woman had instructed, throwing the bag low. It landed on the frozen pavement and slid the last few inches.

The pistol's aim never strayed from her heart as Ellen bent to retrieve the purse and set it on the trunk. With one hand, she slid the zipper open and rooted through the contents, pulling out two plastic-wrapped cigarettes along with the phone. She shoved the Camels back inside.

"What's your password?"

Lindsey recited it.

After Ellen tapped it in, she scrolled through the texts. "That last one wasn't from Brad—but the others were. My. What a devoted husband. You really have him fooled."

"W-what are you talking about?"

Ellen gave her a get-real look. "You and I both know you only married him for his money. You used your . . . assets . . . to buy the life you wanted."

"That's not true. I love him."

"Sure you do." She continued to read the messages, her gaze

flicking back and forth between the cell and her captive. "But he'll understand the difference between true devotion and duplicity after you're gone."

As the woman's comment sank in, Lindsey's jaw dropped. "You're going to kill me and hope he'll fall for you?"

"He did once—until you sidetracked him."

The woman was certifiable.

"And how . . . how are you going to pull this off? You think the law won't hunt you down? You'll end up in prison for the rest of your life."

"Because of an accident? I think not."

Accident?

This couldn't get any more bizarre.

"What kind of accident?"

"You had one of your terrible headaches." The woman tut-tutted. "It was so bad you took extra pills. The medication made you woozy, and while you were crossing this bridge, you ran into the wall. The ice storm will add credence to the scenario, but it would have worked even without that."

"But . . . the impact wasn't hard enough to kill me." She rubbed her temple. It was getting more and more difficult to think.

"That's true. But when you got out to inspect the damage, you lost your balance. Fell over the side of the wall, into the rocky stream. There could be many causes of death. Head trauma . . . drowning . . . internal injuries. It will be interesting to see what the medical examiner decides."

"You really think you'll get away with this?"

"I *know* I will. Once I verify your sad demise, I'll wander out the back way and take a brisk walk through the park to the car dealer on the other side. I'll call a cab from the service department, which will drop me at the café in the mall where I left my car. No one will ever know I was here."

The woman had dotted all the i's and crossed all the t's.

She might actually pull this off.

Another shiver snaked through Lindsey.

She had to keep stalling. Keep thinking. Keep looking for an opportunity to rush her.

"You're wrong about why I m-married Brad, you know. It wasn't for money. I love him."

"Come on, Lindsey. Are you telling me you don't relish the jet set—or should I say helicopter set—life?" She lifted the cell again.

Despite the fogginess in her brain, the woman's question set off a faint alarm bell.

"What do you . . . why did you mention a helicopter?"

Ellen read Brad's text out loud. "'Change in plans. Chuck chartered a helicopter from Palmer Aviation. We're flying to Jeff City. Leaving at 1:30.' Sounds like jet set to me."

The ground shifted beneath Lindsey, and the new wave of dizziness that swept over her had nothing to do with the pills she'd ingested.

Unless Palmer Aviation was having a very busy day, Brad was in the sabotaged helicopter!

She twisted her wrist. Squinted at the blurry face of her watch.

It was one fifty-five.

They'd taken off twenty-five minutes ago.

This couldn't be happening!

"I have to call him." She lurched toward the other woman.

"Stay where you are!" Ellen threw the cell back in the purse and lifted the gun with both hands, backing off a step.

"You don't understand." Lindsey jolted to a stop, heart fluttering in her chest like a trapped bird. "The helicopter . . . it's . . it's going to crash. We have to warn Brad! The pilot has to land. Now!" Hysteria raised her pitch.

Ellen's brow crinkled. "What are you talking about? How would you know that?"

"Because . . . because . . ." Her voice faltered.

She couldn't tell this woman the real reason.

Or maybe she could—if she then turned the tables. Killed Ellen instead of the other way around. She could tell the police the woman had abducted her for . . . for revenge. That Ellen had boasted she'd hired someone to sabotage the helicopter as payback to the man who'd left her. They'd struggled. The gun had gone off. Ellen had died.

It could work.

It *had* to work.

There was no time to come up with an alternative plan.

In fact, it might be too late already—but if it wasn't, every second counted.

Ellen took a step closer, and Lindsey stopped breathing.

"Because what?" The other woman's gaze drilled into hers.

"Because I arranged for that helicopter to crash."

. . . . .

Sweet mercy!

Rick was flying a doomed helicopter.

As the truth slammed into her, Heather's lungs locked.

She and Rick had had it wrong from the beginning.

Brad might be guilty of nefarious activity overseas, but if his wife was the mastermind behind the helicopter sabotage, she must also be responsible for the murders of Boomer and Beth.

And Ellen was just as unbalanced, with her murder plot to finish off the woman who'd married the object of her obsession.

Wrestling her panic into submission, Heather crouched behind the low-hanging boughs of a white pine, every syllable of the conversation seventy feet away coming through loud and clear in the crisp, cold air.

"Why would you want to do such a thing?" It was clear from Ellen's skeptical inflection that she wasn't buying Lindsey's story.

"The pilot was funding an investigation into Brad's activities while he was in the military overseas, and that had to be stopped." Lindsey spoke at a breakneck pace, her frenzied words tumbling over each other. "I didn't want anything to ruin his chance to become governor. Brad wasn't supposed to be on that helicopter. He's going to die if you don't let me text him!"

"You're lying. This is a stall ploy."

"No, it's not!" Lindsey's denial was shrill. Desperate. "You have to believe me! Please!"

Heather pulled out her cell.

She needed law enforcement backup.

Now.

She also needed to warn Rick and get into an optimal position to put these two on ice.

Before she could do anything, Lindsey lunged for Ellen.

A shot exploded, shattering the silent air.

Heather dropped her phone and raced forward, tucking herself as best she could behind the trunk of a towering maple tree thirty feet from the tussling duo. Arms extended, fingers clamped on her Sig, she aimed the weapon at them.

"Stop! Drop the gun! I'm armed!"

The two women jerked toward her, but the struggle continued, bringing them to the edge of the low wall.

There was no way to get a clear line of sight on Ellen.

A second blast echoed through the trees.

Lindsey pitched forward . . . over the edge of the wall. Onto the rocks.

She lay crumpled in the half-frozen stream, unmoving.

Ellen whirled, pistol still clutched in her hand.

More gunfire blasted through the quiet air as Heather squeezed the trigger, the retort slamming her back.

Ellen doubled over. Fell.

She didn't move.

But if she was conscious, danger remained.

Go verify that the threat has been neutralized, Heather. Then check on Lindsey.

Right.

That would be the normal protocol.

Except a sudden, searing pain pierced her arm, and her legs went weak.

Sliding down the trunk of the tree, she dropped to her knees. Looked toward her shoulder.

There was a hole in her jacket sleeve—and the fabric around it was darkening.

She touched the stain.

Her fingers came away red.

Merciful heaven.

She'd been shot.

"Heather!" At the alarmed summons, she roused herself enough to lift her chin from her slumped kneeling position.

Cal was sprinting toward her.

As she tried to control the tremors coursing through her body, he dropped to one knee beside her, mouth set in a grim line. After scrutinizing the sleeve of her coat, he pulled out his phone, punched three numbers, and gave the 911 operator a rapid download.

"Cal." She grabbed his arm, trying to focus on his fuzzy image as the edges of the world began to fade.

"Hold one sec." He finished the call, keeping an eye on the motionless women on and under the bridge. Shoving the phone into his pocket with one hand, he urged her to the ground with the other. "I want to put pressure on the wound." He shed his jacket in two swift motions.

"Cal. Wait."

"Waiting is bad when blood is involved."

"I'm not . . . not bleeding out." The wet spot was spreading, but not at a pace suggesting an artery had been hit.

"Any blood is too much." He positioned her arm flat on the tufts of dormant grass.

"Cal!"

"I'm listening." But he kept working.

"Rick's helicopter has . . . has been sabotaged." She had to employ every ounce of her concentration to form coherent words. "He's in the air . . . now. He has to be . . . warned. Fast. Call Palmer . . . Aviation."

He froze—and the pressure on her arm diminished as he whipped out his phone again. "I'll take care of it."

And he would.

All of the Phoenix PIs could be counted on to do what had to be done—at warp speed.

He issued a few clipped instructions to Nikki, using his no-nonsense homicide-detective voice.

Good man.

Waves of blackness lapped at her—and now that Cal and the team had the ball and were running with it, she could let them suck her under . . . at least for a few minutes.

There wasn't anything else she could do for Rick at the moment.

Except pray the warning wouldn't come too late to save his life . . . and the future she'd begun to hope they might share.

26

At five minutes past two, Rick veered off from the route he'd been following along the Missouri River bottoms and crossed the river at New Haven.

Behind him, his passengers remained engrossed in their work—common among the corporate passengers he ferried around. Few of them paid attention to the landscape below. Not that there was much to see in January, but even in the autumn most travelers were oblivious to the vivid display of fall color unless he pointed it out.

Stretching in his seat, he watched the topography change from flat bottomland to hilly, wooded terrain. This area south of Hermann was especially beautiful in the fall.

Maybe by next autumn, he and Heather would—

His headset crackled to life. "Rick?"

He frowned.

Harvey never called him during a flight unless there was an emergency—and he always used standard radio lingo, never a first name.

"Roger. What's up?"

"You have to land ASAP. Your helicopter's been sabotaged."

Sucking in a breath, he bolted upright in his seat and gave the rolling terrain a fast survey, searching for an open, level spot to touch down. Helicopters and hills didn't mix—and sloping land dense with trees was worse. "Copy that. Do you have details?"

"No."

"Okay. I'll put down as soon as—"

A strong jolt slammed through the cyclic control beneath his hand, and his grip tightened as the aircraft shuddered.

"Is there a problem?" The tense question came from behind him.

"Checking." He kept his tone as even as possible.

"Rick?" Harvey again.

His gaze swept the control panel. "I'm here. Hold."

No warning lights were on. No bells were ringing. All gauges and instruments were normal.

He began a mechanical evaluation, moving the levers and pedals to test their responsiveness.

It didn't take him long to discover the problem.

While he had control of fore/aft cyclic, tail rotor pedal, and collective control, his lateral cyclic was gone.

In other words, he'd lost the ability to bank the aircraft left or right.

Very bad news.

He'd have to make a straight-in approach to whatever terrain was in front of him, using his collective to control the rate of descent and the remaining cyclic to slow the airspeed.

This was going to be dicey.

Especially in this terrain.

"Rick?" Harvey sounded panicked.

"Still here." He briefed the man on the situation. "I'm looking for a place to land—but you know this topography."

"Yeah." The man's response was taut. "I'll alert the appropriate people."

Translation? He was going to call in emergency crews—including ambulances and paramedics.

"Roger."

One of his passengers tapped on his shoulder. "What's going on?"

He muted his mike. "The aircraft has a mechanical malfunction. I'm taking us down."

"Here?" Chuck leaned past him to survey the wooded hills.

"I'm searching for a clearing. Both of you, buckle up."

"There's one over there." The man pointed to the right.

Yeah, there was.

But it wasn't going to help him.

He needed a spot straight in front of him.

And all he saw was woods and hills.

"That won't work. Sit back and buckle up."

At the curt order, the man retreated to his seat.

Fingers tingling, Rick forgot about his passengers and concentrated on the ground.

A small farmer's field came into view on the left.

Why couldn't there be a spot like that directly in his flight path?

If he continued to fly, he might find one—but he had to put down ASAP. He couldn't risk losing any more of his controls. That would be catastrophic.

Three minutes later, a small, open patch of slightly sloping land tucked among the trees came into view. Not an optimal landing site even if he had full control of the helicopter, but it would have to do.

"Harvey—I've got a spot. About eight to ten miles south of Hermann." He gave him a few landmarks.

"Copy." Two beats of silence ticked by. "Good luck, Rick."

"Thanks."

But as he shut off communication and gave the approach his full attention, he knew he'd need a lot more than luck.

He'd need a miracle.

Especially after he cleared the treetops and managed to lower forward groundspeed to a reasonable eighteen knots, only to spot a small depression in the ground that had been invisible until he was just two feet above it.

His gut clenched.

Rough, sloping terrain plus a dip?

Recipe for disaster.

And as he summoned up every ounce of his piloting skills . . . as his skids made contact . . . as the helicopter tipped . . . Harvey's parting words in the hangar scrolled across his mind.

Just bring my Bell back in one piece.

Unfortunately, the odds of that happening were slim to none.

. . . . . .

The jostling of the stretcher as the paramedics hoisted her into an ambulance nudged Heather back to consciousness.

"I have to talk to Cal." The words sounded sluggish to her ears.

What was in her IV, anyway?

"You can talk to him at the hospital." The paramedics didn't miss a beat in their secure-the-patient-in-the-ambulance routine.

"No. Now." She struggled to sit up, but they'd strapped her down.

"Hey. Take it easy." One of them firmly pressed her back. "We don't want any more bleeding."

If they weren't going to listen to her, she'd have to take matters into her own hands.

"Cal!" She yelled at the top of her lungs. The summons didn't come out as loud as she'd hoped—but it startled the paramedics . . . and did the job.

Cal stuck his head in the rear of the ambulance, phone to his ear. "I'm here, Heather."

"Did someone reach Rick?"

"I talked to the owner of Palmer Aviation. He said he'd call him immediately."

"So he's okay?"

"Palmer wasn't aware of any Mayday communication, and Rick hadn't called him to report an emergency. So he thinks we caught this in time."

Thank you, God!

"You can continue this conversation at the hospital." The paramedic shut the door in Cal's face.

Once again, Heather let herself drift.

Everything was going to be fine.

It had to be.

Her future depended on it.

. . . . .

The distant wail of sirens penetrated his brain, and Rick forced his sluggish eyelids open.

He was strapped into his seat in the Bell—but the aircraft was on its side.

No wonder.

That had been the mother of all hard landings.

However . . . while there might be blood dripping off his chin and his left wrist hurt like the devil, he could recover from those kinds of injuries.

Death was more permanent.

And based on the potentially fatal mechanical failure they'd experienced, death had been a very real possibility.

Yet he'd survived.

Had his passengers been as fortunate?

Grunting in pain, he shut off the battery, released his belt, and shifted around to assess the two men.

Weston stared back him, skin chalky, eyes glazed, a large

bump rising on his temple. The man was in shock but didn't appear to be seriously injured.

His campaign manager hadn't fared as well. He didn't have any visible injuries, but he was limp, his restraints taut as he sagged to the side.

"Help is on the way." The reassurance rasped past his throat as the volume of the sirens increased, but he doubted the noise—or his encouragement—registered with either man.

Given the close proximity of emergency assistance and the aches radiating throughout his body, he had to fight the temptation to stay put until the experts arrived.

But while he didn't see any signs of imminent explosion, hanging around a downed aircraft that could have electrical shorts and fuel leaks wasn't the best idea.

Besides, if Chuck wasn't breathing, the paramedics would get here too late to save him.

Favoring his injured arm, and swiping away the blood trickling off his jaw, he maneuvered around, toward his passengers. Hissing through his clenched teeth at the pain, he crawled back, balancing himself as best he could with a bum wrist in a tilted aircraft.

"If you're able to move, you need to get out of the helicopter." He spoke directly into Weston's face as he unlatched the gubernatorial hopeful's restraints and put a shoulder to the passenger door to heave it open.

The man blinked, and his eyes cleared a hair. "Yes. I . . . can do that. I think." He motioned toward his companion. "What about—"

"I've got him."

Weston dipped his head and climbed out awkwardly, opening room for Rick to position himself beside the campaign manager and press his fingers against the man's carotid artery.

He had a pulse—but it was weak.

If he'd suffered internal injuries, it was possible he was bleeding inside.

In the distance, numerous vehicles with flashing lights began bumping over the uneven field.

There was nothing he could do for Chuck except make sure he was given top priority by the medical technicians.

The first responders were already racing toward the helicopter by the time Rick managed to pull himself out of the door with one arm, lower himself to the ground—and survey the aircraft.

His blood ran cold at the sight.

The main rotor blades and tail rotor had shattered, as had the tail boom.

Very few people survived a crash like this.

"Sir." A paramedic touched his shoulder.

He forced himself to swallow past the bile rising in his throat, grabbed the helicopter frame for support, and waved him past. "Worse injuries inside. Take care of him first."

Willing his lungs to inflate, he tried to think about next steps.

Call Heather. Yes. That was what he had to do.

Despite the tremors running through his fingers, he succeeded in digging out his phone and thumbing in her speed dial number.

After four rings, it rolled to voicemail.

Blast.

A helicopter crash would be on the news within minutes—and he did *not* want her hearing about this from someone who had only sketchy facts and didn't know whether there had been any survivors.

He tried again.

Same result.

"Sir . . . why don't you come with me and let us check you out?" A paramedic gave him a practiced sweep.

"I'm okay."

"No, sir, you're not."

As if to validate the man's assessment, a few drops of blood spattered on the frozen ground at Rick's feet.

Maybe he did need minor first aid.

"I think I cut my forehead . . . and bruised my arm." More blood dripped. "Give me a minute to make a phone call and I'll let you do your job." He called Heather again.

"Did you black out, sir?"

"What?" Man, this guy was persistent.

"Did you black out?"

"No . . . I don't think so . . . well, I may have—for a minute or two." Or five. Or ten. He couldn't seem to focus on the numbers on his watch to quantify how long he'd been unconscious.

The phone rolled to voicemail again.

He left a brief message.

But he wanted to talk to her directly.

"I have to try again in a couple of minutes."

The paramedic clamped firm fingers around his upper arm and tried to guide him away from the crippled helicopter. "We'll be glad to make the call for you."

This guy was becoming downright annoying.

However . . . all of a sudden, he didn't feel too hot.

It might not hurt to sit down for a few minutes, let the medic do his job so he'd get off his back.

"I can call while we walk."

The man looked like he was about to protest, but relented with a shrug after studying him for a moment. "Works for me."

Since Heather wasn't answering, Rick keyed in Colin's number with his thumb while cradling his throbbing left wrist against his chest as he walked. Colin would find a way to reach her.

It helped to have friends in the police department.

Colin answered on the first ring.

"Hey—I need you to do me a favor." His pace slowed as the pain increased, and the paramedic gave him a worried scan.

"Name it."

His Treehouse Gang buddy listened in silence as he gave him a quick recap and made his request.

"I'm on it. How badly are you hurt?"

"Not bad." More blood splashed at his feet as the paramedic urged him down onto a collapsible stool. "The medics are checking me out, and I . . . ." The landscape tilted, and Rick frowned.

Weird.

He fumbled for something . . . anything . . . to latch on to that would help stabilize him.

"Rick . . . Rick! Are you there?"

Colin's disembodied voice sounded as if it was coming from a great distance.

"Yeah." He squinted, trying to focus.

"What hospital are they taking you to?"

"I'm not . . . going to a . . . hospital."

The paramedic shined a light in his eyes, and the world tipped again. He tried to hold on to the phone as someone tugged on it, but it slipped from his grasp.

The last thing he remembered was watching the ground rise up to meet him as he pitched forward.

27

Answering questions from a police detective while you were being prepped for surgery wasn't easy.

Heather suddenly had much more empathy for the patients she'd interviewed in hospital ERs.

In her case, though, Mitch Morgan wasn't a stranger. She'd worked with him on a number of cases, and he was a total pro.

"Wrap it up, detective." A nurse bustled in and adjusted the drip on her IV.

"I'll be out of your hair in a minute." Mitch waited until the nurse left again to resume the questions he'd begun firing at her after she'd finished her story.

"Is there anything else of an urgent nature I should know before they put you under?" Pen poised, he waited for her response.

"No." She'd given him as many details of the abduction and shooting as she could recall in view of the morphine the paramedics had administered, which was turning her brain to mush. "I may think of more after I wake up."

He closed his notebook. "I'll swing by in the morning. Let you get a full night's sleep."

"In a hospital?"

One side of his mouth hitched up. "Point taken."

"I don't want to hold you up, but do you think you could get me an update on the two women? And see if you can find Cal?"

"I'll give it a shot."

She was drifting when Mitch returned, Cal on his heels, his expression grave, but she roused herself as he began speaking.

"Ellen Chambers was DOA with two gunshot wounds. Lindsey Weston is in surgery as we speak, in critical condition. Multiple injuries, from what I can gather—including a gunshot wound to the abdomen."

"Did she regain consciousness before surgery?"

"No. We had someone standing by in case she did, but it was a no-go."

Cal moved closer. "I talked to Jordan."

The coil of fear in her stomach uncurled.

That meant he was alive.

The nurse came back in and gave the two men the evil eye. "We're trying to get this woman ready for surgery."

Mitch held up his hands. "We're out of here."

She snorted and adjusted the drip again. "That's what you said five minutes ago."

"This time I mean it."

"What did Rick say when you told him about me?" Heather snagged Cal's sleeve as he turned to leave.

The Phoenix chief shifted. Like he was uncomfortable. "I didn't get a chance to pass on all the news."

Uh-oh.

He was holding back on her.

Her tension ratcheted back up. "Why not? He's okay, isn't he?"

"He will be."

"What does that mean?" Cal began to fuzz out around the edges.

"I'll explain after your surgery."

She wanted to press him. To demand that he spill everything now.

But the words wouldn't come as she began to spiral into a dark vortex.

All she could do was pray that the surge of hope she'd experienced moments ago hadn't been premature.

■ ■ ■ ■ ■

How had he ended up flat on his back being rolled into an emergency room?

As the world came back into focus, Rick tried to sit up.

"Whoa, buddy." A firm hand on his shoulder kept him flat. "We're almost at our destination."

"I don't want to go to the ER."

"Too late. You're already there." The much-too-genial guy wheeling him in grinned. Like they were out for an afternoon stroll in the park.

"I don't need to be here."

"You can discuss that with the docs. You're their responsibility now."

They pushed him into a room.

Before he could continue his argument, Colin appeared in the doorway, twin creases embedded on his forehead.

Kristin edged around him, a worried frown marring her brow too.

"Hey." He summoned up a smile—which took far more effort than it should have. "How did you guys get here so fast?"

"You weren't that far away. They airlifted you to St. Luke's.

And I have a car with a siren—remember." Colin edged aside as a nurse muscled past.

"He swung by en route to pick me up." Kristin touched his arm, exchanging places with a paramedic as the nurse began fussing over him. "How are you?"

"I've been worse. This is just a precaution. I won't be here long."

"I wouldn't count on that." Colin scrutinized him. "You're a mess."

He didn't doubt that—but at least the blood had stopped dripping off his chin.

"Did you get ahold of Heather?"

"Yes."

"You didn't tell her I was heading for the hospital, did you?"

"No."

He exhaled. "Good. Despite what you think, I'll be out of here in an hour. Once they check me over, I'll give her a call, go home and shower, and pay her a visit to reassure her in person that I'm fine."

Colin exchanged a look with Kristin. "She won't be there."

Rick glanced between his two best friends in the world. After all these years, he could read them like a book.

And he was getting the distinct feeling this story didn't have a happy ending.

Bracing, he forced himself to ask the obvious question. "Why won't she be there?"

Kristin rested her hand on his shoulder. "She's here, Rick."

He tried to make sense of that answer.

Failed.

"I thought you said she didn't know I was in the ER?"

"She doesn't. She's here as a patient—but she should be fine. Colin will tell you what happened." Kristin passed the baton to their mutual buddy.

Rick tried to take everything in as his friend gave him the lowdown on the drama that had begun at the yoga studio and ended on Weston's property.

But only one fact fully registered.

Heather had been shot.

"It's an upper-arm wound, Rick. It doesn't appear an artery was involved. The doctors will know more about the extent of the damage after the surgery. But it isn't life-threatening."

He let the news ping around in his head until his brain could absorb it, then sat up and swung his legs around until his feet were dangling.

"Hey! Not so fast." Colin grabbed one arm, and Kristin dashed around him and took the other.

Like sentinels who had no intention of letting him go anywhere.

Not going to work.

"I want to see Heather."

He tried to slide to the floor, but Colin's grip on his working arm tightened.

"Rick, be rational. She's in surgery. There's nothing for you to do except wait . . . and pray . . . and get fixed up yourself. You won't be of much help to her later unless someone takes care of your wrist, a possible concussion, and a laceration that requires a dozen stitches—minimum."

"Colin's right. By the time she's in recovery, you could be finished here and waiting for her when she wakes up," Kristin added.

It was hard to argue with logic—even if his heart was urging him to barrel through the hospital and pace outside the operating room door.

"Fine. I'll wait." He swung his legs back up.

The simple maneuver was way too hard.

"We'll hang with you until you're sprung." Colin wandered over to the wall and claimed a chair.

"And we'll get regular updates for you on Heather." Kristin joined Colin as an aide came in to wheel him to X-ray.

Thank God for friends like these.

"We'll have you back in a jiffy." The man went about his business with no wasted motion.

"I'll hold you to that. I have places to go."

But as the aide wheeled him down the corridor, he found his eyelids drifting shut, even as his mind continued to spin with all the news Colin and Kristin had delivered.

Kidnapping.

Murder.

Sabotage.

So many terrible crimes.

So many diabolical motives.

And Weston's original felony had been the least among them.

Far worse had been Lindsey's ruthless plan to sweep aside all impediments to her husband's ambition, no matter who got hurt, and Ellen's delusional fixation on a man who'd married someone else, along with a sick plot to eliminate her perceived rival.

It was too much for his weary, addled brain to process.

But one thing was clear.

He was glad this chapter in his life was over—and he was anxious to launch the next one.

With Heather by his side.

. . . . .

Someone was holding her hand, the warmth of the tender, reassuring grip chasing the chill from her fingers.

Emitting a contented sigh, Heather opened her eyes.

Rick smiled down at her. "Welcome back."

Back?

She concentrated, letting the events of the past few hours click into place—including the last moments she remembered clearly.

She'd been shot.

And Rick had been in a doomed helicopter.

But she was alive—and so was he.

Except . . . what was underneath that large white dressing on the side of his face? And why was his arm in a sling?

Stomach clenching, she squeezed his hand. "You didn't get the warning in time, did you?"

"No—but I got off easy with a broken wrist, a few stitches, and a slight concussion. You're the one who was shot."

"How bad is it?" She tried to lift her arm, but her muscles ignored the message she was sending.

"The least bad it could be. Neither of your main arteries were hit, there's a small chip in your humerus, you've got a small amount of soft tissue damage, and they'll evaluate your radial nerve later, but they don't think it sustained any significant injury. The doctor said you were lucky. *I* think it's more like a miracle than luck."

"I agree. How come they shared all that with you?"

"They didn't. The doctor told your dad, and he filled me in. He's in the waiting room, chomping at the bit to see you. But he gave me first dibs." Rick winked at her. "I like that man."

"The feeling is mutual." She took a deep breath, trying without much success to clear the fog from her mind. "I know I have a bunch of questions, but my brain isn't cooperating."

"Give the anesthesia a chance to wear off. You can ask them after you're more awake. I'll be here."

"You look like *you* ought to be lying down. Why don't you go home, sleep for a while, and come back later?"

"Nope. You're stuck with me." As if to prove the point, he settled into the chair beside her bed.

She didn't argue.

Instead, she let herself drift off.

True to his word, he was still there an hour later when she resurfaced—and this go-round she was much more clearheaded.

"Hi again." He leaned forward and enfolded her hand in his, his fingers firm and sure and strong.

At such close proximity, it was impossible to miss the fan of creases at the corners of his eyes and the deep grooves on the sides of his mouth.

The man had to be dead on his feet.

"What time is it?"

"Seven o'clock."

"You should go home."

"I will. Later." He stroked the back of her hand with his thumb. "Your dad's been keeping me company. I finally convinced him to go down to the cafeteria and eat dinner."

"Have *you* eaten?"

"Not yet."

"Go get some food."

"Later. Would you like an update on what's been happening while you were out?"

"Yes."

"Weston sustained only bumps and bruises in the crash, but his campaign manager didn't make it. He had severe injuries—including a ruptured spleen. Since he was on a blood thinner, that caused a massive amount of internal bleeding."

Heather cringed.

Another innocent person dead.

"Does Weston know about his wife's involvement?"

"They briefed him here at the hospital."

"How's Lindsey?"

"She made it through surgery, and Weston had a chance to talk to her—but she coded, and they weren't able to revive her."

"Yet the man who started it all walks away." She exhaled.

"Unless CID comes up with sufficient evidence for the authorities to press charges."

"The clock is ticking."

"I know. But even if he escapes an indictment, the life he planned is in ruins."

"Maybe that's punishment enough."

"I won't argue with that. In fact, I'd like to forget all the ugliness for a minute and focus on something much more pleasant before your father gets back."

"Like what?"

"Like this." Leaning close, he stroked a gentle finger down her cheek, then claimed her lips in a tantalizing kiss that was spiced with restrained passion—and all too short.

"Wow." She stared at him as he backed off a few inches.

"That's just a sample. Does it tempt you to want more?"

She put her unencumbered arm around his neck. "I've been wanting more since the day we met."

"Ah. The truth comes out."

"And I'm a woman who goes after what she wants."

"What might that be?"

"You—or at least a chance to find out if we're as compatible as I think we are. What do you want?"

"Exactly the same thing . . . which suggests we *are* compatible."

"In that case, I suggest we spend the next few months confirming your theory."

"I'm in. Let's start with a real dinner date on Saturday—assuming you're up to it."

"I'll be up to it." No matter how many painkillers she had to take. Exerting pressure, she tugged him close again, until his mouth was inches from hers. "But I'd like the appetizer now."

"Happy to oblige, Ms. Shields."

And as he closed the distance between them and gave her a

kiss that made her tingle to the tips of her toes, Heather sent a silent thank-you heavenward for safe passage through the storm—and for the man holding her close, who'd entered her life so unexpectedly and filled it with the promise of sweet tomorrows.

EPILOGUE

"Grab your pot and spoon, Mrs. Jordan. It's three minutes to midnight. We need to get outside to bang in the new year."

Heather pulled on her gloves, snatched up her noisemaking implements, and smiled at her husband of three months. "Thank you for indulging my silly New Year's Eve tradition."

"It's not silly—and I like traditions. I even got you this."

He pulled a small bag out of his pocket and held it up.

Her heart melted. "You remembered my comment last year about confetti."

"Yep. Not homemade—but it'll do the job."

"Are you certain about this?" She inspected the bag. "It will blow all over the camp for months."

"Let it. If any of the kids ask about it, I'll tell them the tale of our romance. It will bolster their faith in true love—and maybe convince them to wait for the right partner to come along."

"I assume you'll leave out the not-so-pleasant parts of our story."

"I'll gloss over all the crimes that were committed—and the injuries. Although the older kids may have seen bits and pieces of the news coverage last January."

That was possible. With all of its soap-opera drama, the story had garnered national headlines.

Even after a year, the memory of those nightmare press photos of Rick's mangled helicopter could startle her awake, pulse pounding. More so after the FAA investigation had concluded that the chances of successfully ditching in that terrain had been miniscule.

But Rick's superb skills—and an assist from above—had foiled Lindsey's plans.

"I wish law enforcement had caught the person who sabotaged the helicopter—and the person or persons who murdered Beth and Boomer." She blew out a frustrated breath.

"Professional saboteurs—and killers—tend to melt into the shadows, according to Colin."

"Sad but true. At least the FAA was able to come up with a plausible theory about *what* the person did to the helicopter."

"Yeah. The notion of reversing the bolt in the cyclic control rod and bell crank assembly—then putting the nut back on with just a few turns—is ingenious in its simplicity. The vibration of the rotors and normal flight turbulence would loosen the nut until it fell off, and then gravity would take over. The bolt would drop out, and the control rod would disconnect from the bell crank."

"Meaning you couldn't turn left or right." Though the technical jargon was beyond her, Heather got the gist of the problem.

"Right. The evil beauty of the plan is that the mechanical failure would have appeared to be the result of negligence."

"And your mechanic would have taken the rap."

"Yes." Rick's eyes narrowed. "And another innocent life would have been ruined."

"But it wasn't. And we had a happy ending too." She tucked her arm through his. "That's more than I can say for Weston."

"Except he's not in prison."

"True." She sighed. "His attorney must have done some fast

talking to swing a deal with CID that allowed him to settle without ever admitting wrongdoing."

"From a practical standpoint, I guess they both considered it the best solution. CID wasn't certain it could come up with sufficient hard evidence for an indictment before the statute of limitations ran out, anyway. With this arrangement, the government's coffers were refilled and Weston didn't have to worry about a possible prison sentence."

"Still . . . his life is a wreck. Since he withdrew from the gubernatorial race and sold his company, he seems to have fallen off the face of the earth."

"You know . . . in an odd sort of way, I feel sorry for him." Rick shook his head. "I can't condone his actions in the Middle East, but can you imagine finding out your ex-girlfriend wanted to kill your wife—who in turn had arranged for multiple deaths to further your political ambitions? Both with motives supposedly fueled by love?"

Heather shivered. "The whole notion sends a chill down my spine despite this quilted coat I put on and that cozy fire you have going." She motioned to the blaze crackling beneath the bough-laden mantel in the cabin she now called home.

"We could always stay inside. It *is* twenty-six degrees out there—and I can think of lots of appealing indoor warm-up methods." He waggled his eyebrows.

"Hold that thought. We can stay up as late as you like once we welcome the new year—and sleep in all day tomorrow if we want to. The next morning too, thanks to the extra day off work Cal gave me. But I don't want to waste this confetti you so thoughtfully supplied."

"Then let's get this party rolling."

He took her arm and guided her toward the back door.

Once they were on the porch, he set his pot and spoon down and left her at the railing as he clomped down the snowy steps.

"Hey! Where are you going?"

"You'll see."

He disappeared around the side of the house.

Half a minute later, he jogged back.

"What was that all about?"

As she asked the question, a distinctive whistling sound drew her gaze toward the lake, where they'd exchanged vows last October under a brilliant blue sky, with the sparkling water and a blaze of fall color as a backdrop.

A few seconds later, three bursts of fireworks filled the inky expanse in rapid succession with a fleeting, glorious display of color.

"Oooohhhh." She breathed more than spoke the exclamation. "That was gorgeous! A private fireworks display. How did you light them and manage to get back here to enjoy it with me?"

"Long fuse. I set it all up earlier." He squinted at his watch. "One minute and counting. Plenty of time to end this year on a high note—and usher in the next one the same way." He plucked her pot and spoon from her gloved fingers and pulled her close.

"I thought we were going to make noise and throw confetti?"

"We are—but I have another festive activity planned first."

"You already shot off fireworks. I wonder what else you could have in mind?" Grinning, she snuggled closer. "Maybe you could demonstrate."

"My pleasure."

He lowered his mouth to hers—and the warmth of his touch not only chased away the chill on her lips, it sent heat rocketing to her extremities.

The fireworks in the sky might be over—but this kind was even better.

And there would be more to come . . . especially after she shared her news.

. . . . .

In the recesses of his awareness, Rick heard a faint echo of guns. His neighbors were celebrating too.

The clock must have ticked over into the new year while he was lost in Heather's eager, all-in kiss that never failed to whip his libido into a frenzy.

It was time to move this party inside and ratchet up the heat.

Slowly disengaging from the kiss, he kept her within the circle of his arms. "I'm losing feeling in my toes. What do you say we bang pots, throw confetti, and hightail it back inside for hot chocolate by the fireplace?"

"Sounds like a plan." Yet she lingered in his embrace, her breath a frosty cloud in the cold air.

"You want me to be the first to break this up?"

"Let's do it together. On the count of three. One . . . two . . . three." She stepped back.

He retrieved their pots and handed her one, along with a spoon.

"Happy New Year!" She banged hers and called out the best wishes at the top of her voice.

He followed her lead.

Once they'd had enough pot banging, he opened the bag of confetti and extended it toward her.

She dived in. "Ready . . . set . . . go!"

They threw handfuls into the air simultaneously, letting the tiny flecks of glittery paper rain down around them.

Heather held out her hand for more, and they repeated the exercise, her delighted laughter ringing through the air.

The happy sound fed his soul.

His wife's ability to find joy in the simplest pleasures was one of the many endearing attributes he'd discovered about her during his six-month courtship and their abbreviated engagement.

It was also one of the many things he loved about her.

Lucky for him, she'd concurred with his rationale to accelerate the wedding.

After all, why wait when they both knew they were meant to be together?

"That was fun." She brushed some confetti from his hair, her irises sparkling. "Dad would have enjoyed this."

He captured her hand. "Next year we can make this a threesome if he's willing to trek out to the country, stay up late, and doesn't get any more notions about taking a cruise to ring in the new year."

"We should definitely count on making it a threesome."

"Did you hear from him again? Is he not liking the cruise?"

"He's loving it. I have a feeling it's going to become a new holiday tradition for him."

Rick cocked his head, trying to reconcile her two seemingly contradictory comments. "Then what do you mean about a threesome? Is there someone else you want to invite to our celebration?"

"Yep." A teasing spark ignited in her eyes. "But he or she may sleep through the fireworks. And they'll be arriving for the party early—like in August."

It took a second for her meaning to sink in, and when it did, Rick's jaw dropped.

"We're having a baby?" His question came out hushed. Reverent.

"Yes. I found out two days ago but decided to wait and share the news while we ushered in the new year."

"A baby." Mouth bowing, he lifted her off her feet and swung her around. "This is a better way to celebrate the new year than pot banging and confetti and fireworks all put together."

"I hope you don't expect a repeat performance every year, though." Laughter tickled her words.

"No, but I wouldn't object to several encores."

"I'll keep that in mind."

He slowly let her slide down his body until she was once again wrapped in his arms . . . close to his heart. "Wait until Colin and Kristin hear this." If his grin got any bigger, his face might split in two. "They may have beat me to the altar, but I'll be first over the line on parenthood."

"Was there a race going on I didn't know about?"

"No. But I don't get to one-up them often. This will be fun." Joy bubbled up inside him as he savored the beautiful face of the woman who'd captured his heart with her courage, kindness, intelligence, sense of humor, and total dedication to every task she undertook. Including marriage.

The day she'd agreed to be his wife had been a gift from God.

And it was one he'd never stop being thankful for.

"Do you know how much I love you?" His throat tightened as he looked down into hazel eyes that were soft with love and tenderness.

"No more than I love you. Let me demonstrate." She rose on tiptoe.

He met her halfway.

Somewhere in the distance, an owl hooted.

Closer at hand, the homey scent of woodsmoke beckoned them inside, where the cozy fire waited to wrap them in warmth.

Up above, the stars twinkled in the firmament, smiling down on them.

All the sights and sounds and scents of this place he called home were endearingly familiar.

Yet on this moonlit night, with the woman he loved in his arms, the little cabin they shared beneath the pines didn't just feel like home.

It felt like heaven.

Read on for a sneak peek of
Starfish Pier,
a Hope Harbor novel

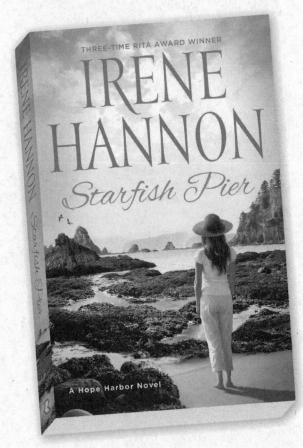

Maybe coming back to Oregon had been a mistake.

Expelling a breath, Steven Roark moved to the stern of the twenty-two-foot fishing boat where he spent his days and double-checked the cleat hitch knot on the mooring line.

Secure.

Which was more than he could say for his place in the world—or in Hope Harbor.

Ducking into the foldaway canvas enclosure that offered a modicum of protection to charter clients on blustery, cold days—like this late March Saturday—he dropped into a deck chair and massaged his forehead.

From a business standpoint, the day had been productive. For this early in the spring, steelheads had been running better than usual on the river at the north end of town, and his customers had left satisfied with their catches. One of them had even hooked a twenty-pounder.

On the personal front, however, the day was a total bust.

Steven leaned forward, flipped the latch on a storage compartment, and retrieved the envelope he'd found in his mailbox yesterday, the address penned in Cindy's fluid, curvy handwriting.

He pulled out the card, reread the printed verse, and skimmed the best wishes jotted inside by his sister-in-law under a crudely drawn smile icon that had to be his nephew's handiwork.

His brother hadn't bothered to sign his own name. Cindy had done the honors for both of them.

Stomach kinking, Steven shoved the card back in the envelope and hunched forward, elbows on knees.

Some birthday.

No one but fish, a couple of pesky seagulls, and three taciturn customers for company. No cake or festive dinner shared with friends or family. No recognition of the day by his kid brother—nor any progress in their relationship.

And if he hadn't made any inroads with Patrick after almost a year, there wasn't much chance his sibling would come around in the future unless the status quo changed.

Steven sighed.

While mustering out of the army had seemed like the right decision twelve months ago after Cindy's disturbing letter arrived in the Middle East, in hindsight—

"Hello? Is anyone on board?"

Steven jerked upright and squinted through the isinglass window.

A slender, thirtysomething woman stood on the dock beside his boat, a folder clutched against her chest. As the gusty wind whipped strands of her longish, light brown hair across her face, she brushed them aside and peered into the deck enclosure.

Given the shadowed interior on this gray day—plus the fog that had rolled in—she might not be able to make out his form.

That left him two options.

He could sink lower and ignore her . . . or give himself a birthday treat and chat with an attractive female for a few minutes.

No contest, in light of the solitary evening that loomed ahead—providing she wasn't here on any bothersome business.

Setting the card aside, he stood, pushed aside the canvas that covered the opening, and emerged into the stern.

The woman hugged the folder tighter and gave him a wary once-over.

Understandable, given his disheveled state after a full day

on the water and the coarse stubble that would be darkening his jaw by now.

"Can I help you?" Taking into account her poised-to-flee posture, he remained where he was.

"Steven Roark?"

"Guilty."

"My name is Holly Miller. May I speak with you for a few minutes?"

"Depends."

Faint creases dented her brow. "On what?"

"On the reason for your visit. I'm not in the mood for a sales pitch."

"I'm not selling anything."

"Then we can talk." For as long as she liked, since he had nothing more exciting to do.

How pathetic that the bright spot of his birthday was a visit from a nervous woman who looked as if she couldn't wait to escape.

But it was better than going home to an empty apartment.

"Um . . ." She surveyed the marina. "Could we sit somewhere? Like . . . back there?" She motioned toward crescent-shaped Dockside Drive, where benches and planters were placed along the sidewalk at the top of the sloping pile of boulders that led to the water.

"I have a few chores to finish here before I leave. Why don't you come on board?"

She gave the craft a dubious sweep. "My sea legs aren't the best."

"There isn't much motion in the marina." Extending a hand, he moved toward her, toning down his usual take-charge manner. Based on her rigid stance, it wouldn't take much to frighten her off. "She's easy to board, and we can sit there." He indicated the unprotected bench seats along the edge of the stern.

It would be warmer—and far less windy—inside the portable enclosure he'd erected for today's charter trip, but despite the windows it was better to stay in the open. He didn't want any trouble, and with all the misconduct allegations flying around these days, why take chances?

"Okay." She swallowed . . . grasped his hand . . . and eased one foot onto the gunwale.

The craft gave an almost imperceptible bob as she transferred her weight, and she gasped. Tightened her grip.

"You're fine. I've got you. Just step down."

She followed his instructions, but the maneuver was downright clumsy, and the instant both her feet were on the deck she groped for the seat and collapsed onto it in an awkward sprawl.

Pretty as his visitor was, the graceful gene had passed her by.

And the pink hue that crept over her cheeks suggested she knew that.

He took a seat at the far end of the stern, leaving plenty of space between them. "You have the floor . . . or the deck." He hiked up one side of his mouth. Holly Miller appeared to be wound up tight as the ubiquitous black turban snails that clung to the rocks on Oregon beaches. Perhaps a touch of humor would help her chill.

Didn't work.

Her lips remained flat—and taut—as she set the folder in her lap, picked a speck of lint off her jeans, and zipped up her windbreaker as far as it would go. "Are you familiar with the Helping Hands volunteer organization here in town?"

"Yes."

"Well, I'm on a committee that's putting together a dinner auction to raise funds for a new pro-life initiative. Everyone involved is soliciting auction items. Reverend Baker at Grace

Christian mentioned you as a potential donor. That's why I'm here."

Steven stifled a groan.

This was the thanks he got for letting Cindy not only pressure him into helping with the holiday food drive at a church to which he didn't even belong, but allowing her to drag him across the room for an introduction to the minister.

Proving the truth of the old adage that no good deed went unpunished.

Worse yet, of all the causes his visitor could be soliciting for, why did it have to be this one?

The irony twisted his gut.

When the silence lengthened, she cleared her throat. "I was, uh, hoping you'd consider donating a charter fishing trip for two—or four, if possible. Everyone we've contacted has been very generous. I spoke this morning with the owner of the Seabird Inn B&B, and he offered a weekend romance package for one of his rooms."

If she was hoping to guilt him into donating, it wasn't going to work.

"What will the money you raise be used for?" He could guess, but the stall tactic would buy him a few seconds to figure out how to decline without sounding like a heartless jerk.

She opened the folder on her lap, withdrew a sheet of paper, and held it out to him. "This explains the effort in detail, but topline, we'll establish a fund to support efforts that protect life in all its stages. One example would be providing financial assistance to abortion alternatives, like paying various expenses for women who agree to carry their babies to term and linking them with adoption agencies. We may also get involved in issues like capital punishment."

He narrowed his eyes. "What's your beef with capital punishment?"

She met his gaze square on. "Killing is killing."

"Putting a guilty person to death is called justice. And it keeps that person from taking other innocent lives."

"A lifetime prison sentence does too."

"At a huge expense to taxpayers."

"How do you put a price on a life?"

"There are practical considerations."

"Also ethical ones."

Squelching the temptation to continue the debate, he skimmed the sheet she'd handed him. This wasn't a subject on which they were going to agree, so why argue on his birthday . . . or extend an encounter that was going south?

This day had been depressing enough.

"Let me think about it." He folded the sheet into a small square, tucked it in the pocket of his jacket, and stood.

She gave a slow blink at his abrupt dismissal—but after a slight hesitation she rose too.

And almost lost her balance.

Again.

He took her arm in a firm grip. "Steady."

"Sorry. I'm a landlubber through and through." She flashed him a shaky smile.

That could be true—but it didn't explain her equilibrium issues.

The same kind Patrick had on occasion.

Yet this woman, with her clear hazel eyes, didn't strike him as the type who would struggle with his brother's problem.

Appearances could be deceiving, though. That's why you had to fact find, then use that evidence to make decisions . . . always keeping the greater good in mind.

At least that's how he'd justified some of his choices in the past.

As Holly tugged free of his hold and turned to disembark, he shifted gears. "Let me go first."

Without waiting for a reply, he hopped onto the dock and held out a hand.

After a nanosecond hesitation, she took it and climbed up onto the seat. Swayed. Stabilized after he tightened his grip.

"One more step." Steven gave a little pull, and she heaved herself up.

He maintained a firm grip until she was on the dock beside him and wiggled her fingers to free them.

Although the lady still didn't appear to be all that sure-footed, he relinquished his hold—but stayed close.

She tucked the folder tight against her chest again. "I appreciate your time today. If you decide to donate, you can contact Helping Hands at the number on the sheet I gave you."

"Could I call you instead?"

The instant the words spilled out, he frowned. Where in blazes had *that* come from? Why would he want to have any further contact with a woman who'd run the other direction if she knew his history?

Her raised eyebrows indicated she was as surprised by the query as he was. "I, uh, suppose I could give you my email."

No backtracking now.

He pulled out his cell. "Ready whenever you are."

As she recited it, he tapped in the professional rather than personal address. "You work for the school district?"

"Yes."

She offered nothing more.

Fair enough. He was a stranger, and she was smart to be cautious.

But he was no threat to her.

Nor was there much chance she'd ever hear from him again.

Willing as he was to support charitable causes, this particular endeavor didn't fit with his history.

He motioned toward Dockside Drive. "I'll walk you to solid ground."

"No." She edged away, leaving a faint, pleasing floral scent in her wake. "I've delayed you from your chores too long already."

"I don't mind."

"Thank you, but I can manage on my own." Her chin rose a notch. "I may not have perfect balance, but I'm perfectly capable of taking care of myself. I'll let you get back to whatever you were doing on your boat."

With that, she pivoted and wobbled down the dock toward Dockside Drive.

Steven folded his arms, reining in the urge to follow along behind her in case she started to tumble. The lady had made it clear she didn't want an arm to hold.

All she wanted was a donation.

Too bad he couldn't accommodate her.

But after everything he'd done, God might smite him with a bolt of lightning if he tried to contribute to a pro-life cause.

AUTHOR'S NOTE

As I've often said, while I write fiction, my novels deal with real-life situations, many of which can't be portrayed accurately without specific—and often complex—technical knowledge. That's why research is so critical to creating credible stories.

Consequently, I spend hours online delving into complicated subject matter. For the average suspense novel, I typically end up with a 75–100 page single-spaced typed reference document. In addition, I often consult experts to add the final polish to my scenarios. For this book, I needed assistance with all things helicopter-related—especially the situation near the end—and four people lent their expertise to help me craft those scenes. They are:

Pilot Terry Wilund, who's logged 18,600 flight hours with the US Army, St. Louis County Police Department, and ARCH Air Medical Service during his forty-two years flying helicopters. Terry also called on the three colleagues listed below for additional input and coordinated all their comments. Thank you, Terry, for taking the lead on this. Your help was invaluable.

Pilot Gale Wolff, who's flown helicopters for both the US Marines and US Navy. After retiring from the military, he became a pilot for ARCH Air Medical Service, where he flew medical helicopters for twenty-one years.

James O'Hara, a US Army helicopter mechanic for ten years, and currently a helicopter mechanic for ARCH Air Medical Service, where he's worked for twenty years.

Robert Veness, a US Navy P-3 "Orion" (anti-submarine air-craft) crew member for four years. He's been a civilian helicopter mechanic for the past forty years, first for a heavy-lift construction company and currently for ARCH Air Medical Service.

You can't find more qualified aviation experts than these gentlemen. Thank you so much, one and all.

I also want to recognize and thank Captain Ed Nestor of the Chesterfield Police Department, who was my first law enforcement source when I began writing suspense more than a dozen years ago. Not only did he graciously answer my questions, he also linked me with other law enforcement professionals who have become trusted and valued sources. The amazing resource network I have today started with Ed—who I met when we sang together in our church choir—and I will be forever grateful to him for his kindness and generosity. Ed passed away last January after a fierce, year-long battle with pancreatic cancer, and will always be deeply missed by those who knew him. Rest in peace, my friend.

Finally, I want to thank all those who've supported my writing career through the years, especially my husband, Tom, to whom this book is dedicated; my mom (in heaven now, but always in my heart) and dad, Dorothy and James Hannon; the readers who buy my books; and the amazing team at Revell, including Dwight Baker, Kristin Kornoelje, Jennifer Leep, Michele Misiak, Karen Steele, and Gayle Raymer.

Looking ahead, I hope you'll join me in April 2020 for another trip to the charming Oregon seaside town of Hope Harbor. In *Starfish Pier*, an ex–Delta Force operator turned charter fisherman and a local teacher find themselves on opposite sides of an issue that threatens to disrupt their placid seaside community. Sparks fly—in more ways than one!

And next October, I'll begin a brand-new series featuring three sisters involved in truth-seeking professions. The stakes are high as they're plunged into dicey situations that lead to danger—and romance.

Thank you for reading *Dark Ambitions*, and I look forward to sharing many more stories with you in the future.

Irene Hannon is the bestselling, award-winning author of more than fifty contemporary romance and romantic suspense novels. She is also a three-time winner of the RITA award—the "Oscar" of romance fiction—from Romance Writers of America and is a member of that organization's elite Hall of Fame.

Her many other awards include National Readers' Choice, Daphne du Maurier, Retailers' Choice, Booksellers' Best, Carol, and Reviewers' Choice from *RT Book Reviews* magazine, which also honored her with a Career Achievement award for her entire body of work. In addition, she is a two-time Christy award finalist.

Millions of her books have been sold worldwide, and her novels have been translated into multiple languages.

Irene, who holds a BA in psychology and an MA in journalism, juggled two careers for many years until she gave up her executive corporate communications position with a Fortune 500 company to write full-time. She is happy to say she has no regrets.

A trained vocalist, Irene has sung the leading role in numerous community musical theater productions and is also a soloist at her church. She and her husband enjoy traveling, long hikes, Saturday mornings at their favorite coffee shop, and spending time with family. They make their home in Missouri.

To learn more about Irene and her books, visit www.irene hannon.com. She enjoys interacting with readers on Facebook and is also active on Twitter and Instagram.

Meet

IRENE HANNON

at www.IreneHannon.com

Learn news, sign up for her mailing list,
and more!

Find her on

Welcome to
Hope Harbor . . .

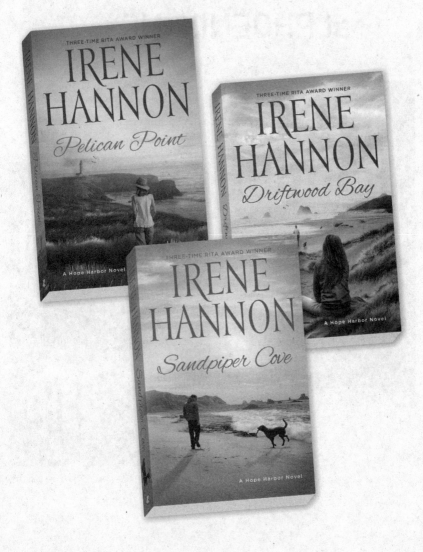

Catch MORE Adventures from the Whole Crew at PHOENIX INC . . .

. . . in the
PRIVATE JUSTICE
Series

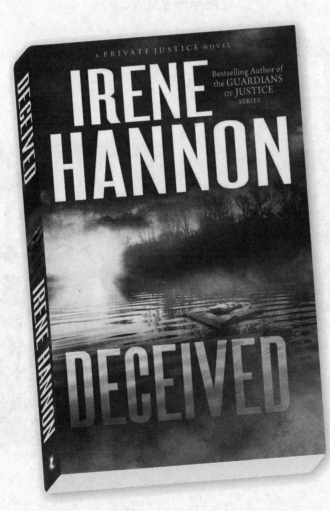

DANGER LURKS AROUND
EVERY CORNER

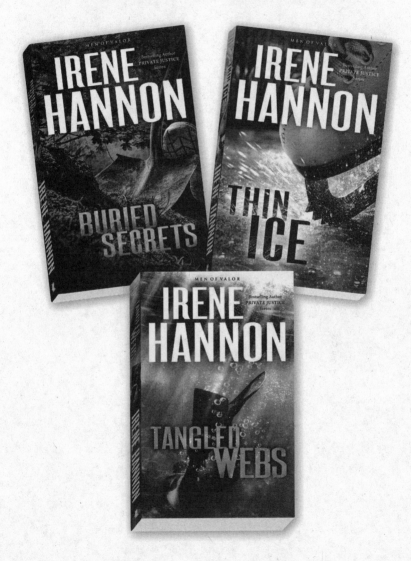

Irene Hannon's Storytelling at Its **Very Best**

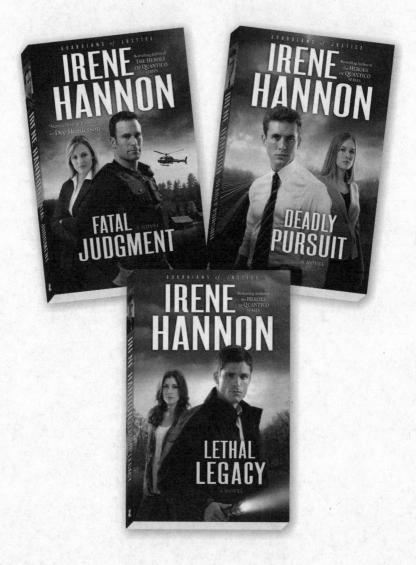

Don't miss Irene Hannon's bestselling
HEROES OF QUANTICO series

"I found someone who writes romantic suspense
better than I do."—Dee Henderson

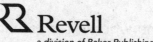